Her
Scream
in the
Silence

Her Scream in the Silence

Carly Moore Mystery

Book Two

Denise Grover Swank

CHAPTER ONE

"Carly! Order up!"

"You made sure to leave off the mustard and lettuce?" I asked Tiny, the ginormous cook at Max's Tavern, smiling to soften my question. "The customer made it *very* clear he'd be taking it out of our tips if we get it wrong."

Tiny placed his hand on the service counter and leveled his gaze with mine. "I can read a ticket."

"I guess it's not you I'm necessarily worried about." I gave a slight nod to the woman struggling to flip a burger on the grill. Tiny had hired the new cook a few days after Bitty, who'd worked under his supervision for years, was shot and killed just outside of the tavern. She'd sold information about me to a man who'd intended to murder me, and he'd immediately turned around and double-crossed her. Despite the steep price she'd paid, Tiny and the rest of the staff saw her action as a bitter betrayal. Once you were accepted at Max's, you were family. And family never turned on each other.

After my own father's betrayal, I knew that was nothing but a sweet lie.

Tiny rolled his eyes. "Sugar didn't have a thing to do with this order."

Sugar was the nickname he'd given her, and we'd all taken to using it even though I was fairly certain that her real name was Phyllis.

Tiny plopped another plate on the counter. "But she had her hands all over *this* one. You can give it to Jerry."

Jerry was a regular at the tavern, and he lived on a very fixed income. I'd learned on my first night that the staff always tried to feed him something extra on the sly, a habit I'd quickly embraced. We'd give him something he hadn't ordered and claim it had been a kitchen screwup. But there had been dozens of actual screwups a day since Sugar had started, and Jerry had gained a good five pounds.

"I already gave him a lunch."

"Well, see if he wants this one too."

Sighing, I picked up both plates. "Jerry might actually put some meat on his bones if we keep this up."

Tiny shot a glare at the woman behind the grill. If Max, the owner of the place, didn't fire her soon, I suspected Tiny would take matters into his own hands and do it himself. Rumor had it that Max had hired her as a favor to someone, but no one seemed to know whom. If Max wasn't careful, he just might lose the best fry cook this side of the Smoky Mountains.

I carried the plates to the dining room. We'd reached the end of the lunch rush, thank goodness, and the space was starting to empty out.

Jerry sat at the bar, and I gave him his food first, cringing as I slid the plate in front of him. "Jerry—"

"How many mistakes can that woman make?" Jerry asked in a whisper.

I made a face. "Apparently a lot of them."

"Why doesn't Tiny fire her?" he asked, using his fork to turn over the tortilla-wrapped object on his plate.

"You mean Max?"

He shot me an irritated look. "Everyone knows Tiny runs the kitchen and Ruth runs the dining room. Max just sits behind the bar and looks good."

I smothered a laugh—I'd never heard Jerry say something so blunt—and Max, who had been standing behind the draft handles, popped his head up. "Somebody say something about me?"

Max Drummond was one fine-looking man and he knew it. Thick blond hair, hazel eyes, and an infectious laugh. He was the good-time guy behind the bar and, rumor had it, between the sheets. Although I hadn't seen him with a single woman since I'd shown up in town at the beginning of November, he was supposedly something of a ladies' man. Ruth liked to bring up all his past indiscretions and rub his nose in them, something he tolerated with good humor. He was only twenty-nine and had plenty of time before he had to worry about settling down...unless he went through the entire under-forty female demographic in the Smoky Mountain town of Drum, Tennessee, before he reached that stage. But my intuition told me that the smooth-talking charmer would still get his pick of girlfriends past.

But now he'd turned his attention to Jerry. "You talkin' about me?"

Three weeks ago, Jerry would have likely hung his head and shied away. But he had recently taken a stand against a man who'd bullied him, and doing so had brought back some of his confidence. He put his fork down and stared Max in the eye. "Phyllis is terrible in the kitchen. You need to fire her."

Max and I both stared at him with dropped jaws. "What?" we asked simultaneously.

"Hey," my cranky customer asked from across the room. "Am I gonna get my food here?"

Great. Mr. Fancy Pants had noticed me dawdling with Jerry while holding his plate of food. Given my short interaction with him, I should have known to serve him first. Within thirty seconds of walking in, he'd grabbed my arm and pulled me away from a table of customers. In a condescending tone, he'd asked about the VIP dining area, as if we might have a secret back room to separate rich people from the riffraff. With a chuckle, I'd told him this was as good as it got. He'd taken a table in the middle and asked for a fresh cloth to wipe down the table and chairs as if the place were dirty instead of very well-worn. I'd obliged, but his attitude had made me spitting mad.

Truth was, I dreaded waiting on him. His expensive dress shirt and pants, silk tie, and Italian leather loafers all screamed that he wasn't from around here, and he wore a perpetual smirk that reinforced that he thought he was too good for our tavern. He reminded me of the people who'd populated my past.

I set his plate in front of him, stretching my smile as wide as possible and forcing a cheery tone. "Here you go, sir. A cheeseburger with no mustard or lettuce, with a side of fries."

His dyed black hair was slicked back, and his face was clean-shaven. There was a hint of crow's feet around his eyes, but something about his forehead suggested he was a frequent Botox customer.

"They're cold," he said, staring up at me with narrowed eyes.

I tried not to shudder.

"You didn't even try them yet," I said in a forced teasing tone, pretending to be oblivious to his insults.

He didn't take his hard gaze from mine, and I realized we were in one of those staring contests my third-grade students had loved to challenge one another to back when I lived another life—the first one who blinked lost.

I knew I should just take his plate back to the kitchen and get a fresh order of fries—"The customer is always right" was the first rule of waiting tables—but I also knew they were still hot enough to burn his tongue. Mr. Fancy Pants got off on scaring people with his thousand-dollar clothes and arrogant attitude. He liked to see people run off with their tails tucked between their legs, but Charlene Moore didn't have a tail to tuck, and I was all out of patience with rich people trying to intimidate and destroy me.

I let my smile fall. "Those fries are just fine. You don't scare me with your condescension. What are you gonna do? Walk out without paying? I'll just give your meal to someone who'll appreciate it."

I should have kept my mouth shut, but he reminded me of my oil baron father and the assholes in his entourage. I might not be strong enough to face Randall Blakely, but I could definitely stand up to this prick.

The man continued to glare at me, but his face was starting to turn red.

I cocked my head to the side to show how unimpressed I was with his temper.

"I see you've met my son's new waitress," a man said from behind me.

Mr. Fancy Pants broke eye contact to glance at the man who was now sliding into the seat across from him.

The silver-haired man wasn't dressed as well as his dining partner, but he made up for it in arrogance and attitude. Bart Drummond was wearing a button-down dress shirt, with his sleeves rolled up to his forearms. It gave the impression he'd been working hard, but what he'd been doing was anyone's guess. The Drummonds had founded Drum over two hundred years ago, but the town had fallen on hard times. Between the shuttering of their lumber yard, the legalization of moonshine, and the loss of their tourist industry after the state park system relocated the entrance to a popular trail down to Balder Mountain, Drum was hurting and hurting bad. According to the locals, Bart Drummond's shine had begun to tarnish.

This was the first time I'd seen Max's father darken the tavern's door.

"Carly," Bart said without bothering to look at me, "could you bother yourself to get me a glass of tea and one of Tiny's world-famous burgers?" Then he turned to his lunch partner and said, "Good to see you, Neil. Did you have any trouble finding the place?"

Anger seethed inside of me. He'd dismissed me as though I were hired help. Okay, so I *was* hired help, but no one enjoyed being treated like dirt. Besides, he had to know I was dating Wyatt, his older son. They were estranged, but it was a small town. Everyone knew.

As I headed to the service counter, I cast a glance at Max, who had been watching our exchange with worried eyes, although I wasn't sure what or whom he was worried about. His father? Me?

I hung up the ticket, still keeping an eye on the two men in the dining room. It looked like Bart was having a business lunch...but at Max's Tavern? Then again, there wasn't really anywhere nicer to eat in this one-stop-sign town. Although Watson's Café, a block down, *nearly* had us beat.

"The fact you're not carrying a plate of food back must mean your cranky customer didn't have any complaints," Tiny called over from the grill.

"He's fine," I lied. "But this is an order for Bart Drummond himself. Said he wants one of your world-famous burgers."

Tiny rushed to the counter, much nimbler than I would have expected from a six-foot-four, two-hundred-and-eighty-pound man. He peered through the opening, trying to get a view of the dining room. "Bart Drummond is *here?*"

"So it *is* unusual?" I asked.

"I ain't seen him in here in years. Not since Max bought the place. Used to see him a lot when Wyatt was runnin' things."

I did a double take. "*What?*"

He shot me a look of surprise. "You didn't know Wyatt used to run the bar?"

"Yeah," I said. "I knew *that* part. I'm referring to the part about Bart comin' in all the time when Wyatt was in charge."

"Wyatt used to be a daddy's boy, through and through. Then the incident happened and... well, they had their falling-out."

Except I'd heard two different versions of the timeline. Wyatt had told me he'd fallen out with his father *before* he was arrested for a DUI and breaking and entering. In fact, he'd been caught trying to steal back a baseball his father had sold out from under him out of spite. Still, most of the townsfolk seemed to think the divide between father and son had come afterward. I had yet to learn the truth.

My past made it hard for me to trust men. My first week in town had been an intense whirlwind, and Wyatt and I had gotten caught up in it, and in each other. Maybe a bit too quickly given everything that had happened. I'd been plagued with nightmares and anxiety after Seth's funeral. So much so that Wyatt had convinced me that we should take a week to process everything before discussing our plan to reveal our fathers' crimes. And at the end of that first week, he'd suggested that we wait another week just to enjoy each other's company.

I'd resisted. My father had destroyed my mother and my former life, and from the sound of it, Bart Drummond wasn't much better. Besides, Wyatt knew so much more about me than I did about him, and all the things I didn't know felt like a barrier between us. But my bluster hadn't come to anything. Wyatt had taken my hand and quietly told me that Hank had heard me screaming the night before, and that had been enough to make me cave. Thanksgiving had been that week too, and since it had been Hank's first holiday without Seth, I'd wanted to make it special. Max went to their parents for dinner, but Wyatt joined Hank and me for turkey, dressing, and all the fixings, with a few diabetic-friendly recipes sprinkled in.

Wyatt and I had agreed to talk over the weekend, but then he'd found out about an auction in Virginia. A couple of tow trucks would go on the block, and the opportunity was too good to be missed, even though he'd offered to do just that. I'd encouraged him to go, even though it hurt a little to do it. We'd talked on the phone a few times, but there'd been a Wyatt-sized hole in my days. Last night, he'd called to say he'd won his bid on a tow truck and would be back in Drum by early evening. He was coming to Hank's after I got off at midnight.

My stomach fluttered in anticipation, and I felt like a high school girl with a crush—an unsettling feeling I'd be a whole lot happier with once he gave me some solid information about his past and his father.

A couple sitting by the window set their napkins down, so I hurried over to deliver their bill. Just as we settled up, a group of road crew guys came in and sat near the big-screen TV that was perpetually tuned to a sports channel. Franklin Tate—known as Tater to most of his friends—was with them. Franklin lived with Ruth, Max's other waitress, in a trailer a few miles up the road from where I was living, but they were secretly looking for a house to purchase.

Max kept casting glances in my direction as I dealt with them.

I knew he wanted me to come over, probably so he could grill me about his father, but I was the only on-duty waitress, and I was currently servicing eight tables. I wondered why he didn't go over himself.

Not long after I served Bart his food, he and his guest left—Bart's burger barely touched—without waiting for the check. I was about to rant to Max about his father dining and dashing, but then I noticed the two twenty-dollar bills on the table, plus a note written on the back of a business card.

Maybe waitressing isn't a good fit for you.

Steamed, I flipped the card over and read, *Neil Carpenter, Synergy Group*, with a Nashville address.

Had Mr. Fancy Pants written the note, or had Bart? And was it wrong for me to pocket the overpayment on the bill without remorse? They'd left a twenty-plus-dollar tip. My only regret was that I hadn't had an opportunity to eavesdrop on their conversation.

Max came over to bus the table just as I was about to leave to check on Franklin's group.

"What did my father want?"

"He was here for a power lunch." I started to pocket the business card, but Max snatched it out of my hand.

"What's my father up to this time?" he asked with a frown as he read the front. "You'd think he'd be lying low after his right-hand man tried to set up an illegal drug business."

His right-hand man, Carson Purdy, was the one who'd killed Bitty. He'd tried to silence me because I'd witnessed the murder of a teenage boy who'd had proof of what he and his accomplices were planning—a coup to unseat the local drug dealer, Todd Bingham. They'd been running a new drug from Atlanta to seal the deal, and Seth Chalmers, the boy they'd killed after he caught them in the act.

Todd Bingham and Bart Drummond were vying for the title of Most Important Man in Drum, Tennessee, although most people thought Bart still wore the crown, mostly because his dealings were aboveboard, while Bingham's were all illegal. I wasn't so sure about that, but it was common knowledge that Bart's large donations to the sheriff's department had likely helped clear him of any wrongdoing in the whole Carson Purdy episode.

"Carly?" Max prodded gently.

"You know what they say. No rest for the wicked."

Worry filled his eyes. "Carly."

I was still having nightmares about everything that had happened, from witnessing poor Seth's murder to the final showdown with Carson, and everything in between. I'd had plenty of dealings with Bingham, owing to his personal investment in the whole mess, and he'd frightened me nearly as much as being held at gunpoint. But Max didn't need to hear that. He seemed to feel guilty, as if he were at fault for putting me up in his motel that first night. So I just waved him off and headed for Franklin's table. As I walked away, I noticed frown lines on his forehead. He was reading the note disparaging my waitressing skills. If Bart Drummond wanted to insult me with twenty-dollar tips, he was free to do so every day of the week and twice on Sunday.

"How's everyone doin'?" I asked Franklin's group when I went to check on them. Like most places, Drum was home to an assortment of people, and Franklin's co-workers were the good kind. "Can I get y'all anything else? Refills? Should I save y'all pieces of Miss Patsy's pie? I gotta warn you—they're goin' fast." While Tiny was a great grill cook, he'd left the baking to Bitty. Without her around to make dessert, Max had gotten Miss Patsy, the Methodist preacher's spinster sister, to start making daily pies for us, and they had been a hit.

Tinker, a man in his forties, leaned back in his chair and rubbed his belly. "I sure as Pete can't pass up a piece of Miss Patsy's pie."

"We've got pumpkin, apple crisp, and pecan today. Miss Patsy seems to be in a fall kind of mood."

Each of the men ordered a slice of pie along with a scoop of ice cream. I was about to head to the back with the ticket when the front door opened. The woman who walked in was tiny— barely five feet tall—and her platinum blonde hair was in two braids that hung a few inches past her shoulders. She had a youthful face with doe eyes, and she was wearing jeans and a bohemian-style blue shirt. A duffel bag was slung over her shoulder.

Max stopped in his tracks when he saw her, his arms full of dirty dishes, a scowl crossing his face.

"Well, I'll be damned," Tinker said, sitting up straighter.

Franklin had stilled as well, casting me a worried glance. "Lula's back."

Which meant I was out of a job.

CHAPTER TWO

I 'd known this job was temporary, but somehow I'd shoved that fact in the back of my mind. Max had always promised me that he'd keep me around when or *if* Lula returned, but the tavern wasn't busy enough for three full-time waitresses.

Lula turned her attention to me, her already large blue eyes widening. "You replaced me, Max?"

The look in Max's eyes softened just a touch. Lula's flightiness was legendary—apparently she'd come and gone too many times to count, usually with no notice—and this last time, she'd gone off to Chattanooga with a truck driver who'd delivered food supplies for Tiny. Max had threatened to not take Lula back, saying she'd left one time too many, but the customers loved her. They'd only warmed up to me because Max and I had both assured them I was temporary.

Panic started to bloom in my chest. I was living under an alias and my father had a five-hundred-thousand-dollar bounty on my head disguised as a reward for my safe return. Wyatt—the only person in Drum who knew I'd been born Caroline Blakely —had convinced me that Drum was one of the safest places I could be…previous murder attempts notwithstanding. He had a point—it was a land lost in time with limited access to internet and even spottier cell phone coverage. It also had absolutely no CCTV cameras. Besides which, the people made me want to stay.

Nevertheless, I had to earn my keep, and Drum wasn't exactly overflowing with jobs.

"He didn't replace you," I said with a wide smile. I stepped closer and offered her my hand. "I'm Carly Moore. I've been filling in for you."

She glanced down at my hand, but instead of taking it, she wrapped her arms around me and pulled me into a tight embrace. "Well, aren't you the sweetest thing!"

Max still stood to the side, and when she released me, she turned and gave him a soft smile. "Hey, Max."

"Don't 'hey, Max,' me," he said, trying to sound gruff, but it came out forced. "You walked out on us, Lula. You left us in a bind. *Again.*"

"I know," she said, casting her gaze on the floor. "I'm sorry. It won't happen again."

"Just because you came back doesn't mean you still have a job. Carly has busted her ass to take up the slack for you. It doesn't seem fair to punish her just because you decided to drop in for another month or two before you take off again," he said in a harsh tone, but I saw the indecision flickering on his face.

He was still holding the dirty plates, so I took them from him.

"Maybe you should have this conversation in the back." I nodded to the table of road crew guys, who were openly staring in curiosity and shock.

Franklin looked plain worried.

"Good idea," Max said. His mouth turned down and he led the way, leaving Lula to follow.

"Hey, Lula," one of the guys said as she walked by, lifting a hand in greeting.

"Good to have you back," Tinker said.

And that was when I knew I'd lost my job. If Max fired Lula, half the men in town would treat me like a pariah. They'd revolt and start going to Watson's.

Max shot them a frown as he kept walking, but Lula waved.

"Hey, Billy. Hey, Tinker and Tater, good to see you." Then she disappeared into the back.

I took the dirty plates to the tray Tiny liked us to dump them in and handed in the ticket for the guys' pies. I waited on another table, then picked up the pie order and headed back to Franklin's table.

"Here you go, gentlemen," I said in a friendly tone as I set the plates in front of them. "Would anyone like some coffee? It'll warm you up before you head back out in the cold."

Billy looked up at me. "What's gonna happen to you now that Lula's back?"

"Don't you worry about me, Billy," I said, forcing a smile. "The good news is that Lula's back and everyone's happy."

Franklin frowned and got up from his seat. "That coffee sounds pretty good, Carly. How about I come back and help you get the cups?"

Franklin knew I was capable of bringing it all out, but I wasn't surprised he wanted to follow me. "Ruth will put this to rights," he said under his breath as we walked to the back together. "Don't you worry."

I shook my head and willed my eyes to stop stinging. "We all knew I started out as a temporary replacement." I turned and offered him a tight smile. "I was lucky this lasted as long as it did."

He leaned closer. "This is bullshit, Carly. You work circles around that girl. She lollygags around, leaving Ruth to pick up the slack." He straightened back up and shook his head. "It ain't right, and Ruth won't get rid of you to keep her."

I placed a hand on Franklin's arm and held his gaze. "It's gonna be all right."

But I had to wonder what Max would do. I wasn't sure there was a right answer here. Lula might not be a great worker, but the patrons loved her, and their loyalty mattered to the establishment.

Max stomped out of his office, Lula following on his heels, and stopped in front of me. "Carly, can I speak to you in my office?"

I shot a quick glance at Lula, who kept her gaze on the floor. That wasn't a good sign.

"Sure," I said, pressing a hand to my stomach to quell my nerves.

I trailed behind him into the room I was sure used to be an oversized closet at one point. He grabbed his office chair and turned it to face the door.

"Have a seat," he said, gesturing toward it.

I did as he instructed, saying, "Nothing good ever came out of those three words."

His lips were pressed into a thin line as he shut the door and sat on the edge of the desk, staring down at me. "I'm takin' Lula back."

My head bobbed as my mind raced. What would I do for work?

"I don't want to, but I'm between a rock and a hard place, Carly," he said in frustration. "Half of my customers love her to pieces."

"I know, Max," I assured him. "They were worried I might be

taking her place, and we both assured them I wasn't." I gave him a tight smile. "I can't be makin' a liar out of the both of us."

"The thing is," he said. "I doubt she'll stick around. The girl has serious wanderlust. She'll be here for a month or two and run off again. I don't want to lose you in the meantime. I know it's not fair to ask, but would you stick around anyway? I'll have to cut your hours, but I'll be sure to have all three of you work on Monday and Thursday nights. And I'll put you on Wednesday lunch shift. We both know that's the best one." He grimaced and leaned forward. "There's just not enough business for three full-time waitresses."

Didn't I know it.

"What choice do I have?" I said with a chuckle. I doubted any other employment opportunities would present themselves. I was still living with Hank Chalmers, helping provide him with medical care and cooking his meals in exchange for room and board, so at least I didn't have many bills. The only regular expenses I had were the gas it took to get to work and back—Wyatt had fixed up Hank's car for me to use—and food that I bought for the household. I could make it work.

I stood and put my hand on Max's arm. "Don't look so worried. I'll be fine."

"Maybe Wyatt can help you out."

My back stiffened. "I'll be just fine," I said in a tight voice as I dropped my arm.

His brows lifted. "Are you and Wyatt havin' problems? I haven't seen him around this last week."

"No," I said, taking a step back, a nearly impossible task given the room was about six feet wide. "But I don't need a man to take care of me. I can take care of myself."

Max grimaced. "I didn't mean…"

"I know what you meant," I said. "And I appreciate you being so worried about me, but I promise I'll be fine. We'll find a way to make it work. When does Lula start?"

"Tonight—if that's okay. With it bein' Thursday and all, I figured there'd be enough tips to spread round."

But we'd all end up with less money at the end of the night.

"I should have just fired her ass," Max said dejectedly.

"We both know you couldn't do that," I said, offering him a more genuine smile than before. "Business would likely suffer, and then all of us would be hurting."

"I'm not takin' her back full-time. I'm makin' her share some of her hours with you," he said.

"I'll take whatever I can get," I said. "I'm just grateful to still be here. I like workin' with y'all too much to leave."

"I meant it when I told you that you're one of us, Carly," he said, his voice tight. "You fit right in. Lula's a flirt, so she's popular with the customers, but she's never been interested in getting too close to us. She comes in and does her job and leaves. We don't know much about her. It's like she's guardin' a lockbox full of secrets."

I ducked my head to hide my shame. I had plenty of secrets I was guarding too, but I knew what he meant. I might have only been a part of the Max's Tavern crew for a few weeks, but Max, Ruth, Tiny, and I had been through hell together. They'd stood by me through the entire nightmare, offering me shelter, comfort, and friendship. I felt a loyalty to them that went bone-deep, yet I still couldn't tell them the truth about my background. Like the fact that my father had planned to marry me off to my lifelong best friend turned betrayer, but only so said best friend could be his successor in an illegal enterprise. After the wedding, they'd planned to have me killed in an accident no one would question.

Although I was fairly certain the freak accident was off the table now. Having given the matter some thought, I suspected they'd use my disappearance to make me look unstable. They'd still want to kill me, but they'd probably make it look like an OD. Or suicide.

"We all have our crosses to bear," I said. "I better get back out there. I think Franklin and his crew are probably ready for their checks." No one had gotten them that coffee, unless Tiny had given it directly to Franklin, but I suspected they'd forgotten about it in the excitement.

I headed for the door and Max called out, "Carly?"

Stopping with my hand on the doorknob, I glanced over my shoulder.

"I meant what I said about you being family. Thanks for being so awesome about all of this."

CHAPTER THREE

Ruth and I had fallen into a routine. I did four lunch shifts and she covered three. We each got one day off a week, and Max had closed the tavern until seven on Thanksgiving last week. Whoever did lunch would stay at the tavern in the slow period between the two shifts, since we were technically open at those times, and leave after the post-dinner cleanup if we were slow and until close if we were busy. Those days ran very long, between nine and twelve hours given the tavern opened at noon and sometimes stayed open as late as midnight, but the midafternoons were slow and Max didn't have a problem with me taking breaks to visit the library or to use his computer in his office. We didn't really get paid much per hour, but he always paid me for the full shift, even on the rare occasions I left for more than an hour.

Ruth was scheduled to come in at five, but I wasn't surprised when she stormed in the back door fifteen minutes early. If anything, I was surprised it had taken her that long.

"Maxwell," she called out with fire in her eyes, standing in the doorway separating the dining area from the back. "Your office. Now."

I'd been sitting at the counter, tallying up the tips while Max sat on a stool behind the bar, reading a paperback western. But he lowered the book and shot me a look that screamed, *Oh shit.*

This was something else Jerry had been right about. Max owned the place, but everyone knew Ruth ran it.

"Now!" she barked. Before she turned the corner, she stopped and pointed her finger at me. "And don't you dare leave this bar!" Then she stomped off.

Max dragged his feet, and it would have been comical if he weren't a twenty-nine-year-old man, deferring to his hired help. But if I'd learned one thing about Max, it was that he was excellent at handling conflict with or between any customers in his tavern—he'd even whipped out a knife to defend me from a drunken lecher—but he couldn't stand to make anyone on his staff unhappy. He tried to placate all of us, attempting to ride the middle ground so he didn't look like he had a favorite—which tended to backfire and make everyone unhappy. Ruth and Tiny had gotten into a spat the week before, but Max had refused to intervene, even though Ruth was clearly in the wrong. (Not that I was stupid enough to tell her.) We'd all walked on eggshells for two days until Ruth had reluctantly apologized, telling Tiny that Franklin had called her out for being a bitch.

In this situation, I understood why Ruth was upset—hell, I was grateful for it—but I had to agree with Max that it wasn't smart to fire Lula. Better to let her quit or run off again on her own terms. I could make it work until that happened.

I headed to the service counter, and Tiny and I jumped when we started hearing muffled shouts.

"Mom and Pop are arguing again," Tiny said with a grin, but I could tell he was as unnerved by it as I was. Especially since I was part of their argument.

Ruth emerged ten minutes later, but Max stayed in his office.

"You," she barked to me as she headed out to the bar. "Come with me."

I shot Tiny a worried look, but he just shrugged and smiled.

I followed her behind the counter.

"I'm running the bar tonight. Max'll help once the football crowd shows up. You and Lula'll wait on the customers through dinner."

"Okay."

She frowned. "Lula ain't me, so you'll likely be pickin' up the slack for her."

"The dinner crowd on Thursday is usually pretty light. I should be okay."

She smacked her hand on the bar, her eyes blazing with anger. "Why the hell aren't you pissed off?"

My eyes flew wide. "About Lula?" I shook my head. "Ruth, when I started, the agreement was that I'd only work until she came back. I'm only glad I get to stay on part-time. I'll take whatever I can get for hours, as long as I'm not hurtin' you."

"Don't worry about me," she said in frustration. "Worry about yourself."

"Maybe she won't stick around," I said, "but in the meantime, at least you'll get more help. And maybe a few days off."

"And a raise," she said fiercely. "Max is payin' us minimum wage in addition to our tips."

I blinked, sure I'd heard wrong. "Are you kidding?"

A grin tugged at her lips as she shrugged. "I tried to get health insurance and paid vacation, but at least I got us a raise."

A new worry hit me. "Can Max afford that?"

"Don't you worry about Max," she said. "He'll be just fine."

She grabbed two shot glasses, set them on the counter, then filled them with whiskey. Picking up the glasses, she handed one to me and kept hers raised. "To better days."

I clinked my glass with hers. I could drink to that. "Amen." We both downed our drinks, and I set the empty shot glass on the counter just as a young couple walked through the door. "Looks like it's time to get back to work."

Ruth made a sour face. "What do you know? It's after five and Lula hasn't shown up for her shift yet." She shook her head. "Get used to it. She's never on time."

I walked around the counter to greet the customers and tell them about Tiny's Thursday night special—chili cheese dogs. (We weren't exactly a classy joint.) As soon as I got their drink orders, a family of five walked in. I invited them to take a seat anywhere they would like. As Lula wasn't here, then I'd be waiting on everyone until she came back or Ruth came out to help.

We got several more customers, and things were hopping before Lula showed up at six.

"I'm sorry, y'all!" she exclaimed as she hurried out from the back, tugging her loose Max's Tavern T-shirt into place as though she'd just pulled it over her head. The flyaway strands of hair sticking out everywhere indicated my thought wasn't off base.

I blinked in surprise. While Ruth and I didn't wear anything obscenely tight, our shirts were much more formfitting. Especially on a football night. Hadn't everyone told me Lula was a flirt?

She hurried over to the bar and her eyes widened. "Where's Max?"

Ruth put a hand on her hip and gave Lula the evil eye. "Catchin' up on paperwork."

"I didn't know you knew how to tend bar, Ruthie," she said, using Tiny's nickname for her.

"There's lots of things you don't know about me, Lula. Maybe if you stuck around long enough, you'd find out a thing or two." Ruth turned her back on her and headed over to the beer taps.

Lula turned to me with hurt eyes. "I think Ruthie's mad at me."

I stared at her in disbelief. Was she for real or was this an act to go along with her innocent-schoolgirl persona? I decided to be generous. "I think Ruth's upset that you keep taking off and leaving her with all the work."

"But you're here now."

"And so are you," I said. "We'll all be making less money. Although Ruth had a discussion with Max earlier, and he agreed to give us all a raise."

Her eyes lit up. "Oh! That's good."

"Yeah," I said. She didn't seem to get it, but I decided to let it go, especially since a group of people had just walked in the door. "How do you want to divide up sections? I've been working your old section, but maybe I should work Ruth's tonight. The Thursday night football crowd will be happy to see you." So happy I wondered if they'd flood her section, leaving me with only the leftover guys who wouldn't fit.

"Okay," she said, her nose scrunched in confusion. "So Ruth's not working tonight?"

Was she really this slow? I didn't see any hint of duplicity—if anything, she seemed distracted and worried—so I softened my tone. "She's working behind the bar, remember? Max'll come out later."

"Oh," she said with a frown, then nodded. "Right."

We got to work, and I watched her with the customers, forgetting things, getting orders wrong, until I finally approached Ruth for some drink refills and asked, "Have you been watching Lula?"

"Like a hawk," she said with scorn on her face.

"Does she usually make this many mistakes?"

"No, this is excessive, even for her."

"Do you think she's nervous because Max kept me on?" Before she could answer, I added, "She didn't seem to grasp that she and I are going to make less money now that there's two of us for one job."

Ruth leveled her gaze on mine. "You are not going to make less money, do you hear me? I'm sure as hell not going to risk losing you over that nitwit." Her expression softened. "I don't dislike Lula. She's a sweet girl and that clueless act is genuine. But you're right about the mistakes. Something's up with her. Let's just keep an eye on her."

"Okay."

She handed me the soft drinks and I took them to the table. At around seven, Wyatt walked through the door, and my stomach fluttered at the sight of him.

He'd come early.

Wyatt Drummond was the epitome of tall, dark, handsome, and mysterious. Even though he still wore his coat, I knew what his strong arms looked and felt like. And his hard chest. And his lips. I'd been thinking about him a sight more than I'd expected considering everything else that was going on in my life.

We'd only been together for a few weeks, but the intensity of my feelings had scared me, and Wyatt had sensed it. While my head knew that Wyatt was different than all the previous men in my life, there was something so closed-off about him, even now, and I wasn't sure I could ever break through his walls. I didn't like feeling so vulnerable. But I hoped things would change tonight.

I flashed him a smile, and the look he gave me made the fluttering turn into an all-out somersault. He started toward an empty table in my usual section, then did a double take when he saw Lula standing next to a table with her notepad in hand.

I motioned for him to come over to a table in Ruth's section, and he spanned the distance between us, stopping just in front of me. Close, but not close enough.

"You're early." My cheeks flushed. I knew I should play this cool, but I couldn't seem to pull it off.

The look on Wyatt's face suggested he felt the same way. "I know we agreed we'd meet at Hank's tonight, but I got back earlier than expected, and I couldn't stay away."

I smiled up at him. "I'm glad you came."

He cast a glance to the other side of the room and a worried frown covered his face. "Lula's back?"

"Yep," I said, forcing a cheerfulness I didn't feel about the situation. "Just got back today."

"Max's keepin' you both on?"

"That's what he says, although Ruth's fit to be tied. She got Max to agree to pay us minimum wage in addition to our tips."

His frown deepened, and I wondered if he worried that I'd be leaving Drum after all.

"I'll be okay, Wyatt. I haven't changed my mind. I'm not going anywhere."

Relief filled his eyes. "I'm glad to hear it."

I gave him a little push toward the chair. "Do you know what you want? Tiny's special is chili cheese dogs."

He grinned. "Don't be telling Hank that. I stopped by his place first and made sure he ate the cauliflower mac and cheese you left for him in the fridge."

My brows shot up. "Did he like it?"

Hank would live off junk food if left to his own devices, but he was diabetic and his right leg had recently been amputated due to his condition. I'd been slipping some diabetic-friendly recipes into my meal planning. I'd even served quinoa stuffing with our Thanksgiving turkey. Since I worked most nights, Wyatt went over to check on him after he got off work to make sure he ate.

"He didn't dislike it. He had two helpings. I ate the rest, so don't be planning on havin' any leftovers when you get home."

I laughed. "I'll consider that a win."

"Expect to hear some complaining anyway."

I shook my head, still grinning. "I can live with it. But if you already ate…"

He moved closer, resting his hand on my hip. Tingles shot through my body at his touch, and I drew in a breath. I'd missed him in more ways than one. I craved him like no other man before him, although I wondered if part of his allure was his promise to help me. He'd painted a future in which I could stop running…and every single part of me wanted that. Still, there was no doubt I was physically attracted to him. Any woman would be.

His eyes darkened and he lowered his voice. "I already told you. I didn't want to wait four more hours to see you."

This man was capable of turning me upside down and inside out, but this wasn't the time or place. "Fine," I said with a hint of a grin. "But sit down and behave. Don't touch me again until I get off."

He grinned back. "I'm not sure I can agree to that."

"I just might kick you out if you become too big of a distraction."

He sat down and leaned back in his seat, wearing a lazy smile. "I'll take my chances."

"You'll have to order something, but I have to warn you.

Tiny's new cook, Sugar, gets more orders wrong than right, so you're taking your chances."

"Get me a chili cheese dog and a draft beer." He shot a glance toward the bar. "And make sure Ruth doesn't spit in it. That seems like the bigger risk."

I laughed as I wrote his order on the ticket. Ruth detested him, although no one would tell me why, the two involved parties included. My best assumption was that it had something to do with the fact that they'd dated briefly years ago, although neither of them had confirmed or denied that.

The front door opened before I could head back to the service counter, and a quick glance told me Jerry had arrived. Wyatt saw him too and motioned for the elderly man to come sit with him. Both of us owed a debt of gratitude to Jerry given the way he'd helped us face down Carson.

"Would you like something for dinner?" I asked as he sat down.

"A burger, fries, and a Coke," Jerry said, slipping off his threadbare coat. I made a mental note to stop by Goodwill when I took Hank to Greeneville the next day for his doctor's appointment.

It occurred to me that Jerry wasn't eating any healthier than Hank used to, and I made another note to bring him some of Hank's extras.

I started to write down his order on a separate sheet, but Wyatt pointed to his chest, letting me know to put it on his tab. Jerry would likely protest, but Wyatt could charm him into agreeing.

A couple of days earlier, Tiny had asked why he hadn't seen Wyatt hanging around. I'd reassured him that Wyatt would likely be in soon enough. Tiny had said *good* with surprising vehemence and then shocked me into silence by calling me an enchantress who'd woken Wyatt up from a long sleep. According to him, Wyatt used to be happy and carefree before his arrest, something he seemed to have lost after his nearly two-year incarceration. He'd come home a loner—quiet, reserved, and serious. A lot like the Wyatt I'd met on the overlook above Drum. I'd laughed and told Tiny that I hadn't known him to be so fanciful, but he'd grinned back. "There's a whole lot you don't know about me, but that doesn't discount the fact that you seem to be bringing Wyatt Drummond back to life."

It was a beautiful compliment, but something about the way Tiny had phrased it had stayed with me. *There's a whole lot you don't know about me.* I got the sense there was a whole lot more to just about everyone I'd met in this small Smoky Mountain town, Wyatt included, but then, I had plenty of my own secrets, so who was I to judge?

I turned in their orders and got Wyatt's beer and Jerry's Coke at the bar.

Ruth shot Wyatt a dark look. "What's he doin' here? I haven't seen him in nearly a week."

"He came for dinner, same as everyone else."

"Not the same as everyone else. He's here for you."

I flashed her a grin. "I'd like to think my sunny disposition brings some of the customers in now."

She laughed and shook her head. "There's more truth to that than you realize, a fact I made sure to point out to Max. He was losin' lunch-crowd business until you showed up. Lula's a hit with the football crowd because of her flirting and sweetness, but the lunch crowd is more inclined to appreciate competent staff with a"—she grinned—"sunny disposition." When she noticed my look of surprise, she said, "Surely you've noticed that business has picked up."

"To be fair," I said. "You warned me in the beginning that it would be slow, but I never saw it because everyone wanted to drop in and see the waitress who'd found Seth's body. They all thought I was a murderer until we caught Carson."

"True enough," she said, handing me Wyatt's mug. "But you're a big draw." She gave me a forced smile. "And notice I didn't spit in Wyatt's beer."

"Why won't you tell me why you two hate each other?"

She frowned. "Hate's a strong word."

"Fine, then you have strong feelings of dislike. Why won't you tell me?"

"Have Wyatt tell you."

"He says to have *you* tell me."

She released a chuckle. "It's water under the bridge, Carly. Let it go."

"But it's hard to do that when my loyalty feels divided."

Her expression softened. "That's sweet of you to say, but what happened between us was long ago. We're both nearly a decade older. I'll only say it involved Heather. Let bygones be bygones, and all that. You two look happy. I won't begrudge you that."

Ruth and Wyatt had dated years ago, during a break in his off-and-on relationship with a woman named Heather. Heather was the woman who'd been with him the night of his arrest. She'd left town after the Drummonds paid her not to testify against him.

I delivered the drinks and settled up with a couple of customers, most of whom seemed intent on leaving before the football crowd showed up.

My section was caught up, but Lula seemed to be behind on bussing her tables.

"Let me give you a hand," I said cheerfully as I started to clear the table next to the one she was working on.

"I don't see how you can keep up with it all," she said in frustration, and I realized she was close to tears.

Her section actually had fewer customers, but she was struggling to make sure everyone was taken care of in a speedy manner.

"It's all about multitasking."

She looked up at me with tears in her eyes. "I really need this job, Carly."

My breath stuck in my chest. Did she want me to quit and give her my hours? Or was she worried her incompetency was going to get her fired? I was going to presume the latter. "I'll help you, Lula. Don't you worry."

"Ruthie's mad at me, and Max'll barely talk to me."

"You know what?" I said in a bright voice. "That's in the past. We're gonna move forward, okay? If you need help multitasking, I can help. I became a master at it when I was a—" I cut myself off as I realized I'd been on the verge of telling her about my past as a third-grade teacher. That was the old me. Caroline Blakely. I'd been Charlene Moore for a month now, and in hiding for even longer, but I still made slips. "I learned it back in retail. I'll help you, so don't you worry."

"Why are you bein' so nice to me?" she asked, swiping her cheek with her hand. "You don't even know me."

"Because, despite their current frustration, Max actually *does* like you and so does Ruth. I trust their judgment. They're just mad that you left them high and dry. If you don't do that again, you'll be fine."

She studied me with deep, soulful eyes, then said, "I won't be goin' anywhere. I need this job, Carly."

"You just do your best," I said. "Come to work on time. Don't run off again. Do your job, and you'll be fine. If you get behind or overwhelmed, I'll help out, okay?"

She threw her arms around me and buried her face into my shoulder. "Thank you, Carly. I knew you were a sweet person the moment I laid eyes on you."

I cast a glance to the bar and caught Ruth's scowl. While I knew that Ruth liked the girl, I also knew her patience was thin.

Pulling free, I said, "Let's get this section cleaned up. The football crowd's due any minute, and they're gonna be so excited to see you."

"Really?" she asked in surprise.

"You bet. They nearly kicked me out my first night, wondering why I was workin' instead of you." I gave her a beaming smile. "So let's clean off the tables, and you can head to the bathroom to fix your mascara so you'll be ready to meet your adoring fans."

"I'm sorry if they were mean to you." Her frown was back. It was like she showed every emotion that fluttered through her head, and I suddenly felt a strong urge to protect her.

"I'm fine. Don't you worry about me. I assured them you'd be back, and all was well with the world." I picked up a stack of plates and held them out to her. "You take these to the back. The Applebaums are ready for their check."

She took the dishes and I took the bill to my customers in the booth, who had shown signs of being ready to leave. Once we were settled, I took Wyatt and Jerry their food.

"What's goin' on with Lula?" Wyatt asked, casting a glance toward her as she bussed another table.

"She's having a rough transition back," I said.

"That girl's touched," Jerry said, turning his gaze on his plate. "Never been right since she almost drowned as a girl. About eight or nine."

"What?" I said in horror. "How awful."

"Her daddy done tried to drown her in the creek that ran at

the back of their property, and her mother shot him with a shot-gun. Heard she had to do CPR on Lula until the ambulance arrived. She ain't been the same since."

Now I felt even more protective of her. "What happened to her mother?"

"Incarcerated on second-degree murder."

Gasping, I turned to Wyatt. "How in the hell did that happen?"

Wyatt's eyes darkened. "Hensen County."

I'd learned that the county was such a cesspool of corruption it was a wonder the whole place didn't stink like a swamp.

"One fight at a time, Carly," Wyatt said in a soothing tone, but his words had the opposite effect. They made me impatient. Although he was the one who'd suggested we take our corrupt fathers down, the idea had made me feel strong for the first time in a long, long while. His promise was one of the main reasons I'd chosen to stay in Drum, but nearly three weeks had passed since Bart Drummond's right-hand man had tried to kill me, Wyatt, Jerry, and Deputy Marco Roland, and we'd done nothing.

Had Wyatt manipulated me? I'd dated a long string of narcis-sists, culminating with Jake, my former best friend and fiancé. Somehow I'd always missed the signs until it was too late.

"So we start tonight?" I pressed.

His expression wavered. "It's been a long day for the both of us."

Another stall, which sounded perfectly reasonable—they all had—but when I added them all together, it made for a pretty clear picture.

It would be a long, long time before this man told me anything.

"Well, it sure would be nice to at least enter the ring on *one* of those fights." I turned around, avoiding the urge to look back, and walked over to help Lula bus the last table.

"Lula, can I ask a favor?"

She looked at me with her large, trusting eyes, and I thought about the horrors she'd faced. Who had taken care of her after her mother had gone to prison? But I shook off my thoughts. Surely that was the last thing she'd want to talk about. "Can you cover Wyatt's table for me?"

"Wyatt Drummond?" she asked, her brow shooting up.

"Yeah," I said, making no secret of pointing to his table. "Over there. It's at the edge of our sections. I can take one of yours in exchange."

"Can you take two?" she asked in nearly a whisper. "Football nights are crazy."

"I'll take as many as you like," I said. "And I'll share the tips with you."

"You don't have to do that, Carly."

"We'll sort it out later," I said. "But you'll be doin' me a huge favor if you handle Wyatt."

"Of course," she said, nodding her head, "I'll do anything for you, Carly. You just have to ask."

I wasn't sure why that worried me.

CHAPTER FOUR

Just as we worked out which two tables I'd cover for her, some of the guys started showing up. When I'd first started working at Max's Tavern, I'd thought it was strange that so few women showed up for football nights, but Ruth had explained the Methodist Church hosted a knitting club on Monday and Thursday nights, although she was fairly certain it involved more wine drinking and gossip than it did knitting.

"Lula's back!" one of the guys shouted, grinning from ear to ear. He was an older man, in his late fifties, and he pulled her into a hug and twirled her around in a full circle.

She let out a squeal. "You put me down, Fred Myers!"

He laughed and set her down as though she were made of glass. "We missed ya, Lula girl."

Her cheeks flushed as she gave him a soft smile. "I missed all y'all too."

"You're not leavin' again anytime soon, are ya?" he asked in a worried tone.

"No, sir," she said solemnly. "I'm stickin' around for good this time."

"Mighty glad to hear it!" Fred exclaimed, then headed over to a table near the TV and out of Lula's section.

More men wandered in to watch the game, all of them enthused to see Lula, and she made the same sheepish look every time. As the night progressed, I realized most of the men treated her kindly and tolerated her slowness and her occasional mistakes with generosity, and I also realized I'd been mistaken about the situation. Before I'd met Lula, Max and Ruth had led me to believe that Lula was popular because she had an ingénue personality. But now I could see that the men genuinely cared about her, and my heart nearly burst.

Wyatt soon figured out that I'd handed him off to Lula, but I ignored his attempts to get my attention. It wouldn't kill him to stew a little bit, and I wasn't sure where I stood right now. I needed time to sort things out.

Around halftime, Todd Bingham walked through the door with his toadies filing in behind him like an entourage, which wasn't far off the mark.

His appearance caught me off guard. I hadn't seen him since he'd shown up in the tavern the night that Carson Purdy had tried to kill me. What was he doing here tonight?

But I understood the second his gaze landed on Lula. The hairs on the back of my neck stood on end even before his gaze turned to me. A grin spread across his face, but it didn't meet his eyes, not that I was surprised. Bingham had been plenty jovial when quizzing me about what I'd seen the night of Seth's murder, but none of it had been genuine. Bingham struck me as a sadist who took perverse pleasure in watching people squirm, and he was clearly waiting for a similar reaction from me now.

He'd wait all fucking night. Todd Bingham had no reason to bother me anymore. He'd unmasked the traitors who'd attempted to steal his business, their identities confirmed by me, and he'd meted out his "justice." Although he'd told me that he would let the final two men run, their bodies had turned up in a ravine down the mountain last week. Further proof, as if I'd needed it, he was not to be trusted.

I cocked my head and gave him a surly gaze. "Are you waitin' for an escort to a table? You know how this works. Find an open table, and you'll be waited on as soon as we get to you."

He didn't like my retort, but I didn't care. I was done letting men intimidate me, even ruffians like Bingham.

I turned my back on him and caught a glimpse of Max, who was now behind the bar, working side by side with Ruth. The scowl on his face suggested he'd noticed my exchange with Bingham, although the roar of the crowd was loud enough to drown out what we'd said. I saw him reach down his right side, and even though the bar hid his body from the waist down, I suspected he was reaching for the hunting knife strapped to his leg. He was expecting trouble. Did he know something about Bingham that I didn't? Was the criminal up to something new? I definitely didn't like the way he'd been watching Lula. I'd be sure to keep an eye on that situation.

I waited on a few customers, placing orders for cheese dogs, nachos, and wings, as well as refilling beers and the occasional whiskey or tequila shots. Those were ordered more frequently on the weekend, when the men were in a more celebratory mood.

When I finally made it to Bingham's table, he was surrounded by his friends—a term I used loosely for the men who always seemed to gather around him like a cloud of gnats. His arms were crossed over his chest, and he stared up at me with an expressionless gaze. "Lula's back."

"You're pretty observant," I sassed back.

"And you're pretty smart-mouthed," he countered, but he didn't look as furious as I'd expected.

"And now that we've gotten reacquainted," I said with my hand on my hip, "how about I take your order?"

"Where's Lula been?" he asked.

"Well, I suppose that's Lula's business, and if she wants you to know, she'll be sure to tell you."

"Then send her right on over so I can get to askin'."

"No can do," I said. "She's got her own section to deal with. You're stuck with me." Then, because I couldn't resist, I added with a bright smile, "And my sunny disposition."

He studied me for a moment, as though trying to figure out if I was for real, then started to laugh. I'd heard him laugh before but only for effect—this laugh was extra proof that the previous ones had all been counterfeit. This one was genuine, and it caught me off guard. Based on the looks of the people around him, they'd been taken by surprise too. When he settled down, his smile faded and his eyes took on a hint of warning. "Let me give you a lesson, little girl. When I ask for something, I expect it to be done."

"Well, shame on your parents for not teaching you that the world doesn't revolve around you. Now do you want to order something on the menu, or should I go take care of my paying customers?"

His eyes darkened and I knew he was done tolerating my back talk. "No one speaks to me that way."

I let out a heavy sigh, but my heart was racing. Todd Bingham was a dangerous man, and I was playing with a freaking bonfire. Even so, I couldn't let him boss me around. He might be a lot rougher than my father, but they had a lot in common—both men were arrogant enough to believe everyone in the world had been put there to serve them and do as they said. Anger billowed in my chest. I'd spent most of my life cowering from my father, trying to stay off his radar, but I was done. I wasn't going to let Bingham tell me what to do, and once I left this town, I was going to find a way to stop my father. With or without Wyatt's help.

I stepped closer, standing over him. "And no one orders me around. *No. One.* Not even you."

He jerked upright, placing one hand on the table and the other at his waist, and it was then I saw the bulge under his shirt, not that I was surprised he was carrying. I'd learned that Drum was a lot like the Wild West, not just because it was hidden away from the rest of the world, but also because most people carried a gun of some type. So far there hadn't been any shoot-outs on Main Street at high noon, but then I'd only been here for a month.

Turn around and walk away, Carly. But I couldn't do it. If I backed down, I'd start the transformation back to Caroline Blakely, the proper daughter of a supposedly respectable man. The woman who'd let so damn much slide. I'd discovered I liked being Carly Moore too much for that.

I narrowed my eyes and glared down at him. "What are you gonna do, Bingham? Shoot me in the bar? Not a good idea. Max is pretty wicked with his knife, and I wouldn't be surprised if his blade was embedded in your chest two seconds after you pull the trigger. Besides, you and I both know there's one more thing that's gonna stop you from touching a single hair on my head— your agreement with Hank Chalmers."

Hank had been the previous drug lord of the area, something I'd learned *after* moving into his house. He'd ceded his territory to Bingham, but there were two iron clauses attached to their agreement. Hank had pledged to stop growing his much coveted high-quality weed, and in exchange, Bingham would never touch Hank's kin. Hank had claimed me as kin, and while that offered me certain protections, I knew Bingham was a little fuzzy with the rules. Still, there was no twisting attempted murder to fit their arrangement.

He lifted both hands to the sides of his head. "You've got an active imagination there, girl."

I didn't back down, still glaring at him. "I have a name and you will use it. You may call me Carly or Ms. Moore. Your pick. If you refuse, then I'll refuse to wait on you."

"I'll just move to Lula's new section."

"Not a chance in hell is that happening."

I wasn't surprised when I heard Max's voice directly behind me. "Is there a problem here?"

Bingham gave me a long, cold stare before lifting his gaze to Max. "*Carly* and I were just getting reacquainted. A lot to catch up on."

"Uh-huh," Max said, putting his hand on my upper arm and pushing me to the side. "So are you all caught up now?"

"Not quite," Bingham said, his gaze following me. "But we've reached an understanding or two."

"Carly?" Max asked, and his tone let me know that all I had to do was say the word and he'd kick Bingham and his men out. Which would likely cause him nearly as many problems as firing Lula.

"I wouldn't be as generous as Bingham about our progress, but I'll concede that we've reached an agreement."

Max looked back and forth between us, uncertainty in his eyes.

"Mr. Bingham," I said with a tight smile. "What can I get for you and your *friends*?"

Bingham's cold, dark eyes penetrated mine. A chill ran down

my spine, but I didn't blink—those third graders had taught me a thing or two.

After about five seconds, he glanced away, looking even more pissed than ever. "Two fingers of whiskey." Two of his men ordered well drinks, while the other four ordered draft beer. Most everyone asked for wings or a burger. Max stood next to me the entire time, and while I appreciated him jumping in to protect me, I felt like I'd been holding my own. We both turned and walked away from the table, and I snuck a quick glance back at Bingham, who had his gaze firmly on my ass.

Gross.

"Carly, a word in my office," Max said in a tight voice.

I searched the room for Lula, my protective instincts kicking into high gear, but I locked eyes with Wyatt first. Somehow I'd forgotten he was in the dining room. For a moment, I wondered if he'd missed the excitement with Bingham—he hadn't intervened, after all—but his ramrod-stiff body and the dark look on his face let me know otherwise.

Lula was at a table next to his. "Just a moment," I told Max, then strode toward her. Wyatt must have thought I was coming to see him, but I ignored him, instead sidling up to Lula and leaning into her ear. "Stay away from Todd Bingham."

She turned to me in surprise. "Why?"

"He wants to talk to you for some reason, and I don't trust him."

She swallowed and worry filled her eyes. "He wants to see me?"

"Do you know why?" I asked.

She didn't answer, instead glancing back at Bingham. She seemed nervous, which made my decision for me.

"Come with me," I said, wrapping an arm around her back

and leading her over to Max, who was waiting at the back door with an exasperated look.

"I wasn't callin' a damn staff meetin'," Max grumbled.

I ignored him and continued on to his office, practically dragging Lula.

"Ruthie won't like that neither one of us is out there," she said in a trembling voice.

"Ruth?" Max snapped. "What about *me*? I'm the damn owner of this place, in case no one's noticed." He turned to me. "Why the hell is Lula back here?"

"Bingham wants to talk to her."

"So?" he asked as though my statement was the most ridiculous thing he'd ever heard. "He likes her. She usually waits on him." He shook his head, narrowing his gaze on me. "Are you saying that big to-do out there was over Bingham wanting Lula to wait on him?"

"That big to-do is because I don't trust him with her. I don't like the way he looked at her."

"Are you serious?" Max demanded. "He looks at everyone that way."

I caught Lula's gaze. "You are not to go near him, okay?"

She nodded, confusion filling her eyes. "I need to get back to work."

"We'll talk later, okay?" I said gently.

"Okay."

Once she left the room, Max turned back to me. "What in tarnation is goin' on? You've known that girl for all of three hours, so why are you acting like a mother hen?"

"I like her."

"I like her too, but her job is waitin' on customers."

"Why are you bein' so stubborn about this? You were on Bingham like white on rice when he was threatening *me*."

"He wasn't threatenin' her, Carly."

I shook my head. "No. I saw the way he was lookin' at her, and something's going on there. Were they a thing in the past?"

"Are you askin' if Bingham was screwin' her? Probably at some point."

I scrunched up my face. "Ew! He's old enough to be her father."

Max shrugged. "He's a powerful man. Women find that attractive."

I wasn't about to touch that subject with a ten-foot pole. "Are you sure Lula went to Chattanooga? Could she have run off because she was scared?"

Max shook his head. "Scared of Bingham? Half the town's scared of Bingham, and if you had any sense in your head, you'd be scared of him too. Which brings me to the whole reason I brought you back here—do not antagonize Todd Bingham."

My jaw dropped open. "You're taking his side on this?"

"I'm not takin' *anyone's* side, but I'm warning you that you do *not* want to make an enemy of that man. He's dangerous, Carly, which you should already know since you had some run-ins with him a few weeks back."

I almost told him about Hank claiming me as kin, but I wasn't sure if his arrangement with Bingham was common knowledge. Information was a currency in this town, and I needed to treat it as such. While I trusted Max to some extent—and *wanted* to trust him more—the only two people I completely trusted in this town were Hank and Wyatt, and I was having major misgivings about the latter. "I'll be fine," I said, lifting my chin and straightening my back. "Are we done now? I need to get back to work."

He gave me a frustrated look, then let out a groan. "Dammit, Carly. I'm not trying to be a bad guy here. I'm worried about you."

I relaxed slightly and gave him a soft smile. "I know. And I'm sorry if I scared you, but I just can't back down to a man like him. They like to use people and then stomp all over them when they're done."

Understanding filled his eyes. "You've dated someone like him."

I noticed the slight furrow in his brow, and I suspected I knew what he was thinking. While my bobbed, shoulder-length auburn hair gave me more of an edge than my previous long blonde hair, I still didn't look like the type of woman who went out with drug czars.

I took a breath. "In a sense, yes. I've dated powerful men who had the resources to hurt me, and I tucked tail and ran." The banked anger inside me, never totally extinguished these days, heated up. "But I'm not runnin' this time, Max. I'm standin' up for myself."

As soon as I finished my pronouncement, I realized I'd given away far too much.

"Ah…" he said with a single bob of his head. "That explains why you're here."

I knew they all had to think it was odd that I'd chosen to stay. Everyone knew I'd only come to Drum in the first place because I'd had the supreme bad luck to break down outside of town. While I'd been stranded because repairing my car would have cost more money than I had, and more money than it was worth, most people would have called friends or family and asked them to wire them money. I'd hunkered down and hadn't called anyone.

"You runnin' from a man, Carly?" he asked gently. "Are you runnin' from someone who hurt you?"

Tears welled in my eyes. This conversation had taken an unexpected turn and his question caught me by surprise.

"I know you're runnin'," he said softly, taking a step closer to me. "All the signs were there, but I never asked because it's none of my business. But you and Bingham…it all makes sense now."

"Please don't tell anyone," I implored, grabbing his forearm to hold him in place until he agreed. "No one can know."

He studied me with new eyes, as though seeing me for the first time. "What's your interest in Lula?" he asked, but then his eyes lit up and he nodded. "You see yourself in her."

I wasn't sure that was entirely true, but it served my purpose to let him think so.

"I really need to get back to work, Max," I said barely above a whisper.

"You've got nothin' to be afraid of, Carly. We take care of our own here."

He'd told me that before, and despite Bitty's betrayal, it had largely proven to be true. But would they still consider me one of their own when they learned that almost everything they knew about me was a lie? Suddenly, I was feeling all kinds of vulnerable and exposed.

He must have seen some of my fear, because he wrapped me in a gentle hug and said, "If some man's comin' to find you, you need to tell me so we can be prepared."

The domestic violence angle worked well for my story, so I went with it. Pulling away, I said, "That's so sweet of you, Max, but he's not gonna come lookin' for me. He's glad to be rid of me."

His eyes narrowed and he cocked his head to the side as he studied my face, as if trying to determine whether I was being truthful. "You know, your Southern accent slips back in from time to time," he finally said, then added for good measure, "and it doesn't sound Georgian. It certainly doesn't sound like anyone I've ever met from Michigan."

I froze in terror. *Shit. Shit. Shit.* Why had I let my guard down?

Max grabbed both of my hands and squeezed. "It's okay, Carly. I don't care if you really came from Georgia or not. Just know that you don't have to keep secrets from me."

"I've got to go."

"Okay, but if you ever want to talk, I'm always here."

"Thanks, Max." I pushed past him and down the hall to the entrance to the dining room, but instead of turning right to check on my customers, I turned left and went out the back door. I wasn't ready to put my game face back on just yet.

I made sure the small rock we used to prop the door open was in place so I wasn't locked out, and pressed my back against the cold brick wall. It was early December, and the air was crisp and cold, giving my body the shock it needed to pull me out of this spiral of dark emotions. The hair on my bare arms stood on end, and I tilted back my head to look up at the cloudless sky. One thing I loved about Drum was the night sky—usually so packed with stars it looked milky, but the rear parking lot lights hid them from view as effectively as city lights did in urban areas. It was easy for the dimmer stars to get lost in the heavens, among a multitude of bright companions. Drum was so small, so secluded from newcomers. I was shining too brightly here, drawing attention to myself.

Maybe it was time to move on.

I didn't realize I was crying until my cheeks stung from the cold. I lifted my hands to wipe them just as the back door opened and Wyatt came out.

"What are you doin' out here?" he asked gently.

"I needed a breather," I said, still looking up at the sky.

"What happened with Bingham?"

"Any other man would have turned caveman when that

happened. Max sure did," I said in an accusatory tone. "But you stayed in your seat." I swiveled my head to look at him, not sure why I was attacking him, other than I was just plain pissed. And overwhelmed. And frightened.

To his credit, he didn't look ruffled. "I was watchin'," he said evenly, "but you were holdin' your own. You're no shrinkin' violet, Carly Moore, and you sure as hell don't need a man to fight your battles for you. Now tell me why you're out here, because I doubt you're moping over Todd Bingham."

Wyatt had a knack for seeing through my walls, which only served to remind me there was so much I didn't know about him. I turned away to look back up at the sky. "Max thinks I'm a domestic violence victim, on the run from an abusive boyfriend. He wanted to know why I was standin' up to Bingham, and I slipped up and told him I wasn't backin' down from men like him again." I shook my head and released a bitter laugh. "Guess I'm not a good candidate for the CIA."

"You're doin' the best you can in a very bad situation," he said, moving next to me and placing his back against the wall, his hands pressed behind him. "Why are you really out here?"

"I keep slippin' up. I'm scared that maybe Drum's too small to hide in and I need to go to a bigger city."

He stood up straighter, then said in surprise, "You're thinkin' about runnin' again."

"I don't know," I said, "but I'm worried I've made myself too visible. Especially after my name and those blurry photos ran in the local paper a few weeks back. When you're on the run, you're supposed to fade into the background. I'm definitely not doin' that here."

"I doubt you're capable of hidin' in the background," he said softly.

"I hid in the background for thirty-one years. I just seem to be incapable of doing it *here*." But to be fair, I was a different person here. Leaving my name and my past behind had allowed me to become the person I'd always wanted to be—the person who'd always hidden inside the shell of Caroline Blakely. "Part of the reason I decided to stay was because you said we'd work together to bring our fathers down, but I can't do squat to help if you don't tell me anything." I turned my head to face him. "What happened between you and your dad?"

Frustration filled his eyes. "Carly…"

I was a fool. Wyatt wasn't going to tell me anything.

I pushed away from the wall with a long sigh. Would I always be fool enough to fall for lines from good-looking men? "I need to get back to work."

He rushed to block the doorway. "Carly, wait. Why are you pushin' me away?"

I shook my head, amazed at his gall. *"Are you serious?* You're the one pushin' *me* away, Wyatt. You know everything about my life, and you've shared next to nothing with me!"

His chest puffed out. "That's not true! Besides, I guessed your secret. You didn't voluntarily share it."

"Yet I suspect if I guessed yours, you wouldn't admit to it."

"I've told you things."

My eyes narrowed, my anger rising. "Sure, you've told me plenty of inconsequential things, but you have yet to tell me anything of importance. I thought we were supposed to be in this together."

His jaw set and I could see a war waging in his eyes, even in the dimly lit parking lot. "I'm tryin' to protect you."

"Bull. Shit," I snapped, poking him in the chest. "I'm not sure who you're really protectin', but it sure as hell isn't me." Then I stormed past him into the bar, so pissed I could kick something.

The men were all watching me when I returned, not that I

was surprised. I'd had my run-in with Bingham, then Max had dragged me to the back. They all probably thought I'd gone off to sulk after being reprimanded. What burned is they weren't wrong, but it made me look weak, something I couldn't afford in this town.

Maybe it really *was* time to move on.

CHAPTER FIVE

Wyatt left soon after that. Part of me was hurt that he'd taken off without saying goodbye. Then I reminded myself he probably thought I didn't want to talk to him. He was right, which only proved I was a hot mess over that man.

What was I doing starting a relationship with everything else going on with my life?

Bingham smirked every time I served his table, as though he thought he'd won the upper hand, but I tolerated his condescension with a smart-ass smile. He left before the game ended, keeping his gaze on Lula, who avoided him like he was a cat ready to pounce on her.

Lula had something Bingham wanted. But what? Had she left town because of him?

Things slowed down enough that Max went back to his office, leaving Ruth behind the bar. I was getting a fourth refill for a man who looked like he had no business driving home when Ruth pinned me with her scrutinizing gaze. "What the hell happened with Bingham?"

"He tried to intimidate me, and I made sure he knew it wouldn't work."

She shook her head, her lips pursed. "Just because you got away from his clutches last time, doesn't mean you're safe, girl. Just leave that man be."

"I'll leave him be when he does the same for me." I lowered my voice. "Did he have something goin' on with Lula?"

Her eyebrows shot up. "What?" But then she shrugged. "Actually, I don't know. The whole time she's been here, she's never once shared who she's sleepin' with."

"How long has she worked here?"

"About a year and a half."

I frowned. "Bingham was watching her like a hawk tonight, and she was downright nervous. Max blew it off, but something's goin' on."

"I'd tell you to ask her, but she's buttoned up tighter than a drum about her personal life. She's friendly and definitely a sweetheart once you get past all the irresponsibility, but she rarely shares anything of any depth."

"But neither do I," I countered.

"You've been here all of a month," Ruth said with a groan. "And you share a hell of a lot more than she does. I know you're slowly changin' Hank's diet—the fact that he's falling for it floors me. I know you're still takin' care of his wound and takin' him to his doctor's appointments. I know what you bought when you went to Target in Greeneville last week. And I know you're dating Wyatt Drummond, and the two of you had an argument that sent him packin'." She leaned closer. "Yeah, I know you have a past you don't talk about, but I don't give a shit about any of that. We've all got our secrets, but you're sharing your real life with me. The here and now, just like I'm sharing mine with you. Even the stuff I don't share with anyone else. She shares nothin'."

Maybe Ruth was right, but I didn't think I could just let this go. I knew anxious when I saw it—I'd spent a good two months staring at it in the mirror.

About a half hour before midnight, Max went up to his apartment, leaving the rest of us to close up. Things had settled down enough that Lula and I sat at a table by the front window and sorted out our tips. She glanced outside and frowned. "It's snowin'."

I turned to look out and saw fat flakes falling from the sky. "I have to bring Hank to Greeneville tomorrow. I hope it doesn't get bad."

Anywhere else, I would have checked the weather app on my phone, but I didn't have cell service up here. I felt completely out of touch with the world.

"Ruth," I called out. "Do you know the forecast for tonight and tomorrow? It's snowing."

"Nope." But she changed the TV to the Weather Channel. Max's Tavern was one of the few places in town that had cable TV, and I was pretty sure that Bart Drummond had something to do with that since he'd owned the place up until Max took over from Wyatt. One of Max's conditions for leaving college to take over the tavern had been a transfer of the title to his name.

"You worried about tomorrow?" she asked, making her way over to us, holding a glass of water.

"Yeah," I said with a frown. "I'm used to drivin' in the snow, but not on mountain roads."

She gave me an inquisitive glance, likely because my cover story was that I'd lived in Atlanta for the last decade after moving from Michigan, which covered the snow comment. Truth was, I'd gained the driving experience while going to college and graduate school in the upper East Coast.

"I can call Franklin and ask him," she said. "He pays attention to that sort of thing, what with workin' on the roads. He needs to know what to wear or if he'll be driving a snowplow, but he usually lets me know if it's in the forecast."

"Nah," I said, "don't bother him. He's likely sleepin'. I'll just check on Max's computer when I put the money in his drawer." A new thought hit me. "If you tend bar the nights the three of us are on shift together, we need to start sharin' our tips with you, Ruth. Max never wanted tips as the bartender, but you need them."

"You let me know if it hurts you too much," Ruth said. "If it does, I'll make Max give us all another raise."

I noticed that Lula was silent through it all, still counting her money with a furrowed brow. She shot another glance out the window and anxiety washed over her face.

"You worried about getting home, Lula?" I asked. "If you want to take off early, I can finish that up for you."

She shook her head. "Nah. I'll be fine."

But the look on her face didn't match her reassurance.

We both finished a few minutes later, and after giving Ruth her share, I took the shares for Tiny and Sugar into Max's office. I turned on the computer and as it booted, I tucked their money into their respective places in the cashbox. The computer screen came to life, and a spreadsheet filled the page, with the title "Max's Tavern November Expense Sheet." Items were listed down the side—food, liquor, wages, utilities, and a few assorted other items like insurance and repairs. The quantities of each entry seemed huge, but I had no idea how much it cost to run a bar. Max had likely been trying to figure out how to offset his increased payout in wages, which made me feel guilty. Maybe it would be better for me to take a few days off and let Lula settle back in. Given time, we'd have a better idea of how to best manage all of this.

I minimized the spreadsheet, then searched the Weather Channel website to check the forecast for the mountains. I was relieved to see the snow was supposed to stop in another hour or so, and that the temperature would be a balmy thirty-four when I drove Hank to Greeneville in the morning.

When I walked out of the office, I found Ruth and Lula in the back room, putting on their coats. Lula's duffel bag sat on the floor next to the employee lockers.

"I'm good to go to Greeneville tomorrow. The snow will be letting up soon and it's going to warm up in the morning," I said. "I'll be back by five. Lula, you still good with working the lunch shift?"

"What?" she asked, sounding distracted while she buttoned her thin coat. The words must have processed after the fact, because she nodded. "Yeah. I'll be here." Then she made a face and asked, "I hate to ask you this, but can one of you drive me home?"

"Where's your car?" Ruth asked in surprise.

"Well," she said, refusing to make eye contact. "Dickie dropped me off here, so I ain't been home yet."

"How were you gonna get home if it wasn't snowin'?" Ruth asked.

"I was gonna walk."

"That's a good six miles, Lula," Ruth protested. "You'd be walkin' in the dark on Highway 25!"

"It's outta your way," Lula said.

"I'll take her," I said eagerly. I was dying to find out more about her. I didn't have high hopes of finding out much after what Ruth had said, but at least I could be kind to her. Maybe I could earn her trust. Something told me I should try—she had the look of someone who needed help, even if she didn't want to ask.

Ruth gave me a dubious look that suggested she knew I had an ulterior motive, but she shook her head and said, "All right. Let's go."

We filed out the back door and she locked the door behind us.

"It feels weird without Max here tellin' us goodbye," Lula said wistfully. "He's *always* here."

"He's here," Ruth said with a hint of irritation. "He's just upstairs."

"You're right," I said. "It *does* feel weird." Truth was, I missed him and his jovial spirit. During down times, Ruth, Max, and I usually hung out and talked. Max was surprisingly well-read, and we'd had several conversations about books.

The windshield of Hank's car had a light dusting of snow, but the windshield wipers got most of it off. The car was slow to heat up, so we waited a couple of minutes to let it warm before I backed up. Ruth had already left and waved goodbye on her way out.

"Thank you so much for doin' this," Lula said.

"Would you have really walked?" I asked.

"I considered askin' Max if I could stay at the motel, but I gotta get home to get my car anyway."

"Anytime you need a ride, you just let me know, okay?" I said. "I don't mind, Lula. Really."

"Thanks," she said, staring out the windshield. I got the impression she was embarrassed.

I started backing up and said, "Okay, where to?"

"Head toward Ewing," she said.

Once I pulled out of the parking lot, I turned right onto Highway 25, the road that ran through town and connected Drum to Greeneville. After half a minute of silence, I said, "How long have you lived in Drum?"

"Oh," she said in surprise. "My whole life. I was born in my daddy's shack."

"No wonder you have wanderlust," I said. "Stuck here your whole life. You probably want to see the world."

"I used to want to," she said, looking close to tears, "but that's not why I was gone."

"Oh?" I said. "Where did you go?"

"I was visiting my momma in prison."

"Oh." I hadn't expected that.

"I don't like drivin' that far, so I caught a ride with Dickie to Chattanooga. He arranged for his friend to give me a ride to Nashville."

"Why on earth didn't you tell Max and Ruth that?" I asked. "I'm sure they would have understood."

"The less people know, the better," she said.

"But you're telling me."

She turned to look at me with her wide, innocent eyes. "Because I can tell you're different."

I wasn't sure what that meant, but I'd take it. "Why don't you want it to get out?"

She pressed her lips together.

"What's your mother in prison for?" I asked, knowing full well, but I didn't want her to think I'd been gossiping about her. Besides, part of me was still hoping Jerry might have gotten it wrong.

"For murderin' my daddy," she said blankly. "He was drownin' me in the creek and my momma stopped him."

I let out an appalled gasp. A genuine one. Even though I'd anticipated her answer, it was horrifying to hear her state the facts so matter-of-factly. "How old were you?"

"Eight. My momma got fifteen years, and she's about to get

out due to good behavior. She says she's comin' for me once she gets out and we're goin' to Cali-fornia."

I smiled at the way she pronounced the state. "I hear it's sunny there."

But I also remembered what she'd said to the patrons—that she planned on staying for good this time. Had that just been talk? Or did part of her think her mother's plan would never come to fruition?

"And warm," she said. "I don't want my baby sleepin' in that drafty shack."

Baby?

I nearly let out a gasp as my gaze dropped to her stomach and then lifted to her face. Was that why Todd Bingham had been watching her all night? Was he the baby's father?

Horror filled her eyes, and she turned to me, grabbing my arm in desperation. "*Please* don't tell anyone. Momma says I have to keep it a secret."

"I won't tell anyone," I assured her. "But why won't you tell Ruth and Max? I'm sure they'd help you."

She shook her head. "Momma says not to trust them. Not to trust anyone until she gets home."

Did her mother know much about them? If she'd gone to prison soon after the incident, Max and Ruth would have been in their teens. Maybe she'd just told Lula not to trust people in general. "They're gonna find out once you start showing," I said, then realized this was why she'd worn a baggy shirt. "How far along are you?"

"I dunno," she admitted. "Momma thinks the baby's comin' February or March."

A quick calculation put her at five or six months pregnant. "Have you been to a doctor, Lula?"

She shook her head.

"Lula, honey, you have to go get checked out. You need to make sure your baby is safe and healthy."

"Momma said she'll be home before I have the baby and she'll help me. Just like the midwife helped her have me."

I had no intention of letting her go her entire pregnancy without visiting a doctor, but I'd press the issue later.

"Who took care of you after your momma was arrested?"

"I lived with my aunt—my momma's sister—but she died when I was sixteen. My daddy's family didn't want to have anything to do with me. So then it was just me, and I moved back out to the shack."

"Do you live alone?"

She turned to me with suspicious eyes. "Yeah. But I've got a shotgun that belonged to my daddy. My aunt took it and anything of worth after Momma was arrested. Good thing too, since people took a bunch of our stuff."

Had people scavenged her house? I decided to try approaching the topic I was really interested in, especially now that I knew her news. "Why was Bingham watching you all night?"

She sat perfectly still.

"Look," I said. "I know Todd Bingham scares half the town, but he doesn't scare me."

"He should," she said, barely above a whisper. "He kills people. Or makes them disappear. Same difference."

I knew that to be true from firsthand experience. "I know, but Bingham's a bully. And the best way to deal with a bully is to stand up to them."

"Is that what you were doin' tonight?" she asked.

"That's exactly what I was doin'," I said. "Until Max went and screwed it all up."

"He was just lookin' out for you," she said. "He likes you."

"He likes all of us," I said. "And he wants us to be safe, which is why he jumped in, even though I had it covered."

"Are you really datin' Wyatt Drummond?" she asked, changing topics, although I was pretty sure it wasn't intentional.

"Yeah," I said reluctantly. I had a lot to consider regarding my relationship with Wyatt.

"Do you know he hasn't had a single girlfriend since he came back from prison?"

"So I've heard."

"I'd never seen him in the bar before," she mused. "Everybody says he and Max are fightin', and I ain't never seen 'em together, so it must be true."

"Do you know what they're fighting about?" I asked, feeling horrible for pumping her for information. She was so naive, it felt plain wrong. It was an indication of how desperate I'd become.

"Something to do with their daddy is all I ever heard." She pointed to a county road coming up. "Turn left up here."

I slowed down to make the turn. The snow had started sticking to the road, and I had no intention of crashing into a tree.

Once I'd safely made the turn, she said, "Go about two miles and then turn left again. I'll tell you when we're close."

"Okay."

"Is Wyatt a good kisser?" she asked, and I damn near ran off the road.

"What?"

"He's got really great lips...not too thin and not too full. I'd never seen him up close until tonight. He's good at just about everything he does, so it stands to reason that he's a good kisser. So is he?"

"Yeah," I conceded. "He's a great kisser."

"And how is he in bed?"

I was grateful it was dark enough to hide the blush that was burning my cheeks. "Lula! I'm not gonna answer that."

"Oh, come on," she teased. "I'm not as innocent as I look."

"I would guess not considering you're having a baby, but I'm still not going to tell you. Some things are private." And then there was the fact I hadn't slept with Wyatt yet. The next time I slept with a man, I needed to be sure I could trust him with my heart *and* my life, and while he'd proven the latter, he had yet to prove the former. "Time to change the topic."

She laughed. "How'd you end up in Drum, anyway?"

"My car broke down and Wyatt towed it into town. I started working at the tavern because you were gone and I was flat broke. Figured I could make enough money to pay for the repairs, but it ended up being too expensive. I ended up staying because I had nowhere else to go."

"That explains how you hooked up with Wyatt. Half the girls in this town would like to start something with him. Maybe he was lookin' for something different."

If she knew about his recent romantic relationships—or apparent lack thereof—maybe she knew about past ones too. "I heard he dated Ruth years ago."

"Really?" she said, sounding excited. "I had no idea."

"Do you know anything about anyone else he dated?"

"Shouldn't you be askin' Wyatt these questions?"

Her question stoked my anger—but not at her. And not just at Wyatt either. I should never have opened myself up to someone who refused to do the same. He'd had plenty of opportunities to let me in. For him to keep such much information secret was unconscionable, especially given the fact that I'd told him about all of the men who'd used me in the past, Jake first and foremost among them. He had to know how much it would hurt me. Why had I tolerated that?

When it came to Wyatt, I couldn't trust myself—which meant I'd do best to remove myself from the situation. "You're right, Lula. He should be the one to tell me. You've helped me make a huge decision. Thank you."

"I did?" she burst out in shock. "Wow."

"Now, about Bingham," I said, realizing I was running short on time. "Why was he watching you like he was?"

Her voice shook. "He thinks I know something."

"He thought I knew something too," I said. "And he tried to bully and intimidate me, but I stood up to him. And you can too."

"No. We need to let it go."

"Maybe we should go to Max with this. He can help you. He helped *me*."

"No!" she shouted in panic. "You can't tell Max."

"Why can't we tell Max about Bingham?" I paused, then asked what I'd been wondering since I learned she was expecting. "Is Bingham your baby's father?"

"I'm not talkin' about this," Lula said. "Please, please, *please* don't tell Max!"

The worry in her tone caught me off guard. Was she afraid of Max? "I won't. I promise."

"Thank you," she said, collapsing into the seat. "Thank you."

We were quiet for a moment. Then she pointed to a turnoff up ahead. "Turn there."

I turned left onto a snow-covered one-car lane that snaked through a narrow gap in the trees.

"I can get out and walk from here," she said. "I'm scared you're gonna get stuck."

"I don't feel right leaving you here, Lula. You haven't been home for a month. At least let me walk with you to make sure everything at your house is okay." Especially after what she'd said about scavengers.

She shook her head. "Nah, I'll be fine. I was gonna walk home anyway, remember?"

She went to open the door, and I asked, "Are you taking prenatal vitamins?"

"What?"

"I'm going to Greeneville tomorrow. I can pick some up for you, if you like."

Her mouth dropped open. "You would do that for me?"

"I suspect they might not carry them at the Dollar General. This way you'll be set. And I won't give them to you in front of Max or Ruth, so no need to worry, okay?"

Tears filled her eyes. "Thank you, Carly."

I thought about her being out here all alone. I suspected Todd Bingham knew where she lived, regardless of whether they'd had an affair. "Hey," I said as an idea popped into my head. "How about you grab some stuff and I'll take you home with me."

"Why?"

"I'm worried about you being here all alone. You could stay with me and Hank tonight, and we'll figure out what to do tomorrow."

Her eyes grew wide. "You're living with Hank Chalmers?"

"Yeah," I said, confused at her reaction. "Is that a problem?"

"I'm fine," she said, but she opened the door as though her pants were on fire. "Thanks for the ride."

She was already out the door when I called after her. "Lula! Wait!"

She paused with her hand on the edge of the door, ready to close it. Her eyes were wide with fear.

"Lula, are you afraid of Hank?"

She shook her head vigorously. "No. I'm fine. I'll see you tomorrow."

"Lula! *Wait!*" She hesitated again, and I said, "I'd like to be your friend. I want to earn your trust. If you're scared of someone, I can help you. I *want* to help you."

She smiled, but her chin trembled. "I'm fine. I'm not scared of anyone. I want to be your friend too. We'll talk tomorrow."

Then she shut the door and hurried down the lane.

CHAPTER SIX

I waited until she was out of sight, then backed up and headed to Hank's. The roads were getting slippery, and the drive up the mountain toward White Rabbit Holler was treacherous in some spots. But I slowed to a crawl and drove carefully, relieved when Hank's mailbox finally came into view.

At least until I saw Wyatt's truck parked out in front of the house.

I parked the car, and Wyatt was out the front door before I reached the front porch.

"I was about to go after you," he said. "I worried that you might have run off the road. What took so long? I called Max and he said y'all left the bar almost an hour ago."

"What are you doin' here?" I demanded.

He looked taken back by my sharp tone. "I didn't feel right about how we left things."

"You mean you didn't like that I called you out on your bullshit."

He looked properly chastised. "Carly…"

I shook my head. "No. No more excuses, Wyatt. If we're really going to start a relationship, then we can't have these big secrets between us."

"You don't understand—"

I held my hand up to stop him. "No, I don't. And if that's your only answer, then you should just leave."

I started to walk past him, but he wrapped an arm around me and tugged me back.

"Carly."

My resolve began to weaken—his touch tended to do that to me—but I knew I had to stand firm. I couldn't let my good sense be overruled by hormones. Pulling free from him, I said, "Let me go, Wyatt."

"Will you please let me explain?" he pleaded, sounding panicked.

I put a hand on my hip. "Will your explanation include any of the answers I want?"

"I want to talk about what happened between you and Bingham first."

He was changing the subject again, but I'd address this giant elephant before shifting back to the main topic. "It's simple. Todd Bingham does what he wants, and he treats people like shit for fun."

"No," he said. "Not always. I asked Lula and she told me his behavior in the tavern tonight was unusual. What did he want?"

"Stop," I said. "I'm not telling you anything else until you tell me *something*, Wyatt."

"Carly…"

"You promised me," I said, leaning in closer and lowering my voice. Sound carried out here. "You told me we'd bring them down. I want that. I *need* it. Now, are you going to tell me or not?"

A war waged in his eyes, but I wasn't sure if it was because he was trying to decide whether to start sharing or if he was preparing himself for a fight. "Not yet."

"Not yet," I repeated. Was I being unreasonable? I was asking him to share his most intimate secrets. It had taken me two months to share my whole story with my friends from Arkansas. But my connection with Wyatt was deeper and more intimate. If he told the wrong person the things he knew about my past, I'd be murdered, and yet he refused to take me into his confidence.

Be smart, Carly. Don't let another man screw you over.

I stared up at his emotionless face and took a step back, raising my hands in surrender. "You know what? I've had enough. I'm not doing this anymore. Until you're willing to be more open with me, we're done."

His eyes flew wide. "Carly!"

He reached for me and I took another step back, needing distance from him so I could stand firm.

"You know how hard it is for me to trust, especially after Jake." My voice broke, and I couldn't stop my tears. "He was my best friend for my entire life, and he betrayed me, Wyatt. Betrayed and destroyed me."

He shook his head, looking shell-shocked. "No. Not destroyed."

I released a bitter laugh. "Okay, he was saving that part until after he got a wedding ring on my finger."

"Carly…"

"Give me something, Wyatt. Give me a reason other than the bogus excuse that you're trying to protect me." When he didn't respond, I gasped from the burst of pain in my chest. "You don't trust me," I said, giving voice to the doubt that had been simmering below the surface for the past two weeks.

"Carly, it's just that—"

I wasn't sure what else he would have said because I walked

past him into the house and shut the door, locking it before he tried to follow me inside.

"Carly!" he shouted through the door. "Please let me explain."

I shook my head, even though he couldn't see me. *No.* I was done letting people screw me over.

"Carly!" he shouted again, banging on the door. He had a key, so he could open it at any time. Apparently he was respecting my boundaries, which softened my resolve. Some.

Hank appeared in the hall, one crutch under his armpit and his rifle in the other hand. He wore a white T-shirt and a pair of blue pajama pants with the right pant leg cut off below his knee. His gray hair was smooshed on one side, and it hit me that I should take him to get a haircut when we were in Greeneville.

"What the hell's goin' on?" he grumped. "Who's out there?"

"Wyatt," I said, trying not to cry. "I'm sorry we woke you."

"Why's he outside bangin' on the door?"

"I refused to talk to him and told him to leave."

Hank gave a sharp nod, then hobbled toward the door faster than one would have thought possible for a one-legged man. He jerked it open, and the relief on Wyatt's face quickly turned to confusion.

"She don't wanna talk to you."

"Hank, if she would just—"

"It's damn near one in the morning," Hank snapped. "She don't wanna talk to you, Drummond, so go home."

But the ground beyond Wyatt was covered in snow, and I knew those roads were slippery. Even now, I didn't like the thought of him driving on them.

"If he doesn't want to drive in the snow, he can sleep on the sofa," I said in a firm voice. "But I'm goin' to bed."

I didn't wait to hear his answer, instead heading to my room. Closing the door, I sat on the edge of the bed and started to cry, but it pissed me off. I'd started to let him into my heart after all, something I shouldn't have done so easily.

How could I have been so stupid *again*?

I heard Wyatt's truck roar to life, the sound fading as he drove away. Seconds later, a soft knock rapped on the door, and Hank said, "He's gone."

"Thank you," I said, hating that I'd let Hank be the one to run him off. Grateful that he'd taken my side without knowing any of the details.

"You okay, girl?" he asked in a softer tone than I was used to from him.

"No," I said, a sob rising in my throat. "But I will be."

"Do I need to go kick Wyatt Drummond's ass?"

A laugh bubbled up, and I stood and opened the door. Hank was standing there with one crutch and no shotgun. "No," I said with a watery smile. "I can handle him on my own."

"I know you can, girl," he said, his voice turning gruff. "But just because you *can* doesn't mean you have to do it alone. Say the word, and I'll step in and have a go at him. You're my family now."

To my horror, I started crying again. How had I been lucky enough to find him?

I expected Hank to turn and run, but kindness filled his eyes. "Wyatt Drummond is a stubborn man who grew up with the belief that women should be protected. I learned different from my Mary, but his momma lives in his daddy's shadow."

Which meant Hank had heard a lot of our conversation, not that I was surprised. The walls and doors in this house were thin.

"Even after everything we went through together with Carson Purdy?" I asked in disbelief as I sat down on the bed. But my mind wandered back to Wyatt's explanation for why he hadn't jumped into my spat with Bingham. I knew Hank was reading this wrong. Wyatt wasn't old-fashioned. He just didn't trust me. "It doesn't matter."

"Wyatt may be stubborn, but he's a good man, Carly," he said, hobbling back to the doorway.

"What does that mean?" I asked. "What makes a good man?"

"I sure as hell wouldn't know," Hank scoffed. "I definitely ain't one."

I thought about Lula's reaction to the news that I was staying with Hank. Had he been something like Bingham back in the day? He hadn't hesitated to shoot the intruder who'd attacked me —one of Seth's killers—but that had been self-defense. I had trouble seeing him hurting anyone for any other reason.

"Whatever you were like in the past, you're a good man now," I said, looking up at him.

"Nah. You just see what you want to see," he said with a sigh. "I done plenty bad. So has Wyatt. And I suspect so have you. But the levels of bad are different for all of us. Mine just happen to be worse than the lot of you."

I wondered what he meant by that, but part of me didn't want to know. I'd meant it—the Hank I knew was a good man.

"Wyatt knows about my past. I shared it all with him, but he refuses to tell me anything substantial about his," I said, realizing I was opening a can of worms. Hank still didn't know about my former life. I'd tried to tell him once, but he'd cut me off, insisting that I keep my secrets—it didn't matter where I came from, it only mattered that I was here now.

"Secrets are like currency in Drum," he'd said. "You're sellin' pieces of yourself when you share them. Be careful who you sell 'em to."

Hank only knew me as the woman who'd held his dying grandson's hand and then had the tenacity to track down his killers since the sheriff's department wasn't to be trusted. "I've been with men who held secrets from me, and those secrets nearly got me killed. He knows this, yet he still refuses to trust me." I shook my head. "I'm done playin' the fool. I'm done beggin' and pleadin' with him. I'm just done."

He limped over and placed a hand on my shoulder. "It's never a good idea to make a decision when you're tired and upset. You need to sleep on it."

I nodded, but I knew I wasn't going to change my mind. Unless Wyatt came clean—with all of it—we were done.

CHAPTER SEVEN

We got an early start the next morning. I was worried about the road conditions, but most of the snow had melted, leaving behind only a few slippery patches. Hank's appointment was at ten, and the appointment went well, although Hank seemed resistant to the doctor's suggestion that he get an artificial leg.

"I ain't got the money for somethin' like that," Hank said after we left the office an hour later and got into the car.

"You're on Medicare, Hank. Surely they'll pay for part of it. At least find out how much it would cost you out of pocket before you decide against it."

"If I get a fake leg, I'll have to come down here to Greeneville several times a week," he said, refusing to look at me. "It's too much trouble."

"You know I'll bring you."

"I ain't gonna ask you to do that," he scoffed. "You're working at the tavern most days."

"Not anymore," I said. "Lula came back."

He turned to me in surprise. "You lost your job?"

"No, Max wants me to keep working part-time."

He frowned. "And you're just now tellin' me this?"

"It doesn't matter. Max thinks Lula will take off sooner rather than later," I said with hesitation.

"Sounds like you disagree with that."

"I took her home last night. That's why I was late getting back. Sounds like she's not planning on going anywhere, at least not until her mother gets out of prison this spring."

"Louise is gettin' out?" he asked, sitting up in his seat.

I shot him a glance. "You know her?"

"I know most people in this town. The good *and* the bad."

"Are you saying Lula's mother is a bad person?"

He made a sour face. "She killed her husband."

"Because he was drowning Lula."

He snorted. "Is that what you heard?"

"Yeah, from Jerry and from Lula herself. Jerry said Lula's mother had to do CPR on her until the ambulance arrived." I turned to him with narrowed eyes. "Are you saying it didn't happen that way?"

"I'm saying I'm sure there's more to the story than most people know. Now take me to Popeyes Chicken for lunch. I'm starvin'."

"Popeyes isn't good for your diabetes, Hank."

"If I can't have fried chicken, mashed potatoes, and biscuits, then life ain't worth livin'."

He had a point. I loved those things too, and I supposed everything was okay in moderation, so I headed to Popeyes. We sat inside and ate more greasy food than either of us had a right to. I tried to get him to tell me more about Lula and her parents, but he just gave me a pointed look and said, "The past is better left where it belongs. You of all people know that."

The way he said it made me think he knew more about me

than he let on, but then he quickly changed the subject by complaining about the temperature in the doctor's waiting room.

When we finished eating, we headed to Target. Hank sat in the Starbucks seating area while I shopped for some warmer clothes, a coat for Jerry (I decided he deserved a new one for what he'd done), socks and new underwear for Hank (his were so old and ratty, I planned on throwing them away as soon as we got home), some toiletries for both of us, and a box of hair dye to cover my blonde roots. Ruth had asked me to pick up a few items for her, so I got those as well as Lula's vitamins. After I checked out—cringing at the total—I found Hank in his chair, dozing against the window.

It made me consider giving up my grocery store stop, but fresh fruits and vegetables were hard to find in Drum, and Hank's next appointment wasn't for another two weeks. So Hank stayed in the car and napped some more while I shopped, which I decided was a good thing. I'd been sneaking increasingly healthier food into his diet, and I didn't want him figuring it out during my shopping excursion.

By the time I finished, it was around one thirty, and since Hank refused to let me take him to get his hair cut, saying he was good for another month (I figured I'd try my hand at giving him a haircut later at home), I decided to head back to Drum. It hit me that I'd have to go without cell phone service for a couple of weeks before Hank and I came back to Greeneville, so I made a quick check of my burner phone to see if I'd gotten any texts or calls since I'd last checked it a few hours earlier. I felt a little silly for checking again. My friends in Henryetta knew it was too dangerous to get in touch with me, and vice versa, unless something major happened. Hearing nothing was actually the better scenario, or so I told myself. Truth was, I missed them. But I had a new life, a new home, and I had to accept that.

While there was nothing from Arkansas, there was a call *and* a message from Max's Tavern, which caught me off guard. I had no idea why Max would be calling me on my day off. I expected to hear his voice in the voicemail, but it was Ruth who said, "What a surprise…Lula didn't show today. I told Max she's done. I know you're in Greeneville, but in case you were makin' plans around your new part-time schedule, cancel 'em."

I stared down at my phone to check the time of the call. 1:05. Max must have called Ruth in to cover the lunch shift, but where was Lula?

I called the tavern as I pulled out of the parking lot.

"Have you heard from Lula?" I blurted out as soon as Max answered.

"Well, hello to you too," he grumped. "And no. Haven't heard a word, but that's typical Lula behavior."

"Have you called her?" I asked. "What if she had car trouble?"

"She hasn't got a phone," he said. "And Ruth doesn't want to hear a single excuse. Lula took off again after she swore she was stickin' around this time." I could hear the disappointment in his voice.

"I don't think she took off, Max," I said. "Last night she told me she really needs to keep her job until her mother gets released from prison next spring." Lula hadn't wanted Max to know, but I figured she'd be all right with me telling him if it meant I could help her keep her job. Besides, I was genuinely worried that she hadn't shown up for her shift, and I needed Max to take my concerns seriously.

"Her momma's gettin' out? I had no idea."

"That's where she went. To Nashville to see her mother in prison."

"What?" he asked, sounding shocked. "It took three weeks?"

"The delivery driver gave her a ride to Chattanooga, and one of his friends ran her up to Nashville. I have no idea why it took so long."

"Why in the hell wouldn't she tell me?" He didn't disguise the pain in his voice.

"I don't know."

"And why would she tell you, a woman she just met?"

"I don't know, Max. I told her I was worried about Bingham's interest in her, and I suspect she told me about her mother to change the subject." When he remained silent, I said, "I pass the turnoff to her property on the way back to Drum. How about I stop by and make sure she's okay?"

"Ruth won't care," he said, sounding glum, and part of me wanted to tell him that he was technically the boss, not Ruth. As much as I liked her, she could be too judgmental. But then again, I was more like Max—a big softy. We tended to give people the benefit of the doubt, and it often bit us in the ass.

"Nevertheless, I'm going to check on her. I'm worried."

"Okay," he said, and I heard the relief in his voice. "Let me know what you find out."

Hank had been quiet during my call, but when I put my phone back into my purse, he turned to me. "The Baker girl took off again?"

"No," I said. "She didn't show for work, but I don't think she left town."

"Yer plannin' to go by her place, ain't ya? I want to be back in time to see *Ellen*."

I rolled my eyes. For being a semi-gruff man in his late sixties, he sure loved his daytime TV. "It won't take that long. You'll still be home in time to see *Ellen*."

"Well, all right then."

He fell asleep again on the drive back up the mountain, so he wasn't paying attention when I turned onto the county road toward Lula's house.

The narrow drive, snaking through the trees, was still partially covered with snow, and I was worried about driving down it in Hank's rear-wheel drive car, so I pulled into the gravel entrance and put the car in park. When I started to open the door, Hank roused. "What's goin' on? Where are you goin'?"

"I'm at the entrance to the lane to Lula's house, but I worried that the car might get stuck, and I sure as hell don't want to call Wyatt Drummond to pull us out." Not that we'd even be able to call him. Even more incentive to leave the car close to the road.

"You're gonna hike down that snowy road in those shoes?" he asked, glancing down at my ankle boots.

"I bought a pair of snow boots at Target," I said. "I'll wear them."

He frowned, clearly not approving of this plan, but he didn't protest.

I got out and popped the trunk, digging the boots out of a bag and pulling hard on the stretchy band that held them together to separate them. Once they broke free, I sat on the edge of the trunk and changed into my new boots.

I gave Hank a wave before I started down the road, but he unrolled the window and said, "Maybe I should come with you."

That sounded like the worst idea ever, but I didn't want to hurt his feelings, so I said, "If I find anything looks off, I'll come back, and we'll get Marco."

Marco was still on medical leave from his gunshot wounds, but I knew he was up and driving, although I suspected that was against the doctor's orders. Given the fact that the Hensen County Sheriff's Department was as crooked as a dog's hind leg, Marco was one of the only deputies I trusted. The other was

Marta White, the detective who had handled the investigation of Bitty's and Carson's deaths, but I wasn't sure this warranted a detective yet.

I knew I might be borrowing trouble. Maybe Lula couldn't get her car started. Or maybe she'd had some kind of accident and was stuck in her house. The latter was a possibility given the fact she lived alone, far from the road, and lacked a phone.

I picked up my pace.

I walked about a hundred feet before the lane ended at a small plot of open land and a run-down house. Lula had called it a shack, and that seemed fitting. It was a one-story structure with aged wood planks for walls, and matching wood shingles for the roof. The roof extended over a porch that ran the length of the front of the house, but the roof sagged on one side and several of the porch floorboards were missing. The whole thing looked like it would fall down with a strong wind.

A small compact, rust-covered car was parked in front of the structure, and the land behind the house dipped slightly toward a narrow babbling brook. I wondered if it was the same creek where Lula's father had allegedly tried to drown her. It didn't look deep enough now, but I suspected it contained more water in the spring.

There weren't any lights on in the house, but then again, I didn't see any electrical lines. It was no wonder Lula didn't have a phone. I was fairly sure she didn't have electricity.

"Lula?" I called out as I approached the house. One thing I'd learned about the people living on Balder Mountain was they took protecting their homes seriously, and their security system of choice was a 12-gauge shotgun. She'd already told me she had one. "Lula, it's Carly. Are you home?"

When I didn't hear her answer, I moved closer. "I'm coming up to the front porch."

The wood planks sagged under my weight, and I gingerly made my way to the front door and knocked. "Lula? Are you in there?"

When she didn't answer, I knocked a couple more times before trying the doorknob.

Surprisingly, the door was unlocked, so I slowly pushed it in, then took a step inside the dark house. "Lula?"

It took a second for my eyes to adjust to the dim light, but then I scanned the room, realizing it was literally a one-room house. A bed was in the far corner—a mattress tucked into an old, dilapidated wooden frame. The bed was unmade, the covers thrown back as though Lula had gotten up in a hurry and hadn't touched the bedding since. A tall chest of drawers was next to it, a still-glowing kerosene lantern on top.

A cookstove was across from the bed, close to the front door. On the wall opposite the bed was a line of cabinets with a porcelain sink equipped with a pump handle. No refrigerator. No dishwasher. Also no bathroom. There was a ladder to a loft in the peak of the roof, and I could see a small bed up there. Had that been Lula's room when she was a girl? The front of the house had two single-pane windows. There was a window in the kitchen area, facing the creek, and another window in the back wall. Red-and-white checkered fabric was nailed into the wood plank walls above them to serve as makeshift curtains.

The room was warmer than outside but not by much. I could feel some heat radiating from the woodstove and used the sleeve of my coat to open the cast iron door. The interior was filled with glowing embers. Lula had lit a fire, but it looked like it had been hours since she'd added more wood. The few logs on the floor next to the stove suggested it wasn't because she'd run out of fuel.

"Lula?" I called out even though I knew she wasn't home. I

climbed the ladder partway to the loft, but it was empty except for a twin mattress that sat on the floor, and several boxes.

A gnawing worry burrowed in my gut. Lula hadn't wandered off again. Either something had scared her away—or someone had taken her.

CHAPTER EIGHT

After I took a picture of the lamp with my crappy cell phone, I extinguished the flame. The place looked even more abandoned in the dark, but I checked around the property just to be sure, even opening the outhouse door and nearly falling over from the stench.

I hurried back to the road, trying to figure out the fastest way to reach Marco. I considered making the call from the tavern, which would allow me to inform Max and Ruth of what I'd found, but I still needed to take Hank and the groceries home.

When I reached the car, I contemplated changing back into my ankle boots, but it was so cold and wet I decided to leave on my muddy snow boots.

"Did you find her?" Hank asked.

"No," I said. "And it looked like she'd left without planning to."

"How do you know that?" he asked.

I told him what I'd found, and he frowned. "That don't necessarily mean nothing. The girl's not playin' with a full deck."

I thought about her many mistakes the night before, and while I suspected he was right, something felt off about this.

"What are you gonna do?" he asked.

"Take you home and call Marco."

"You're really bringin' in the sheriff?" he asked in surprise.

"No, I'm calling *my friend* Marco, who happens to be a deputy sheriff. However, he's on medical leave right now, so it will be one friend calling another."

"Uh-huh," he grunted.

"What does that mean?" I asked.

"You can't help yourself. You think she's some poor dumb girl and you feel the need to help her." When I started to protest—mostly because he'd called her dumb—he held up a hand. "It ain't an insult, so calm down. You're just like my Mary." He paused for a moment, then added softly, "You remind me of her. You're both so alike—headstrong but softhearted."

"Thank you, Hank."

"I didn't say it was necessarily a good thing. My Mary got burned a time or two, and given this girl's history, I'm worried you'll get burned too."

"All I'm doing is calling Marco," I said. "We'll see what he says and go from there."

"Uh-huh."

I didn't think Marco could handle the case since he was on leave, but surely he could refer me to someone he trusted in his department. Although I'd downplayed the situation for Hank, I thought something reeked about this, and I intended to do what I could to make sure Lula was safe.

We headed back home, passing Wyatt's garage on the way. An ache filled my heart, and I wondered how I'd let myself get so attached to him. What a fool. I needed to cut all ties so I wouldn't be tempted, a difficult task given that we lived in a town with a population of about 2,200 people. My old car was still in the parking lot behind the building. "I need to ask Wyatt to sell my car for parts."

"Or you could get Bingham to steal it so you can file an insurance claim," Hank muttered, staring out the window.

"I thought Bingham was the local drug dealer."

"Bingham believes in diversification," Hank said. "He ran the chop shop before he took over the drug business. After I relinquished my business, he got himself a cook from Chicago, but he can't grow weed like I could." A hint of a smile lit up his eyes.

"A few weeks ago, Wyatt thought that Bingham had asked you to grow pot for him. Is that an issue for him?"

He chuckled. "He's asked a time or two, but I always turn him down. I ain't got the stamina for it no more."

"Do you think Bingham will pressure you into it?" I asked.

"He ain't got nothin' to pressure me with. You and Wyatt are off-limits. I ain't got nothin' else left."

I wasn't so sure about that. Bingham had found a work-around with Hank's grandson—he'd helped Seth spy on the rival drug dealers because Seth had come to him rather than the other way around—which meant he wasn't above thinking outside the box. "Bingham was watching Lula last night, and not in a good way. Got any idea why?"

"You hear me, girly, you need to stay *far* away from Todd Bingham. You got lucky last time, but the next time might not end in a happily ever after."

I laughed. "Are you callin' this a happily ever after?"

"You're alive, ain't ya? That looks mighty happy to me."

I had to admit that he had a point, but I wouldn't go so far as to call it a fairy-tale ending. Not after my breakup with Wyatt. I needed to focus on more important things. "Back to Lula—"

"I ain't got no idea why he was glarin' at her. Rumor has it he's got him some prostitutes. Maybe she worked for him on the side."

"I don't see how that's possible," I said. "Not with the hours Ruth and I work."

"Then maybe it's drugs. Like I said, the girl's not right in the head. Maybe she tried to rip 'im off."

"Maybe..." I mused. But that didn't seem likely either.

"It makes no nevermind to you what he was glarin' at her for. That's *their* business, not yours."

I disagreed with that, but I could see there was no convincing him. His only concern in this situation was my safety. "I'm just trying to figure out what to tell my friend Marco."

Hank snorted so hard I thought he was going to spit out his tonsils. After that, I couldn't get him to spill anything else about Bingham or Lula. Knowing him, I decided I'd just have to bide my time and ask him later.

When we got home, Hank went inside as I carried in the food and Target bags, leaving Ruth's purchases in the car. Hank settled into his recliner and turned on the television, grumbling that he'd missed the first few minutes of *Ellen*. I made him test his blood sugar, and not surprisingly, he needed a dose of insulin, so I got him squared away before heading to the kitchen.

I found Marco's phone number on my cell phone, which was pretty much a glorified phone book in the mountains, and dialed it into Hank's rotary phone. Since the phone had a long cord that would allow me plenty of leeway to move around the kitchen, I started putting away the groceries while I waited for him to pick up.

Marco answered after a couple of rings, breathless. "Carly? What's up?"

"You got a minute?" I asked as I put a container of almond milk in the back of the fridge, trying to hide it from Hank.

"For you? You bet."

Marco and I had barely known each other before our big showdown with Carson Purdy. Beyond the fact that we were both around the same age, we didn't have much in common—he was a good ole boy who lived to hunt and fish, and I was a former city girl who thought the outdoors was best observed through a window. But life-and-death situations had a way of bringing unlikely people together.

Marco had been shot twice by Carson in an attempt to protect me. I'd tried to drag Marco to the safety of his car. I hadn't been successful, and Carson had nearly shot him again—we both had Jerry to thank for our lives—but Marco had claimed most people would have taken off and left him to fend for himself. I'd countered that if most of the people he knew would have left him behind in a life-or-death situation, then he needed to find better company. We'd been friends ever since.

"What do you know about Lula?" I asked.

"Lula Baker who works at the tavern? I heard she was back. I planned to come in tonight to see her."

The way he said it made me think she was one of his many conquests in the area. Like Max, Marco was too handsome for his own good, with his blond hair, blue-green eyes, and his roguish looks. I'd taken him to dinner to celebrate his release from the hospital, and judging from the half a dozen women who'd greeted him with starry eyes, Marco Roland was a popular man with the ladies. No wonder he and Max were such good friends.

"Don't waste your gas money," I said. "She's gone."

"Already?" he asked in dismay.

"Yeah, except I don't think she left on her own, Marco."

"Well, she usually hitches a ride," he said. "Her car's shit. I told her once to have Wyatt look at it, but she claimed it was fine. I'm pretty sure she had one of the Grisham boys look at it."

I wondered why she hadn't asked Wyatt. Was it money? She couldn't have many expenses living where she did, and a car was a necessity in these parts. Had she been sending all her money to her mother? "If she hitched a ride, I'm not sure it was voluntary, or at least she left in a hurry."

"What makes you say that?"

"I dropped by her house, which is a generous description of where she lives."

"I take it she wasn't there?" After I described what I'd found, he asked, "What exactly are you askin' for, Carly?"

"I'm askin' you which deputy I should call. We both know that a good many of them are corrupt. I want someone who will really look into this."

"Then your answer is none of 'em," he said. "But not for the reason you think. Lula's got a history of runnin' off, and she hasn't even been gone twenty-four hours, let alone the forty-eight we tend to wait."

"I'm telling you, Marco. She didn't run off. She told me last night that she needed her job at least until the spring when her mother gets out of prison."

"That doesn't mean nothin', Carly. Not with Lula."

"She told me something else. Something I promised to keep secret. But it makes me believe she wouldn't leave. And on top of that, Todd Bingham was watching her like a hawk last night. Was there bad blood between them?"

"Not that I know of, and from what I saw about six months ago, I'd say it was more like *hot* blood."

"What did you see?"

"Seriously, Carly?" he groaned good-naturedly. "I never took you as the kind of girl who'd want to know the details of other people's sex lives."

"They were havin' sex? You're sure you didn't misconstrue it?"

"He had her pinned to the brick wall behind the tavern, drivin' her home, if you know what I mean, his bare ass shinin' in the moonlight. She seemed to be enjoyin' every minute of it, so I turned tail and ran back inside for another beer. When she came back in about five minutes later, she had the look of a satisfied woman."

My face heated. "I could have done without *that* image."

"Hey, you asked if I was sure."

I had, and now adrenaline zipped through my blood. So they *had* been an item of some kind, even if it was just for one night, and if she was about five months pregnant, it very well could be his child. Had Bingham kidnapped her so he could keep his kid? Or…

I couldn't help thinking about Rose. She was carrying the baby of the local crime lord, and he hadn't exactly celebrated the news. What if Bingham hadn't taken it well?

Lula had told me herself that Bingham made people disappear. And now Lula was gone.

Except she'd been adamant about keeping her pregnancy secret, and I didn't feel I could break her trust and tell Marco. Not without knowing more about the situation.

"Marco," I pleaded, not above begging. "Will you *please* have someone look into this? I have a really bad feeling."

After a moment of silence, he sighed and said, "I can't turn it over to anyone, because no one will look into it. Not now, and likely not even after forty-eight hours. She's just run off too many times before."

Just when I was about to thank him for his time and hang up, he added, "But I'll help you."

His response caught me by surprise. "You're still on medical leave."

"That's right, which means this won't be an official investigation. It'll just be two friends checkin' on her."

"Thank you, Marco!"

"Don't thank me yet," he said. "For now, I'm only committin' to checkin' her house."

Something I'd already done, although he was bound to notice more than I would.

"We'll figure out where to go from there," he continued, "*if* we go somewhere from there. How soon can you meet me at Lula's house?"

I glanced around the kitchen. I'd only put half the food away and still had to make Hank's dinner. Or did I? After Hank's release from the hospital, Wyatt and I had agreed to share the responsibility of taking care of him. Surely he could do his part.

I mentally added up how long it would take me to finish with the groceries, grab my work shirt, and drive to Lula's. "About thirty minutes. Do you need directions?"

"Nah," he said, "I ain't never been to her house, but I know the turnoff. I'll meet you in a half hour."

I hung up the phone and called the garage, my stomach clenching at the thought of talking to Wyatt. I prayed that his employee, Junior, answered instead.

Of course, luck was against me.

"Drummond Auto Repair and Towing," Wyatt answered.

My breath caught in my throat. Why did I have to like him so much? Why did my body react to him like it had never reacted to anyone else? Why couldn't he be more forthcoming?

"Wyatt, it's Carly."

I heard him exhale in relief. "I'm glad you called. I was givin' you some space, but I planned to come see you tonight."

"Were you coming to tell me your secrets?" I asked, my voice stiff.

He hesitated. "Carly…"

"I'm not calling about me," I said. "Hank and I just got back from Greeneville, and I don't have time to make him dinner before I leave. Can you come to Hank's and make sure he eats something healthy? He had Popeyes for lunch, so he really needs to eat something on his diet."

"Yeah, but I still want to see you."

"Don't be coming to the tavern expecting to talk to me," I said. "It's Friday night and we'll be busy. And unless you're planning on sharing at least one of your secrets, don't bother talking to me when you get to Hank's either."

"I need a little time, Carly, if you'd just—"

I had no idea what else he planned to say, since I hung up. I had bigger issues to contend with than my love life. I needed to focus on what had happened to Lula, because I was sure it was nothing good.

CHAPTER NINE

Marco's black Ford Explorer was parked perpendicular to Lula's driveway, his engine running. Making a U-turn, I parked along the side of the street in front of him. I got out and walked to his driver's side, wearing my snow boots.

He rolled down his window and said, "Get in. We'll drive down to her house in my car."

I walked around the other side and climbed in, nearly salivating over the heated leather seats. I'd had a nice car in my other life—an Acura with a luxury interior and a nice stereo system.

Caroline Blakely would never have thought she'd end up searching a one-room shack for a pregnant waitress who'd been sleeping with a dangerous drug dealer.

He backed up, then turned down the lane, coming to a halt within a few feet of pulling in.

"Did you drive down here before?" he asked, pointing to the drive that was still partially snow-covered.

I wouldn't have noticed, but now that he mentioned it, I saw some patterns in the mud.

A chill zipped down my spine.

"No. I parked on the street because I was worried I'd get stuck. I didn't drive down last night either. I dropped her off and watched her walk toward the house."

He stared out at the lane. "You don't say. Then I wonder how those tire tracks got there." Reaching into the backseat, he grabbed a nice digital camera with a long lens. He flipped a switch, turning it on. "Do me a favor and take some photos of those tire tracks."

I didn't have to ask why he needed the help. The crutches in the back confirmed that he was still using them, and likely would for weeks to come. "Yeah. Of course, but I thought you weren't investigating."

"I'm not," he countered good-naturedly. "But if this does turn out to be something, then I'm not destroyin' any evidence. I can't walk down there, but I can drive on the side and preserve some of the tracks. We'll get photos of the rest."

"Okay," I said.

"Focus on getting photos of the right side of the lane. That's where I plan to drive."

"Okay," I repeated and opened the door as I looped the camera strap around my neck.

Staying to the right, I started snapping photos of the barely visible tracks. The tires had been wide, and now that I was looking, I could see several sections of mud embedded with tire treads. I took a ton of photos, then headed back to Marco's SUV, handing him the camera once I was inside.

"Are these good?"

He scanned the screen, quickly shuffling through the images. "They'll work for now. When we come back out, I want you to get closer to those tread marks in the mud."

"Yeah. Of course."

He gave me a tight smile. "Let's go check out the cabin."

He backed up, giving himself more room to maneuver, and then drove slowly down the side of the lane, so far to the right of the lane that tree branches scraped the side of his vehicle.

When the shack came into view, Marco's jaw tightened. "Shit. I can't believe she was livin' like this."

"She told me she's been living here alone since she was sixteen."

He stared at the house for a few seconds, his forehead wrinkling. Finally, he released another heavy sigh. "Okay. Let's go check it out."

He opened his car door and started to get out.

"Let me get your crutches," I said as I hopped out. But by the time I made it around the car, Marco was already standing at the back door, grabbing his crutches from the backseat.

He grinned when he glanced up. "I'm a pretty self-sufficient guy. Much to the ladies' dismay. A few of them would love nothin' more than to wait on me hand and foot."

"Most men would love that," I teased.

"Not this guy. I make no secret that I like a good tumble in the sheets and no commitment." He got the crutches positioned under his armpits, then shut the door. "Okay, let's go."

I expected him to make slow going of getting to the house, but he'd obviously regained quite a bit of strength since I'd last seen him—a surprising feat given he was also recovering from an abdominal wound.

"The porch is rotten in a lot of places," I warned him, "so be careful."

"Yeah," he said with a frown. "I can see that."

I walked up first, testing the floorboards so he knew where it was safe to step. I knocked on the door again, calling out Lula's name to be sure she hadn't returned, then opened it so Marco could hop across the porch of doom into the house.

The room was darker than before, in part because I'd extinguished the lantern and in part because the sun was already setting behind the trees and hill on the western side.

"I don't have my phone to use as a flashlight," I said.

"I rarely carry my phone on me since it doesn't do much good in these parts," he said as he practically vaulted in the room. He likely didn't want to take any chances on the porch. "But I guess you're used to good phone service after living in Atlanta."

He was talking about my fake past.

His statement seemed innocent enough, but it still caught me off guard. "You have no idea."

Hobbling over to the potbelly stove, he reached for the side of it, stopping just short of touching the surface. "Yeah, it's warm." He grabbed a fireplace poker leaning against the wall, then opened the stove and prodded the coals. "There's no central heat in this place. She might have left embers to keep the place warm until she came home."

"The lantern on the chest of drawers was lit," I said, moving toward it. "I extinguished it before I left. I didn't want to risk her house burning down."

He glanced around with a grimace. "Doesn't look like she'd lose much if it did."

While I could see where he was coming from, it *was* her home.

"I think someone came and got her," I said. "And she left in a hurry—look." I pointed to a hook on the wall behind the door. "That's the jacket she was wearing last night."

Marco spun around to look it over. "This thing can barely be considered a coat. She probably grabbed a heavier one before heading out into the snow. Did you see footprints outside when you approached before?"

I cringed. "I didn't look. But where's her shotgun?"

"What?"

"She told me she has a shotgun for protection, but I don't see one and there aren't many places to store one."

Marco leaned on his crutch while his gaze scanned the room. "There." He nodded to the front door. "There's a couple of nails protruding from the logs. I bet she kept it there."

I went over to exam it and frowned. They didn't look like much, just a couple of large nails jutting a couple of inches out of a log. I was going to have to take his word for it. "If her gun's missing and she left without her jacket and didn't douse the lantern…"

"Let's take a peek at those prints now," he said in a grim voice.

Getting outside was trickier for him than getting in, but he reached the bottom step, his mouth pinched tight with pain.

"You're doing too much, Marco," I said, feeling guilty.

"I was bored staring at those same four walls. I'm glad to be out," he said, focusing his attention on the snow. "Which way did you walk coming in and out?

"I should have been more careful," I admitted, feeling terrible. "I think I walked just about everywhere."

"But you didn't drive, right? You parked on the road and walked in?"

"Yeah."

His brow furrowed as he studied the partially snow-covered ground. "I don't see any tire marks, which means whoever drove down the lane didn't drive all the way in."

"Why not?" I asked. "Do you think they were worried about getting stuck?"

He shook his head. "No. Those tire marks you showed me

were from a truck. The double tire marks so close together suggests a big one—a dually."

"What's a dually?"

He chuckled. "You really ain't from around here. It's a pickup with an extra set of tires in the back. It's good for hauling trailers or heavy loads. There's quite a few guys up in these parts who fancy themselves NASCAR drivers. They'll haul their pieces of shit a couple of hours to the Smoky Mountain Speedway in Maryville or North Carolina or if they're any good, like the Grisham boys, down to Georgia." He grinned. "This is the land of NASCAR, Carly. You'll need to pick a team come spring."

"A team?"

"Max'll start showin' NASCAR races at the tavern. Everyone has a favorite driver. The guys'll expect you to pick one."

"They don't ask me about football."

"That's because it's football. NASCAR's a religion down here." He laughed when he saw my face. "Don't you worry. Max and I will get you up to speed enough to pick a driver and rattle off a few stats. It'll help with your tips." He pushed out a long breath, rubbing his chin in a way that told me he wasn't completely unaffected by being here. "In any case, back to more serious matters…like the reason the truck likely didn't pull up to the house. I would say they were hopin' for the element of surprise, except you can hear everything out here. Especially if it was a dually. Lula would have heard the engine." He hopped off the step into the yard. "Makes me think they were blockin' her in."

"You mean her car?" I asked. "So she couldn't drive away?"

"Yeah, but she could have run on foot." He turned to look at me. "You think you can show me where you walked?"

I nodded, both relieved he was taking this seriously and worried sick for Lula.

"Get the camera out of the Explorer. We'll take photos if we find something suspicious."

I hurried to the SUV and grabbed the camera, then returned to find him several feet away from the porch, studying the ground. Embedded in the snow was a large, heavy-tread footprint. No way that belonged to Lula, or me for that matter.

"Put this on the ground next to that print and take a photo."

He handed me a quarter, and I gave him a strange look as I took it.

"It's to show the size of the print. If we turn these photos in to the evidence lab, they'll be able to compare the size of the print to the quarter to determine the shoe size."

I set the quarter down and snapped several photos, then showed them to Marco to make sure they were good enough.

He nodded and scanned the ground. "It's too damn bad the snow's mostly melted on this section because it looks like the man walked right up to the porch, but I don't see any sign of 'im walkin' away, and I sure don't see any smaller prints. I suspect the snow they crossed over on the way back to the truck has all melted."

"I can't believe I didn't notice any prints before," I said, feeling like a fool.

"They were likely in the shadows," Marco said, "and the prints are mostly gone. It just looks like patchy ground. I was specifically lookin' for them."

"So you think someone kidnapped her?" I asked, my stomach falling to my feet.

"I don't know." He shook his head and turned to me. "But there's not a deputy who will take this as a case. Just because the truck parked at the end of the drive doesn't mean she was kidnapped. In fact, all the times she's run off, she never once took her own car. All of that is gonna be held against her."

We walked around the back of the house to look for more prints, only finding the ones I'd left earlier.

"She has an outhouse?" he asked in dismay.

"It stinks to high heaven," I said, wrinkling my nose. When he gave me a horrified look, I added, "I was looking for Lula, not *using* it."

"I know people live like this around these parts. Hell, I've come across 'em on calls, but I never once guessed that Lula lived this way."

"Does Max know?" Marco and Max were best friends, and if anyone would know, it would be Max.

He shook his head. "I don't think so. Otherwise, I suspect he would have done somethin' about it. That boy has a good heart. More so than most people realize."

"I've seen it," I said. I'd experienced it firsthand after Seth's murder. I'd left my unregistered gun next to Seth's body, and even though he'd only known me for a matter of hours, Max had intended to recover and hide it from the sheriff deputies…He would have too, except Jerry had gotten to it first. He'd used it to stop Carson Purdy, and now it was locked up tight in the Hensen County Sheriff's evidence room. Jerry had told them he'd found it behind the motel, so they were none the wiser that it was mine.

But in the days that had followed Seth's murder, Max had been worried enough about my safety that he'd given me a gun for protection to replace it. (Which had also ended up in the sheriff's evidence room, although this one was linked to both me and Max.) And Max always, always protected Ruth and me from irate customers. He was a good man…The only thing that made me nervous about him was his connection with his father, but it occurred to me that Marco might know a thing or two about that.

"How close is Max to his father?"

"They're amicable," he said carefully.

"Amicable can mean a lot of things."

"Are they best buds? No. Bart Drummond never fostered a close relationship with his boys."

That didn't fit with what Tiny had said about Wyatt. Then again, I knew people had different perceptions of shared events. I wasn't ready to dismiss his observations just yet.

"How long have you known Max?" I asked as we started walking around the shack toward the SUV.

Marco chuckled. "Since kindergarten. We went through all thirteen years of school together, and I suppose that wasn't enough, because we roomed together in college. But he left the university at the beginning of his senior year after Wyatt got arrested and quit the family business. Max had to take over."

"What made Max decide to go to college when Wyatt didn't?"

"Max presumed Wyatt would inherit it all. That's what his father told him. That left Max with a whole lot of nothing. So he decided to forge his own path. He was determined to get a business degree and open his own business, but then his daddy came callin' and Max gave it all up to come home."

"Did he *want* to come home?"

"Didn't matter," Marco said as we reached his Explorer. "If Bart told them boys to jump, they jumped."

"Does Max resent his father?" It struck me that his father might not be the only one he resented for hijacking his future. "Does he resent Wyatt for giving it all up and leaving it to him to take up the mantle?" Was that the cause of the brothers' rift?

"Those are two very good questions I don't have the answers to," he said, then opened his car door and tossed his crutches into the backseat. When I got inside, he asked, "Why the interest? What does Wyatt say about all of this?"

"Wyatt refuses to tell me anything about anything. In fact, Wyatt and I are done."

"When the hell did that happen?" he asked. "And more importantly, *why?*"

"It doesn't matter."

He sent me an ornery grin. "So does that mean you're available now?"

I laughed, but my heart hurt at the reminder. "Too soon, Marco."

"Well, if you're lookin' for a fling, I'm your guy."

Laughing again, more softly this time, I said, "I'm not really a fling kind of woman."

His grin spread, his eyes lighting up. "I guessed that about ya, but you can't blame a guy for tryin'." He backed up the SUV and turned around, heading toward the lane. Just like before, he drove close to the trees, as far off the drive as possible.

"What are we going to do about Lula?" I asked.

He shot me a quick glance before returning his gaze to the road. "There's nothing to be done. I told you that already."

"No, you told me no deputies will take the case seriously, but you and I both believe she didn't voluntarily leave."

His hand shot up into the air like a stop sign. "Now, hold on there! I never committed to that theory."

"You and I both know that someone in a big truck came to her house and took her with them. What do you plan to do about it?"

"In case you've forgotten, I'm still on medical leave." But his hesitation seemed a little forced, as if he thought we shouldn't look into this rather than that we'd be wasting our time. I wondered if he was concerned that Todd Bingham might be tied to Lula's disappearing act.

"And you told me that you're bored to death."

"I can't investigate a case while I'm on leave, Carly."

"Well, then let's cut to the chase. I don't think it will take us long to figure out who took her," I said, my voice firm. "All it's gonna take is paying someone a visit."

His back stiffened and his eyes flew wide. "Oh, hell no, Carly Moore. You are *not* gonna go talk to Todd Bingham!"

"He's the most logical person to have taken her, and I plan to ask him where she is."

"He's liable to shoot you the moment you show up on his doorstep."

I gave him a fake sweet smile. "Not if a certain off-duty deputy drives me to his front door."

"No," he said with a firm shake of his head. "No fuckin' way."

"Then I'll go on my own. Now tell me where to find him."

"There's no way I'm sending you to your death!"

"He's not going to kill me, Marco. He and Hank worked out some kind of deal that protects me from Bingham. If he hurts me, Hank will have his head."

Marco narrowed his eyes. "How the hell did Hank Chalmers work out a deal like that?" He was shaking his head before I could respond. "Never mind. I don't want to know. And I'm not takin' you, so give up this fool idea right now."

I shot him a glare. "You *do* realize that I can find him with or without your help. All I have to do is head back to town and start askin' people."

"You'd really consider visitin' him on your own?"

"If he's got Lula, you bet your ass I will."

Marco released a loud groan, shaking his head in disgust. "I'm gonna regret this decision, but fine. I'll do it, but that will be the end of it, you hear?"

I flashed him a smile, never agreeing, but hoping he didn't figure that out.

"Get in your car and drive it to Max's," he said, obviously unhappy. "We'll leave your car there, and I'll run you out to Bingham's. But I'm tellin' you, you're playin' with fire."

"Then I guess I need to bring a fire extinguisher," I said with fake enthusiasm as I got out of his car.

Now I just needed to figure out what that was.

CHAPTER TEN

Marco followed me into town, then let his SUV idle on the street while he waited for me to park my car in the tavern's back parking lot.

When I approached his car and opened the passenger door, he said, "I take it you haven't changed your mind yet?"

"Nope," I said, refusing to look him in the eye as I said it. Truthfully, I'd had plenty of second thoughts about meeting Bingham face-to-face away from the watchful eyes of Hank and Max. Sure, we'd had a one-on-one meeting at the library with no one else around, but this was different. I was barging onto Bingham's turf uninvited.

"This is the craziest thing I've ever done, Carly Moore," Marco said as he pulled away from the curb. "I didn't take *you* for the crazy type. Maybe that's why Wyatt broke up with you."

I nearly corrected him about who'd broken up with whom, but decided it wasn't worth the trouble. "Guess you'll have to ask Wyatt yourself."

I paid close attention to where he drove, noting that he took Highway 25 out toward White Rabbit Holler but he turned right onto a county road a couple of miles before I usually turned left. We drove another few minutes before I realized we weren't on a county road. This was private property.

"Does Bingham own this land?"

"It's been in his family for generations. The Binghams used to give the Drummonds a run for their money back in the day—as recent as the Prohibition era, making moonshine—but Floyd Bingham, Todd's daddy, was the laziest man around and a mean drunk to boot. Ran it all into the ground."

"Guess all this privacy makes it easier for Todd to make people disappear," I teased, but I was so nervous it came out flat.

"I wouldn't be surprised if he had a few bodies buried on his land," Marco said, slowing down as he approached a gravel road and turned left. "And some of 'em were probably left by his father. He may have been lazy, but he was an evil son of a bitch." He shook his head. "Max and me went to school with Todd's younger brother, Rodney, and one day Rodney stopped comin'. They sent a truant officer to find out where he was, but Floyd said that Rodney had run off to live with his momma down in Hickory, North Carolina. Ain't nobody believed that for a minute. Todd's momma died of mysterious circumstances when Todd was about twelve—then Floyd remarried a young thing a few months later. Rumor had it she was barely sixteen. After a few years, I guess she'd had enough beatin' and rapin' because she took off in the middle of the night and left Rodney behind. Kid was about five. Floyd told everyone that she wanted no part of her former life, especially not some snot-nosed kid. Everyone suspected her only way to escape was to leave her son."

"Did anyone verify his story? Make sure he didn't kill her?"

"Not that I know of," he said. "When Rodney disappeared, the sheriff's department poked around a bit, but what could they do? The boy was gone. Todd backed up his daddy's claim that the kid had gone to live with his mother. No one ever could find her to ask. Max and me and the other kids were sure Floyd had gotten carried away with one of his infamous beatin's and killed the poor kid, but we had no way to prove it and the sheriff's department wanted to wipe their hands of the whole thing. I'm pretty sure they saw him as one less future hoodlum to deal with, especially since his older brother was already givin' them a run for their money."

I was so horrified by the thought that Bingham's father had likely killed his son and both of his wives and gotten away with it that it took a moment before Marco's last statement sank in. "I looked Todd Bingham up on the internet and there was no mention of any arrests. Did I miss something?"

"You didn't miss a thing. He might not have been on the internet, but he's definitely been on *our* radar. He's got a juvie record, and while he kept stirring up shit after he hit eighteen, he was smart enough to make sure it was never linked back to him." Marco turned to me. "Bingham's wicked smart, Carly. And with his father's history, he's damn dangerous. Do *not* underestimate him."

I nodded. He was only confirming what I'd already suspected. "How old were you when Rodney disappeared?"

"Third grade. I think he was eight."

I did a quick mental calculation in my head. "So Todd Bingham was twenty-three."

"That sounds about right."

I had so many other questions, but a multiple building complex came into view, so I limited myself to the most pressing one. "What happened to their father? Is he still alive?"

"Nope. He died about six months later. Tripped into a wood-chipper. I hear it was grisly."

"Fell into a woodchipper?" I asked in surprise. "Did anyone really believe that?"

"I doubt it, but I don't think anyone was too sorry to see him go, so they took the word of the lone eyewitness."

"And who was that?" I asked.

"Todd Bingham himself," he said, giving me a sideways glance as he pulled up in front of a house that was at the front of the property. A large metal building was about fifty feet to the right of the house, surrounded by too many old cars to count on either side. Several more of them were parked behind it, going back as far as I could see. Another smaller building sat a bit farther back. I couldn't tell if it was a shed or an old barn.

"What did Floyd do for a living?" I asked, an idea formulating in my head.

"Ran that junkyard you're lookin' at. Todd took it over and made it into a chop shop. The paperwork claims he's doin' it on cars he owns or was hired to work on, but we know he's stealin' 'em too. We just haven't caught him yet."

More like they were turning the other cheek.

"Have you figured out how you're gonna approach him yet?" Marco asked.

"I'm gonna ask him to buy my car." I got out, heading up to the front porch of the bungalow-style house that had probably seen its glory days back in the Prohibition era. With the faded and peeling paint, it was obvious Bingham wasn't going for curb appeal.

I knocked on the door and waited, peering around for any sign of Lula. Nothing popped out, not that I'd really expected it to be so easy. Bingham might feel safe and secluded out here, but he wasn't stupid enough to chain her to his front porch.

The door opened and Bingham filled the doorway. I'd

somehow forgotten how big he was, or maybe he only seemed bigger because I wasn't in a safe zone.

He held a beer can in his hand and wore a pair of jeans and a T-shirt that read, *The South Lives*.

"Well, well, well," he smirked. "This is quite the surprise. What brings you to darken my doorstep, *Ms. Moore?*" He said my name in a snide tone.

"I want to scrap my old car, and I want to know how much you'll give me for it."

He nodded to Marco's SUV, which was parked perpendicular to the house. "You needed a sheriff deputy escort for that?"

So he'd recognized Marco. I'd been counting on it. "Marco and I were takin' a nice drive so he could get out of the house, and when he mentioned you lived down this way, I suggested we stop."

He laughed. "Is that so?" Leaning his shoulder into the door-frame, he said, "I already offered to buy your car, but your boyfriend said no."

"What?" This was the first I'd heard of it—the first I'd even heard of Wyatt talking to Bingham—and I couldn't hide my shock.

His brows shot up. "He didn't tell you, huh? I'm surprised—not about his refusal to sell it to me. He's never sold me nothin' since he bought that business. But I am surprised he didn't tell you that I'd offered. I took it that you two had a more *modern* relationship."

The last thing I intended to do was discuss my relationship— or lack thereof—with Wyatt. "Wyatt Drummond doesn't run my life or the fate of my car. I'm ready to be done with it, so I want to work out an arrangement." I peered past him into his living room, which was full of faded, vintage-style furniture. "You gonna invite me in to discuss it?"

His eyes narrowed. "You know, this has the look and feel of entrapment all over it. Have you become a deputy sheriff, Carly Moore?"

I puffed out my chest and lifted my chin as I propped my hands on my hips. "Got something to hide, Todd Bingham?"

He started laughing. "I never know what's gonna come out of that smart mouth of yours." The laughter faded, and his mouth settled into a harsh line. "But the answer is no. I never conduct business in my house. We can do this out here because it will be short and sweet. I can offer you a thousand dollars."

I shook my head. "Nope. Not enough. I need a new car, so I need more money than that."

"Sounds like a personal problem, sweetheart. Not mine. Take it or leave it."

"Fine," I said, dropping my arms. "I'll leave it."

I turned to walk toward the steps, but he called out good-naturedly, "Well now, hold on there."

I paused and half-turned back to him. "You ready to stop insultin' me?"

He chuckled. "I've got a business to run here. Can't blame a man for lowballin'. Name a price."

The problem was I hadn't looked up the value of my car because I'd trusted Wyatt to handle it. Whenever I'd brought up my car, he'd told me there was no hurry and he was looking into finding a buyer. Why hadn't he told me that Bingham had made an offer? It might be a wreck on wheels, but I was the one who got to decide what to do with it, not him. His silence on the matter only reinforced the fact that I could rely on only one person—me.

I decided to shoot high and negotiate to the middle. "Six thousand."

With a sly grin, he shook his head. "I never took you for a dreamer, Ms. Moore."

I was surprised he was following the rules of etiquette I'd set up the night before. But Marco was right—Todd Bingham was wicked smart, and I knew he was playing some long game...but what was his prize?

"I'm just a woman who needs to replace her car."

"That hunk of junk ain't worth six grand. Try again."

"Five."

Rolling his eyes, he moved closer and leaned his shoulder against one of the posts on the porch, crossing his arms. "It's obvious you didn't do any homework on what your car's worth, so why are you really here?"

Shit. I wasn't about to play my Lula hand yet, so I pulled out the only other card I had, as much as it killed me to tell this man anything about my personal life. "Because I'm no longer with Wyatt Drummond. I'm using Hank's car, which doesn't feel entirely right, so I want to get a new one, which means I need money from the old one. Considering it's not exactly easy to do internet research in this town, and I'm not speakin' to the one person who might have that information, I decided to come to the source and muddle my way through."

His eyes brightened with interest, but not because he looked like he wanted to ask for a place on my dance card, more in a *this is information I need* kind of way. "Well now, if that's the case, I think I might be able to help you out."

"Which case is that?" I asked, partially afraid of the answer.

"Wyatt Drummond is no friend of mine, and if you left him, I'll be more than happy to help you."

So many questions sprang to life...which one did I pick? Curiosity got the best of me.

"What makes you think *I* broke up with *him*?" I asked in a sassy tone.

He chuckled, his laugh this time sounding slightly genuine. "Hell, anyone can see he's crazy about you. There's no way he broke up with you."

"You never struck me as a romantic, Mr. Bingham."

He quirked an eyebrow. "Not a romantic. An observer. I didn't get to where I am by bein' passive like my lazy-ass father. I paid attention to my surroundings. I took advantage of opportunities others missed because they weren't payin' attention."

"And you built this empire," I said, gesturing toward the junkyard.

Tilting his head to the side, he regarded me with cold eyes. "You lookin' down your pretty little nose at me and what I built, Ms. Moore?"

"Not at all," I said. "Despite your humble abode, I suspect you're quite a wealthy man. You just know the value of a dollar. I heard you inherited this from your father and built it into what it is now."

"You've been askin' around about me? I'm not sure whether to be flattered or insulted." The tone in his voice insinuated he'd already chosen the latter.

"You're a powerful man, Mr. Bingham. You proved that after Seth died. The sheriff's department didn't seek justice for that boy's murder. You and I did." Sadly, it was a true statement, although Bingham hadn't been in it for altruistic reasons. "You and I both know that while everyone thinks Bart Drummond is runnin' the town, including the man himself, you've been yankin' it out from under him."

His eyes narrowed as though he was trying to figure out my endgame. I had a point, but I'd taken a meandering path to get there.

"And what's your point?"

"You said you study people...well, the same is true of me. I see you buildin' this empire, and I have to wonder what your motivation is. People do things for a reason."

His body stiffened, and I knew I was now treading on dangerous ground.

"And what do you think motivates me?" he asked.

"I don't know," I admitted. "I don't know enough about you, but I wouldn't say it's to pass your empire down to your son or daughter since you don't seem to have one."

"So you *have* been askin' about me?"

It was a lucky guess that had thankfully struck home. "I think it's good to learn everything I can about the important people around me." I shifted my weight. "So does that factor into your plans for the future?"

"Kids?" He couldn't have observed me any closer if he'd had a microscope.

"Why are you askin' if I want kids?" Then his eyes lit up. "You just broke up with Wyatt Drummond, the son of a powerful man, and now you're sniffin' around here askin' if I want kids?" His arms dropped to his sides. "Got a thing for bad boys, Ms. Moore?"

"What?" I asked in shock. "No, you fool."

"You came in here talking about the two of us workin' together as a team and me being such a powerful man. Everything you've said suggests you're interested in me, and you decided to make the first move."

Oh. *God.* "No," I said as calmly as possible in case he took my horrified reaction the wrong way. "That is *not* it." *Dammit.* I needed to cut to the chase. "Why were you watching Lula like a hawk last night?"

The confusion on his face was almost laughable. "What?"

"You were watching her, and she was nervous as all get-out.

Why?"

His confusion quickly faded to anger. "That's none of your damn business."

"It is given she's missing, and she was scared to death of *you*."

Surprise flickered in his eyes. "Lula took off again." As was usually the case with Bingham, anger quickly took center stage. "Damn that bitch."

"You didn't have anything to do with her disappearance?"

"What?" he practically shouted. "Hell, no. That girl takes off at the drop of a dime, only she left town quicker than usual this time." He shook his head and released a string of curses.

"Sounds like she has something you want," I said.

He had turned away from me a little, as if he didn't want me to see his face, but he swiveled his head to look at me. "Why the interest in Lula? From what I heard, you just met her yesterday."

"Let's just say we hit it off, and I feel the need to protect her."

"From me," he said dryly.

"From anyone who aims to hurt her."

"Sounds like she took care of that on her own by takin' off again," Bingham said.

"No," I said. "I'm sure she was taken. I don't believe she went willingly."

"And where's your proof?" he asked.

That was it. I didn't really have any. It wasn't outside the realm of possibility that someone had dropped by, asked her if she wanted a ride somewhere, and taken her of her own free will. But that didn't seem to fit with the talk we'd had last night. "That's not for you to worry about."

He smirked, and it was obvious he didn't think I had any. "Why don't you get the sheriff involved?" He gestured to Marco's SUV. "And I'm not talkin' about your off-duty escort there."

Marco had his gaze pinned on the both of us.

"Because you and I both know they won't do a damn thing about it."

"That's because there's nothin' to be done," he said. "She ran off. End of story."

"Why is she scared of you?"

"Hell if I know," he said with a shrug. "I treated her damn fine when we were together, but then her mother found out and told her to end it. So she did."

So their tryst hadn't been a one-time thing. I wasn't surprised to hear her mother had influenced her to end it. It sounded like she ran Lula's life from behind bars. "Do you know how often Lula goes to see her?"

"Her mother? Never. She kept in touch with letters and the occasional phone call she accepted at Max's."

Obviously Lula hadn't shared much with Bingham, making me wonder how close they actually were. "How long were you together?"

"What is this, twenty questions?" he asked, sounding irritated, but I could see a hint of concern in his eyes. "Three months, but it was on-again, off-again the entire time. We broke up this summer. I wanted to keep it quiet and Lula had no problem with it."

"Why'd you keep it a secret?" I asked.

"To protect her. I already knew that people looked down on her, and this would only add fuel to the fire. Besides, it was nothin' serious." But the look on his face suggested otherwise.

Once again, I found myself thinking about Rose. Her relationship with Skeeter Malcolm had been a carefully kept secret. I suspected Skeeter cared about Rose more than he let on too, and he'd made dangerous choices because of it. "Did you take the breakup well?"

"Hell no, I didn't. It was a stupid-ass reason, but I couldn't force her to be with me, now could I? So I had to accept it."

But did he? It sounded like his father's way of treating women was to abuse them into doing whatever he wanted. What if the apple hadn't fallen far from the tree?

"So why was she anxious around you last night?" I asked again.

"Hell if I know," he barked. "You should have asked her."

"I did and she refused to tell me. She only told me not to piss you off because you kill people or make them disappear."

The sly Todd Bingham I knew slipped back into place, and he gave me a lopsided grin. "Well, you know that firsthand, now don't you, Ms. Moore? Seems to me I helped you and Hank make someone disappear as a favor."

"Seems to me that Hank did *you* the favor," I said, risking a glance at Marco to see if he'd heard. If he had, he wasn't reacting. Bingham had disposed of the body of the intruder Hank had shot, but he'd benefited from the situation too. He'd wanted to know which of his men had turned traitor. Turned out the man who'd helped kill Seth and tried to kill me was one of his guys.

"I don't know why Lula was afraid of me," he said in a low, rumbling tone that let me know he'd about reached his limit. "I only know I treated that woman like a queen when we were together, and she ended it for a bullshit reason. Did I treat her like peaches and cream after? No, but I wasn't going to make her disappear, if that's what you're insinuating." He took a step closer, puffing out his chest. "Now I think it's time for you to leave."

I stared up at him. "I'm going to find out what happened to her."

"Good luck with that," he said. "If she already left, she might not be comin' back this time." Then he turned his back on me and walked through the door.

CHAPTER ELEVEN

When I got back in Marco's SUV, he didn't waste any time pulling away from Bingham's house.

"The fact you're still alive is a good sign," Marco said, flying down the long driveway. "Unless he's comin' for you later."

I rolled my eyes. "He's not comin' for me later."

"Did you really ask him to buy your car?"

"I did, and we were workin' out a deal before we got side-tracked...*dammit*." I really *had* wanted to sell him my car.

"Well, I'm sure as hell not goin' back, so you're shit out of luck." He shot me a glance. "Did you find out anything?"

"He admitted that he and Lula had a thing that lasted about three months. Lula's mother made her break up with him. He said that he wanted to keep their relationship quiet." I narrowed my eyes at him. "Ruth apparently didn't even know about it. You didn't tell her or Max?"

"Hell, no. I'm no gossip. The only reason I'm tellin' you now is because it might play into her takin' off." He hesitated, then said, "But there's more."

I shifted in the seat to get a better look at him.

When he was sure he had my attention, he said, "Lula seemed off a few weeks after I saw her and Bingham. I could see something was eatin' at her, so I started askin' questions. She confessed she had broken up with someone and was worried about his reaction. I wondered if it was Bingham, but she didn't volunteer, and I didn't ask. I told her she could hang out at my place for a few nights, and she looked relieved."

Lula had broken up with Bingham about six months ago, and she'd spent several nights with Marco, which meant…

"Marco," I said in a tight voice. "Did you sleep with her?"

"You're seriously askin' me that question?" he asked, sounding offended.

"I'm not judging, but your answer is important."

"I still don't see what business it is of yours."

"What's the big deal? You've admitted to having multiple partners," I said.

"Just because I've slept with more than a handful of women doesn't mean I'm gonna go posting their names on social media."

"I'm not asking for a roster, Marco, and it's not like I'm going to tell Bingham, if that's what you're worried about."

"Why is it so important to know if I slept with her last summer?" he asked, growing irritated.

"It just *is*, Marco," I said, torn between my promise to Lula and the need to know if he was a potential father to her baby.

He shot me another look, and then his eyes widened slightly. "Wait. You *know* something. What aren't you tellin' me?"

I countered his question with my own. "Will you help me find her?"

"Do you have any more leads?" he asked in frustration. "Because this seemed to be our only one. Unless you tell me what you're holdin' back."

"You have to swear you won't tell another soul."

"Okay."

"No, you have to *swear* it, Marco."

"Okay, I swear."

I still wasn't sure if I should tell him, but I needed to find Lula, and he was the only person liable to help me. Which meant I had to take the risk. "Lula's pregnant."

The car swerved to the right as he jerked his head to face me, but he quickly corrected it. "She's *what?*"

"She's five or six months pregnant. She's not sure how far along she is because she hasn't gone to see a doctor...which means she doesn't know when she got pregnant. So Bingham could be the father, or if *you* slept with her..."

He shook his head. "It's not me."

"So you didn't sleep with her?"

"It's not me, Carly," he said, keeping his eyes on the road. "Let's just leave it at that."

I would have felt more relieved if he'd flat out denied sleeping with her, but it was obvious this was the best I was going to get. "So Bingham's in the running for the father, but I don't think he knows about her pregnancy. Could there be anyone else?"

"Why are you askin' me?" he asked defensively.

"You seem to know more about her personal life than Ruth does."

A frown tilted his mouth down. "Ruth is hard on 'er. She thinks Lula's slow and dimwitted, and she's hurt her feelin's more times than I can count. Lula purposefully keeps her personal life from Ruth because she doesn't want her to rip it apart."

I felt disloyal for even thinking it, but I suspected Marco was probably right. I'd seen their dynamic play out the night before at the tavern. "Surely Lula has someone she talks to. A friend she confides in."

"As you've figured out, working at the tavern doesn't leave much time for socializin', but last I heard, her closest friend is Greta Hightower."

I repeated her name. "Where have I heard that name before?"

"She's a waitress at Watson's," he said.

I shook my head, working it over. "That's not it." I snapped my fingers and pointed at him. "Max slept with her and pissed her off."

Marco cringed. "Yeah, Max mentioned something about that."

"Do you think you can talk to her?"

He snorted. "I'm not sure she'll talk to me. I'm guilty by association with Max."

"Then there's no way she'll talk to me. I work for him. And then there's the fact I've been filling in for her best friend at the tavern. She might be one of the people who think I'm trying to steal Lula's job."

"Maybe you can butter her up by talkin' bad about Max."

I was already shaking my head. "Max has been more than generous to me. I won't do that to him."

"Well, you took Lula home last night, and you're lookin' for her now. Surely she'll want to help you find her."

"If she trusts me. It's all about trust, Marco."

"Yeah," he said, the corner of his mouth twitching up, "but you have a way of makin' people trust you, Carly. Just be honest with her and she'll see that you're on the up and up."

I glanced at the clock on the dashboard. "Well, I won't be talking to her tonight. I'm barely going to get to work on time as it is, but I'm off tomorrow afternoon." I gave him a sly smile. "What are you doing tomorrow morning?"

"Why do I think it's going to Watson's Café for breakfast with you?"

"Because you're more than just a pretty face, Marco Roland."

"Ha!" he said with a laugh. "Try convincin' my boss of that."

"You'll prove it to him by finding Lula."

"She still could have taken off again, Carly."

"Maybe," I conceded, because I'd had a few moments of doubt. "But my gut tells me that someone took her. And I feel really guilty about going to work knowing she's in trouble."

He nodded. "Yeah, me too, but you have to promise me you won't go off and try looking into this by yourself. It's too damn dangerous, Carly."

"You're going to help?"

"Only if we do it together."

"Really?" This felt too good to be true. I'd been prepared to make a half dozen other arguments to turn him around.

"Look," he said. "It's like I told you, I've got nothing but time on my hands, and I'm worried about her too. I could get in trouble running an investigation on my own while I'm on medical leave, but if you're searchin' with me, it's just two people lookin' for a friend."

I raked my bottom lip with my teeth. "Do you think I should call in sick to work tonight?"

"If we had a solid lead to follow, then yeah, maybe. But we're chasin' our tails at this point, and it's Friday night. Max and Ruth need you. Plus, maybe you can pick up information from the customers."

He had a point, but I still hated the idea of doing nothing until tomorrow. If someone had taken Lula against her will, we didn't have much time to help her. Given she was gone, I'd be pulling a double on Sunday and Monday. Tomorrow would be my only chance to look into her disappearance for the next few days.

When I raised my concerns to Marco, he released a long groan. "How about this? I'll drop you off at Watson's so you can see if Greta's there. But I've got the waitress schedule there down pat, and she's typically off on Fridays."

I narrowed my eyes. "You know the waitresses' schedules?"

"Hey," he said defensively. "When I'm on shift, I usually eat lunch there."

"Not Max's?"

He grinned. "I can't look like I have favorites."

I snorted. "Let me guess—they hire pretty waitresses."

His grin lit up his eyes as he stole a glance in my direction. "It certainly doesn't hurt."

When we got into town, he found a parking space on Main Street, a few shops down from Watson's Café.

"You don't have to wait for me, Marco," I said. "I can just walk down to the tavern when I'm finished."

"I'll stick around in case she's there. I want to see what you find out."

"Okay." I got out and strode down the nearly deserted sidewalk to the café, tugging my jacket tighter around me. The wind had picked up, and it was colder than it had been earlier. I wondered if another storm was moving in. That wouldn't bode well for my search for Lula. I'd been warned that the mountain roads sometimes became impassable when there was a heavy snow. I'd already stocked Hank's cupboards with enough staples to keep us fed for a week if, or more likely *when*, that happened.

The smell of fresh apple pie hit me full in the face when I walked through the door to Watson's, and my stomach grumbled. I took a second to orient myself. Although I'd had their breakfast sandwiches, I'd never been inside the café before, but I'd walked past it a dozen or so times on my way to the library.

The dining area was smaller than in Max's Tavern, and the tight space was crammed with tables, but the walls were a pale blue and the large windows made it seem lighter and airier. Only a handful of tables had customers—a group of teens and an older couple. I didn't see any waitstaff, but as I walked toward the back, a woman called out, "Just take a seat anywhere."

"Thanks…" I said, realizing I should have come up with a script. "I can't stay, but I was hoping to put in a to-go order." I hadn't intended to get anything, but now I was starving and it gave me an excuse for being here. Even if Greta wasn't working, the other waitstaff might know something useful about Lula.

A young woman popped out of the back. "Sure thing." She was wearing a pink waitress dress with a white collar, plus white sneakers with white cuffed socks. Thank goodness Max didn't make us wear anything so cheesy. Her head tilted as she studied me, her long blonde ponytail swishing to the side. "Say, aren't you the new waitress at Max's?"

"Sure am," I said in a cheery voice. "Marco Roland tells me he eats here all the time, so I thought I'd pick up something for the both of us."

Her blue eyes narrowed, but it looked more like confusion than any sort of malicious intent. "I thought you were datin' Wyatt Drummond."

Word sure did get around in a small town. "I'm not seeing him anymore." It wasn't her business, but I needed information from her, so I hoped my own transparency would help. "And before you ask, no, I haven't set my sights on Marco," I added with a laugh. "We're just friends."

"I heard you saved his life."

My cheeks flushed with embarrassment. "There was a lot of mutual savin' goin' on that night."

"I guess something like that would bind people together," she said with a soulful look.

"Yeah," I admitted. "It does." I pulled my mouth into a wider smile. "Say, do you have a menu I can look over?"

"What was I thinkin'?" she said with a laugh, then grabbed a menu off a table. "Here you go, but if you're not sure what to get Marco, he usually gets the double cheeseburger and double fries."

I took the menu from her and quickly scanned it, shaking my head. "Why am I not surprised he goes for all the grease?"

"Right?" she asked with a laugh. "If I ate all those calories every day, I'd gain twenty pounds."

"Well, he's still recovering from his gunshot wounds, so let's give him his comfort food," I said. "And I'll take a club sandwich and a side salad with ranch dressing." Max's Tavern didn't have salads, and while I didn't have high hopes for this one, some vegetables would be nice, even if it turned out to consist mostly of tasteless iceberg lettuce.

"Good choice," she said, pulling a small notepad out of her pocket and writing the order down. "I'm Greta, by the way."

My mouth nearly dropped open, and it took me a second to process who she was and figure out how to react. I stuck out my hand. "I'm Carly. Nice to meet you."

She gave me an odd look but loosely shook my hand.

I laughed. "Sorry. I guess you already knew my name."

"Yeah," she said with a grin. "I did. Let me put your order in. Have a seat if you like." She gestured to an empty booth next to where we stood.

I slid into the seat, relieved she didn't seem to hold a grudge against me, but I still wasn't sure how to handle my questions about Lula. Given that Greta didn't seem so sour on Marco after all, I should have probably left this to him. Maybe she'd forgiven him after his near-death experience. I was sure his good looks didn't hurt.

Greta came back out and took the seat opposite me. "I told Fred I was takin' a break."

I took a quick glance at the room, then said, "Seems like a good time to take one."

She gave me a conspiratorial grin. "Well, I've only been workin' about a half hour, but the dinner rush'll hit soon enough, and then I'll be hopping for the rest of my shift. I figured you and I could get to know each other a little since you and Lula are workin' together."

"I confess that I was worried you'd think I was trying to steal Lula's job," I admitted.

She leaned back in her seat, getting comfortable. "I'll admit it crossed my mind, but then she came in yesterday and said you were super sweet and you two were job sharin'." She leaned closer. "Thanks for not stealin' it out from under her. I heard Max was fit to be tied this last time."

"I wouldn't do that," I said, "but do you know why she left in the first place?"

She made a face and shot a glance at the table of teenagers. "What does it matter?"

"Max and Ruth are none too happy that she keeps runnin' off, but I figure they'll be more understandin' if she has a good reason."

"There's no need to worry about that now," Greta said with a wave of dismissal. "She's back now."

"Greta," I said slowly, "Lula's gone again."

She stared at me as though I'd sprouted a unicorn head. "What are you talkin' about? She just got back yesterday."

"I know," I said, "but she didn't show for her shift at noon today. I was worried that maybe she had car trouble, so I went to her place this afternoon and she wasn't there."

She frowned and I could see she was still processing what I'd said. "That doesn't mean she took off."

"Her car was out front, and she'd left a lantern on and a fire burning in her woodstove. Seems like she'd know better than to leave the place like that if someone came to pick her up. I brought Marco back with me, and she was still gone."

She began to gnaw on her bottom lip.

"Given her history, he said no deputy will look into it. At least not this soon, and likely not at all. But the two of us looked at her property together. There were tracks in the snow, plus tire prints from a big dually truck. Someone was out there."

"Well, that makes sense," she said, shifting to the side as she tucked a leg under the other on the seat. "If her car was still there."

"So you think she left willingly?" I asked. "Even though she knew if she didn't show up for her shift at noon today she would likely be fired?"

"Lula *is* impulsive," she said, staring at a spot of dried ketchup on the Formica-topped table, but her statement lacked conviction.

"Do you know who might have picked her up?"

"It could have been anyone," she said, still keeping her gaze on the table.

"Does she have a boyfriend right now? Could he have picked her up?"

She snorted. "Lula doesn't do boyfriends. Her mother's convinced her that all men are jerks, that she should get what she needs and move on."

"So she's made her way through a lot of men," I said thoughtfully.

Her face jerked up, her eyes blazing. "Lula is *not* a slut."

Horrified, I shook my head. "No. I don't think that. I'm sorry if I unintentionally gave that impression."

Her shoulders relaxed, but only slightly.

"I'm just trying to figure out if she left her home willingly, because I have this gut instinct that she's in trouble."

Greta narrowed her eyes. "Why would you care? You hardly know her, and on top of that, your hours are gonna get cut now that she's back. Sounds like if anyone had motive to take her, it was you."

My heart jumped. Crap. I hadn't even considered that I might be a suspect, but as far as I knew, I *was* the last one to have seen her alive.

It occurred to me belatedly that my reaction to her comment had probably made me look guilty. Leaning forward, I lowered my voice and said, "Look, you're right—I barely know Lula. I only met her yesterday afternoon, but she's probably one of the sweetest people I've ever met. Todd Bingham came in with his motley crew and made her anxious. It didn't help that he kept staring at her. I could tell he worried her, and since I'm older than her, I guess my big sister instincts kicked in. So I put him in my section so she didn't have to deal with him." To prove to her that Lula, at least, trusted me, I added, "Then I drove her home in the snow because she didn't have a car."

"She said she was going to have Max drive her home," Greta said, her tone softening, but her guard was still up.

I understood. It wasn't smart to blindly trust the citizens of Drum. There were many lines in the sand, and the wind was always blowing. Someone loyal to Bart Drummond one week might fall in line with Bingham the next, especially since Bart's right-hand man had killed so many people. I wasn't sure where Greta's loyalty lay, but I was hoping it was with her friend.

"With our new shared hours, Max was upstairs," I said. "She asked Ruth for a ride home, but I offered."

Frown lines creased her forehead. "She must have been desperate if she asked Ruth. That woman has it in for her."

Marco had said something similar, although not quite in those terms. I understood why Ruth struggled with Lula—her behavior was frustrating, and sometimes it required the people around her to work twice as hard. Still, there was something about Lula that made me want to save her from that one-room shack. To protect her from her mother. To show her that she had more worth than the men she slept with. To help her make sure her baby was healthy and had a safe delivery.

But I had to find her first. And hope to God she was still alive.

I shuddered and Greta's eyes narrowed even more.

"You have no reason to trust me," I said. "I'm new to town, and now I'm asking about your friend after I told you she's missing. It's suspicious. I have no idea how to prove myself to you, but I hope you can see my sincerity. I think she's in trouble and I'm trying to find her. I'll do everything in my power to save her job and help her with the baby."

Greta gasped and jerked backward, her back slamming into her seat.

Oh crap. "You didn't know she was pregnant?"

"You *did?*"

I gave her a sad smile. "She let it slip. I take it she's five or six months along. Her mother apparently wants her to deliver the baby in that uninsulated shack. Without a midwife or any medical supervision. I knew I couldn't change her mind, at least not during the drive to her house, but I did get her to agree to take prenatal vitamins if I got them in Greenville this morning."

Greta watched me for a few seconds. "I should have thought of the prenatal vitamins."

"My friend is pregnant. She was kind of beside herself when she found out she was two months pregnant and hadn't taken any. I guess it really stuck in my subconscious."

Greta relaxed a little. "I told Lula that her mother's crazy. She needs a doctor, but she won't listen."

"How long have you known?"

"Not long," she reluctantly admitted. "She told me in October, a few weeks before she took off last time. Honestly, I don't think she'd known that long herself. Her periods have always been irregular. In fact, she thought she couldn't get pregnant, so she's never been too careful."

"That's why she's not sure about the due date?" I asked.

She nodded.

"Did she tell you who the father was?"

Her eyes hardened. "How is that any of your business?"

"Because the father could be unhappy he's about to be a daddy. Maybe he's the one who carted her off."

"The father doesn't know."

"But you know who the father is?"

She inhaled a deep breath and slowly pushed it out. I could tell she was buying herself a few seconds to consider her response. "I don't feel comfortable telling you anything else."

I resisted the urge to groan. While she'd shared helpful information, none of it would help me find Lula.

"I know you don't trust me," I said. "And I understand why—truly, I do. But Marco and I are the only ones who think she didn't leave on her own, which means the sheriff's department won't look into it, and Max will never give me time off to search. I only have tomorrow to look for her, from morning until early evening, so the more I know, the better my chances."

"Marco doesn't think she ran off?"

"No, which is why he's helping me."

Her frown deepened. "If Marco's involved, I can't tell you anything."

"Was she doing something illegal, or was she associatin' with people who wouldn't like a deputy sniffing around?"

"Both."

I sat back, pressing my lips together as I thought her predicament through. "Marco assures me he's just looking as a friend. He's still on medical leave, so this isn't official."

She snorted. "What else would you expect a cop to say? It's unofficial until he finds something good."

She had a point.

"Marco protected her," I said, still hoping to convince her. "A few months ago. She stayed with him after an ugly breakup. Why would he have given her a place to stay if he was so interested in busting her?"

Her frown deepened.

"Especially when it likely put him on Todd Bingham's bad side."

Her jaw dropped like a trapdoor, but she quickly recovered, jerking her gaze around the room.

"Who told you she was seein' him?" she whisper-shouted as she leaned forward.

"Bingham himself."

Her face paled.

"So Bingham's the father?"

Leaning an elbow on the table, she covered her mouth with her fingers. I could tell she was frantically sifting through her options. She landed on belligerence. "I don't believe you. Bingham doesn't talk about his personal business with anyone, let alone an outsider."

She had a point, and now that I thought about it, I had to wonder why he'd been so open. Had I caught him by surprise? That seemed highly unlikely. Todd Bingham hadn't gotten where he was today by being sloppy.

"I don't know what to tell you," I said. "I knew she was scared of him last night, and now she's missing. He seemed to be a likely suspect, so I paid him a visit."

She shook her head in disgust. "You're either reckless or a fool, and neither option is good."

I suspected I was both.

"Greta, yer order's up," a man called from the back.

Greta slid out of the booth as quickly as if a zombie were trying to bite her on the butt. I reluctantly followed her, and she grabbed the bag from the server's ledge and thrust it at me. "That'll be $14.60."

Reaching into my purse, I pulled out a twenty-dollar bill and handed it to her, but when she grabbed hold of it, I didn't let go.

"I know you don't trust me, Greta, but I swear I only want to protect Lula. If you can think of anything that will help me find her, I'm begging you to tell me."

Her response was a glare.

I'd screwed this up. I should have given my approach more thought, but I hadn't, and now Lula would pay the price.

My voice wavered as I pushed past the lump in my throat. "If you change your mind, I'll be at the tavern until it closes. You can come by and see me or you can call. I'll stop whatever I'm doing to talk."

Her determination seemed to waver for a second, but then the steely resolve returned to her eyes. She tugged harder on the bill and I released it, making her stumble backward a half step.

"I'll get your change," she snapped.

"Keep it," I said as I turned my back to her and headed out the door

I was back at square one, and I only had myself to blame.

CHAPTER TWELVE

arco was tapping his thumb on the steering wheel when I walked up to his Explorer, singing along to a country song I didn't recognize. I opened the door and climbed in, grateful for the warmth of the interior.

"That took a while," he said, turning down the volume so the music was in the background. "But I won't complain since it looks like you brought food."

I was about to tell him that some of it was for me, but a quick glance at his dashboard clock confirmed it was 5:02. If I walked in with food from Watson's, Ruth would have my hide.

I shoved the bag at him. "Greta was there. She'd just started the dinner shift."

"No shit!" he exclaimed in excitement. "What did you find out?"

"Not much." I spilled our conversation.

"Okay," he said. "You didn't get confirmation that Bingham is the baby's father, but it wasn't nothing. We filled in a few blanks."

"But I didn't get anything that will help us find her," I protested in frustration.

"Don't you worry, little bulldog," he said with a grin as he peered into the bag. "We're not givin' up. I'll pick you up at Hank's at nine, and we'll drop by Watson's for breakfast, just like we planned. I know for a fact she's workin' the Saturday morning breakfast shift. We'll keep tryin' until we wear her down. It might take a few days, but she'll spill."

"Thanks for not tossin' in the towel," I said in relief.

"Slow and steady wins the race," he said as he popped a couple of french fries into his mouth. "Ain't you never read the tortoise and the hare story?"

Nostalgia washed through me, sweet and sappy, tugging me back into my grief over the life I'd lost. It had been part of my third-grade language unit on fables. I'd been a good teacher, but I'd never teach again unless I found some way to deal with my father. Fat chance of that. Wyatt had changed his mind, and I couldn't even get Greta to talk to me. Tears tracked down my cheeks, and I reached up to wipe them.

"Ah, Carly," Marco said, pulling me into an awkward hug on the front seat of his SUV. "We'll find her. Don't give up yet."

"Thank you, Marco." As I pulled away, I gave him a quick kiss on the cheek. "I got dinner for myself too, but I think Ruth will pitch a fit since I'm late, so you can have it."

He peered into the bag and crinkled his nose. "What's in the cup?"

I leaned over to look. "My side salad, but there's also a club sandwich."

"A salad?" he said with disgust, as though I was trying to get him to snack on rat poison.

"Yes," I teased with a groan. "You should give it a try." I opened the door and started to get out. "I'll see you tomorrow. Don't overdo it tonight since you've been so busy today."

"Yes, Mom," he said with a chuckle.

I grinned back at him, rolling my eyes. When I turned around, I ran smack-dab into Junior, the mechanic who worked for Wyatt.

He grabbed my arm to keep me from falling on my butt.

"Oh hey, Junior," I said, taking a step back. "How are you? How's Ginger? I heard Maria had a bad cold last week." Junior's wife helped out with Hank sometimes, and although Hank was a sixty-eight-year-old former drug dealer, he was as big of a gossip as any female busybody. And he told me everything he learned.

"Maria's on the mend and back at preschool, thanks for asking. Also, thanks for hiring Ginger to clean Hank's house. We could really use the money and, well…" His cheeks flushed. "Thanks."

Hire her to clean Hank's house? Hank would never have made such an arrangement. For one, he didn't have the money, and for another, I earned my room and board by cooking, cleaning, and helping take care of Hank. If someone was cleaning his house, that meant I wasn't meeting my end of the bargain.

"Is there a problem?" Junior asked with a worried look.

"No, none at all," I said. "And I should be thanking Ginger. With all my hours at the tavern, some days I struggle to keep up." Was Hank unhappy with my contribution? He hadn't said anything, and he definitely wasn't shy about expressing his opinions.

"Wyatt said it would make it easier for you."

That put a twist in my stomach. Had Wyatt done it to help me, or did he want to win me back? Did it matter?

Junior looked appeased, even if I was far from it. "I hate to run off on you," I said, taking a step backward and pointing down the sidewalk toward the tavern. "But I'm already late. It was good seeing you, Junior!"

"You too, Carly."

I hurried down the sidewalk, realizing I should have had Marco drop me off to save time and body heat. I couldn't hightail it straight into the tavern either, because my work shirt was still in my car around back, along with Ruth's purchases—and surely Ruth would be less pissed if I came bearing gifts—so toward my car I sprinted, working a stitch into my side. Just as I was about to turn the corner to the tavern's back parking lot, a man in a dress coat exited one of the rooms at the Alpine Inn and got into the driver's seat of an idling black BMW sedan.

It was Neil Carpenter, the man Bart Drummond had met for lunch.

What in the world was a guy like that doing in the negative-one-star-rated Alpine Inn?

He backed his car out and turned right, heading east, toward White Rabbit Holler and the overlook.

According to his business card, Neil Carpenter was from Nashville. What was he doing on a road that would land him in North Carolina in about fifteen minutes?

He didn't seem to notice me as he passed, and even though I knew I needed to get to work, I was beyond curious about what he'd been doing.

On a whim, I bolted across the street and across the motel parking lot.

The brick building was L-shaped. The office was on the street, at the end of the short part of the L, but it was permanently closed, with a sign instructing guests to check in across the street at the tavern. Max ran the place for his father and rented the first two units to permanent guests—Jerry and a man they called Big Joe. Their rooms and two others were next to the office, and twelve units made up the longer section of the building. (The first room on the long side started with 8 instead of 5.)

The fateful night I'd witnessed Seth's murder, I'd been on the end in 20. Seth had been hiding in 17.

Neil Carpenter had come out of room 16.

My stomach cramped as I marched up to the door. Maybe I was acting crazy, but I wouldn't rest until I knew why he'd been hanging out at the seedy Alpine Inn. I was sure it had something to do with Bart, and my distrust for the Drummond patriarch went beyond my broken agreement with Wyatt. I strongly suspected Bart had been involved with Carson Purdy's scheme, which meant he was partly responsible for Seth's death. That gave me a reason all my own for wanting him to see justice.

If Bart's crony was coming out of the Alpine Inn, it couldn't be for respectable purposes. Maybe this was the first step to figuring out what he was up to.

Steeling my back, I rapped on the door, realizing that there was a good chance no one would answer. And for a few seconds no one did. I was about to turn around and head over to the tavern when the door cracked open, revealing a young woman's face and scantily clad body. She was wearing a pair of red lace panties and a thin white tank top that left nothing about her breasts to the imagination.

"You came back…" Her voice trailed off when she saw me, her smile morphing into a glare. "I know you. You're Max's new waitress. What are you doin' here?"

I had absolutely no idea who she was, which made me uncomfortable. "I'm sorry for the intrusion. I was looking for someone else."

Her eyes widened in surprise. "Are you workin' in the motel now that Lula's back?"

Working in the motel? For one wild second, I thought she was asking me if I was doing housekeeping. Then her meaning penetrated, and so did her reason for being here.

"No," I said. "I was lookin' for Jerry."

"Jerry?" she asked in disgust. "He's down in number two."

"Thanks," I said, already backing away. My mind was whirring. I'd heard the rooms at the Alpine Inn sometimes rented by the hour, but I'd thought that meant people brought lovers or prostitutes there. Not that a prostitution ring was run out of the motel.

Max managed the motel. Did this mean he was a pimp?

The idea made me queasy, but I decided to give him the benefit of the doubt. He didn't own the motel, just ran it for his father. For all I knew, Bart had some rooms blocked off for his prostitution ring, and Max was none the wiser.

And I was an utter fool if I believed a word of it.

I didn't have time to dwell. I'd never been this late before, and I had little to show for it. It would have been quicker to head through the front door, but I still needed to get my Max's Tavern T-shirt, plus I still wanted to get Ruth's bag as a peace offering. So I stopped by the car, grabbing Jerry's coat too, and then headed through the back door with the key Max had recently given me. I hung up my coat and was about to strip off my black long-sleeved T-shirt, but the thought of putting my cold uniform shirt against my bare skin made me shiver. I tugged it over my head instead, going for a layered look.

Ruth was bussing a table by the kitchen. Her gaze jerked up as I came through the doorway. "You're late!"

"Sorry," I said as I tied my small apron around my waist and scanned the room to assess what needed to be done. Three middle-aged men nursed beers at a table by the window. Not busy yet.

Whew. That appeased my guilt, but Ruth was still madder than a wet hornet.

She propped a hand on her hip, then said with plenty of attitude, "Now that you've met Lula, you think you can start pulling her shenanigans?"

I gasped in surprise. She'd never spoken to me so hatefully before, and my first instinct was to snap back. Sure, I was seven minutes late, but she wasn't overwhelmed, and my tardiness wasn't a habit. But I suspected she'd been stewing about Lula all afternoon, especially since she was the one who'd had to cover her shift, and she was ready to vent.

I was the lucky recipient.

Max had been sitting on a stool behind the bar, reading a book, but he popped his head up, his eyes alert, looking ready to spring into action.

I moved directly in front of her, then calmly said, "Ruth, I'm sorry I was late, and I'm sorry you had to cover for Lula today. I'm not trying to take advantage of you or Max. It was an honest mistake."

Her eyes were still blazing, and she looked like she wanted to pounce, but my apology had stolen some of her steam. "Don't make a habit of it."

"I won't," I said. "And the things you asked for from Target are in the back." I grinned. "I even got you something you didn't request."

Her eyes widened, and she looked stunned. "You got me a surprise?"

"Yeah," I said. "Why don't you go in the back and check it out? I'll finish bussing this table."

Several emotions flitted across her face, but sadness was the one that stuck. "God, you must think I'm a bitch."

"I think you're stressed out and human. Now go take a break and check out your surprise."

She headed into the back while I cleared the table. After I

dropped off the dishes at the door to the kitchen, I headed behind the bar to check in with Max.

"Good job handlin' Ruth," he said, glancing up from his book. "You must be a shaman or a spirit walker."

I snorted. "I thought those people dealt with the dead."

"They wrangle evil spirits."

"I think it's a bit much to compare Ruth to an evil spirit," I said with a grin.

He grinned back. "Says the woman who wasn't working with Warpath Ruth all afternoon."

"Sorry," I said, then leaned closer, wondering which issue to bring up first—Lula or the business across the street. I went with the safest. "Max, I don't think Lula ran off."

He perked up, lowering his paperback western to the counter. "What makes you say that?"

"I went to her house to check on her."

He looked startled and was about to respond when Ruth emerged from the back, smiling from ear to ear.

"If you think this excuses you bein' late..." she grumbled.

"I don't," I said, "and I promise I won't make a habit of it." I knew she wanted to know why I was late, but I couldn't risk pissing her off. She'd never approve of me looking for Lula, and if she knew I was snooping across the street, she'd tell me to mind my own business. While I didn't need her permission to investigate either mystery, I also didn't want to antagonize her.

"What'd you get her?" Max asked, genuinely curious.

"Girly things," Ruth said, beaming.

Max's upper lip curled in revulsion. "Gross. I don't want to hear about tampons."

I busted out laughing, but Ruth was disgusted. "Why in the hell would I be so happy over tampons?"

"Damned if I know how the female mind works," he said,

crossing his arms over his chest.

"She got me *bath bombs.* Lavender and mint. I'd told her that I'd read about them in *Women's Day* magazine, and she picked up a few for me."

The way she stated it made me think people didn't usually give her little gifts. I made a mental note to give her more. I shrugged. "It was nothing. I saw them and remembered you mentioned wanting to try one."

"It's perfect." She reached out and grabbed my hand, squeezing as she made a face. "I'm sorry I was such a bitch. I feel terrible."

"Bombs, huh?" Max said. "Does this mean you wouldn't have been so bitchy if I'd run down the street and picked up a grenade from the army surplus store?"

When I turned to look at him, his eyes were dancing with mischief.

"You try getting me a grenade, Maxwell Drummond, and just watch where I put it," she said in a stern voice, but I could tell she was fighting off another grin.

"Don't you worry about it," I said. "You had a shitty afternoon. But I'm here now." The door opened and a group of six walked in. "If you want, take a quick break before all hell breaks loose again. I've got it covered."

"You're the best." She headed to the back, and I was about to walk around the bar, but Max caught my eye.

"So what will it be? Shaman or spirit walker? Or maybe just miracle worker? I like that."

I laughed. Leave it to Max to make me laugh after a crappy day. "I'll settle for Queen Carly." Cocking my head, I gave him a smug look. "I like it. It rolls off the tongue."

Chuckling, he said, "That title already belongs to Ruth, and I'm not havin' any part of that battle."

I took the new customers' orders and checked on the three guys still nursing their nearly empty beers. I offered to get them refills and asked if they wanted a basket of wings and fries to munch on. To my surprise, they did.

Max waggled his eyebrows and mouthed, *Miracle worker.*

I mouthed back, *Suggestive sales.*

God, I really hoped Max wasn't a pimp.

I didn't have time to dwell on it. More customers showed up, and Ruth came out after a twenty-minute break. Then Max took a break as the dinner customers thinned out. The drinking crowd had started to show up in full force by the time Wyatt rolled in at around eight, wearing a dark look.

He scanned the room until his gaze landed on me.

Even though I was furious with him, my body still reacted to the sight of him.

This was why I didn't trust myself with men. It would be so easy to back down, to accept what he was willing to give me, but I needed to be strong. If I let myself fall for him, I'd go head over heels, and there was no way I was doing that unless he gave me answers.

He strode right up to me as though he was on a mission. I wondered if he'd try to take me into his arms and kiss me—and what I'd do if he did—but he stopped just short of me. "Are you in your usual section?"

I could lie to him, but I wasn't fifteen and I didn't want to play games. "Yes."

He gave me a brisk nod, then headed to the bar and slipped onto a stool next to Jerry. The bar was Max's territory.

What the hell?

Ruth gave me a questioning look, which was when I realized I still hadn't told her about our breakup. My heart ached at the thought.

More people came in, and while Fridays were always busy, the place wasn't usually this packed. Even so, I noticed right away when a woman I'd never seen at Max's walked in through the door.

Greta Hightower, wearing a pair of jeans and a thick gray sweater with no coat, made her way to the half-filled bar, taking an open seat a few stools down from Wyatt and slightly to the side of the beer taps.

Max's eyes practically popped out of his head. I nearly laughed, but I prayed she wasn't there to see him. There was only one way to find out.

When I slid behind the counter to talk to Max, he was setting beers in front of a couple at the far end of the bar, but he kept sneaking glances at Greta. I leaned into his ear and asked, "Is that the infamous Greta?"

He turned to me in surprise. "Yeah."

"Tell me the truth, Max. Do you want to see her again or not?"

"I…uh…" he sputtered.

"Undecided?"

He was silent for a moment before he softly said, "Yeah, I'd like to see her again, but I messed everything up."

I pulled my notepad from my apron and handed it to him. "Cover my section."

"I can't do that!" he protested, sliding back a step and refusing to take it.

"Bullshit. Cover my section. I'll see how agreeable she is to goin' on an actual date with you that doesn't involve moonshine and skinny dippin'."

He scowled, but he snatched the order pad from my hand and pointed to the stack of tickets on the counter. "Most of the orders are beers. You can handle the shots, but some stuck-up fool thinks we're a fancy night club and ordered an old-fashioned. You know how to make one of those?"

"No."

"Neither do I. Make it up as you go." With that, he headed out onto the floor.

I could feel Wyatt's eyes watching me, and a quick glance in his direction confirmed it. Heat washed through my body, but I told myself that he was like strawberry shortcake: utterly delicious and, courtesy of my strawberry allergy, guaranteed to give me hives.

Just because something tasted good didn't mean it was good for me.

Ignoring him, I walked over to Greta and gave her a bright, customer-friendly smile. "What can I get you?"

She glanced at the wall behind me, studying the beers on tap. "What do you recommend?"

"Are you a beer drinker?" I asked. "Or are you more into fruity drinks? Ruth and I have been playing around with a drink we're creating. It's a frozen drink with pineapple juice and rum. I know it's cold, but the deliciousness makes up for it."

"That sounds good," she said, looking nervous as she glanced around the room. "If it's not too much trouble."

"No trouble at all," I said breezily, but I suspected Max would shoot me a death stare once he realized I'd moved Greta's drink to the front of the line. Especially since it was so labor-intensive.

Ruth walked behind the bar with a handful of tickets as I poured pineapple juice into the blender full of ice. Her brows shot up. "Are you making our Pineapple Sunrise Surprise?"

I twisted my mouth to the side, unsure how she'd take this. "Maybe…"

"Who ordered that?" she asked, glancing around. "And why are you working the bar?" Her gaze landed on Greta and understanding washed over her face. She lowered her voice so Greta couldn't hear. "That chickenshit."

I hated that she thought so little of him, so I said, "It was my idea. I think he'd like to see her again, but he feels like an asshole for treating her poorly. I'm gonna see where he stands."

"By butterin' her up with our drink?"

I made a hesitant face. "Yeah...?"

She narrowed her eyes, then nodded. "I approve. I wish I'd thought of it myself. But move my tickets in front of Max's," she said, slapping them on the counter. "He doesn't need the tips."

I nearly told her his tips were my tips, but she turned and headed back to the kitchen.

I added the rum and coconut milk to the mixture before setting it on the base to blend. While I waited, I pulled a few more beers and set them on a tray with a ticket. At least I'd filled one of the tickets, although there were at least half a dozen more. Talking to Greta was more important. I poured the pineapple drink into a tall glass, added a straw, and set it in front of her. "If we had any of those fancy umbrellas, I would have added one."

She took a sip and her eyes lit up. "Girl, as long as it tastes this good, you could put it in a red Solo cup and I'd be happy."

"I haven't seen you in here before," I said, moving on to the next ticket.

"Shh..." she said, closing her eyes as she took another sip. "Don't spoil my good mood."

"Okay, but I can't stay behind the counter for long." While Max was making the rounds with his easygoing smile, I could tell some of my customers were getting pissed. And soon the people around the bar would be rioting for their drinks.

She was quiet for nearly a minute before she said, "I've been thinkin' about what you said."

"I said a lot of things," I said, my stomach a bundle of nerves.

She shot me a dark scowl. "About Lula."

It had all been about Lula, but I knew better than to point that out.

"I asked around about you," she said, then took a sip through her straw.

"Oh?" I said in surprise, my brain scrambling to figure out whom she might have asked. Just about everyone who knew anything about me was in this room.

"I wanted to know if I could trust you."

"And?"

Rather than answer, she focused on sipping her drink, which was going down entirely too fast. But I didn't really need her to share. I doubted she would have shown up to gloat if she'd heard through the grapevine that I was a terrible person. She was here because I'd been deemed trustworthy.

She leaned closer and caught my eye. "When Lula left for Chattanooga, she was deliverin' a package."

I hadn't seen that one coming. "What kind of package?"

She glanced around, then leaned even closer. "She wouldn't say. Trust me, I asked."

"Was it for Bingham?"

She paused for a moment. "I'm not sure."

But the look in her eyes told me she still didn't trust me enough to be truthful. Which suggested this might be related to one of the illegal activities she'd mentioned.

I took a breath. "Greta, did Lula mention that she was going to run off again?"

She shook her head adamantly. "No. She told me she was stickin' around because she needed the job. Because of...you know."

I nodded. "Have you heard from her at all today?" When she

shook her head, I said, "Do you know why she was scared of Bingham last night?"

She shook her head. "Your guess is as good as mine."

"What do you know about her breakup with him?"

"Not a thing. Just because we're friends doesn't mean she shares everything with me." She took another sip of her drink, then glanced up at me. "Yesterday afternoon, I asked about her trip, but she refused to tell me anything about it other than insisting she was done. No more runnin' packages."

"Is that what she was doin' every time she left?" I asked. "Running packages?"

Greta pressed her lips together as though locking Lula's secret into a vault.

"Greta, I want to help her, but you have to tell me what you know."

"Why?" she asked with more vitriol than I'd expected. Especially since *she'd* come to *me*. "You'll have more hours if she stays away. Maybe you want her gone for good. Or maybe you're workin' with Marco to get her into trouble."

"No, Greta," I said in a soft, calm voice. "I swear to you that I don't have a malicious reason for looking into this. I'm worried about her."

"Why?" she shot back. "You work with her for a few hours, and suddenly you're attached to her? You think you can save her?"

Save her? I cocked my head. "Save her from what?"

She glanced down at her nearly empty drink as though trying to decide if keeping her secrets was worth ditching her drink. When she lifted her gaze, her eyes pleaded for understanding. "I want to trust you, Carly, really I do, but I'm still not sure you have her best interest in mind. I just can't see why you'd go to this much trouble for someone you barely know."

I understood her concern. It was a legitimate question. She didn't know me from Adam, and I hardly knew Lula at all. How could I explain my reasons to her when I hardly understood them myself?

My mind flashed to Rose and Neely Kate coming up to my broken-down car by the side of the road.

"I think maybe I'm helping her because I was recently in a very difficult situation, and strangers came to my aid. Maybe I'm just payin' it forward." When she didn't bolt, I added, "When I took Lula home last night, she seemed scared, but she refused to tell me why. I asked her about Bingham, but she didn't say much other than that he could make people disappear. Which makes him suspect number one. But when I talked to him this afternoon, he didn't let on that he knew she was pregnant. Maybe she was delivering a package for him and something went wrong?"

If Lula had botched some kind of delivery for him, she had a legit reason to be worried. At the same time, I doubted she would have come back at all, let alone stayed by herself in that cabin, knowing Bingham might come gunning for her.

"He might not be the daddy," Greta said so softly I barely heard her.

I wasn't surprised, but I needed more to go on. "Who else could it be?"

"You can't tell anyone," she said, leaning forward again and grabbing my wrist in a tight hold. "Swear it."

I couldn't tell her I planned to share what I learned with Marco. She clearly didn't trust him. At the same time, I didn't want to lie to her.

Her hold tightened, her fingernails digging into my flesh. "Swear."

"I swear I won't tell anyone." I hated the constraint, but it was obvious she wasn't going to tell me otherwise. I'd have to find a work-around.

"She was seeing someone else around the same time, but I'm not sure who. I wasn't even sure she was seein' Bingham until you verified it."

"Why wouldn't she tell you?" I asked. "You two are obviously close."

"Her crazy-ass mother puts all kinds of ideas into her head. She keeps telling Lula not to trust anyone, even me. Lula still tells me things, just not everything."

"Do you have any clues to help me track this other guy down?"

"All I know is that he was supposedly a man of importance." She made a face. "That's what she called him. A man of importance. She doesn't talk like that, so I figured he was the one who told her that. Other than that, I only know that he was older and she used to meet him at the Mountain View Lodge outside of Ewing." Pushing out a sigh, she said, "Lula has daddy issues."

I supposed having a father who'd tried to drown you would do that to a person.

"Do you know when she first started seeing him? Or the last time?"

"The last time I know of was back in September. She met him several times that month. As to *when* it started…I'm guessing early summer? I know she asked to borrow a bikini in June because he was taking her to the lodge and they have a hot tub. She wanted to look good."

"And you loaned it to her?"

"I almost didn't since she was so stingy with details. She finally confessed that he was married. He'd sworn her to secrecy. In fact, I don't think her momma even knew about him."

"What about Bingham? Did he know about the other man?"

"I'm not sure they overlapped. I can't imagine he'd handle sharin' well." She shrugged. "Either way, I suspect he never knew. I don't think she met her Ewing guy all that often in the beginning, and the only reason I knew was because of the bikini. She's pretty good at keepin' secrets."

So I'd gathered.

"Do you know if she broke it off with the Ewing guy?"

"I honestly have no idea, but I can't help but think it ended. By October, she didn't seem to go to Ewing all that often anymore, and she just seemed sad."

"Hidin' a pregnancy might do that to a person," I said, deep in thought.

"True." She glanced over her shoulder and her face lost color. "I have to go." She grabbed her purse, which was hanging from the stool back.

"Wait," I pleaded. "What else do you know?"

Her fingers were shaking as she pulled her wallet out of her purse. Why was she so spooked? I glanced around the room, half-expecting Bingham to be glaring at us, but I didn't see him or any of his known associates. No one else seemed to be sending threatening glances our way either.

"Greta," I said, abandoning the draft station and moving directly in front of her. "Why are you so scared?"

Shaking her head, she handed me a ten-dollar bill. "Will this cover it?"

"Where are you parked?" I asked.

"Uh...down the street. Behind the café."

"I'm gonna have Wyatt walk you to your car."

Her brows shot up and she cast a quick sideways glance in his direction. "I thought you weren't dating anymore."

"We're not, but he's a good man."

Too bad he wasn't good for me.

CHAPTER THIRTEEN

I hurried down to Wyatt. My traitorous eyes took in his mussed dark hair and those lips I'd kissed. He looked jarred by my sudden appearance, not that I could blame him.

"I need you to do me a favor."

"Okay," he said without hesitation.

"Don't you want to know what it is first?"

"Nope. You only have to ask, and I'll do it."

Was he trying to win me back? Dammit. Between this and his bit of kindness with Ginger, I was almost weak enough to consider it. *Focus, Carly.* "I need you to walk Greta to her car."

His brow lifted slightly. "Has she had too much to drink?"

"No, she's a bit spooked, is all. Can you do it?"

"Of course," he said, already getting off his stool and slipping on his jacket. "Does she want me to take her home?"

I cast a backward glance at her as she stared at her now-empty glass. Which was when it occurred to me that I was sending the wrong brother. What with our talk about Lula, I'd completely forgotten to ask Greta about Max.

Holding up my hand, I said, "Wait a minute." Then I hurried around the counter and intercepted Max as he made his way to the counter with several tickets. "If you want a chance to win her back, you've got a shot at playing hero, but you need to grab your coat right now."

He shook his head as though trying to clear it. "What are you talking about?"

"Greta's worried about walking to her car alone."

His back straightened—Enforcer Max had made an appearance. "Why?"

"I don't know. I was going to have another guy do it, but I thought maybe—"

He shoved the notepad at me. "On it."

He made a beeline toward her, leaning in to say something across the bar. She listened then nodded, shooting me a questioning look.

I smiled and relief filled her eyes.

Two birds with one stone. I was good.

Max wrapped an arm around her back and led her away. I hurried back to the bar to fill the rest of the orders, scanning the crowd to see if anyone made a move to follow them. I wasn't surprised when I saw Wyatt shift to Greta's seat in front of the beer taps.

"What was that about?" he asked as I filled a mug from the draft.

I gave the room one last look before I turned to him. "Honestly? I don't know. One minute she was fine, but next she wasn't. I think she saw something—someone—who scared her. I have no idea who."

"And the Max situation?"

"Let's just say I think they like each other. They got a little misstart, and I gave them a push in the right direction."

"Is that how you'd classify us? A misstart?"

"You ready to talk yet?"

"And are you going to move on to someone else if I'm not?" he asked in a gruff tone.

"What are you talkin' about? Why would you ask me that?"

"Junior said he saw you with Marco. And that you two were… close."

What would he have seen? Our hug? Me kissing Marco's cheek? I could see how it might be misconstrued. "I never realized Junior was such a gossip."

"So it's true," he said, sounding pissed. "You *were* with Marco."

"*With him* could be taken two different ways, Wyatt, and frankly, if you and I aren't together, neither one of them matters to you."

The pain in his eyes nearly made me cave.

I was being harsh, and I knew it, yet he needed to hear the truth. "You know how to fix this."

"I can't. What little I can tell you won't be enough to appease you, and I don't have permission to tell you the rest."

Permission? "Who are you protecting?"

He leaned over the bar and held my gaze, his eyes pleading with me. "I'm askin' you to trust me, Carly."

"So I'm just supposed to accept that I shared everything with you and you're not going to tell me *anything*?" I asked, incredulous.

"I know it sounds bad."

I couldn't believe we were having the exact same conversation *again*, and in public no less. I shook my head. "I'm not doin' this."

"Were you with Marco today?"

My mouth dropped open. "I never took you for the controlling type, Wyatt Drummond."

"And I never thought you'd be shallow enough to stage something with Marco in an attempt to make me jealous and force my hand."

I gasped and I could see the instant regret in his eyes.

"Do you really think so little of me?" I asked, my voice breaking.

He cringed and ran his hand over his head. "No. But…if you…"

I shook my head, fighting tears. "You need to go."

"Carly."

"No. You need to go. *Now.*"

"I didn't mean it, Carly. I was angry and hurt, and I—"

"I'm hurt too, and you don't see me accusing you of awful things."

"Aren't you, though?" he asked. "I did everything in my power to save and protect you. If that doesn't earn your trust, what will?"

He had a point, and my heart broke. "I trust you with my life, Wyatt. I have no doubt you would take a bullet for me, but you *know* that men have lied and kept secrets from me. You *know* how much that has hurt me. The only way we can make this work is if you're open and honest with me, yet you refuse to do that. Hell, I don't even know about your past girlfriends, because ninety percent of your life is a mystery you're keeping in a locked vault."

His jaw twitched, but he remained silent.

"I like you, Wyatt. I like you more than I've ever liked a man before, but I have to be smart. I have to protect my heart. And my life. Which means that unless you start sharing things, we're not going to work, so we might as well call it now."

His eyes turned glassy, and my chest hurt so much I struggled to draw a breath.

He gave me a soft nod before sliding off the stool. When he walked out the door, he took most of my heart with him.

"Where are the orders, Carly?" Ruth bellowed as she approached the bar. "I've got some thirsty customers, your section is completely uncovered after Max's disappearin' act, and you're havin' a heart-to-heart with your boyfriend?"

She was right. We'd chosen a completely inappropriate time and place for our conversation, even if Jerry was the only person within earshot.

Her eyes widened when she saw my face. "Oh shit. What happened?"

Shaking my head, I started pulling beers again. "Sorry. You're right about all of it. I'll catch up. Give me a moment."

"What did he do?" she asked in a semi-growl.

"We just figured out that we're not gonna work," I said, placing a mug on the bar. "Better to find out now than later."

Her scowl told me she wasn't falling for my explanation, but we were too busy for a longer talk.

I ignored her and poured all my energy into filling the drink orders. Max returned about twenty minutes later, and it was hard to gauge how his walk with Greta had gone based on the solemn look on his face. She might have confided why she was upset, or she might have given him the brush-off.

He slipped behind the counter to take my place, not offering any information. I was too busy trying to contain my own heartache to stick around and ask.

Plastering on my brightest smile, I touched base with my tables, offering free baskets of wings and fries to soothe some irritated patrons. Within a half hour, all was well and my tables were happy and pleasantly inebriated.

I couldn't help wondering how they were getting home since there were no taxis or Ubers in Drum.

Max sent Ruth home around eleven since she had been there all day and was working the lunch shift the next day. We were still busy after she left, but Max sent Tiny home too, and he and I managed the crowd until he kicked the stragglers out at two a.m. He still hadn't said more than a word to me, so as soon as he locked the front door, I called out, "You've been keepin' me in suspense all night, Max. Tell me what happened."

"What happened is I made a shit-ton of money tonight. That's what happened."

I propped a hand on my hip. "You know I'm talking about Greta."

"I walked her to her car and then I came back," he said as he stopped at a table and began collecting empty mugs.

"You were gone much longer than it would have taken to walk behind Watson's and come back."

He shot me an exasperated look. "Don't you think you've inserted yourself into this situation enough?"

I lifted a brow. "So you didn't want to walk her to her car?"

A lazy grin spread across his face. "Now, I never said that."

"Are you gonna see her again?"

"Only time will tell," he said, then turned serious. "She told me you've been askin' a lot of questions about Lula."

"And I already told you that I don't think she left voluntarily this time. I'm trying to figure out what happened to her."

"You're wastin' your time, Carly." He didn't look happy to be admitting it.

"Maybe," I said, "but it's my time to waste."

"Well, don't be lettin' Ruth know you're lookin', and definitely don't be late again because of your sleuthin'. The last thing you want is to face her legendary wrath." He pointed a finger at me. "And yeah, I know you were late because you were talkin' to Greta over at the café."

I decided to throw caution to the wind. "Actually, I was late because I dropped by the Alpine Inn."

"Were you lookin' for Jerry?"

Crap. That reminded me that I hadn't given Jerry his new coat. "No," I said, slowly. "I saw your father's associate leave one of the rooms."

"My father's associate?" He looked genuinely confused.

"The one he met here the other day. Neil Carpenter."

He set the glass in his hand on the table and turned to face me, his face devoid of expression. "Why are you snoopin' on my father's business associate?"

Ah, crap. Good question. "It just looked odd, is all. He's an upstanding businessman in a fancy suit. The last place I expected to see him was emerging from a room in the Alpine Inn."

His eyes flashed with fury. "How does that concern you, Carly?"

His reaction caught me off guard. Although I'd seen Max angry, it had always been a righteous sort of anger—against men who disrespected Ruth and me and other women at the bar. He'd certainly never been this pissed at me.

"It just seemed odd," I said defensively.

"It's none of your damned business! Just like me and Greta are none of your business! And where Lula went is none of your business! You live here for a few weeks and suddenly you think you need to be stickin' your nose in things that have nothin' to do with you?" He shook his head and pointed a finger at me again. "Leave it all the fuck alone!"

I took a step back in total shock. Max couldn't have hurt me worse if he'd slapped me.

His face hardened. "Go home."

I gestured to the dirty tables around us. "But we're not done cleaning up."

"Go. Home."

He didn't have to tell me a third time. I spun around and practically sprinted to the back and got the hell out of there.

I wondered if I'd have a job tomorrow.

CHAPTER FOURTEEN

I tried to sleep, but I was too upset about Max, so I lay awake for over an hour, wondering if he was right. Was I overstepping? I admitted that I was by investigating what Neil Carpenter had been doing at the motel. And perhaps I'd overreached when I'd asked Max if he wanted to walk Greta to her car, but he could have said no.

But Lula…that was the one that puzzled me. Why would he care if I looked for her? Wouldn't he want me to find her?

I finally fell into a fitful sleep, but I woke with a headache when the alarm went off at seven.

Hank was already up, which was no surprise since he was an early riser. His stitches had all been removed, so I no longer had to change his bandages and clean his wound, but his compression bandage still needed to be changed. Hank had trouble doing it himself. He'd tried to insist that I no longer needed to massage around the incision area, something I did to break down the scar tissue, but I'd refused to let it go. If he ever changed his mind about getting a prosthesis, a thick layer of scar tissue would make it painful to wear. I hated to think his pride and stubbornness might cause him trouble later.

He was bundled up in his jacket and sitting on the porch with a cup of coffee, watching several small gray and green birds eating sunflower seeds out of a bird feeder Wyatt had installed for him a couple of weeks ago. A single crutch was leaning against the wall.

He glanced up at me standing in the open doorway. "You're up early after bein' out so late last night."

So he'd heard me come in.

I wrapped my arms around my chest to ward off the cold. "We were busy last night. Max kept us open until two, and even then, he had to kick everyone out."

"Are you goin' to work at noon?"

"No," I said, watching the birds. "What are those?"

"Pine siskin. They're like goldfinches. They were Mary's favorite."

His wife had died several years ago, and it was obvious he still missed her. Just like he missed his daughter, who'd died last year, and his grandson, Seth.

The appearance of the bird feeder had surprised me, if only because Hank hadn't struck me as the bird-watching type, but I often found him watching it. It occurred to me that Hank might like a bird-watching book so he could identify the species he didn't recognize. If I asked him, he'd tell me not to bother, but I knew he'd accept it if it just appeared.

Was that another sign of me butting into someone else's business?

Max's accusation was making me question everything.

"Marco is picking me up at nine, so would you rather have me change your bandage before or after I dye my hair?"

There was no hiding what I was up to when I dyed it. The

smell filled the house. I'd expected Hank to ask questions the first time, especially since the color hadn't really changed much. The upkeep was intended to mask my roots, not change my look.

His mouth turned down into a scowl. "Neither."

"I'm not leavin' until we change your bandage," I said in a no-nonsense tone. "But I'll let you stay out here to watch the birds while I start on my hair."

"Where are you goin' with that deputy?"

"We're going out to breakfast." I'd gotten plenty of information from Greta the night before, however, and it occurred to me that our trip to Watson's was no longer needed. I'd ask Marco what he wanted to do once he showed up.

I waited a second to see if Hank had more questions before I went back inside. I poured a cup of coffee, then carried it to the bathroom and examined the roots of my hair.

My hair was naturally blonde, but I dyed it auburn to help disguise my appearance. My hair grew fast, and I really didn't want people asking questions, so I'd decided to dye it every few weeks. Last time I'd just touched up the roots, but the original color had begun to fade, so I'd do an all-over color this time. After I changed into a dark T-shirt that I'd bought at the Dollar General for this purpose, I mixed up the dye and applied it to my roots, then covered the rest of my hair.

I had forty-five minutes to kill, so I made Hank some protein pancakes. (Which I was sure he only liked because he didn't know they were a healthier option.) He said he wanted to eat on the porch since the entire house stank of hair dye, so I handed him his plate and refreshed his coffee. I headed back inside and started changing the sheets—which was when I remembered Wyatt's arrangement with Ginger. When was that supposed to start?

Since I was going to be gone all day, I chopped up some

vegetables and covered them with olive oil, then seasoned some chicken breasts and put them all on a foil-lined cookie sheet. I realized that I'd made enough for Wyatt too, and my heart hurt again. If I kept living with Hank, I'd have to keep seeing Wyatt, but I didn't want to move out. I genuinely liked living with Hank. Sure, the house was kind of a dump, and he could be a cranky old coot, but I cared about him. He made me feel needed. Necessary. Maybe it was selfish, but after feeling invisible and replaceable most of my life, I liked being indispensable.

By the time I got the food into the oven, it was past time to rinse out my hair, so I washed it off in the tub and showered. When I blow-dried my hair, it was a lot darker than before, but it didn't look bad. Just different and with less undertones. It looked like a home dye job. I swallowed my disappointment. I didn't have the time or money to pay someone to professionally dye it. I'd have to suck it up. It was only hair.

I was getting dressed in my room when I heard an engine outside. A quick glance at my phone read 8:46, which meant Marco was early. I still hadn't changed Hank's compression bandage and massaged his stump. I hurriedly stuffed my work shirt, a thermal tee, and a pair of athletic shoes into a bag, then headed out to the living room. I was hoping I still had a job.

To my surprise, Wyatt was standing next to the sofa, holding a box of donuts.

His gaze shifted to me and the longing in his eyes made my knees weak. "Carly, I said some things last night that were totally out of line."

My gaze dropped to the box of donuts. I'd mentioned in passing a week ago that I'd kill for a box of donuts, and here he was with some.

"You were right," he said, contrition covering his face. "It's not fair to tell you absolutely nothing about my past when you've been so upfront with me about yours." He took a step forward. "I don't want to lose you, Carly. You're too important to me."

"But you also said I'd never be happy with how little you can tell me." I glanced around. "Is Hank still outside? I need to change his compression bandage."

"He's watchin' the birds. Which means we have time to discuss this now." His gaze landed on my bag and his body went rigid. "Where are you goin'?"

"This is for work tonight." I sighed. "If I still have a job."

"Why wouldn't you? Did Lula come back?"

I made a face. Me and my big mouth.

The oven timer went off, so I dropped the bag on the sofa as I walked past him into the kitchen. "I made something for Hank's lunch and dinner. Also, there's still some vegetable lasagna from the other night if he'd rather have something else."

"Where are you goin'? Why do you think you might be out of a job?"

I grabbed the potholders and opened the oven door. "Max and I got into an argument."

"Over what?" he asked, sounding incredulous.

Pushing out a breath, I said, "It's not important. I'm probably overreacting."

"Did he tell you that you were fired?"

"No, but we were cleaning up the bar, and he told me in no uncertain terms to drop what I was doin' and leave."

He set the box of donuts down on the table and rubbed his jaw. "What were you arguin' about?"

"Max thinks I'm sticking my nose where it doesn't belong."

"You mean askin' him to walk Greta to her car?"

"Among other things," I said, setting the cookie sheet on the stove top. "I need to leave before this cools down. If you're sticking around, can you portion it out into these containers?" I asked, pointing to four plastic bowls with lids that I'd already set out on the counter. "There's enough for you too."

"Yeah," he said with a frown. "Of course. But where are you goin' that has you in such a hurry?"

"Carly!" Hank called out from the front porch. "Your date's here."

Well, crap.

Wyatt's brow practically shot up to his hairline. "Your what?"

"It's not a date, Wyatt."

His entire body stiffened. "Who's here to pick you up?"

There was no easy way to tell him this. Might as well rip off the Band-Aid. "Marco."

His jaw tensed. "Marco."

"Like I said, it's not a date."

"Well, whatever it is, you're takin' your work clothes, so you're clearly plannin' on spendin' all day with him."

Crap. I hadn't thought this through. If Marco dropped me off at the tavern, I wouldn't have a way home. I could ask Ruth, but she'd probably get off early since she was going in at noon, and asking Max for a ride probably wasn't a good idea.

"Can you give me a ride home tonight?"

His eyes narrowed. "So you *are* spendin' the entire day with him?"

"Yeah," I said, starting to get pissed. "I am. Lula's missin' and he's helpin' me look for her."

"Yeah," he said in disgust, "I bet he is."

"What the hell does that mean?"

"We all know that if Lula took off, she's nowhere around here. He's playin' you, Carly."

I put my hand on my hip. "Excuse me?"

"He's pandering to you so he can spend time with you."

I released a short laugh. "Are you seriously suggesting Marco is makin' up a reason to spend time with me?"

"Why is that so unbelievable?" he asked. "You're a beautiful woman, Carly Moore. He'd be a fool not to want you."

"What makes you think that he can't respect me and Lula as people enough to genuinely want to help? And did you forget that Marco almost died trying to save us from Carson?"

He hesitated and I could see the thoughts shifting across his face, followed by dawning recognition. "Shit, I didn't mean to imply…"

He looked so contrite I couldn't hide my smile.

"What's so damn funny?"

"You." Poor word choices aside, I didn't actually think Wyatt was misogynistic. He'd always seemed to respect me. And although the timing wasn't right, I genuinely did want to know why he was here this morning—who he was protecting and what he was now willing to share.

I reached up and gave him a soft kiss. "This doesn't mean we're back together. It means I'm willing to hear what you have to tell me. Tonight. When you pick me up from the tavern at midnight to bring me home."

I started to walk away, but he grabbed my arms and hauled me back, pulling me to his chest and kissing me with fierce possession.

When he lifted his head, I stared up at him in a daze. This man made me feel things I hadn't known I was capable of feeling.

His dark brown eyes held mine in an intense gaze. "That was to remind you that I fight for what's mine," he said in a husky tone.

"And I suspect it was partially for my benefit as well." Marco was leaning on his crutches by the front door, dressed in a pair of jeans and a dark gray jacket. He had a perfect view of the two of us in the kitchen doorway, and a tickled grin lit up his eyes.

I wasn't sure whether to be amused by Wyatt's insecurity or irritated that he was trying to stake his claim.

I pulled away from him, deciding not to address it at all. "I haven't changed Hank's compression bandage. And he needs someone to massage around the incision site. He hates it, but it'll help the scarring and dispel some of the phantom pain, even though he might have convinced you otherwise."

His grimace was confirmation I'd guessed right on that one. "Consider it done."

Marco set his crutches against the wall and lifted my coat off the coat-tree. Balancing on one leg, he held it open for me to put on.

"Say, Wyatt," I said as I slipped my arms into the coat. "Did you hire Ginger to clean the house?"

"Yeah," he said in a rough voice, his gaze on Marco. "You've been workin' so many hours. It seemed like a lot, especially since you've been cooking and paying for the meals, so it's a win for both of you, especially since Junior's youngest is racking up some medical bills they're struggling to pay."

"But cleaning the house is part of my bargain with Hank. Have you told him?"

"Not yet. I'll do it today, but he'll be all right with it. He likes Ginger and he appreciates everything you do."

I nodded. "Okay."

I still didn't feel right, but I wasn't going to argue about it in front of Marco. They were doing enough posturing already.

Marco grabbed his crutches and nodded to the door. "Shall we? I'm starvin'."

I picked up my bag and purse and followed him out. He was

already down the porch steps when I got outside, so I gave Hank a quick goodbye and headed for Marco's SUV.

Wyatt leaned against a post, watching me get into Marco's Explorer. Once I was in, I dropped my bag of clothes onto the backseat.

Marco tossed his crutches into the back, then jumped up into the driver's seat. After he started the engine, he gave Wyatt a flippant wave and a grin.

Wyatt scowled in return.

"Sorry about him," I said as Marco backed up and headed to the street.

"I thought you said you two broke up," he said.

"We're not back together, if that's what you're suggesting."

He chuckled. "You sure Wyatt got that memo?"

I groaned. "It's complicated."

"Hey," he said with a laugh. "No skin off my back, either way. But Wyatt can be a stubborn ass, and I like you, Carly, so my brotherly advice is don't take any shit from him."

"Thanks. I won't. I'm basically givin' him another chance to make things right and share his past. If he doesn't come clean, it's really over."

"You sure that's gonna work?" he asked. "Because you two seem to have trouble stayin' away from each other."

The thought had occurred to me. "Well, if Max actually fires me, then leavin' Drum might be the answer."

"You're thinkin' about leavin' Drum?" he asked in surprise. "And why would Max fire you?"

"There's something else I need to tell you. Greta paid me a visit at the bar last night."

He shifted in his seat and shot me a glance. "What?"

I filled him in on what she'd told me about the second possible father of Lula's baby.

"So you want to head to Ewing?"

"Yeah, I hope that's okay."

"We have the whole day," he said. "So we can go where we need to go."

"We'd planned on eating breakfast at Watson's"—indeed, he was already driving there—"but I doubt Greta has anything else to share, so we don't have to go there now."

"Hell yeah, we're still goin' there," he said as though I'd suggested we stop breathing. "They have the best biscuits and gravy in Hensen County. We can't let you pass up the opportunity to try 'em, especially since you're talkin' about leavin' Drum. Now tell me what happened with Max."

"Don't you want to talk about the mystery man?"

"We can talk about him over breakfast. I want to hear what happened with Max."

So I told him about Greta getting scared at the end of our chat, plus how I'd arranged for Max to walk her to her car.

"So she gave him the brush-off and he blamed you?"

"No. That wasn't what ticked him off, but he added my interference to his list of grievances." I took a breath. "He was mostly pissed because I went over to investigate after I saw one of his father's business associates leaving the Alpine Inn."

"You did *what*?" he asked. "What in the world possessed you to do that?"

It was on the tip of my tongue to tell him the real reason. Wyatt refused to let me in, and I was trying to get dirt on Bart Drummond. But I doubted that explanation would fly with Marco. "He and Bart had lunch at the tavern a few days ago, and he was a real jerk. I guess I was just being nosy."

"Bart was at the tavern?" he asked in surprise.

"Yeah. I heard it was unusual."

"I doubt he's been there more than a handful of times in the past few years. Who was this guy?"

"He's from Nashville. I have no idea why he was here or what their business was about."

His brow furrowed. "Now I know why Max was pissed. You scared the shit out of him."

"Why?"

"Carly, Bart Drummond is not a man to trifle with."

"You sound like you're talking about Todd Bingham."

"Don't play stupid," he said. "You know Bart is his own brand of dangerous. Diggin' into his business is no better than diggin' into Bingham's. It might even be worse."

"Then why don't you do something about it, Marco? Aren't you a deputy sheriff?" I couldn't help my accusatory tone.

My accusation rolled off Marco like water off a duck's back. "Because Bart Drummond has lined so many pockets at so many levels that it would be pointless to arrest him. The DA would never prosecute. And if the DA *did* decide to press charges, there's every chance he'd get a judge who was beholden to him too."

"So Bart Drummond has enough money to get away with whatever he wants," I said in disgust.

"No," he said slowly. "Not money per se. The Drummonds used to be a lot richer when Max and I were kids. But he holds power. Influence. So while his bank account is a lot lighter than it used to be, he's still in control. He's the master of favors. He'll do a favor for you, and at some point, he'll ask you to do a favor for him. You wouldn't believe the number of people we've arrested who were doin' Bart Drummond's dirty work. They take the fall, then refuse to name him, which lets him get away with murder. Sometimes literally."

That hit close to home. Carson Purdy had been Bart's right-hand man. Was this proof he'd been working on his behalf after all? If so, Bart had told Carson to kill me. But Carson had almost killed Wyatt as well. Had it been on Bart's orders?

"Why wouldn't they rat him out?" I asked.

"Fear. Rumor has it that he has secrets on just about everyone in town."

A cold sweat broke out on my neck. If he ever found out *my* secret, I was in big trouble. "So if y'all know what he's doing, why isn't anyone tryin' to stop it?"

"No one's foolish enough to attempt it. And the sheriff is stinkier than a three-day-old sock." When he saw I wasn't appeased, he said, "Look, even if the system weren't rigged in Bart's favor, he's got all these stooges doin' his dirty work. And without them testifyin', there's no proof."

"You make it seem so hopeless," I said. "You're a sheriff deputy, Marco. You're supposed to want to right wrongs and get the bad guys."

"And I do, Carly, trust me. Don't think Bart hasn't tried to buy my support. It takes some fancy sidestepping on my part to stay out of his clutches, although I'm sure Max has played some part in that as well."

Max. My heart ached knowing he was upset with me. While I didn't want to lose my job, it hurt more to think I may have lost a friend. "I know Wyatt has broken away from his father, but I'm not sure where Max stands. I know he runs the inn for Bart, but what else is he involved in?"

Marco had told me they were amicable, but that didn't tell me anything about their business dealings.

"Honestly, Carly, I don't know. It's one of those don't ask, don't tell situations. The less I know, the better."

"When I knocked on the motel door last night, a woman

answered. I'm pretty sure she was a..." I struggled to come up with a word that didn't sound demeaning.

"A prostitute," he said bluntly.

I grimaced. "Yeah." I took a breath and steeled my back. "I know Bart owns the inn and Max manages it. Does one of them run a prostitution ring out of it?"

"Jesus, Carly," he blurted out. "Did you ask Max that?"

My cheeks flushed. "No, but he knows I was snoopin'. Hank said he thinks Bingham operates a prostitution ring. Would he dare to run it out of Alpine Inn?"

And what did it mean if Neil Carpenter had paid a visit to one of Bingham's working girls?

Marco cursed under his breath. "I have no idea what goes on in that motel, and I want to keep it that way."

"Which means you're protecting Bart."

"No," he said with a groan. "It means I'm stayin' out of my best friend's business."

"Doesn't that defeat the purpose of your job?" I asked with plenty of snark.

He swiveled his head to take a long look at me before turning back to the road. "It must be nice livin' in an ivory tower."

"What the hell does that mean?" I asked.

"In case you haven't noticed, things are different here in Drum. There's not such a clear delineation between black and white, good and bad. For fuck's sake, you're livin' with a man who ran the biggest marijuana empire in East Tennessee. Who are you to judge?"

My mouth dropped open in shock.

"Come on," he said in a gruff tone. "You had to know."

"I knew he was a drug dealer before Bingham took over."

"He wasn't just a drug dealer, Carly. He was a major distributor, and he owned his own share of deputies back in the day.

Bingham just took it to the next level." He cast me a wry look. "Allegedly."

I sighed. Marco was right. Hank wasn't a perfect man, yet I struggled to see him as a hardened criminal. But he'd killed a man to defend me, and now Marco was telling me he used to have deputies in his pocket. He'd been more than a two-bit player.

"Hank and Bingham are beside the point," he said, "although I still say you're far too nonchalant about Bingham. My point is that you do not want to poke the bear known as Bart Drummond. Which is likely why Max freaked out on you. He likes you and wants to make sure you stay safe. He proved that after you found Seth in the parking lot."

"I know."

"So Max was probably more scared than mad, because if his father finds out you were lookin' into his business, there's no tellin' what he'll do."

After my encounter with Carson, plus other whisperings I'd heard, I was pretty sure I knew. "Do you believe Carson was workin' on his own, independent of Bart?"

He was silent for a moment. "I don't know. The ground under Bart's feet isn't as stable as it used to be. Seein' Bingham's success might have made Carson a little power-hungry. Bart's not known for bein' boss of the year, if you know what I mean." He snuck a glance at me. "There's a good possibility Carson was workin' independently."

I wasn't sure whether to be relieved or worried.

"And if Carson *was* trying to start his own empire," Marco continued, "I suspect Bart will make an example of the next person who tries to cross him. Every attack on his power makes him lose face, whether or not it's successful."

We were silent for a moment, both of us contemplating that.

Then Marco asked, "What did Max say that makes you think he might fire you?"

I shifted on the seat to face him. "Max told me that I had no business sticking my nose into *anything*. Even trying to find Lula. He told me to butt out of everyone's business. Then he told me to leave."

"He kicked you out in front of customers?"

"No, it was after we closed. But the dining room needed bussing, and I hadn't tallied up my tips. I just left them on his desk and took off."

He was silent for a moment. "He's not gonna fire you, Carly," he finally said. "But don't be surprised if he sits you down and lectures you about leavin' everything to do with his father alone." He gestured out the windshield as he drove into town. "Enough about Bart Drummond. I'm ready to get me some biscuits and gravy."

The diner was busy, but thankfully we got the last empty table. I didn't recognize the two waitresses who were working the room, though, and there was no sign of Greta.

One of the frenzied waitresses dropped off a couple of menus. "We're short-staffed, but I'll bring your waters and silverware in a moment. Coffee?"

She started moving on before I could answer.

"Yes. Please," I called after her. I needed all the caffeine I could get.

"Where's Greta?" Marco asked as he glanced around.

"I don't know. She said she was working today. She mentioned it again last night at the tavern."

"Maybe she called in sick," he said with a frown.

"Maybe." But I couldn't shake the thought that she'd been scared last night. Based on the dark look on Marco's face, he was dwelling on it too.

The waitress returned a few minutes later, balancing two coffee cups and a carafe of coffee. She set them on the table, then put two napkin-wrapped sets of silverware down beside them.

"Hey, Angie, where's Greta?" Marco asked, trying to sound nonchalant. "I thought she was workin' today."

The waitress shook her head. "No-show."

"She didn't call in?" I asked, my stomach seizing.

"Nope. And a hell of a day to do it. We're busier than a whorehouse during a church revival."

I couldn't help wondering if that meant they were busier or slower than usual.

"Did you call and check on her?" Marco asked, trying to look like a concerned friend and not a deputy interviewing her.

"Sure did. Her sister said she never came home last night."

"Say, can we have her sister's number?" Marco asked.

She narrowed her eyes. "What for?"

"I heard Melody was selling eggs. I was wanting to buy some."

"Yeah," Angie said. "I'll get it for you after I put your order in."

"We're gonna need our food to go," Marco said. "Pronto."

Marco ordered three orders of biscuits and gravy, a couple of side orders of bacon, hash browns, and a cinnamon roll.

"You must be really hungry," I said, trying to sound funny, but it fell flat.

"You know who the third order's for, so start girding your loins."

"Gird my loins?" I asked, trying to find the humor in his phrase, but my guts were churning.

"Wyatt doesn't hold the market on Drummond stubbornness. I suspect Max hasn't had enough time to cool down, but we're gonna go see him anyway."

"He's not going to like us waking him up. I suspect he was working until at least three."

"Tough shit," he said, his jaw tightening. "We need to ask him some questions."

About Greta. He was really going to be pissed at me now. But Max might have been the last person to see her, and we needed to know if she'd said anything. For all we knew, her life could depend on it.

But I couldn't help remembering the way Max had lashed out at me after returning from walking her to her car. Some small part of me wondered if he knew more than he was letting on.

A new thought hit me like a bolt of lightning. What if Max was protecting someone?

What if the married man of importance Lula had been seeing was none other than Bart Drummond?

CHAPTER FIFTEEN

Marco may have asked for the food pronto, but it still took nearly fifteen minutes for the server to bring it over. I thought he might want to discuss matters, but he seemed lost in thought and I wasn't so sure it was a good idea to talk about things in public, especially with the tables so close together. When Angie brought our bags and Melody's phone number, Marco already had his money out to pay for the food. When I protested, he said I could pay for lunch.

I grabbed the food bags and headed to the entrance, holding the door open so Marco could hop outside.

"Should we go see Melody first?" I asked. "I mean, if Greta stayed somewhere else last night, there's no reason for us to risk pissing Max off."

He shook his head. "I know for a fact Greta doesn't have a boyfriend right now. My gut tells me we need to talk to Max first, then Melody."

"Marco," I said, feeling sick to my stomach. "Do you think…?"

"We just need to talk to Max," he said in a no-nonsense tone. I had to give him credit for insisting we go to Max first, especially since I knew how Max was likely to react, but surely it also meant he believed in his friend's innocence.

"Okay," I said with a nod. "I'm going to walk, but why don't you drive down and park behind the tavern? It will be easier on your leg."

"You don't want to ride with me?" he asked in surprise.

"No. I need a little fresh air to clear my head."

I took off toward the tavern, my stomach sinking deeper with every step I took.

Max was my friend. I didn't want to think badly of him, but something strange was going on. Marco was right about one thing—hearing about Neil Carpenter had set Max off. It had also made him pissed about the whole Lula thing, when he hadn't much cared about it before. But why?

Well, no borrowing trouble until we talked to him.

By the time I made it to the parking lot, Marco had already parked and was heading, slowly, toward the back door.

"I presume you've got keys?" he asked.

"Yeah." I handed the take-out bags to him, then dug the keys out of my purse. After I unlocked the door, I took the bags and held the door open.

"I bet he's asleep," I said as I followed him in and let the door close behind me. "I don't think I should be the one waking him up."

"I've got that part covered."

I gave him a nervous glance. "How are you going to get up those stairs?"

"Don't you worry about that. Go start a pot of coffee."

Coffee was a good idea. Max was going to need plenty of it. Shoot, *I* needed it. I set the food bags on the counter in the kitchen and then found Tiny's stash of industrial-strength coffee and started some brewing.

I heard clomping on the stairs going up to the apartment. Marco hadn't explicitly asked me to stay downstairs, and I figured I should probably hear what they said to each other. I couldn't forget that Max was the son in good graces with his father, and Marco was Max's best friend. There were motivations at work I didn't understand. Besides, I'd never been up to Max's apartment before, and I had to admit I was curious. Grabbing the take-out food bags, I started up the narrow stairwell, wondering how Marco had made it up with his crutches.

When I reached the landing at the top, I found the door to the left partially ajar. I pushed my way through the opening into a large, loft-style living room facing the street. It ran the full width of the building and had an industrial look. I could see that a wall had been ripped out—the wood base was still attached to the unfinished wood floor. Opposite the wall of windows was a kitchen that looked like it had come from a salvage yard—old cabinets that obviously were not original yet were so worn I couldn't figure out why they had been dragged in, a newer stainless steel refrigerator, and an old avocado-colored stove.

The walls on either side of the space were brick, and I could see the ceiling had been ripped out, exposing wood beams, but they weren't evenly spaced and looked like they needed to be ripped out rather than salvaged.

As far as seating went, the large living room only had a brown sofa and a fake brown leather recliner. Against the far wall was a long wood cabinet that held a TV that was likely too small for such an oversized room.

Bart Drummond had money, yet none of the businesses he owned seemed to be thriving, and both of his sons lived frugally. At least, if I ignored the fact that Wyatt had paid for Seth's funeral and somehow found the money to buy his garage after getting out of prison.

Max was lying on his side on the sofa, shirtless and wearing a pair of jeans. His arm hung over the edge, his hand resting on the hardwood floor next to a nearly empty bottle of Jim Beam.

Marco was standing next to him, poking his shoulder with the tip of a crutch. "Wake up."

The room was so bright from the uncovered windows it was hard to believe Max was still asleep. I suspected the Jim Beam had something to do with it.

Max grunted and batted the crutch away. He tried to roll over to face the back of the sofa, but Marco put the tip of his crutch against the sofa cushion, blocking him. "Wake up, Max."

"Leave me the fuck alone," Max slurred, batting at the crutch again.

I inched deeper into the living room, reluctant to leave even though I felt like I was intruding.

"We need to talk to you," Marco said in what I presumed was his deputy voice.

"I don't have anything to say," Max mumbled with his face buried in the cushions.

"I'm not playin' around, Max," Marco said, sounding pissed. "Get up."

Max finally shifted to look at him, blinking as if the light had suddenly flooded the apartment. "What the fuck is so important that you had to wake me up at this ungodly hour?"

"Ungodly hour?" Marco asked. "It's nine thirty in the morning. Don't you need to be up to open the tavern in about two and a half hours?"

"Exactly. Which means I should be able to get another two good hours of sleep." Max buried his face deeper into the sofa cushion.

"I need to talk to you about Greta Hightower."

Max released a long groan. "That damned Carly needs to stay out of everyone's business."

"I'm giving you five minutes to get your shit together, then you can have some biscuits and gravy and hash browns from Watson's Café."

"That's *your* favorite breakfast from Watson's, not mine," Max said, his face still buried. "And if I eat anything right now, I'll puke it up in thirty seconds."

"You now have four minutes and fifty seconds," Marco said. "And then we'll give you a hot cup of coffee to help clear your head." He gave me a pointed look.

I set the bags on the kitchen counter, then turned around and headed back downstairs. Max was groaning as he tried to sit up, and I was pretty sure he hadn't realized I was there.

The pot was finishing up, so I fixed a tray with three coffee cups, creamer, and the carafe, and brought it up to the loft.

When I walked into the living room, Marco was sitting on the square coffee table with a Styrofoam container, digging into his breakfast. His crutches were propped against the table behind him. He glanced up at me. "He's in the bathroom. Pukin'."

Sure enough, I heard the sound of retching.

I made a face. "How can you sit there eating while he's throwing up less than twenty feet away?"

He grinned as he shoved another bite into his mouth.

I set the coffee tray on the kitchen counter, poured him a cup of coffee, then handed it to him. "You took it black at the café…"

He snatched the cup and took a sip, then yelped like a scalded cat. "It's hot."

"I just made it. Of course it's hot."

The toilet flushed and I heard running water. A few seconds later, Max appeared in the door. His eyes widened when he saw me. "What's she doin' here?"

"Bringin' you coffee," Marco said good-naturedly. "Now come sit down so we can have a chat."

"Only if you get that shit out of my face," Max said in disgust, waving to the Styrofoam container as he sat back down on the sofa.

I poured coffee and creamer into one of the cups, then took it over to him.

He accepted the mug, but he refused to look at me. "You gettin' Marco to fight your battles for ya, Carly?"

"No," I said, trying to stifle my anger. "We're here for an entirely different matter."

"Seems like you're a few people short for an intervention," Max said dryly, then took a tentative sip of his coffee.

"We're here because I need to know what happened when you walked Greta to her car," Marco said in a breezy tone. He followed it up by taking a big bite of biscuit.

"Are you kiddin' me?" Max spat. "You woke me up to grill me about my love life?"

I'd noticed that Marco had withheld the part about Greta not showing up to work today.

Did that mean he was suspicious too?

I inhaled deeply. What was I thinking? This was Max. He wouldn't hurt a fly.

But that wasn't precisely true. I knew he'd hurt people before, but he only took his anger out on people who deserved it.

There was no way he had anything to do with Lula's or Greta's disappearances.

So why hadn't Marco just come out and told him the truth?

Max shot a look of disgust at his best friend. "And I'm not sayin' another word until you get that shit out of my face. Otherwise, I won't be responsible for barfin' on your shoes."

Marco shoveled a couple of final bites into his mouth before holding the container out toward me.

I was about to snap and tell him I wasn't here to wait on him, which was when I remembered the bullet wound in his leg. Grumbling under my breath, I snatched his trash from him and dumped it. He nodded at the other bags, so I handed him the one with the hash browns and bacon.

He reached inside and pulled a piece of bacon out of the smaller container. "Grease is great for hangovers, Maxwell. Now tell me what happened when you walked Greta to her car."

Max snatched the piece of bacon from Marco and took a bite. "I asked her why she was scared, but she brushed it off, so then I told her why I hadn't called her after our previous rendezvous. I asked if she'd be willing to go out with me again. She didn't say yes, but she didn't say no. She just said she'd come by the tavern next week." He took another sip of his coffee. "There. Are you happy now? That hardly seems like a good reason for disturbin' my sleep."

"Did she say when she'd come by to see you?" Marco asked.

"Were you listening to me?" He snorted. "She said she'd come by next week."

"Did she say where she was goin'?" Marco asked.

"No, but I presumed she was goin' home." His eyes narrowed. "Why are you askin' me all these questions?"

Marco was silent for a moment. "Greta didn't show up for her shift at Watson's today."

Max took a bite of the bacon, then said, "She called in sick? Are you warnin' me that she has some nasty virus she might have passed to me?"

"No," Marco said. "I'm telling you that she didn't show up to work. No callin' in sick. She was just a no-show. Her sister told Angie she never came home last night."

The color leached from Max's face, and he tossed what was left of his bacon on the coffee table.

"You're sure she didn't mention anything about what had scared her at the bar?" Marco asked.

"Why did you stick your nose in this, Carly?" Max shouted. "You had to stir up a hornet's nest by lookin' for Lula. You couldn't leave it alone."

"Don't just blame her," Marco said. "We're *both* lookin' into Lula's disappearance."

"What the fuck, Marco?" Max asked in disgust. "*Why?*"

"Because I think Carly's right. I think someone took her this time."

"Then you're both fools." He stood and set his cup on an end table. "You need to leave it all alone!"

"I can't do that, Max," Marco said, regret heavy in his voice.

That set Max off.

"Get out," he said, pointing to the door. "*Get out!*" He began to pace the middle of the floor, unsteady on his feet.

Marco grabbed his crutches and stood up. "What the hell is goin' on here, Max?"

"*You,*" Max said, turning his fury on his friend. "You should know better."

Marco's face went expressionless. "What does that mean?"

Max shook his head, then swung his attention to me. "And you? You're fired."

"Max," Marco protested. "Think this through."

"You stay the fuck out of it!" Max shouted. "I'll hire and fire whoever the hell I want!"

I'd never seen him so angry, but I also saw past the anger. I saw a man wracked with guilt. "Max, please." My voice broke. "I don't care about the job. I care about *you.*"

His face lost even more color, and he looked like he was close to throwing up again.

"You've been nothin' but trouble since you showed up on my doorstep, Carly, and I'm done." He waved his hand toward me and nearly fell over, and I realized he was still drunk. But it didn't matter. His words had hurt me to the core.

"Max," Marco said slowly, "Do you know what happened to Lula?"

"I am not havin' this discussion at nine thirty in the morning while I'm fightin' a hangover from hell."

Marco's entire demeanor changed, and if I had been Max, I would have thought twice about sassing him. "Why are you so shit-faced drunk, Max?"

"That's none of your goddamned business," Max snapped.

"You only get drunk like this when something's eating at you," Marco said, and I could see he was struggling between being Max's friend and Deputy Roland.

"Get out," Max said in a cold, dead voice

"Max," Marco said, lowering his voice and hobbling closer. "You're like a brother to me, man. You can tell me what's goin' on."

Max's gaze dropped to the floor for a couple of seconds, and when it rose back up to Marco, he looked like he was carrying the weight of the world on his shoulders. "You haven't wanted to know what's been goin' on in my life since I came back home. Why're you gonna start now?"

Marco looked stricken. "Max."

Turning to me, Max looked me in the eye. "You don't belong here. Go home, Carly Moore, if that's even your name. Leave Drum, and never look back."

His words didn't hold the heat or anger I would have expected. He sounded like I'd utterly exhausted him.

He couldn't have hurt me worse if he'd plunged a knife to my chest.

Marco's eyes widened, and he glanced back and forth between us in confusion.

Defeat washed over Max so hard, he looked like he was about to crumple to the floor. He shook his head and stumbled backward two steps. "I'm goin' to bed."

Then he walked down the hall, leaving Marco and me wondering what in the hell had just happened.

CHAPTER SIXTEEN

"Come on, Carly. Let's go," Marco said, but I could see his indecision.

Tears stung my eyes as I stared at the spot where Max had gone around the corner. "I don't want to leave him like this."

"Max needs sleep right now. He can be a mean drunk just like his…" His words trailed off and he pivoted on his crutches. "He needs to sleep it off."

"Just like who, Marco?"

"Let it go, Carly."

"Let *what* go? Max? Lula and Greta? What just happened here? Should I leave town with my tail tucked between my legs?"

"No," he countered. "And that's not what Max wants either, trust me. He's totally shit-faced. When he sobers up, he'll apologize to the both of us. If he even remembers any of this. You'll still have your job, and it will be like this never happened. Now, let's go."

There was no way I could pretend like this had never happened. Especially since Max had been acting so guilty.

He knew something about Lula.

We went downstairs, which was slow going for Marco. When he got to the bottom, he headed to the bar, and I wondered if he was going to pour himself a drink at nearly ten a.m., but instead he grabbed the phone out from under the counter. He dialed a number from memory and waited.

"Tiny? This is Marco. Y'all might need to close today. Max is havin' another episode." He paused for a moment. "Yeah. How about I put up a sign? Will you call Ruth?" He paused again. "Nah, I'll take care of lettin' Carly know." A couple of seconds passed. "I'll check on him later and let you know."

Marco hung up and leaned on the counter for several seconds, looking like he was on the verge of breaking down. Finally, he turned to me, his eyes glassy. "Max is a lot of things, but he's not a murderer or a kidnapper."

I nearly broke into tears. "I've only known him for a little while, and even *I* know that."

"I'm strugglin' here, Carly. Max knows more than he's tellin' us."

"I know." I swallowed. "I'm sorry I dragged you into this."

That snapped him out of his limbo, and he returned the phone to its place under the counter. "No. I'm even more determined to find out what happened. If for no other reason than to clear his conscience."

But if Max knew something about Lula's disappearance, was easing his conscience possible?

"We need to hang a sign," Marco said, looking weary. "Can you make it and tape it in the window?"

"Yeah. Sure." But the more I thought about all of this, the more it didn't feel right. Marco acted like this had happened before. He'd told Tiny that Max was having *another* episode. Was Max an alcoholic who had downward spirals that shut him off from the world temporarily?

How often did this happen?

Had anyone tried to intervene?

I got a sheet of printer paper, a marker, and tape from Max's office, then took them out to the dining room. Sitting down at a table, I uncapped the marker and said, "What do you want it to say?"

"Closed due to illness," he said in a tight voice.

I started writing, the tip of the marker making a squeaky noise on the white paper. "No reopening date?"

"No. Better to wait and see how long it takes for him to hit bottom first."

My chest tightened. "So this *has* happened before."

He hesitated. "A time or two."

"How long does it last?"

"Usually a few days, but one time a few years ago it lingered for a full week. Ruth was fit to be tied with that one."

I looked up at him. "Marco, it sounds like Max is an alcoholic."

He shook his head. "Max has had a shit life, and an even shittier father. Wyatt may have escaped that man's hold, but Max is trapped in a headlock. Some days he can't handle the stress and the pressure and he…escapes."

"Seems like a shitty way to live. He did not look like he was enjoying his little vacay from life."

"It *is* a shitty way to live, and he's doin' the best he can given the circumstances." I heard an edge of irritation in his voice.

"And what are those?"

"He was never supposed to live this life. He had plans. Dreams. His mother had set money aside for him to start a business after college graduation. We were going to go to Nashville. He was going to start a live-music tavern, and I was going to help him. But then his daddy came callin', sayin' the golden boy had fallen from his throne and the spare was now the heir. Max was just supposed to drop everything and jump."

"And he did," I said. "He dropped out of school and came home."

"That bastard wouldn't even let him finish his last semester," Marco said in disgust. "Wouldn't wait three months. He had to go home *now*."

"Why didn't he say no?" I asked.

Marco released a bitter laugh. "You don't say no to Bart Drummond, especially if you're a Drummond boy."

"But he wasn't living here. He'd already escaped. He could have finished school and carried on with his plans."

"And he likely would have if not for one person."

"Who?"

"I was with Max when he got the call. In a stone-cold voice, he told his father to go to hell. But then Emily came to Knoxville a few days later. She just showed up at the front door to our apartment. She told me that she needed to speak to Max alone and could I please give them some privacy. If it had been Bart, I would have told him to go fuck himself, but it was Emily, so I left.

When I came back an hour later, Max was drunker than shit. Sure, he's always been a drinker, but that night he got blackout drunk. He was trashed. I asked him what had happened, and he said he didn't want to talk about it. He was like that for three days, didn't go to class, didn't shower or leave the apartment, just drank himself into a stupor. Then I came home from class one afternoon and found him packing up his clothes. When I asked what he was doing, he told me he was goin' home."

"What did she say to change his mind?"

"I have no idea. He refused to tell me, but once he'd made the decision to go home, there was no reasoning with him."

"You came back too," I said.

"Not until after I graduated a few months later."

"But you didn't have to come back," I said. "You could have escaped."

"Without Max?" He shook his head and sagged into his crutches. "I meant what I said upstairs. We're like brothers. More so than his real one."

Part of me wanted to defend Wyatt, but from what he'd told me himself, the brothers hadn't spoken for years until Seth's death.

Marco let out a long sigh. "Hang the sign. We've got an investigation to run."

"So we're not letting this go?"

"No," he said, his voice gruff.

"But this isn't an official investigation. Now that Greta's gone too, the sheriff's department might take this situation seriously. Do you want me to call them?"

"No," he said, so sharply I jumped.

He rubbed his forehead, then added, "Not yet. It's too soon for them to look into Greta, and we both know they won't do anything about Lula."

"Do you think Greta was kidnapped for knowing too much about Lula?"

"I don't know," he said with a sigh. "We need to go see Melody and get more answers."

I agreed, but I couldn't help wondering if he was now trying to find Lula and Greta to protect his friend, because I was certain Max was involved in this somehow. It was only a matter of how deep.

CHAPTER SEVENTEEN

Marco may have gotten Melody's number, but he didn't call her before we left the tavern. I didn't question him —he was the deputy, and he knew her besides. He likely had his reasons. On the way to Ewing, we passed the state park where we'd had our showdown with Carson Purdy. Marco cast a quick glance in that direction and a tiny shudder rippled through his body.

I put a hand on his arm, and he reached his left hand over his chest to cover mine. He only kept it there for a moment, and neither of us said a word, but the unspoken message sunk in deep. We shared a bond after that night. But I wondered if this would break it.

Marco would always be loyal to Max. I was loyal to him too, but Marco and Max shared a deep-seated connection that seemed to transcend man-made laws.

Was that why Marco had gone into law enforcement? To protect Max?

I wouldn't let myself dwell on the fact that Max had fired me.

As drunk as he'd been, Marco might be right: he might not remember firing me. But I would.

A few miles past the state park, Marco turned left on a narrow road that didn't even have a street sign.

Trees edged up to the sides of the road, and its gravel shoulder couldn't be wider than about six inches. We were out in the middle of nowhere, but then again, everywhere out here felt like the middle of nowhere.

After we'd driven about a half mile and only passed three houses, I asked, "How'd you know how to get here without an address?"

"Oh, Melody Hightower's been on my radar for a while now. I didn't have her phone number, though, so it seemed like a good excuse to get it from Angie."

I was about to ask why he was aware of her, but he'd just pulled up to a rusted mobile home nestled in a clearing in the trees. A chicken coop sat next to the house, surrounded by thin wire, and over a dozen chickens squawked at us as we got out of the truck. The entire yard was a giant mud bath.

Why hadn't I thought to bring my snow boots? When I opened the door and stepped down, my foot sank a good inch. Leaning into the hood of the Explorer, I made my way to the front of the vehicle. Marco was having trouble finding purchase with his crutches as he tried to get to the front porch.

I was about to call him back, worried he'd fall and hurt his leg even more, when the front door opened. A woman wearing a pink fuzzy robe and slippers appeared in the opening, pointing a shotgun in our direction.

"What are you doing on my land?" she called out in a scratchy voice that sounded like it should have belonged to someone who'd smoked for thirty years. Her short blonde hair was sticking up every which way, and she looked about as far from the collected, polished Greta as a person could get.

"Melody," Marco called out, lifting his hands up to the side of his head. "It's me. Marco Roland."

She frowned and squinted at him. I got the impression she needed glasses.

"What are *you* doin' here, Marco?" She sounded leery, and perhaps with just cause—if she knew his name, she likely also knew he was a deputy sheriff, and she had the look of a woman who liked to skirt the law.

No wonder Marco knew where she lived.

"I'm here to ask you about Greta. Put your gun away."

She seemed to consider his request, but it didn't stop her from walking out onto the porch and resting the barrel of the gun on her shoulder. A medium-sized golden dog slipped out of the door and stood by her side, the hair on its back rump standing on end. It released a low growl.

"Easy, Critter," she murmured.

Critter was a forty- to fifty-pound mutt that looked like a Frankenstein that had been given the worst attributes of several breeds—an underbite, short golden hair, and a four-inch-long tail with a tuft of hair on the end. Its head looked disproportionately small, and its back legs seemed longer than the front.

"Where's your uniform?" Melody asked. "And who's she?"

"I'm not here on official business," he said, taking a step closer. His crutch slid and he struggled to maintain his balance. "And this here's Carly. She's Max's new waitress, fillin' in for Lula while she's gone."

She looked down her nose at me. Literally. But her gaze seemed unfocused. Was she high? "Greta said Lula came back."

"She did, but she's gone again," Marco said. "We're tryin' to find her."

"What's that got to do with Greta?"

"We're not sure," Marco said. "Can we come inside and talk?"

Melody's face scrunched as she considered his request. Then she said, "No. Right here suits me just fine."

It suited me too. I wasn't sure I could make it the rest of the way to the porch without falling on my face, and Marco wouldn't fare much better. Then there was the fact that I just plain didn't trust her. There was no telling what she'd do to us inside.

Marco seemed to take her answer in stride. "I heard that Greta never came home last night. Is that unusual?"

"Not when she has a man," Melody said, resting her hand on the porch railing. The dog sniffed at her slipper, and she gave him a kick.

I grimaced as the dog let out a yelp and skittered a couple of feet behind her.

Marco ignored the dog and asked, "Does Greta have a man right now?"

"Nope."

"Any idea where she could be?" I asked.

She turned her hardened gaze on me. "Who are you again?"

"Carly. Carly Moore." I considered moving closer to offer my hand for a shake, but I didn't think falling on my butt would make a good impression. Besides, she didn't seem the mannerly type.

"Well, Carly Moore, I'm not sure why it's any of your business where my sister is."

"Carly's helpin' me out," Marco said, shooting me a look that said, *Let me handle this*. When he turned back to Melody, he said, "Has Greta felt threatened?"

That got Melody's attention. "How do you mean?"

"Has she said anything about someone watchin' her?" Marco

asked. "Or someone warnin' her to be quiet or threatening to hurt her?"

"Nope."

"Was Greta excited about Lula bein' back?" I asked.

Marco shot me a dirty look again.

"She ain't got many friends," Melody said. "Anyone smart moves on from this godforsaken place."

"Why hasn't Greta moved on?" I asked.

Melody was silent for a moment. "She stayed to help me. I got me a pack of kids and my man ran off. She helps bring in money."

As if on cue, a little boy's dirty face appeared between two curtains in the window.

"So she was happy to have her friend back?" I asked.

"Lula told her she was stickin' around for a while, but Greta was worried her ex would run her off again."

"Her ex?" I asked trying not to sound too excited at the prospect of getting a new piece of information. "Do you know who that is?"

She shook her head. "Shoot, Greta doesn't know him from Adam. She only knows he's some married bigwig. But Lula stopped seeing him a while back, and then someone came around the café last week, asking about Lula."

"Wait," I said, "if she didn't know who Lula was seeing, then how did she know it was Lula's ex?"

"Because it weren't Lula's ex," Melody said as though I was too stupid to understand. "It was someone askin' on her ex's behalf."

Why hadn't Greta shared that information? "Did she know who the messenger was?"

"She said he worked up in Ewing."

So she knew something about him. Was that because she'd recognized him, or had he introduced himself?

"Did she say where?" Marco asked.

She hesitated, then shook her head. "No."

Marco leaned into his right crutch, and he seemed to be having trouble keeping his balance in the slippery mud. "Melody, do you have a photo of Greta I can show around?"

For the first time, Melody looked worried. "Show around where?"

"I'm not sure yet, but it could prove helpful."

"Do you think something bad's happened to her?" she asked, coming down a step.

"I don't know," Marco said. "You might be a better judge of that. You don't seem all that worried. If she doesn't have a boyfriend, where did you think she was last night?"

Melody pressed her lips together, then said, "I'll get you that picture."

She spun around and went into the house, but Critter stayed in place.

Marco tipped his head toward me and said in a hushed tone, "Something's off here."

"Yeah," I said. "Why isn't she worried? And why didn't she answer when you asked where she thinks Greta might be?"

"She either knows where Greta is or she knows who intercepted her."

"You mean took her," I whispered.

He made a face. "I'm hoping she's shacked up with an ex somewhere, but I suspect that's wishful thinking. Still, I'm gonna ask her about Greta's exes just in case."

"Good idea."

Melody came back a few minutes later, holding on to a photograph. "I found one."

She went to the bottom of the steps and held it out to us, making it obvious we were going to have to wade through the mud to get it—meaning, *I* would wade through the mud to get it.

As I slogged my way over, Marco asked, "While we're here, can you give me the names and numbers of some of Greta's ex-boyfriends?"

She pulled the folded photo back as I tried to reach for it. "Why?"

"We're hopin' to find her, so we're gonna ask around."

She held the photo to her chest and narrowed her eyes. "You need to stay away from Tim Hines. That man is trouble."

"So Tim Hines is one of her exes?" Marco asked. "When did they break up?"

"About three months ago. She was sleeping with another guy, but it didn't work out."

"Do you have a name for the other guy?"

"Nah, she said it was a one-time thing, but based on the way she moped around, I could tell it was more than that for her."

Was she talking about Max?

"Did she break up with Tim Hines because of the other guy?" Marco asked.

"Nah, she broke up with him because he's an asshole, but he always suspected she moved on to someone else. He couldn't imagine she'd prefer to be sleepin' alone than dealin' with his bullshit."

"How long was she with Tim?" Marco asked.

"I don't know," she said, sounding frustrated. "Less than a year, I guess. Maybe nine months?"

"Did she live with him?" Marco asked.

"Not at first. She was livin' with me, helpin' with the kids, but then she moved in with him after she and me had a fight. It happened around the end of the school year because she weren't here to fix the lunches for the kids for the last-day-of-school picnic. But she came back from time to time, usually with some kind of bruises on her arms and once on her face. One time after she came back—toward the end of the summer—she had these awful bruises on her back, like someone had hit her with something long and skinny."

"Like a belt," Marco said in a tight voice.

Melody lifted her hand to her chin with a look of deep concentration. "Yeah. That sounds about right."

"Did she go back to him after that?"

"She did, but she was back about a week later, sportin' a nasty black eye. She admitted he'd hit her, and said she was done bein' his punchin' bag."

"How'd he take that news?" Marco asked.

"Not well. He came over nearly every night, trying to get her to come out, but he gave up after a week or two."

"Did he try to break in or become violent?"

"Nah," she said. "I mean, he yelled plenty, and sometimes he'd come here drunk and throw things at the trailer. He broke that there window," she said, pointing to the boarded window to her right. "But he never tried to force his way in. And after a few hours, he eventually left."

"How many times do you think he came over?" Marco asked.

"I don't know. Seven? Ten? Enough to be annoying as shit, especially after he broke the window. I told Greta she either needed to tell him to go away or go back to him, because I was getting tired of his shit."

What a lovely sister.

"Did she confront him?" Marco asked.

"I don't know, but she said she'd take care of it, and he only came back one time after that."

I couldn't help wondering what had convinced him to stop.

Given the expression on Marco's face, he was wondering the same thing.

"Did he pester her at work?" he asked.

"Oh, no," she said, waving the photo. "Old Mr. Watson wouldn't put up with that shit. He even watched her in the parking lot to make sure Tim didn't bother her comin' and goin' from her car."

Marco nodded and seemed to be considering what she'd told us.

"But we ain't heard hide nor hair of Tim in months. Since mid-August or so. What's he got to do with any of this?"

Marco ignored her question. "You're sure Greta wasn't seein' anyone else over the last year? Just Tim and the one-time guy? Was there someone new recently? Someone who could have made Tim jealous?"

"No one I know about, but she ain't one to share her life and *her feelings*," she said, emphasizing the last part with derision. "You know?"

Marco looked her dead in the eye, his body stiff. "Yeah. I know."

"You think she took off?" Melody asked. "I'm goin' out tonight, and she was supposed to watch the kids."

"Honestly, Melody," Marco said in a tone drier than burnt toast, "I have no earthly idea."

"You gonna look for her?" she asked in a hopeful tone. Marco's delivery had gone right over her head.

"Not in an official capacity," Marco said. "I'm still on medical leave. I'm just here checking on a friend. But if you think she's in danger, you should call the sheriff and report her missin'."

"Why don't you do it?" she asked with a mixture of fear and anger in her eyes.

"Because I doubt they'll listen to me." He tilted his head in my direction. "Now, if you'll hand that photo over to Carly, we'll be gettin' out of your hair."

Melody glanced down at the now-crumpled photo, the hard lines of her face softening for a moment before she reluctantly handed it to me. "I still don't know why *you're* mixed up in this."

I opened my mouth to answer, still not sure what I intended to say, but Marco beat me to it. "She's helpin' me. I got to know Greta pretty well at the café. I eat there several times a week when I'm on duty, and since I'm still recoverin', Carly offered to help."

I took the photo and tried to give Melody a genuine smile, but I was still struggling to read her. Was she actually worried about her sister's well-being, or did she feel inconvenienced by the disappearance of her built-in babysitter? I suspected it was the latter.

I backed up several steps, having formed the impression it might not be a good idea to turn my back to the woman in such close physical proximity. When I was several feet away, I turned around to check on Marco. His crutches were sliding, and he was struggling to maintain his balance.

I knew perception was everything on this mountain, and in most instances, I would have left Marco to flounder, simply because it could be seen as a mark on his manhood if he were to accept assistance, but he'd told Melody I was there because of his injuries, and the tension on his face told me he was not only struggling but hurting too.

I moved next to him and took his left crutch, then slung his arm over my shoulder. "I'm gonna drive."

I half-expected him to protest, but instead he leaned into me and let me lead him to the passenger door. I opened it and helped him maneuver so he could hop up. Since the crutches were a muddy mess, I put them in the cargo area before getting in on the driver's side.

Melody studied us as though she were watching a carnival sideshow.

"Where do you want to go now?" I asked as I pushed the button to start the SUV. Marco had the key fob in his pocket. "We didn't get Tim Hines's address." I backed out onto the road and headed toward the highway.

Melody stayed on the step, watching us leave.

"We don't need Tim Hines's address," he said, his entire body tense. "I know where he lives."

I was about to ask him how he knew, but Marco's obvious pain was my number one priority at the moment. "You're over-doing it, Marco." When he didn't protest, I became even more concerned. "How bad is your pain?"

"I just need to take a couple of pills," he said. "But they're at home."

"Okay," I said. "We'll drop by your house so you can take some. We also need to talk to Mr. Watson at some point."

"If he's there," he said, shifting his leg and pushing his seat further back to extend his leg. "He doesn't stick around a lot on the weekends."

We'd deal with that later. I was still worried about Marco. "Where are you hurting?"

He leaned back in his seat and closed his eyes. "Everywhere, but I tweaked my leg while slopping around in that mud. What's she doin'? Plannin' on hostin' a mud-wrestling match?"

I didn't answer, knowing he just needed to vent.

He took a few breaths, then said, "While Tim Hines is suspi-cious, I think someone else is involved. You said Greta saw something that scared her in the tavern, but if she saw Tim, I think she'd be more inclined to stick around than to run. Safety in numbers."

A quick glance showed me he still had his eyes closed. "Yeah. I agree. It was more like she was scared she'd been seen talking to me and wanted to get away as soon as possible."

"If I got ahold of a photo of Tim Hines, could you tell me if you think he was there last night?"

"Yeah, but we were really busy. Even if he was there, he might not have been in my section. I'm not sure I would have noticed him."

"Fair enough," he said. "But it can't hurt to look. Besides, you probably know most of the regulars by now, right?"

"Yeah."

We had more to discuss, but I kept silent for a few moments, staring at the road and giving him time to get comfortable. When his breathing became steadier, I said, "I keep thinking about Melody saying Tim stopped coming by. I can't imagine he would have listened to reason. Do you think Greta got someone to run interference for her? Maybe Mr. Watson since he was looking out for her."

He made a face, but his eyes remained closed. "Doubtful. Mr. Watson is over seventy years old. While he's tough on his own turf, I doubt he'd have much influence off his property, but I *do* know of someone with enough influence to get him to stop." He shifted to look at me, finally opening his eyes. "Tim Hines is an alleged associate of Todd Bingham."

I swallowed the lump of dread in my throat.

No matter where we looked, all roads led to Bingham.

CHAPTER EIGHTEEN

"You think Greta got Bingham to stop Tim from bothering her?" I asked in shock. "Why would he do that?"

"*That* is the question of the hour. What would Greta have that Todd Bingham wanted?"

I paused. "Information about Lula?"

"Maybe. Or maybe information that would help him in his business ventures. I bet you a hundred bucks Melody won't call the sheriff about her sister. She can't afford to have them snoopin' around. In fact, I suspect she's scrubbin' down her trailer as we speak."

My stomach knotted. "You think Melody hurt her sister?"

"No, not in this instance. I've suspected she's sellin' drugs for a while now. A few months ago, I found a link connecting her to the operation Carson Purdy was runnin'."

"But all of those men were killed. Isn't that operation done for?"

"There's no tellin' if that was all of them, but Tim was stalkin' Greta back in August, when Carson and his people were gearing up their operation. Bingham would have found any information about her sister helpful."

"So Greta either sold out her sister or her best friend."

"Or she could have given him information about Hines, but the miserable bastard is still alive and kickin', so that one's more doubtful."

"Bingham would have killed him?"

"Depends on the level of betrayal, but yeah. Bingham's a stone-cold killer, and you need to bear that in mind." Something about the way he said it led me to believe he hadn't yet finished his thought.

I turned slightly to glance at him. "You think I should talk to him again."

"I don't know yet. He didn't threaten you yesterday, and you seemed to get away with mouthin' off to him at the tavern, but the man has his limits. Ones you might test if you drop by to start askin' questions about Greta."

Facing Bingham scared the shit out of me. I had to think this through.

"One possibility is that Tim Hines took Greta," I said, "but that seems unlikely. I think he would have needed a trigger, but so far we haven't established one. And if it was Tim, it seems unlikely Greta's disappearance is related to Lula. I don't know about you, but I doubt it's coincidental two best friends went missing in the same forty-eight-hour period."

"My thoughts too."

"Let's say Greta did go to Bingham for help with Tim. What does that have to do with her disappearance now?" I asked.

"If it was Bingham who helped her in August, and if the price was information about Lula, he might be watchin' Greta now. Maybe he doesn't want her passin' anything along to you."

I felt like I was going to be sick. If that was the case, I'd gotten Greta kidnapped.

"And if that's so, goin' back to see him is a fool's errand," Marco said.

We were silent again, and I let all the possibilities run through my head. "Does Greta have any other association with Bingham?"

"Not that I know of, but that doesn't necessarily mean anything."

"And then there's the second possible father to consider," I said. "And the man who stopped by the café to ask Greta about Lula."

Marco nodded. "I think we need to stop by Watson's before we head to my place."

"Are you sure that's a good idea, Marco? You're in pain for one thing, and we're a muddy mess for another."

"I've got another pair of shoes in the back," he said. "We just need to wash off my crutches and get some new shoes for you."

"I have shoes in my bag," I said, another lump forming in my throat. "For my shift tonight." I still couldn't believe Max had fired me, but maybe he had a point. What if my snooping had gotten Greta kidnapped or killed?

"He's gonna hire you back, Carly."

"I don't know, Marco. I've never seen him so pissed."

"I've been thinkin' about it. He wasn't pissed. He was scared."

"Of what?"

"I don't know, but I don't think he was scared for himself. He was scared for you."

"Because I'm lookin' into Lula's disappearance." I took a deep breath, preparing to share my suspicions. "Do you think this has to do with his father? Greta said Lula was sleeping with a man of importance. Could it have been Bart Drummond?"

He pursed his lips, considering it, then said, "I don't know. She's not really his type."

"He has a type?" I asked, unsure why I was so surprised by the confirmation that he slept around. Didn't powerful men sleep around with young women just because they could? My father had become the exact same way after my mother died.

"Bart Drummond sleeps around, but he usually does it out of town. Rumor has it one of his paramours confronted Max's mother at the tavern when the boys were younger. He was more careful after that."

"Lula *was* meetin' her second guy in Ewing. Is that out of town enough?"

"Bart usually went to Asheville or Greeneville. But he's getting older and Emily goes out less often than she used to. He might be gettin' lazier."

"So Max might have known his father was sleepin' with Lula. Maybe he knows or suspects his father had something to do with her disappearance, and he's worried we'll uncover it and put ourselves in danger."

"Possibly."

"Where do we focus our attention first?" I asked. "I feel torn in too many directions."

"I think we should focus on Greta right now. I think we can work on the assumption their disappearances are connected, and hers is fresher, which likely means we'll find more clues."

"And if they're not connected?" I asked. "Do we stop lookin' for her and go back to Lula?" I wasn't sure I felt good about making that call.

The look on Marco's face suggested he didn't feel comfortable making it either. "Let's cross that bridge when we get to it."

We were approaching Drum, so Marco told me to stop at the back of Wyatt's garage.

I shot him a dark look. "Why?"

"Because he has a hose out back that he'll let us use." He grinned. "You could ask the man to drive to Knoxville to get you an ice cream cone, and not only would he do it, but he'd figure out a way to keep it from melting before he handed it to you. He'll let us use the hose."

I groaned.

"He's got it bad for you, Carly. But if you prefer to go to the tavern and wash up in Tiny's kitchen, I'll follow your lead."

Tiny wouldn't let us bring dirty dishes into the kitchen. He'd lose his mind if I took muddy crutches in there—didn't matter that we were closed for the day.

"No way," I said. "Can you imagine Tiny's fury if we tried such a thing?" I shook my head. "Wyatt's garage it is."

Of course his truck was there, but so was Junior's car. When I pulled up behind the building, I could hear a power tool running in the garage. Maybe we could wash off Marco's crutches and leave before we were noticed. While I did want to talk to Wyatt tonight, I didn't want to do it now, especially right after his brother had fired me.

I left the engine on and opened my door. "Stay here. I'll do it."

Marco just closed his eyes and grimaced as though a new wave of pain had hit him. I planned to look over his wounds when we got to his house. While I was hardly a nurse, I'd learned a thing or two from caring for Hank and Violet.

I grabbed the crutches out of the back, then walked around to the passenger side and opened the door.

Marco cracked his eyes open.

"I'm gonna take off your shoes," I said. "You need to change them anyway, so I might as well wash them off here."

He looked hesitant to agree.

"What?"

"They're Air Ones."

"Is that supposed to mean something to me?" I said wryly.

"They're nearly two-hundred-dollar shoes."

"Then what were you doing wearing them in the mud?" But I knew the answer to that, so I said, "Never mind. Don't worry. I promise to be careful."

He reluctantly nodded his head. I made quick work of untying his shoes. When I slipped off the second one, he cried out in pain, which made me seriously doubt he would be able to continue today. Maybe we should take a break. I'd wanted to cram as much investigating as possible into one day because of my work schedule on Sunday and Monday, but now I had all the time in the world.

I blinked away tears. Losing my job was nothing compared to this mess unfolding around us, and it wouldn't help anyone if I fell apart now.

A heavy-duty black garden hose was connected to an outside water spigot, so I turned on the water and started to spray the ends of Marco's crutches.

I wasn't surprised when Wyatt walked out the back door a few seconds later. He propped his hands on his hips and took in what I was doing. "Do I want to know?"

"Probably not."

"Why isn't Marco cleaning his own crutches?"

"He slipped in some mud and I think he hurt himself."

Worry filled his eyes, and he glanced back at the SUV. "Is he okay?"

"Honestly? I don't know, but he wants to go somewhere before I take him back home, so we thought it best to hose these down."

"And your boots?" he asked, his voice turning husky as he took a step closer.

"I have my tennis shoes in the car."

"But are your boots ruined?" he asked.

I snuck a glance at them. "Maybe."

He took the hose from me. "Why don't you clean them inside? I'll finish this up."

"You don't have to do that, Wyatt."

"I know, but I want to."

I gave him a warm smile. "Thanks."

Taking Marco's shoes, I headed back to the car and grabbed my bag. Marco hadn't moved a muscle, and he didn't react other than to flinch when I closed the door again. Not good.

I'd only been in Wyatt's garage once before, and on my first visit, I'd stayed in the waiting area. Just one more reminder that there was so much I didn't know about him.

Junior was leaning over an engine, but he looked up when I walked through the door.

"Hey, Carly," he said, but I saw hesitation in his eyes. He thought he'd seen me getting cozy with Marco.

"Wyatt said I could wash off some shoes inside. Where would be the best place to do that?"

He stood up, his gaze shifting pointedly to the larger pair of shoes. He no longer looked quite so friendly.

I didn't owe Junior an explanation, but I also didn't want to make an enemy. "I know you think I'm cheating on Wyatt."

He held up his hand. "It's none of my business."

"Clearly it is," I said, moving closer. "And while Wyatt and I are still trying to figure things out, I'm only hanging out with Marco to look for Lula. She's missing again."

"She does that," he said, his guard still up.

"This time is different. Now, if you could show me where I can clean these up?"

He motioned behind him to a large sink against the wall.

"Thanks." I walked over, my heels echoing in the concrete space. I could clearly hear the water running outside. No wonder Wyatt had come outside in 3.2 seconds flat.

I turned on the water and tentatively put Marco's shoe under the stream, picking up a brush from the back ledge of the sink and lightly scrubbing at the mud.

"Why do you think Lula's leavin' is different this time?" Junior asked.

"I can't tell you the specifics," I said, still facing the sink, "but there were some suspicious things out on her property." And, because the rest was bound to come out soon anyway, I added, "And now her best friend is missing."

"Greta?" he asked in surprise.

I turned completely around to face him. "You know that they're best friends?"

"Ginger is Greta's cousin. What happened?"

Did Marco know about their connection?

"Marco and I went to talk to Greta this morning at the café, and one of the waitresses told us she hadn't come in. She hadn't even called in sick. So Marco and I went out to talk to her sister, and Melody confirmed that she didn't come home last night."

Disgust washed over his face. "She's a piece of work."

"We gathered that. She didn't seem to think it was a big deal, even though she admitted she has no idea where Greta could be."

"Melody only thinks of herself. She'll be concerned soon enough when Greta's not there to watch her kids."

"I'm really worried about her," I said. "Marco told Melody to report Greta as missing to the sheriff's department, but he doubts she'll do it."

"Mel's dealin' pot and meth. She won't want the sheriff sniffin' around the trailer."

"That's what Marco said. We're on our way to talk to Mr.

Watson and the rest of the staff at the café." I paused. "How close are Ginger and Greta?"

"Not as close as Ginger would like. Melody has a way of destroyin' everything in her path, other people's relationships included."

"Would Ginger be open to talking to us about Greta?"

"Sure, but I'm not sure how helpful she'll be." He paused and shook his head. "So no one's called the sheriff to report her missin'?"

"Maybe we can convince Mr. Watson to do it," I said. "I get the impression it's unusual for her to skip work without calling in."

"Yeah," he said absently. "Let me know if he won't do it. I can have Ginger call, but they aren't very likely to take it seriously since Ginger only talks to her every other week or so." His eyes narrowed. "Marco's with the sheriff's department. Why doesn't he file the report?"

"He's still on medical leave. I'm pretty sure he only agreed to help me because he was bored sitting at home. I think I got him tied up in more than he bargained for." I turned back to finish scrubbing the shoe.

"Do you want me to call Ginger and let her know you want to talk to her? It would be easier if you dropped by the house since she's got all the kids."

I suspected Marco might be done for the day after we visited the café. I'd promised him I wouldn't investigate without him, but talking to Ginger would be like chatting with an acquaintance. We didn't know each other well, but she seemed safe. Especially since she was about to start cleaning Hank's house. "That would be great. I'll probably come by later this afternoon."

Once I finished with Marco's shoes, I moved on to mine. The mud had already started to dry and cake, so I struggled to get them unzipped, but once I had them off and got a good look at them, I wondered if they were ruined after all. I doubted water and a scrub brush could fix this.

Wyatt walked in while I was finishing the second boot, but he only nodded to me and walked into an office with a window overlooking the garage. I suddenly worried why he'd been out there so long. Had he confronted Marco? He wasn't in any shape to be interrogated.

And then there was the fact that Wyatt had essentially ignored me just now. Had Marco said something to piss him off? Or was this some kind of test? Did he expect me to hunt him down? I was much too tired for games, but I still had to tell Wyatt I wouldn't need a ride home tonight after all, so I put on my clean shoes and headed toward the office. The door was mostly closed, but I heard him talking in a low voice about a carburetor and belt. The situation suggested he wanted privacy, and with Marco fading fast, I couldn't wait long. So I headed over to Junior, Marco's damp shoes hanging from my fingers. I'd stuffed mine into the bag.

"Hey, Junior," I said. "Will you tell Wyatt thank you for the use of his water?"

Junior smiled, apparently appeased that I wasn't cuckolding his boss. "Yeah."

"And also tell him I don't need a ride home tonight. I'll explain why later."

"Sure thing, Carly. I told Ginger you'd drop by to talk to her, and she said she'd be there all day."

"Thanks, Junior." I headed out the door, surprised when I saw a large black pickup truck parked several feet away from Marco's SUV, the front end facing me. A rugged man with dark hair was standing in front of the truck. The crutches were nowhere to be found.

I hurried over to the Explorer and opened the back, although the stranger was standing uncomfortably close. I was relieved to see the crutches when I tossed in my bag and Marco's shoes. I pulled his clean shoes out of his bag, then took another look at the guy as I closed the hatch.

He had narrowed his focus on me, and it didn't look like friendly interest.

Had I made another enemy? I wasn't sure I could afford any more.

CHAPTER NINETEEN

I decided the best way to handle Truck Guy was to ignore him. I got into the car and glanced over at Marco, who was sound asleep, his face pale.

Marco was in no shape to be going anywhere but his own bed. He was done for the day.

Shifting the vehicle into drive, I pulled out and Marco stirred. "You finished?"

"Yeah, and I have someone else to talk to about Greta. Turns out Junior's wife is her cousin, and she's willing to tell us anything she knows."

He tried to sit up and released a cry of pain. "Sorry." He took a deep breath. "Maybe she'll have another lead."

"I think we should just take you home, Marco."

"No," he said, gripping the armrest on the door. "We'll stop by Watson's first. Then you can take me home to get my pills."

I had no intention of bringing him back out with me after I took him home, but I was keeping that plan to myself for now. The car I used was back at Hank's, so I'd be stuck out there, but I'd figure that part out later.

"Okay," I said amicably. "We'll stop at Watson's, but don't you dare pass out on me, because I am not carryin' your body around."

"I'm not gonna pass out," he grumped. I'd been joking, but his face was so pale I wondered if it was a legitimate concern.

I was lucky enough to find a spot directly in front of the café. I got Marco's crutches out of the back, put his clean shoes on his feet, and helped him out onto the sidewalk.

"If I didn't know any better, I'd suspect you had experience with one-legged men," he teased, but his voice was strained.

"Been practicing," I said, opening the door. "But let's not overdo it in here. We can always come back later." Or I could come without him, since this seemed like a safe interview too.

I'd expected him to wave me off, but he had to be hurting even more than I'd thought because he nodded before slowly hobbling in. The café wasn't nearly as busy as it had been in the morning. Marco took the first available booth close to the front door, and practically fell onto the vinyl seat. He extended his left leg, putting his foot onto the seat next to me.

"You're back," Angie said cheerfully as she headed over to us pulling out her notepad.

"We couldn't stay away," Marco said with a big grin. "Can you believe Carly had never had Watson's food until last night? Now she can't get enough of it."

That wasn't true. I'd had their breakfast before, and Marco had ended up with my dinner last night, but I wasn't about to correct him.

"Know what you want?" Angie asked. "The special today is meatloaf."

"Sign me up," Marco said a little too jubilantly. I knew he was trying to sell that he was okay, but it only made me more worried.

I decided to get the meal I'd ordered the night before. "I'll take a club sandwich and a salad with ranch dressing," I said, then looked Marco in the eye. "But I think we should get our food to go."

He studied me for a long second, and I was sure he was about to correct me, but then the corner of his lip tipped up into a hint of a grin. "You heard the lady."

"You two an item?" Angie asked, glancing back and forth between us.

"Yep," Marco said with a wink at the same time, I said, "No."

Angie looked rightfully confused, so I added, "Marco's such a jokester. We're just friends."

She looked us over once more. "Y'all want drinks while you wait?"

Marco ordered water and I got iced tea. When she walked away, I leaned in closer and lowered my voice. "Marco, maybe we should do this tomorrow."

"We're already here, and besides, I'm hungry." But his eyes looked glazed and his cheeks were flushed.

I leaned over the table and pressed the back of my hand to his forehead and then his cheek. Both were slightly warm, and I wasn't sure if he had a low-grade fever or if he was just warm from the exertion of getting inside.

He grinned. "You playin' nursemaid?"

"I've had plenty of practice with Hank."

Closing his eyes, he slumped down in the seat and rested his head back. Within about twenty seconds, I was sure he was asleep.

Angie was standing in the back with another waitress, who looked a couple of decades older. I slid out of the booth, taking care not to disturb Marco, and headed to the back.

"Is there a bathroom back here?" I asked, deciding to ease my way into this.

"Right there," said the other woman, whose name tag read Sheila. She thumbed to a door down the hall.

"Oops," I said with a laugh. "Right in front of me."

I hurried into the bathroom and decided to use the facilities while I could. When I came out a few minutes later, Sheila was waiting on a table, but Angie was still standing in the back.

"Did you ever hear from Greta?" I asked.

"Nope," she said with a frown.

"Marco was pretty worried, so we paid her sister a visit to see if she knew anything."

"Did she?" Angie asked and I could see a hint of worry in her eyes.

I stepped closer and lowered my voice. "No. She doesn't know where she is, but she doesn't seem all that concerned."

She shook her head, her lips pressed into a thin line. "Melody doesn't give a shit about that girl. Only keeps her around for babysitting and makes her hand over most of her paychecks for room and board."

That didn't sound all that surprising. "She said Greta hasn't had a boyfriend since Tim Hines. Do you know if that's true?"

She gave me the once-over. "How do you know Greta?"

"I confess, I only just met her yesterday. I came by Watson's to ask her some questions about Lula, and then she stopped by the tavern to talk. I think she saw someone who frightened her, because she looked scared and left in a hurry. I had Max walk her to her car, and now she's missing." I took a breath. "I'm worried."

Angie didn't respond, but she looked worried too.

"Melody said someone came in last week asking Greta about Lula. Do you know anything about that?"

She picked up a pitcher of water. "I'll come over to your booth in a minute."

It wasn't exactly a promise of anything, and her expression was blank, but it was the best I was going to get.

"Okay," I said. "Thanks." When I sat back down, Marco stirred. "How are you feeling?"

"Like shit." He tried to sit up but slouched back down in his seat.

"I think you need to go to the doctor, Marco."

"I just need a pain pill and sleep."

I hoped that would fix it, but I wasn't so sure. Then again, he'd seemed fine until our mud adventure, and that had come after the exertion of climbing up and down Max's narrow staircase, not to mention the emotional strain of arguing with his best friend. Marco had been shot twice three weeks ago. He was on medical leave for a reason.

Angie was refilling water glasses around the room, and she came to our table last. She didn't waste any time getting down to business.

"Greta told me that a man was in here asking for Lula," she said in a hushed tone. "But Lula was still gone, and Greta told him so. The bastard didn't like her answer, so he left and stuck her with the bill for his pie and coffee. Watson's pretty strict with that stuff, so the guy's bill came out of her tips."

A reminder that Max was a great boss...when he wasn't drunk and pissed at me.

"Did she know who he was?" I asked.

"She said she didn't recognize him."

"Did you believe her?" I asked.

She hesitated. "I don't know. I'm not sure why she would lie, but *something* was off."

"Did *you* see him?" Marco asked.

She gave him a long look. "You look like shit."

"Thanks," he grunted.

"I mean, you didn't look so great when you came in, but now you look like shit."

"Thanks," he repeated, his tone even surlier.

"And no," she said. "I didn't see him. I wasn't here. She told me about it the next day. He came in right before closing."

"Did she tell you what he said?" I asked. "Specifically?"

"He told her he was lookin' for Lula. That her boyfriend was willin' to pay big money for info about where she might be. Greta didn't know, but she wouldn't have told him anyway."

"Did Greta tell you who the guy was workin' for?" Marco asked.

She shifted her attention to him. "No. But she was worried, and we speculated who Lula's guy could be. There were some rumors that it might have been Todd Bingham, but the messenger wasn't one of Bingham's guys. She said she was certain she'd seen him in Ewing but couldn't remember where."

"How often does she go to Ewing?"

"Once or twice a week."

"Does she go to the same places when she's there?" Marco asked. "Knowin' that might help us narrow down who he is and who sent him."

"Oh, that's easy," Angie said. "She visits her nana at the old folks' home."

I shot a glance at Marco, then looked back at her. "Do you know the name of it?"

"It's the only one in town," Angie said. "Greener Pastures, or something like that."

"Does she go anywhere else while she's there?" Marco asked.

"I don't think so. Maybe the grocery store. The drugstore. That kind of thing. But she mostly goes to see her nana."

Maybe the messenger visited someone at the nursing home, but we had no name or photo to help ID him. It would be a shot in the dark. But what if someone had sent him there to watch Greta? We needed to go to the old folks' home and ask around.

"Oh," she said, "she *did* describe him. She wanted me to be on the lookout for him, but it was so generic I'm not sure it'll help."

"*Anything* would help," I said.

Angie nodded. "She said he had dark brown hair, brown eyes, and a pale complexion. He was medium height and had stubble on his face, no beard. When he left, he tried to tower over her, but she said he wasn't much taller than her, so likely about five-seven, five-eight." Then she added, "Oh! And he wore a gold chain around his neck."

"That's great, Angie," Marco said. "Thank you."

"No problem. Anything to help."

"We appreciate it," I said, then shifted the angle of our questioning. "Say, Melody told us a bit about Greta's ex, Tim Hines. Did she talk about him much?"

"I know he beat her from time to time and was physically and verbally abusive, but I didn't find out until after she left him. She did a good job of hiding it."

"Is there a chance they got back together?" Marco asked.

She started to answer, then stopped. "I'd like to say no, but she acts like she's been keeping a secret the last few weeks, so maybe. But when they were together before, he came in fairly regularly to eat. I thought it was sweet at the time, but now I'm pretty sure he was keepin' tabs on her. You know how those controlling assholes are. But if they're back together, he hasn't been in to watch her."

"And no one else has been in to watch her either?" Marco asked.

"I don't think so. I remember the regulars." She flashed Marco a grin. "Like you. And I ain't seen anyone new hangin' around, let alone someone who's been watching her."

"What if she didn't want to go home to Melody?" I said. "Like maybe she'd had enough and needed a break. Where would she go?"

"She ain't got many friends around here anymore. A lot of girls she and Lula went to school with moved away. But if she wanted to hide out somewhere, she might have stayed with her cousin Ginger."

And we knew she wasn't there.

The customers a couple of tables over were making subtle signs that they were ready to leave. Angie noticed and started to head over.

"One more thing," Marco said. "Is Mr. Watson here? I'd like to ask him a few questions."

"He took off until Tuesday. He and his wife went down to Atlanta to visit their kids."

Leaning forward, he said, "Then I need to ask you a huge favor. Melody won't report her sister missing, and the call needs to come from someone who knows Greta's schedule."

"But you're a deputy," Angie said in shock. "I thought you were already investigating."

"We are," Marco admitted. "But it's not official. Someone needs to officially report her missing and see if they'll start lookin' for her. They'll likely make you wait for forty-eight hours, but at least she'll be on their radar."

She nodded. "Yeah. Sure." She glanced over at the table of customers. "I've gotta take care of 'em."

"Of course," I said.

Sheila brought our food over, and Marco and I quizzed her about Greta. But Sheila seemed to keep her nose out of everybody's business, so I wasn't surprised she didn't know much.

Marco left business cards for both of them and asked them to call him if they remembered anything else. He also asked Angie to let him know what the sheriff said after she called to report Greta missing.

I laid enough cash on the table to cover the bill and tip, then helped Marco out of the booth and into the SUV. He fell asleep again and didn't wake up until I pulled up in front of his cabin. It was on the cute side for being a bachelor pad. He had a porch that ran along the front of the house—which was only about twenty to twenty-five feet wide. The front door was on the left, and a large window on the right had two Adirondack chairs centered in front of it. The front of the house had a narrow view of the valley toward Greeneville, and I suspected he'd paid good money for the two-bedroom house and the view...good money for Balder Mountain, anyway. There was no telling how much that was.

"Marco," I said, touching his arm lightly.

He stirred slightly, then opened his eyes, trying to focus on my face.

"You're home," I said. "Let's get you inside."

"Yeah," he said, trying to sit up and reaching for his door handle.

"Just wait for me." I jumped out and got his crutches from the back, then met him at the open passenger door.

"Do you have any idea how embarrassin' this is?" he asked, his cheeks flushed as I helped him slide off the seat and onto the ground.

I handed him one crutch and wrapped his left arm around my shoulders, taking his weight. "Marco, you were shot a little over three weeks ago. You had major surgery. It takes time to recover from that. I'm pushing you too much."

He grunted and took a labored step. It took longer than it

should have to get him up the three steps and into the house. Once we were inside, I helped lower him to the sofa, then ran outside for our lunch and his shoes.

When I got back, he was dozing sitting up. I was about to tell him to lie down, but the cuffs of his jeans were caked in mud, and I wanted to examine his wounds.

"Marco, we need to take off your jeans."

A grin spread across his face, but his eyes remained closed. "As many times as I've dreamed of you saying those exact words, I'm not in the mood."

"Very funny," I said sarcastically. "I want to look at your leg."

He started to fumble with the button of his jeans, so I sat next to him and pushed his hands away.

"If you tell anyone I undressed you, I'll call you a bald-faced liar," I said.

"Your secret is safe with me."

I got the button undone and the zipper pulled down, careful not to accidentally touch something sensitive underneath. Then I grabbed the fabric at his hips and tugged down as he lifted his butt off the sofa. It took some finagling, but I finally got his jeans past his hips and started to tug them down his legs. I tried not to look at his snug navy boxer briefs.

"God, you suck at undressing a man," he said through gritted teeth. "I guess Wyatt doesn't care about your lack of finesse."

I wasn't about to tell him Wyatt and I hadn't gotten to that point in our relationship.

"Most men are more able and willing," I said, carefully pulling the material over his bandaged leg.

"Who said I wasn't willing?" he asked, cracking an eye to look at me.

"You. Just a few seconds ago."

Once the jeans were at his ankles, I carefully pulled them free, then turned my attention to his left thigh. An elastic band that reminded me of Hank's compression bandages was completely wrapped around his leg. It was stained with blood.

"When was the last time you changed your bandage?" I asked.

"This morning."

"Does it still drain?"

"No."

Pushing out a breath, I got to my feet. "I'm going to unwrap it and look it over. Then put a fresh bandage on. Where are the clean ones?"

For a second, I thought he was going to protest, but he slumped deeper into the cushions. "The bathroom."

"And your pain pills?"

"Same."

I headed into the bathroom and found the bandages, pills, and a thermometer so I could check his temp. I set them on his coffee table, then got him a glass of water from the kitchen—the design purposefully rustic compared to Max's, which simply looked old.

He was dozing again when I went back, so I woke him up to take a pill. Since he wasn't in any shape to go anywhere, even back to his bedroom, I grabbed a couple of pillows from his bed and brought them to the sofa, putting them at one end. I helped him lie down, making sure his left leg was closest to the edge.

"Here, put this in your mouth." He started to make a comment, but I took advantage of his parted lips and stuck the thermometer under his tongue. Then I got to work unwrapping his leg.

A jagged scar marked his thigh—a hole the doctors had apparently sutured closed. His stitches had been removed, but a small section of the wound appeared to have parted and was oozing blood. I checked the back of his leg for the exit wound and found it to be okay. I put antibiotic ointment on a square, then placed it over the open wound before rewrapping his leg with a clean ace bandage.

The thermometer beeped, and he took it out of his mouth. "98.4. No fever." He tossed it onto the table next to him. "You sure you're not a nurse?"

"Nope, but I *do* have some nursing care experience." I glanced up to his face. "I'm going to look at the wound on your abdomen." When he didn't protest, I lifted his shirt, stopping for a fraction of a second when I noticed the ripple of his abdominal muscles. I pushed on quickly, hoping he wouldn't notice my reaction.

A dressing was taped to his side.

"I only have that bandage to cover the incision," he said with his eyes closed. "My shirt irritates it if it's not covered."

"I'll be sure to replace it." I carefully peeled the bandage away and took in the sight of his jagged incision. Since the bullet had gone straight through his leg, they'd cleaned it up with minimal surgery, but his abdomen had been a different matter. He'd been in surgery for hours, and they'd removed his spleen as well as repaired other damage. I could see the pink puckered scar from the drain they'd removed a week after surgery.

A stark reminder that he'd been shot saving me and Wyatt. Tears stung my eyes. Marco had almost died because Carson had wanted to kill me.

"Hey," he said in a husky voice, and I lifted my gaze to his. "I was shot in the line of duty."

I released a short laugh and wiped the tears off my cheeks with the back of my hand.

"So it was nothing personal?"

"Then? I was just doin' my job, Carly."

The *and now?* hung heavy between us. We'd become friends,

but the way he was looking at me now made me worry he was feeling something more, which was laughable. Marco Roland did *not* settle down.

"You have a small tear in your front leg wound, but this one looks good. Where's most of your pain?"

"Both my leg and my side, but I tweaked something in my gut when I slid in the mud," he admitted. "I'm supposed to limit the use of my crutches because of my side wound."

"*Marco.*" I looked at the abdominal wound again. What if slipping around in the mud had torn something loose inside? Not to mention he'd gone up and down those stairs and traipsed everywhere else.

He closed his eyes again. "I knew you'd go without me."

My heavy heart pressed on my lungs, making it difficult to take a breath. "Go to sleep. Rest."

I hated that he was in so much pain. I felt even worse that he'd done it for me. Again.

CHAPTER TWENTY

I covered him with an afghan and put his food in the fridge, then took my lunch out to his front porch, sitting down in one of the chairs to enjoy the view while I ate. I could see why he liked it here. While I enjoyed spending what little free time I had on Hank's front porch, Marco's view was ten times nicer.

I started to eat my sandwich, my stomach churning with worry. I had no idea what signs pointed to internal bleeding, but we were nearly an hour away from a medical facility that could take care of him. I didn't even have internet to look it up on WebMD.

I only choked down half my sandwich and a couple of bites of the salad before I gave up and went inside to search for his discharge paperwork. I checked the bathroom, where he kept all his supplies, and found it tucked behind a box of bandages. He had a cordless landline, so I took the phone outside and called the phone number listed on the papers. The call went to an answering service. They told me the doctor would call me back, but I didn't know Marco's number, so I had to find my cell phone—my glorified address book in this rural mountain town

—and look it up. I worried that all the opening and closing of the front door would disturb Marco, but he was out cold.

Desperate for something to do, I picked up Marco's jeans and found a pair of sweats in his drawer that mostly fit me. After I took everything out of his pockets and put them on his dresser, I tossed both of our jeans in his washer along with another pair I found in his dirty laundry. I would have done some housework to occupy my time, but Marco kept a tidy house and other than some laundry and a few dirty dishes in the sink, there wasn't much to do.

Except…I'd been hoping to talk to Ginger this afternoon, and I realized I could probably do that over the phone. I found her number in my cell phone, then used Marco's cordless phone to make the call on his porch.

Ginger answered after a couple of rings, sounding breathless.

"Ginger, this is Carly. Did I call at a bad time?"

"With three kids underfoot, there's never a perfect time," she said. "Junior said you might be stopping by."

"That was the plan, but Marco overdid things today, so I brought him home. Now he's taking a nap, and I'm out at his house without my car."

"Do you need someone to come pick you up?"

"Maybe later," I conceded. "But for now, I'm sticking around to make sure he's okay. I've put in a call to his doctor, and I'm waiting to hear back."

"Well, if there's anything I can do to help…"

"Thanks," I said. "I'm hoping you can help with something else. I'm not sure what Junior told you, but Marco and I are worried about Greta. She didn't show up to work this morning, and I hear that's not like her."

"It's not. She really likes that job, and she wouldn't screw it up. Even if she decided to play hooky, she'd pretend to be sick."

"If she was scared, do you know where she might have gone?"

She was silent for a moment. "Why would she be scared?" Her voice rose in pitch. "Is that damn Tim Hines stalkin' her again?"

"I don't know," I admitted. "I've heard he stalked her this summer. Do you know why he stopped back then?"

"I don't have a clue. She just said he stopped comin' round."

"Did she say if she got someone to intercede for her?"

"Who would do that?"

"I don't know," I said, not wanting to volunteer any information and sway her answers. "Do you know if she's been seeing anyone recently?"

"No. I know she had that one-night stand with Max back at the end of the summer, and then she said she was taking a break from men."

"I know Lula is her best friend, but does she have anyone else she might turn to?"

"Other than me, not really," Ginger said. "All her friends moved away. Oh, wait. One of them recently came back to sort through her parents' things after they moved to Florida. They took what they wanted and left the rest for her to deal with."

"You're kidding," I said. "That sounds like a nightmare."

"They gave her the house too. It ain't worth much, but something is better than nothin'. Her name's Leann Burton."

"Do you have a number for Leann?" I asked.

"Last I heard, she doesn't have a landline. If you want to talk to her, you'll have to drop by and hope she's there."

"Do you have an address?"

"More like directions," she said, then proceeded to give me detailed instructions on how to find her place off the highway to Ewing.

"Did Greta tell you anything about Lula?" I asked.

"You'll have to be more specific."

"Did she tell you that Lula had come back?"

"No. I had no idea. Does that mean you're out of a job? *Crap.* Does this mean Wyatt doesn't want me to clean Hank's house anymore?"

"That's between you and Wyatt," I said. "And Lula took off the very next day. Marco and I were trying to find her—then Greta disappeared too."

"I called the sheriff's office like Junior suggested, but they won't do nothing since it hasn't been more than forty-eight hours."

My stomach cramped. Angie had said she'd call them too, so the pressure was on—but they likely wouldn't do anything for another day and a half. That meant that Marco and I were currently the only ones looking for her, and Marco was out of commission for the foreseeable future.

"Do you have a grandmother in a nursing home in Ewing?" I asked. "Angie said Greta went up there a few times a week to see her nana."

"Yeah, Nana Thelma. She and Greta are pretty close. I don't get up there all that much because of the kids." Her excuse was understandable, but I still heard the guilt in her voice.

"Do you think your nana would be open to me paying a visit?"

"You think Nana Thelma knows something about Greta bein' missin'?" she asked, a little incredulous.

"I don't know," I said, wondering how much I should tell her. "But I know a man stopped by the café last week asking about Lula, and he made Greta uncomfortable. She told Angie she recognized him from Ewing, but she wasn't sure where she'd seen him before. I figured I'd check out the places where she spends the most time. Ask around about him."

The phone beeped with an incoming call, and caller ID said it was a medical clinic. "Ginger, Marco's doctor is on the other line. Thanks for all your help."

"When you find Greta, tell her to call me."

"I will." I hung up and transferred to the other line. "Hello?"

"Carly? This is Dr. Freeman."

"Thank you for calling me back."

"From what the service told me, Marco's in severe pain after doing a lot of physical activity? Why don't you fill me in yourself?"

I told him some of the things Marco had done, including our mud adventure, leaving out the fact we were investigating two missing women. "He just got so tired out of nowhere. It scared me, and I wondered if he might have hurt himself."

"We did some extensive work in his abdomen, so there *is* a possibility of internal damage and bleeding. Does he have pain in his abdomen? And if so, in one spot or all over?"

"He has pain in his leg, but he says it's mostly his abdomen."

He was silent for a moment. "Have you checked his blood pressure?"

"No."

"If you have a blood pressure cuff, take his pressure. If it's running low, bring him in to the ER, but I suspect his pain and exhaustion are from overdoing it. He underwent major trauma, and it's going to take some time for his body to heal. But if you have any more questions or concerns, feel free to call me back. Or if you think he's getting worse, bring him to the ER."

"Thank you, Dr. Freeman."

As I hung up, I realized that I needed to get a blood pressure cuff, which meant I had to head back to town. I'd need to leave Marco alone for a little while in order to properly take care of him.

I went back inside to check on him. His breathing was steady, but he still looked pale. I kneeled next to the sofa and lightly pinched his wrist to check his pulse with my fingertips. It seemed strong enough at first touch, but I held on tight, counting the beats to be sure.

He stirred slightly and murmured, "Are you sure you're not a nurse?"

There was no way I was telling him that I'd cared for a dying woman before fumbling my way to Drum. It didn't fit with my Carly Moore cover, and besides, it wasn't liable to reassure him. "Shh, I'm trying to count your heartbeats."

He lay still for a few moments, and although I didn't have a watch with a second hand to count off the seconds, I could tell his heartbeat was steady and strong. "I talked to your doctor, and he says to monitor your blood pressure. You don't have a blood pressure cuff, do you?"

He opened his eyes wider to give me an incredulous look. "Why would I have a blood pressure cuff?"

"I had to ask." I started to get up, then squatted back down. "You're not going to chastise me for calling your doctor?"

"I've learned that you do what you want, and you did it because you care about me." He took a breath. "You want to go get a blood pressure cuff, don't you?"

"But I don't want to leave you alone."

"I was alone when I came home from the hospital," he said. "Go get the blood pressure cuff if it makes you feel better. I'll be okay."

I hadn't even thought to check if he'd had any help after his release. Now I felt terrible.

"What's got you upset?" he asked with a frown.

"Don't you have any family around?"

He took a moment before he said, "None worth speakin' of, but I'm fine. I've got Max. I've got friends. I'm good. Someone would have stayed if I'd asked, but I didn't. All of that's to say if I was okay then, I'm totally fine now. Now go get some money out of my wallet and pick up that blood pressure cuff. I'm gonna go back to sleep."

"I don't have a car."

"Take mine. The keys are in my pocket."

I headed to his room and grabbed his keys and his cell phone, which I'd retrieved from his jeans before throwing them in the washer. I left his wallet. I didn't feel right taking his money. Besides, I figured Hank could use a blood pressure cuff, so I'd keep it for him.

There was a floor-length mirror in the bedroom, and I caught a glimpse of my reflection. With my jeans in the washing machine, I was wearing jogger pants that barely fit, paired with a sweater that definitely didn't match. I considered running by Hank's for a change of clothes or putting on my Max's Tavern T-shirt, but right now I felt I had no right to wear it. So I searched Marco's drawers until I found a well-worn University of Tennessee long-sleeved T-shirt. It was too big for me, and I had to roll up the sleeves, but the ensemble looked better than what I'd had on before. Besides, I was running to the Dollar General in Drum. I could have worn a gunnysack and been fine.

I set Marco's cell phone and the cordless landline receiver on the coffee table next to the sofa and made sure his crutches were within reach in case he needed to get up. Before I headed out the door, I refilled his glass of water and set it down next to the phone.

There were only a few keys on his key fob, and I was lucky enough to pick the one that locked the front door on the first try. I got in the Explorer and headed back into Drum.

Dollar General was packed on a Saturday afternoon. I searched the shelves in the small health section for a blood pressure cuff, but when I couldn't find one, I tracked down an employee.

"We don't carry nothin' like that, hon," she said, clearly frazzled. "Yer gonna have to head down to Ewing."

Ewing. That would be an hour-and-a-half round trip. "Do you have a pay phone?"

"Outside."

Pay phones were a whole new world to me. I considered running over to the tavern to use the phone there, but I figured Max and I needed as much space from each other as possible. So I dug a quarter out of my wallet, inserted it into the slot, then called Ginger.

"Hello?" she asked, sounding leery.

"Ginger, it's Carly. Did you mean it when you offered to help with Marco?"

"Sure," she said, but I heard the hesitation in her voice.

"You don't have to do anything, but I need to head to Ewing to pick up something at Walgreens. I'm going to call him as soon as I get cell phone coverage there, but if I can't reach him, can I call you and have Junior or someone go check on him?" I'd briefly considered calling Max, but I wasn't sure he'd talk to me, and for all I knew, he was sleeping off his hangover. Or drinking again. Wyatt was out. He'd been far too jealous that morning.

She gasped. "Oh, my word. Is Marco okay?"

"The doctor thinks he just overdid it, but I can't help worrying about him."

"Of course. I'll be here. Just call, and I'll have Junior run up there to check."

"Thanks."

I drove Marco's Explorer to Ewing, wondering if I should have made a quick trip to Hank's to pick up his car. It didn't feel right driving Marco's vehicle and using his gas, but I reminded myself that I was making the trip for him. Nevertheless, I wondered what people would think if they saw me driving his SUV, especially since I was wearing a baggy outfit that obviously belonged to a man. Did I care? Did it matter?

When I pulled into the Walgreens parking lot, I dug my phone out of my purse and checked my cell service. Two bars. Drum had absolutely no coverage, but I'd discovered that Ewing had spotty areas, and I'd lucked out. I called Marco, and it took him several rings to answer.

"Hello?" He sounded groggy, like he'd just woken up.

"Hey, Marco," I said. "I had to go to Ewing to get the monitor, but since I'm going to be gone longer than I expected, I wanted to check on you."

"I'm fine," he said, sounding grumpy. "I was sleeping."

"How's your pain? Better? Worse?"

"I'm fine, Carly. Stop worryin'."

That was asking for the impossible. "This shouldn't take too long. I'll be back before you know it."

"Don't hurry on my account," he said. "I'll probably sleep a little while longer, then heat up my meatloaf for dinner."

"If you have any problems before I get back, you can call Ginger. She said she would send Junior to come check on you."

"Junior? Why in the hell would you send Junior out to check on me? *I'm fine.*"

I was beginning to think I'd overreacted, but Marco wasn't the best patient. I suspected he was grumpy because he was in pain.

"Of course you are," I said. "But call her anyway if you have any problems. Okay?"

"If I have any problems, I'll call one of my friends," he snapped. "I'll see you when you get back." Then he hung up.

I was pissing people off left and right today. But I knew

Marco wasn't angry with me. He was in pain and likely frustrated. I took comfort in knowing that I didn't have to rush back—it didn't seem like he was going to hemorrhage to death while I was gone. I wondered if this was a completely wasted trip, but I still thought a blood pressure cuff was a good idea for Hank. I wasn't sure why I hadn't thought of it earlier. Besides which, I'd wanted to come to Ewing anyway. If Marco was feeling okay and wanted to sleep, I could stop by the nursing home before heading back.

Since I wasn't in a hurry, I took my time, perusing the cosmetics and skin care aisle. Carly Moore was two years younger than Caroline Blakely. I wondered if I should up my skin-care game. I picked out a new eye cream, then put it back when I realized it cost about thirty bucks. Budgeting was new to me, and I still had a lot to learn. I picked out a different one, under ten dollars, and moved on to the hair aisle. While my dye job had covered my roots, it wasn't great. Maybe I could find a YouTube video to teach me how to make it look more natural.

What did it matter if I didn't have a job to pay for any of it?

What did Max know about Lula and Greta? Could I forgive him when I found out?

If Max doesn't give me back my job, I might have to leave.

I was surprised by the melancholy that washed over me. I'd become pretty attached to some of the people in Drum.

I found the section with blood pressure cuffs and stood in front of the shelves, trying to decide whether to get a wrist or armband model. For the millionth time, I wished I had a smart phone so I could use the internet.

"Carly?" I heard a small feminine voice ask to my left.

I glanced up, wondering who had recognized me in Ewing, and I couldn't hide my shock when I found myself face-to-face with Emily Drummond. She looked frailer than I remembered at

Seth's funeral. She'd tied a blue scarf around her head, and dark circles underscored her pale blue eyes. Her skin hung off of her skeletal frame, but I could see the kindness in her eyes, a sharp contrast to the man she was married to.

Her face lit up with delight. "Oh, it *is* you."

"Hello," I said, so caught off guard that I had no idea what else to say. I grabbed the box in front of me and put it in my basket, not even paying attention to which one I'd picked up.

"Is that for Hank?" she asked. "Max said you were taking care of him."

"Actually," I said, recovering from the shock of seeing her. "It's for Marco. The sheriff deputy who Carson shot." But of course she knew him. He and Max had been best friends for years. The story he'd told me filtered back—how Emily had come to their apartment to speak to Max, how she'd said something to convince Max to come home from college early.

Her sunken eyes clouded. "When I heard…" Her voice trailed off and the pain on her face made it clear she, at least, had possessed no knowledge of Carson's schemes. "I'm so sorry."

"Thank you." Part of me wanted to tell her it was okay, but it wasn't, so instead I said, "It wasn't your fault."

Her gaze dropped to the floor, and it stayed there for a couple of seconds before she lifted her face. Tears shimmered in her eyes. "Marco is like a second son. When I heard what Carson had done…" She shook her head. "I still can't believe he shot Marco. Carson *knew* him. Had watched him grow up. To shoot him in cold blood like that…"

"He shot at Wyatt too," I said, my voice thick. "He wouldn't have batted an eye at killing him."

"To get to you," a man behind me said in a dry voice.

I involuntarily flinched, but I shouldn't have been surprised Bart Drummond was with her. Emily looked like she'd blow over in a strong wind. It was a wonder she was out of her house at all. She probably didn't go anywhere alone anymore.

I slowly turned to my side as Bart walked past me to get to his wife, and his words finally penetrated. He was attempting to make this all about me. "Carson was cleaning up loose ends," I said, turning the blame where it squarely belonged. "I was a loose end."

"And my son and Max's best friend were caught in the cross-fire," he said in a voice so cold goosebumps broke out on my arm.

Emily turned and patted her husband's arm, but she looked like she was being careful not to upset him. "No, she's right. This wasn't personal for Carson. It was a man cleaning up his mess." Tears filled her eyes again. "Because I can't let myself believe he'd purposely target Wyatt and Marco."

Bart wrapped an arm around Emily's back. "Now you're upset, love."

The look he gave me made it clear who he blamed for that.

She leaned into him and gave me a smile, but I saw hesitation in her eyes. A reserve that hadn't been there before her husband had joined us. What was it like to be married to such a man? I hadn't been able to ask my own mother, and part of me wished I could ask Emily.

"I hear you're working for Max at the tavern," she said. "He has such lovely things to say about you."

I wasn't sure how to respond given he'd fired me a few hours earlier, but the last thing I wanted to do was give Bart the satis-faction of saying so. He was the one who'd started this whole mess, somewhere down the line. I lifted my gaze to his as I answered. "Max is a wonderful boss. I'm very lucky."

"Lucky," Bart said. "Do you consider yourself lucky, *Carly*?"

The blood fled from my head, and I had a moment of dizzi-ness as the truth slammed into me.

He knew. He knew who I was.

Everything in me screamed *run*, but anger and my pride made my back straighten. "I believe luck is what you make of it."

"A good philosophy," he said. His mouth stretched into a grin, but his eyes were cold. "One I share. You never know when something interestin' will fall in your lap, but what really matters is what you do with it."

Oh, he definitely knew.

Did I leave town? Did I try to reason with him? Maybe this would be the linchpin that convinced Wyatt to finally share his secrets. Because my desire to bring Bart Drummond to justice had just gotten a whole lot more personal.

Emily shook her head and glanced up at her husband. "Don't bore poor Carly with your work talk, Bart."

"Despite her…interesting manner of dressing, Carly seems to have a level head on her shoulders," Bart said with a chuckle. "I'm sure she's findin' our conversation quite interestin'."

I'd wondered when he'd make a dig at my oversized clothes.

"Speaking of work talk," I said with a smile I hoped didn't look too forced. "It was lovely meeting your business associate at the tavern this week. Neil Carpenter?" I added, as though to jog his memory. Really, I wanted him to know I'd remembered the man's name. "I was surprised to see him in Drum yesterday. Across the street from the tavern. I had the impression he'd gone back to Nashville."

Bart's left eye twitched. "I'm not sure how you came up with that impression. Neil's been workin' on a special project for me."

"Bart's puttin' in a new resort and spa," Emily said. "He'll close the small one outside of Ewing."

"You own the spa in Ewing?" I asked. This was the link I needed to tie Lula to Bart.

"I'm not sure you can call the Mountain View Lodge much of

a spa," he said dismissively. "The new resort will be much grander."

"But he'll hire all the old staff," Emily said. "I insisted on it."

"If they choose to come, dear." Bart patted her arm. "They may not want to make the drive."

"And where will the resort be located?" I asked, trying to buy some time. I wanted to ask Bart questions about Lula, but a direct approach seemed too dangerous, and I didn't want to insult Emily.

"Well, that's been a source of contention," Bart said with a sly grin. "I'm puttin' it on the edge of the vast Drummond property, but it borders Bingham land." He made a dismissive gesture. "That's all worked out now."

"Bart just found out he won the court case this week," Emily said. "They'll break ground in the spring."

"How exciting," I said with fake enthusiasm. "How soon do you think it will open? I'm sure you'll be needing staff." I held Bart's gaze. "Lula might be lookin' for a job since she and Ruth don't seem to be seein' eye to eye these days."

To his credit, Bart didn't show a reaction.

"Poor Lula," Emily said. "What an awful thing, to have one parent who kills the other." That stung, although I could tell it wasn't an intentional barb—Bart might know my secret, or at least part of it, but he wasn't the sharing type. But what she said next completely reclaimed my attention. "Quite the mess. I couldn't help but feel partially responsible."

"How so?" I asked in surprise.

"I'm sure Carly's not interested in Balder Mountain gossip," Bart said. "That's ancient history now."

"Oh, no," I said. "I'm a history buff. And besides, I figure the more I know about the people and the town, the better I'll fit in."

"Louise dropped by the house lookin' for Bart that day. She

said something about Hank that I didn't understand. I asked her to repeat herself, but she seemed *so* upset." She looked off in the distance, seemingly lost in thought, then asked, "How is Hank doin', by the way?"

"His leg is healing nicely," I said, my mind reeling from what she'd said about Hank. Especially since Hank had seemed so cagey about the incident when we'd discussed it the day before. "But he misses Seth terribly."

"How can you stand livin' out at that shack?" she asked. "I hear it's haunted up there from all the…" Her voice trailed off as though she couldn't bring herself to finish.

I blinked in surprise. "I have yet to meet any ghosts."

If there *was* a ghost, I'd expect it to be the man Hank had killed in my defense.

"Don't pay Emily any mind," Bart said good-naturedly. "She's a believer in the supernatural. Me," he said, holding my gaze, "I'm a firm believer in the here and now, and I believe you and I have some business to discuss. Perhaps we can get together next week. Whenever your schedule will allow."

I had no doubt about the topic—my real identity—but if he wasn't going to turn me in to my father, then I must have something he wanted. Part of me was scared to find out what that was.

"Perhaps you can get Wyatt to bring you," Emily said, sounding wistful.

"No," Bart said, "I have a business proposition for Carly, and I think it's best if she has no outside influence. In fact," he added, "I think it's best if you don't mention this to anyone. *Especially* my sons."

My fake smile spread a small fraction of an inch to acknowledge I'd heard his request, but I wasn't about to agree to it. I needed to give this some thought, but a seed of hope formed inside me. This would influence Wyatt to take me into his confidence, wouldn't it? Surely he'd want to help protect me.

"I'll be in touch," Bart said.

"Maybe you can stay for tea when you come," Emily said. "We hardly get visitors out to the house these days."

"I'm sure that Carly will have to run off as soon as our meeting is done," Bart said. "She's a very *busy* woman."

Did he know I was looking for Lula? I wouldn't be surprised. Even if his power had waned, Bart Drummond seemed to have his finger on the pulse of everything that happened in Drum. Was that why he wanted to meet with me? To convince me to stop my search? If so, why not send Emily to another area of the store and convince me now? No, it was something else entirely.

"Mrs. Drummond?" a woman from the pharmacy counter called out. "Your prescription is ready."

"Oh," Emily said, looking flustered. "My doctor called in a new prescription for my nausea. I hope this one works." Then she added, "It was so lovely seeing you. I do hope you'll find time to stay for tea when you stop by to see Bart."

"Don't worry," Bart said with a shit-eating grin that looked eerily familiar, likely because I'd seen a nearly identical grin on Max's face countless times. "We'll be seeing a whole lot more of Carly." Then he steered her around me and headed to the pharmacy counter.

I didn't like the sound of that. What did Bart have planned for me?

But I'd been dismissed, which I was one hundred percent good with. I really didn't want to chat with Bart, and I had places to go before I headed back to Drum.

After I went to the nursing home, I was paying a visit to Mountain View Lodge.

CHAPTER TWENTY-ONE

Greener Pastures was on the other side of Ewing, at the top of a steep slope. It seemed dangerous to keep a bunch of elderly people next to such a sharp incline, but then again, the brick building looked like it had originally been intended as a bomb shelter. I doubted they got out much.

The front doors opened to a wide hall that led to a large room with multiple tables set up to my right. A few older women sat at one of the tables, working on a jigsaw puzzle. To my left was a nursing station desk with an older woman tapping on her smartphone. She barely looked up when I stopped in front of her. "Can I help you?"

"I'm here to see Miss Thelma."

"Thelma Baines or Thelma Tureen?" she asked, her attention still on her phone.

"Uh...I'm not sure. Her granddaughter Greta comes to see her all the time. Her granddaughter Ginger said it would be okay to stop by for a visit."

"Honey, ain't nobody gonna stop you. Head on back." She

made a vague gesture toward her right. "Thelma Tureen's in room 26."

"Thank you." I turned and walked down the hall, passing a wall plastered in headshots of the various employees, or so I assumed, but my attention was captured by a man in a wheelchair who seemed catatonic. My heart ached, and I considered stopping to check on him, but I was already leaving Marco longer than I'd planned. I needed to talk to Thelma and get out of here.

The door to 26 was open, and a woman with short, pure white hair sat in a rocking chair in the corner with a red quilt over her lap, knitting. She looked up with a friendly smile. "Hello. Are you looking for Virginia? They put her in the room next door."

"No," I said, taking a step into the room. "If you're Thelma, I'm here to see you."

Her smile widened. "Come on in." She squinted up at me. "Do I know you?"

"No, ma'am. I'm Carly Moore, a friend of Greta and Ginger's." I was proud of myself for not fumbling around, trying to remember to use my new last name. It had become more and more natural over the past weeks.

She placed her knitting in her lap. "Oh, yes, Ginger called to tell me you'd be stopping by. I haven't seen her in a month or so, but she's busy with those babies. Greta comes to see me though. She shows me pictures of Ginger and her kiddos."

I noticed she didn't mention Melody.

"That sounds like Greta," I said, only then realizing I'd put myself in an impossible situation. Was I really going to tell this elderly woman that her granddaughter was missing? It seemed obvious Ginger hadn't told her.

"Carly, please sit," she said, gesturing toward a chair next to the wall at the foot of the bed.

I gingerly took a seat, my nerves starting to get the better of me. "Miss Thelma, has Greta mentioned anything about Tim Hines to you?"

Her mouth puckered with disapproval. "Nasty fellow."

"So I've gathered."

"You haven't met him?" she asked in surprise.

"No. I've only heard about him. I just moved to Drum about a month ago."

"Oh, dear," she said sympathetically. "People don't usually come to stay in Drum. They prefer to leave."

"Do you know if Greta wants to leave?"

She blinked in surprise. "I guess I hadn't considered that."

"She's never mentioned it? Like maybe she wanted to escape Tim?"

"No. She said she talked to someone who convinced him to leave her alone. But still, now that I think about it, I doubt she wants to stay in the area." Pain filled her eyes. "She knows how lonely I get, and she comes more often than most people's families do." She glanced up at me. "What if she's only stayed because of me?"

"I know that she loves you very much," I said. "And I know she also loves her job. I'm sure she doesn't see staying in the area as a chore. Plus she helps Melody with her kids."

"But she's lonely. That Tim is a nasty piece of work, and her new fella didn't work out. Good eligible men are hard to come by in these parts. Too many of 'em have dirtied their hands in some illegal mess or another. And she might love those kids, but Melody treats her terribly, and she can't afford to move out on her own."

"What about living with Lula?" I asked. I couldn't see anyone purposely living in that hellhole, but they could have moved somewhere better together.

Tears filled her eyes. "She said Lula's been growing more distant over the last year. Plus the girl keeps runnin' off. Deliverin' those packages."

"Greta told you about the packages?"

She nodded.

"Do you know who she was delivering them for?"

"No, but she suspected it was tied to Lula's mother."

"Her mother?" I asked in surprise. "How so?"

She shook her head, looking troubled. "She wasn't sure. She said it was just a gut feeling, but Greta doesn't trust that woman one bit. Says she's usin' poor Lula. It worries Greta somethin' fierce."

A new thought hit me. "You said Greta spoke to someone who got Tim to leave her alone. Do you think Greta might have tried to get help for Lula too?"

"What do you mean?"

"Do you think she might have tried to convince the person behind the packages to leave Lula alone? Or that she maybe got someone else to do the convincin' for her?"

She frowned. "That sounds like something Greta would do."

Did the packages belong to Bingham? Was that why Bingham had been giving Lula the evil eye at the tavern? Had he expected payment or a report of some kind? But how would Greta fit into that theory?

"You said most of the men around here have done illegal things," I said. "I know Todd Bingham has his chop shop and drug business. Carson Purdy was trying to start his own drug empire. I suspect many of the young men in town have had dealings with one of them. Was it always like that in Drum?"

"Well, I ain't been privy to that world in quite some time, but when I was younger, Hank Chalmers and Bart Drummond ran it all. Bart with his moonshine and Hank with his pot and his pills. Then meth and Oxy entered the scene and Hank saw what it did to people and wanted no part of it."

"And he gave the business to Todd Bingham?"

"Gave it? Oh, no. Hank made himself a tidy profit, I'm quite sure."

If Hank made a huge profit, then why was he living in such squalor? I'd heard people talk about his supposed fortune, but I'd always assumed they were being foolish.

"And Todd Bingham's father was involved in illegal activities too, wasn't he?" I said. "Marco recently filled me in. Said he was a terrible man."

She nodded with a faraway look. "We were all sure Floyd had killed both of his wives and his son. Sweet child too, that little Rodney." She shook her head and clucked. "But the good Lord saw fit to give that man a proper earthly punishment on his way to hell." She cast me a sideways glance. "Fell into a woodchipper."

"So I've heard." And I was certain God had nothing to do with it unless you considered Todd Bingham to be His instrument.

"Floyd Bingham was a scary man, but he kept to his property and left the rest of the world alone. Sure, he had his own thing goin', but it wasn't on the scale that Bart and Hank ran things."

"And then Todd took over."

She waved a hand. "I didn't pay any attention to him. I hardly paid attention to Floyd, other than noticing how poorly he treated his wives. By the time Todd Bingham's name started bein' whispered more and more, I was too busy with my own life to care. My husband got sick and I spent a good five years with my head down and taking care of him. And by the time Daniel died, I kind of stopped carin' about everything." She gave me a quivering smile. "That's what got me here. Not carin'. But

Greta, she cares enough for the both of us. She's what keeps me goin'"

And now she was missing. I needed to tell Thelma, but I couldn't bring myself to do it yet. "Do you remember anything about Lula's mother shooting her father?"

"Oh, honey. *Everyone* remembers that nightmare. But many of us remember it all differently."

I'd seen the truth of that, but no one had really explained it to me. Since she was being so helpful, I figured I might as well ask. "How so?"

"I've never heard anything from any real source, mind you. I've only heard what other people supposedly know, so take what I tell you with a grain of salt."

"Okay…"

"Walter Baker was a worthless piece of shit," she spat, then gave me a knowing look. "That's not speculation. That there is pure fact."

I'd seen their homestead and knew what he'd supposedly done to Lula. I wasn't about to argue with her.

"Rumor had it that he did a job for Hank, but he screwed it up somehow. Some people say Hank shot him in cold blood, then pinned the whole thing on Louise. Tried to drown Lula because she witnessed the murder."

I couldn't help remembering how terrified Lula had looked when I'd mentioned Hank's name. I'd seen him shoot a man without blinking an eye, but I couldn't imagine him drowning a child. Not the man I knew. "Do you think that's true?"

"Shoot, no," she said with a wave of dismissal. "Hank would never have hurt a child. If anything, Hank only hired the man to help him provide for Lula and Louise. They were poor as dirt. But I have no trouble believing Walter screwed it up."

"What were the other rumors?"

"That Walter was doin' a job for Bart Drummond, and things went south. That Bart had him killed."

"Do you think that's a possibility?"

"Why would Louise take the fall?" Thelma asked. "And killing isn't really Bart's style. At least not so openly. The few times dead people have been linked to him, there was a murderer who *wasn't* tied to him."

"Because he called in a favor," I said to myself.

"What?" she asked. "You know about Bart's favors?"

"Only a little," I confessed.

"You sure know a lot about that town considering you've only been there a month."

"I'm a fast learner. What do you know about Bart's favors?"

"Makin' a deal with Bart Drummond is like makin' a deal with the devil himself," she said. "Some people call him a crossroads demon." Her brow shot up. "You know what that is?"

"When you go to an intersection and summon a demon for a favor? Only you have to sell your soul to get it."

She nodded. "That's right. Except instead of goin' to a crossroads, you'd show up on Bart Drummond's back doorstep." Shaking her head, she clucked again. "Only the truly desperate seek a deal with *that* devil."

"They'd take the fall for him in a murder," I said. "Because he'd already have their souls."

"Yep." She pushed out a sigh. "I don't hear about Bart's favors all that often anymore. He doesn't have the power that he once had. He's an old man now, although I doubt he'll go quietly into the night."

"I just saw him and Emily at Walgreens before I came to see you," I said. "They said they'll be breaking ground soon on a new resort."

"I heard they were doin' something like that," she said in a disapproving tone. "But they need to just let Drum die. It's a town full of evil and discontent. Just let it die."

I wasn't sure I agreed with her attitude, but I hadn't lived there for six or seven decades either.

Connections formed in my head, one thing linking to another. Emily had mentioned that Lula's mother had shown up at their doorstep right before the murder. Had she asked for a favor? Had she killed her husband for Bart and claimed he was drowning Lula to justify it?

"What about Todd Bingham?" I asked. "If I do my math right, he was running his father's business by the time Lula's father was shot."

"He was much too small-fry to be any part of *that* mess," Thelma said.

I wasn't so sure. Todd Bingham was ambitious and arrogant. I doubted he would have had the patience to wait long before starting a campaign to get his share of the pie. What if he'd inserted himself into it somehow? If Louise knew about it, it would explain why she'd been so adamant that Lula cut ties with him. But that was all speculation, and one thing I knew from listening to all those true crime podcasts was that you never presumed someone guilty or innocent. You only followed the facts and the clues.

Thelma had given me a wealth of information. We now had multiple avenues to search, but I needed to figure out what to tackle next. While I still wanted to check out the resort, I wasn't sure that was the best use of my time. Bart Drummond seemed like a prime suspect, but Bingham was tied to this thing every which way I looked. Greta may not have recognized the man at the café as part of his enterprise, but that didn't mean he wasn't. Bingham didn't strike me as the sort to publicize all of his connections. I couldn't chase every lead at once, and I had to use my time wisely. Besides, I didn't even have a photo of Lula. How was I going to ask about her at the spa?

My second week in town, out of curiosity, I'd tried to look her up on Facebook, but like most people in Drum, she didn't have a Facebook account. Or IG. Or Twitter. With no internet to update their status, what was the point? It occurred to me that the lack of social media breadcrumbs tossed around in Tweets and Insta posts probably made things harder for local law enforcement.

"Thank you, Miss Thelma," I said, getting to my feet. "This has been so helpful."

"Something's happened to my Greta, hasn't it?" she asked, but her voice was strong. "Ginger didn't say why you wanted to talk to me."

I took a breath. "Yes, ma'am. She didn't come home last night, and she didn't show up to work today. Lula disappeared the night before, and I don't think she took off voluntarily this time. I think whoever took Lula may have taken Greta."

"Why?" she asked, her back stiffening.

I needed to own up to my own role in all of this. "Because I was asking Greta questions about Lula, trying to figure out what had happened. I think I may have poked a bear and put Greta in harm's way." My voice broke. "I'm so very sorry."

Her chin lifted and fire filled her eyes. "You listen here. Greta was doin' what she does best—takin' care of someone. She was looking out for her friend as best she could. And now you're lookin' out for the both of 'em." Her eyes hardened. "So you watch your back and find 'em, you hear?"

I nodded solemnly. "Yes, ma'am."

I left her room and headed toward the door, but the wall of headshots caught my attention again. The man in the wheelchair was gone, giving me better access to it. Above the photos was a sign that read, *Greener Pastures Employees*, but it was a photo of a man off to the side, under a title of *New Hires*, that caught my attention.

He wore blue scrubs and had a serious expression. Underneath his photo read *Shane Jones, Janitor*.

He had dark brown hair and a heavy gold chain around his neck.

He was the man I'd seen out back at Wyatt's garage, and I'd bet my new winter coat he was also the man who'd paid Greta a visit.

CHAPTER TWENTY-TWO

I snapped a photo of his headshot, then hurried over to the front desk. "Excuse me," I said to the woman, who was still watching something on her screen. "Can you answer a question for me?"

"No, you can't eat dinner with your loved one," she said with a look of irritation. "It's liver and onion night and the chef only made enough for the residents."

I nearly gagged. "I don't want to eat here. I have a question about the wall of photos."

She shook her head with a look of disgust. "I'm busy, and it's self-explanatory."

Busy watching Netflix, from the look of it.

"Miss," a woman called out behind me. "We can help you."

I spun around to look at the two women still working on the jigsaw puzzle. One of them was motioning for me to come over. Her fluffy gray hair reminded me of a cotton ball. When I approached her, she motioned to a chair between her and her friend.

"Sharon won't help you," Cotton Ball said. "She's too busy watching *The Witcher*."

"She's got a thing for Harry Cavill," the other woman said, cramming a puzzle piece into a spot that clearly wasn't a fit. "Especially with his shirt off."

"You mean Henry," Cotton Ball said.

Her friend rolled her eyes. "Whatever."

"You were asking about the wall of photos?" Cotton Ball asked. "It throws a lot of people off. Those are photos of all the employees. They have such a high staff turnover rate that the residents get confused about who works here and who's just visiting. So now they post photos with names and their jobs so we'll know."

"Makes sense," I said.

The second woman made a "hmph" sound, but I suspected she was perpetually grumpy.

"What do you know about Shane Jones?" I asked. "The new janitor?"

"He only started a few weeks ago."

"What do you make of him?" I asked.

"He's quiet," Grumpy Lady said. "And that's good enough for me."

Cotton Ball rolled her eyes. "He's quiet, but it's because he's casin' the joint. Things keep disappearing. Watches. Rings. Just last week Thelma's granddaughter's wallet disappeared."

"Greta Hightower?" I asked in surprise.

"You know her?" Cotton Ball asked.

"She was visitin' Thelma, you nincompoop," Grumpy Lady said. "Didn't you hear her ask Sharon?" She picked up another puzzle piece, having given up on the first. "And Greta's wallet wasn't stolen—it was found in the restroom."

"And how did it get in the restroom?" Cotton Ball asked belligerently.

Grumpy Lady lifted her gaze to me and peered over the top of her reading glasses. "Nothin' was missin'. Not even her money. They say it fell out when she went in there to pee."

"She didn't use the restroom that day," Cotton Ball said in exasperation. "Someone took it."

"So you think this new guy is stealing things?" I asked.

"If anyone took her wallet, it was Minnie Horton," Grumpy Lady said, shaking her head. "Everyone knows she's a klepto."

"Minnie was out with her daughter," Cotton Ball said. "And besides, that boy was watching Greta on her last two visits."

"So he's got a thing for her," Grumpy Lady said. "Young love."

"More like young stalker," Cotton Ball said, her mouth pursed liked she'd sucked on a lemon. "I've seen *You*."

I tried to squash my jealousy that Cotton Ball and Sharon had better access to streaming services than I did. "Do you know where Shane worked before?"

Cotton Ball nodded her head with a knowing look. "He said he came from pharmaceutical sales."

Drugs. Nobody went from pharmaceutical sales to janitorial work. Not if it had been a legit sales job.

Had Bingham encouraged Shane to get a job here to spy on Greta?

"Thank you so much for your help," I said as I stood. "Good luck with your puzzle."

"There's three pieces missin'," Grumpy Lady said, focusing on another piece. "We've done it five times now. We're just killin' time until we die."

She was just a ray of sunshine, but I made a mental note to pick up some puzzles at the Dollar General and drop them by the next time I was in Ewing.

As soon as I got outside, I sorted through everything I'd learned. Shane Jones *had* to work for Bingham, which meant I needed to talk to Bingham again at some point. There was no way I was letting Marco come with me today or even tomorrow, yet I was smart enough not to try going alone.

I needed to find out more about Shane Jones, and given that I'd seen him at the garage, the most logical person to ask was Wyatt. If he thought I was getting into something dangerous, I had no doubt he would try to stop me, but I'd have to take my chances.

Once I got into Marco's car, I pulled out my cell phone and checked my service. Three bars. I called Wyatt's garage first, but it rang multiple times before going to his answering machine. Same thing with his home phone number, but I left a message this time.

"Hey, Wyatt, it's Carly. I came to Ewing to get a blood pressure cuff for Marco, and while I was in town, I stopped by the nursing home to visit Greta's grandmother. I saw a photo of a guy who was behind your shop this morning. I was hoping to ask you some questions about him. I'm heading back to Marco's now, so I'll try your home number or Hank's number later."

Since the spa seemed like a pointless venture and I was still worried about Marco, I headed back to Drum. I was tense for most of the drive, imagining Shane Jones's pickup truck at every turn, but no one tried to run me off the road or even cut me off. I made it back to Drum safely.

My makeshift sign was still on the front door at Max's Tavern, and I struggled to block the replay of my morning with Max. I was torn between wanting to smooth things over with him and worrying that he was guilty of something that would ruin our friendship forever.

It was getting dark by the time I pulled up in front of Marco's house, but a light glowed through the window. When I walked inside, Marco was sitting up on the sofa and he shot me a scowl. "Did you drive to Timbuktu to get the damn thing?"

I shut the door behind me. "Well, hello to you too."

"I was gettin' worried, Carly. You were gone forever."

I sat in the chair next to the sofa. "You didn't seem in a hurry, so I went by the nursing home and talked to Greta's grandmother. While I was there, I saw a wall of photos, and one of them was of the guy who was hanging out behind Wyatt's garage this morning. He started working at the nursing home a few weeks ago. I'm sure he's the same guy who visited Greta at the diner, and according to one of the residents, he stole her wallet while she was visiting her grandmother and then left it in the restroom."

He stared at me wide-eyed. "What? What guy behind Wyatt's garage?"

"You were really out of it," I said, then filled him in about seeing the guy at Wyatt's, talking to Greta, going to the nursing home, and what I'd learned from Thelma and the other women.

"Shane Jones," he said more to himself than me. "I have a friend in the department who can run his name through the system and see if he has any priors. That is, if it's not an alias."

"We know he drives a black pickup," I added.

"Did you get the plate number?"

"No, but I think Wyatt talked to him. The guy showed up after I went inside, and Wyatt stayed out there longer than it would take to hose off your crutches. I thought maybe he was talking to you, but you were out of it."

"Sure was."

I told him about Wyatt's call.

"I suspect the guy dropped by inquiring about parts," Marco said. "But it's odd that he went straight to the back to do it."

"Maybe Wyatt knows him or got some information from him."

"I'll call my friend Ken, and then you call Wyatt."

As he started to reach for the phone, I said, "I went all the way to Ewing to get this blood pressure cuff, so I'm going to actually use it before you make that call."

But it was obvious that a long nap was exactly what he'd needed. His color was back and the dark circles under his eyes were gone. Still, the way he was carefully moving around told me the pain hadn't completely abated.

He sat back in his seat and held his left arm out straight. "Okay, Nurse Carly."

I opened the box and wrapped the cuff around his arm. "I ran into someone at the Walgreens in Ewing." I looked up and held his blue-green eyes. "Two someones... Emily and Bart Drummond."

He held perfectly still, and I was pretty sure it wasn't because of the cuff around his arm, filling with air. "What happened?"

I'd started this conversation, but I wasn't sure I wanted to follow through with it. Marco didn't know about my life as Caroline Blakely. If I told him about Bart's invitation, he'd want to know what Bart had on me, and I wasn't ready to tell him. While I trusted Marco, the fewer people who knew, the safer I'd be. "Emily was pleased to see me. Bart...he was harder to read."

"That's Bart for you. How did Emily look?"

"Thin. Tired. She was picking up a new prescription for her nausea."

He frowned. "She's had a rough go of it with this round of chemo. Max is worried about her."

"He never talks about it."

The cuff stopped filling with air and began to deflate.

"He's great at compartmentalizing," Marco said.

"Maybe not as great as you both seem to think since he gets shit-faced drunk as a coping mechanism." I looked at the blood pressure reading. "122 over 76. Perfect."

"See?" he said. "I told you I'm fine. I was just tired."

"Emily did make a comment about Lula that I found interesting. She said Lula's mother showed up on their doorstep the day she shot her husband. Louise was looking for Bart, apparently, but she also said something about Hank."

His brow shot up. "Hank was involved in it?"

"I don't know. Emily doesn't remember what she said, but it made me wonder if Louise showed up to ask Bart for a favor."

A frown creased his forehead. "She would have to be pretty desperate to resort to that."

"My thoughts exactly, which is why I need to get Hank to talk. He seemed pretty surprised to hear Louise was getting out soon. And he seemed a little off when I brought it up….like maybe he knew more than he was sharing."

He looked deep in thought, so I stood and said, "Call your friend, and I'll heat up your food from Watson's."

I transferred the food from the Styrofoam container to a plate and put it in the microwave. Marco might be feeling better, but I still didn't think he should go back out anytime soon. Still, I couldn't stand the thought of doing nothing. Not when Lula and Greta were missing. I'd heard that the longer someone was missing, the greater the chance they weren't coming back alive. Time was of the essence.

No one else was going to look for those two women. Could I really just wait?

The microwave dinged, and I removed the plate and started to bring it to the living room, but Marco was up and hopping to his small kitchen table.

"Ken said he'd look up Shane Jones and get back to me, but it might not be until tomorrow." He glanced at the plate, then back at me. "You gonna eat too?"

"I ate earlier. I probably should get back to Hank. You and I can't do anything more tonight, but I can ask Wyatt what he knows about Shane Jones and talk to Hank about his version of what happened to Lula and her parents."

He was quiet for a moment. "You'll fill me in on what you find out?"

I grinned. "Only if you tell me what you find out from Ken."

"Deal."

"I also have to find a ride to Hank's, but I'm hoping Wyatt will play taxi."

"I can take you home, Carly," he said, his voice full of guilt.

"You need to stay here and rest, and Wyatt and I are due for a good chat anyway."

His eyes twinkled. "Is that what the kids are calling it these days?"

I groaned and walked into the living room to pick up the cordless phone. "You're obviously feeling better."

"I'll be ready to go back out tomorrow," he said quietly.

"Let's just wait and see." I called Wyatt's home number and got his machine again, so I hung up and called Hank's number.

"Hey, Hank," I said when he answered. "Have you seen Wyatt this afternoon?"

"He came here lookin' for you. Then Junior called and Wyatt took off."

Frustration washed through me. Why hadn't I gotten stranded in a town that had cell phone towers? "How long ago was that?"

"I dunno. Maybe fifteen minutes."

I didn't want to call Ruth, and Hank couldn't drive. If push came to shove, I could get Marco to take me back, but he needed to stay home and rest. Selfishly, I wanted him to help me continue the investigation as soon as possible—which meant he needed to do as little as possible tonight. "And Wyatt didn't say where he was going?"

"Nope, just took off like a bat out of hell."

"Dammit."

"Hey, Carly," Marco said, sounding pretty pleased with himself. "I know where Wyatt is, and he's not lookin' like Mr. Mary Sunshine."

Sure enough, when I opened the front door, he was bounding up the steps with a dark look on his face.

CHAPTER TWENTY-THREE

"Wyatt. How did you find me?" I asked, but I knew the answer before I finished the question. According to Hank, Wyatt had bolted after talking to Junior. Junior had found out from Ginger.

He stopped on the porch a couple of feet in front of me. "What the hell's goin' on with Max? The tavern is closed, and when I went in to find out why, Max was drunk off his ass. But he *was* coherent enough to go on and on about how he fired you for stickin' your nose where it doesn't belong."

"I don't want to miss the good stuff," Marco called out good-naturedly. "Come on in, Wyatt."

Wyatt gave me a look that let me know he was waiting for my permission, so I stepped aside and let him in. The motion jarred my arm, and I realized I was still holding the phone.

"Hank?" I said into the receiver. "Wyatt's here. I'll be home soon."

"I thought you were workin' tonight."

"Not tonight. I'll explain later." I ended the call and replaced the receiver on the phone's base as Wyatt took a seat at the kitchen table across from Marco.

Wyatt looked Marco dead in the eye. "What's goin' on with Max?"

So he wasn't mad at me. He was upset about his brother.

Fair enough. So was I.

"Good question," Marco said as he scooped up some mashed potatoes with his fork and took a bite. He was trying to play nonchalant, but it was plain as day that he was as upset as Wyatt.

"I know you and Carly went to see him this morning. Why's he so upset that you're lookin' for Lula?"

"I don't know," Marco said, setting down his fork. "But you and I both know he only gets like this when something's eatin' at him."

Wyatt was silent for a moment, then said in a voice so low I could barely hear him, "Do you think Max had something to do with Lula's disappearance?"

"No," Marco said confidently. "He would never hurt her."

I didn't believe it either, but I had to wonder why he was so upset. Everyone else believed she'd just taken off again. While he'd questioned why I thought differently, he hadn't tried to dissuade me. He'd told me to keep it from Ruth. He hadn't gotten truly upset until I said something about Neil Carpenter.

"But you think he's involved anyway," Wyatt said in a low growl.

Marco gave me a questioning look, then turned back to Wyatt and said, "We've come across some information about Lula that we're not at liberty to divulge."

The message was loud and clear. Do *not* tell Wyatt Lula was pregnant.

I expected Wyatt to get angry, but instead he tapped the tip of his finger against the tabletop and toggled his attention between the both of us.

"I wasn't under the impression this was an official investigation," he said in a lazy voice, yet I saw the tension in his shoulders.

"It's not," Marco conceded.

Wyatt released a short laugh. "You sure *act* like you're treating this as an official investigation. You're just not checkin' with the sheriff's department." He glanced away before turning back to Marco, his jaw tight. "Is my brother a *person of interest* in Lula's and Greta's disappearances?"

I was taken aback that he knew about Greta, but then of course he did. He'd known where to find me because of Ginger. But his language—*person of interest* and *official investigation*—was even more jarring. This had started as Marco and I trying to find Lula, and he was right. It had turned into something more.

Marco started to say something, then swallowed it. "We're not at liberty to say."

Wyatt's entire body vibrated with anger. "You're supposed to be his best friend."

Marco held his gaze. "Not all of us cover up crimes because of our personal relationships."

Wyatt jumped to his feet, his chest heaving. "You don't know what you're talkin' about, Roland."

"Maybe I know exactly what I'm talkin' about."

For several long seconds, I thought Wyatt was going to jump him, but then he took a step back, his hands clenched at his sides. "Carly. It's time to go."

My mouth dropped open in disbelief. "Excuse me?"

"I said it's time to go," he said through gritted teeth.

My back stiffened. "That caveman attitude might work on the women in Drum, but it's not gonna fly with me."

"So you're gonna stay here with Marco?" he asked. "Because Ginger made it sound like he was at death's door, yet he seems just fine, eating his meatloaf and mashed potatoes."

I stared at him, at a loss for words.

"Drummond," Marco said in a calm voice, still seated in his chair. "Carly and I need to discuss our case. You may wait outside, and if she changes her mind about goin' with you, so be it. Otherwise, I'll take her to Hank's, after I gain even more strength from my meatloaf and mashed potato fortification." He flashed a grin.

Propping my hands on my hips, I shot Wyatt a deadly glare. "I won't be changing my mind."

"Nevertheless," Marco said in a reasonable tone, "he can wait outside while we speak, and he's free to stay on my property until we're done."

Wyatt looked furious, but he spun around and headed out the front door, slamming it behind him.

"I'm not leavin' with him, Marco," I spat in fury. "Telling him he can stay is a waste of breath."

"He thinks we're doin' something dangerous and he's worried about you. I have to wonder if he's right." He shot me a cockeyed grin. "I'm tired of craning my neck to look up at you. Sit down so we're eye level."

I flopped on the chair, still furious. I suspected Marco might be right, but that still didn't give Wyatt the right to treat me like a child.

"Let's talk about the case for a minute," he said. "Wyatt accused us of considering Max a person of interest. Do *you* consider him a person of interest?"

"It would explain some of his behavior," I said, running my hand through my short hair. "But I can't believe he would hurt her," I added. "Either of them."

"You know you're not supposed to try to make the narrative fit the clues, right?" he asked gently. He paused and then said in a softer tone, "If this were an official investigation, I'd never be allowed to take part. They'd say I'm too close to a person of interest, and they'd be right. We're both too close to the situation. I've known Max for nearly twenty-five years, and I can't believe he'd do anything like this either."

Tears burned my eyes. "So what do we do? Do we stop looking?"

"No, but we need to be extra careful about how we handle Max. Be aware of our bias."

I saw the agony in his eyes. This was killing him. "You're a good man, Marco Roland, and a damned good detective. They're crazy for not taking you more seriously."

Emotion washed over his face, and he took a second before he said, "You're not so bad yourself. We make a good team." He shot a glance toward the front door. "He's not wrong that this is gettin' dangerous for you. Shane Jones was watchin' us at the garage, and it wouldn't have been hard for him to find us at the café. He could have followed you to Ewing. Maybe he even saw you at the nursing home. If he thinks you're gettin' close, you might be the next woman to disappear."

A lump of fear filled my gut. "I know."

"A sheriff deputy on medical leave disappearin' is gonna cause a stir, especially since I was shot in the Carson Purdy case and there are ties to Bart. But a waitress who's been in town for a month? If she disappears, they won't pay much attention. They'll figure you left town just like you dropped in, which means you're not safe."

"You want me to stop lookin' into this," I said, surprised at how hurt I felt.

"No," he said slowly. "I think it's too late for that. You're tied to it now, not to mention that I meant what I said—we make a good team."

"But you want me to go with Wyatt. That's why you told him to stay."

"If someone shows up lookin' for you, I'm not sure how much good I'll be at protectin' you."

"Maybe I don't need protecting," I countered. "I'm a damned good shot. And let's not forget that I was tryin' to protect you from Carson."

He flashed a tight grin. "True enough, but I still think you should go with him. Hank may be one-legged, but I suspect he won't put up with bullshit on his property, which will make him one hell of a bulldog."

Marco had no idea.

"And Wyatt would throw himself in front of a grenade to protect you."

I suspected he was right. "I'm not sure if we're going to get back together. If I leave with him for the sake of protection, then I'll feel like I'm using him."

"So tell him that up front." He leaned closer. "Tell him you're pissed about how he handled this, and you're not sure it's gonna work out. But I know Wyatt Drummond. He's as loyal as the day is long. It's one of his greatest strengths. It's also his greatest weakness."

The way he said that last sentence set off something in my brain. "You know more about what happened between Wyatt and his parents."

"You need to talk to Wyatt about that, Carly."

"I've tried," I confessed. "He knows some deep, dark secrets about my past. Things that could get me killed, yet he won't share a single thing with me."

Worry crinkled his eyes. "You're in another danger besides this situation?"

I released a harsh laugh. "Doesn't it seem strange to you that my car broke down and I just stayed?"

He cocked his head. "Your car didn't break down? You were a plant?"

"No, I actually *did* have the supreme bad luck of getting stranded here. And it was true I was stuck here, but you and I both know I could have left. In fact, I considered hopping on a bus and getting the hell out of here during Seth's murder investigation."

"But you stayed," he said. "Was it for Wyatt? Hank? Because you like Max, Ruth, and Tiny?"

"All of the above," I said quietly. "But I'm also hiding, Marco."

He drew in a short breath. "Are we talkin' a domestic violence situation, or are you runnin' away from a legal matter?"

"I've done nothing illegal," I said. "So you can wipe that concern from your conscience. It's more similar to the first. The people looking for me have the means to find me. Money. Resources." I leaned in closer and held his gaze. "There are no CCTV cameras in Drum. I have a new identity. I thought I would be relatively safe here, so I stayed." But that wasn't quite the full story, so I added, "But I only stayed because of the people. I could have gone off the grid somewhere else. At least I have friends here."

He studied me as though I'd sprouted a second head. "I have a ton of questions, but I won't ask most of them because you would have shared the information if you'd wanted me to have it, so let's go with this one. The way you said *relatively safe* makes me think your identity has been compromised. Has it?"

"Remember what I told you about running into Bart Drummond? He wants to meet with me next week. And the way he said my name…he knows it's not my real one. He knows I'm in hiding." When Marco didn't say anything, I added, "In hindsight, I should have seen it coming. He seemed intrigued by me at the funeral. It stands to reason that he would have had me investigated."

"And you think he's going to blackmail you with it?"

"Possibly. The other option is to give me up, but if he planned on turning me over, I'm not sure why he'd go to the trouble of warning me first. Besides, I doubt he's really interested in half a million dollars."

Marco blinked and then his eyes bugged out. *"Half a million dollars?"*

"Thinkin' about turnin' me in, Marco?" I asked in a dry tone, my accent slipping in.

He turned serious. "Who the hell wants you that badly, Carly?"

I remained silent. I realized he could find out easily enough, but the lack of internet or cell phone service would make it harder.

"How would Bart know someone's lookin' for you?"

"It's public information," I said. "A few weeks ago, the person hunting me offered a large reward for my 'safe' return." I used air quotes around *safe*.

"If they're willing to go public, surely there's no danger?"

I got to my feet. "Look, I realize it's a lot to take in, and I know you want more information. You have no idea how much I appreciate your restraint. But trust me when I say he will find a way to make it look like an accident. A car crash. A drug overdose. I won't last long once he has me back."

He ran a hand over his head, looking like he was about to be sick. "Jesus, Carly. Who the hell were you mixed up with? Must be one hell of an ex."

I released a bitter laugh. "You have no idea."

He frowned and pushed out a breath. "Let Wyatt take you home. I'll pick you up tomorrow morning at nine, and we'll get back to investigating. We can come up with a plan in the morning."

"As much as I'd like to think otherwise, you have no business going out tomorrow, Marco. You need to stay home and rest."

"I'll rest tonight." He planted his hands on the table and got up to stand on his right foot. "I'll pick you up at nine."

"Okay." I knew I should insist he stay home, but I'd go crazy sitting around all day, worried about Lula and Greta, and his warning hadn't fallen on deaf ears. It would be foolish of me to go out alone. I'd just have to make sure he took it easier tomorrow.

I picked up my purse and coat from the coffee table and headed for the door. Wyatt was leaning with his back against the front of his pickup truck. He pushed away when he saw me, but his gaze darkened as he took in Marco hopping out behind me and holding on to the doorframe.

"You be careful tonight, Carly," Marco called out. "Call me if you have any sign of trouble."

I knew exactly what he was up to—trying to stoke Wyatt's protective instinct.

"I don't need you to fight my battles, Marco," I called out as I marched toward Wyatt's truck.

I heard him chuckle.

Wyatt looked pissed, but he just stomped to his side of the truck and got inside as I did. Yep, he was pissed. He was usually eager to open car doors for me.

Marco waved with a grin as Wyatt started the truck and backed up. We were both silent until he pulled out onto the road.

"You gonna tell me what's goin' on?" he finally asked.

"You gonna treat me like a grown woman and not a four-year-old girl?" I countered.

"Carly…"

I shifted in my seat to face him. "I don't get it. A couple of nights ago, you trusted me to handle Todd Bingham on my own. Why don't you trust me with this?"

"It's not that I don't trust you," he said. "But I don't think you appreciate the danger you're puttin' yourself in."

"What made you so concerned about it? Your visit with Max?"

"That and your conversation about Shane Jones." He shrugged off my look of disapproval. "It's not like I was trying to eavesdrop. Marco's louder than an auctioneer. And he did tell me to wait right outside."

"Marco has a deputy friend looking into him."

"Why was this guy following you?" he asked. "Because his excuse for dropping by the garage was total bullshit."

"He wanted a carburetor?" I asked. He shot me a quick glance, his brow raised, and I explained, "I stopped by your office before I left, but your door was partially closed. I heard you on the phone asking about one, but I didn't wait because of Marco."

"Who looked just fine when I walked in a few minutes ago."

"Come on, Wyatt. You saw him behind the garage, and he got a lot worse after we left. I was so worried about him that I called his doctor, who told me to watch for signs of internal bleeding, which was why I went to Ewing for a blood pressure cuff. In any case, Marco slept for at least a couple of hours, and by the time I got back, he looked much better."

When he didn't respond, I said, "He was shot less than a

month ago. He had major surgery and his spleen was removed. He did too much today, and it wiped him out. He wasn't trying to pull a fast one on me, for whatever reason you've concocted in your head."

"Are you gonna stop investigatin' Lula's disappearance?"

"No," I said flatly. "Marco's going to pick me up tomorrow morning, and we're going to keep looking into it."

"Why don't you let the sheriff's department handle it?"

"Because they won't," I said, starting to get angry, but I knew my anger was only partially for him. A good portion of it was reserved for the sheriff's department. "Both Ginger and Angie at Watson's Café reported Greta's disappearance, and last I heard, they wouldn't look into it."

"They won't look into it *yet*," he said, "Junior told me, but the forty-eight hours should be up soon. They'll get started then."

"You really *believe* that? Because I've seen how the sheriff's department works around here. Even if they do take the case, I doubt they'll give it half as much attention as we've given it."

"It's too dangerous, Carly."

It *was* dangerous, and I wasn't stupid. It scared the snot out of me.

But I was getting used to being scared. I'd been running for months now, and I'd risked my life attempting to find justice for Seth. Fear was a given. And something else was motivating me now, something I couldn't possibly ignore. A lump filled my throat.

"Greta's gone because of me, Wyatt." My voice broke. "Someone took her because I was asking questions about Lula. I'm responsible for her being taken."

I'd been trying not to think about it, but the thought had been there with me all day.

His voice softened. "You are *not* responsible, Carly."

"No one would have taken her if I hadn't been asking questions."

He was silent for a moment, and when he spoke, all the fight had bled out of him. "Do you really think Max is part of all this?"

"He's part of it in some way. We just haven't figured out how."

And part of me didn't want to.

CHAPTER TWENTY-FOUR

We were silent for the rest of the drive. I was trying to make all the information Marco and I had found fit together, and I was sure Wyatt was thinking about what we'd told him. He might be estranged from his brother, but it was obvious that he cared.

When Wyatt pulled up in front of Hank's house, he turned off the engine and started to open the door but stopped when he realized I wasn't moving.

He shifted sideways to face me, the vinyl under his legs creaking.

I kept my gaze fixed on the windshield. "Why are you and Max at odds? You were close as kids. What happened to tear you apart?"

He sat still for so long I didn't think he was going to answer, but he finally said, "It's not one thing. It's the culmination of a lot of things. Our father always treated us differently. Max called me the golden boy. He claimed I could do no wrong in our father's eyes, while Max was always in trouble."

He shifted in his seat again, stretching out his legs and resting his wrist on the steering wheel while he released a bitter laugh. "It was true. Our father always made it clear I would take over the family businesses, and he prepared me for it from a young age. He didn't spend any time on Max. In my father's eyes, there was no point to it. So Max saw no point in trying to follow the rules.

"Believe it or not, we were still close. We were still brothers, and I understood his pain." He took a breath. "It helped when Max went away to college. Even though he had Marco as a tether to this place, it was the first time he'd finally had a chance to live his life out from underneath the shadow of the Drum legacy. Nobody gave a shit that his family owned the middling Drummond distillery, and the logging business was long gone. Max was finally free, and he thrived there. He was making plans to move to Nashville with Marco after graduation. He was happy."

"So what happened? Your arrest?"

"Like I said, a lot of things. He resented that our father forced him to come home to take over the bar."

"But how could he force him?" I asked. "He was in his last semester of college. If Bart threatened to cut him off financially, Max could have found a job to help cover the rent and food."

"Max's relationship with our father has always been complicated. While Max hated the way he was treated, part of him still wanted our father to love him. So when Bart came callin', my brother came runnin' home."

I shook my head. "No. It wasn't that easy for him. He didn't come back until your mother went to see him."

Wyatt's body froze. "What?"

"You didn't know?" I asked. "That's the story Marco told me. He got your dad's call and blew him off. But your mother came to see him, and he went on a bender. He left to go home a few days after that."

Wyatt sat still, staring out the windshield. "I have to go."

"You have to go talk to Max?" I waited several seconds for him to respond, and when he didn't, I shook my head and reached for the door handle. "Screw you, Wyatt." Jerking the door open, I jumped out and slammed it shut behind me.

He was out of the truck and at the front of the hood before I got there. "What the hell, Carly? You want me to open up, and I did, but it's still not enough?"

Shaking with frustration, I shouted, "No! It's not enough. I asked a yes or no question, and you refused to answer. A yes or no question about whether you're going to see your brother!"

"This is complicated!" he shouted. "And believe it or not, it's not all about you!"

I took a step back as though he'd slapped me. "I don't want it to be all about me, Wyatt. I want it to be about you too, but you won't let me in!" I released a pent-up groan of frustration. "Go see Max, but don't come back until you're actually willing to talk, because I'm tired of playing this stupid game."

I brushed past him and raced up the porch steps, then went inside and slammed the door behind me.

Hank stared up at me from his recliner, his mouth open, but I didn't give him an explanation, just stomped into my room and paced and stewed for a good ten minutes. When I finally settled down, I took a deep breath and headed out to the kitchen.

"I'll start heating up your dinner," I said as I walked through the living room. An old movie was playing on the television.

I poured a glass of water from the pitcher in the fridge and stared out the window while I sipped it.

I had to leave Drum.

I'd lost my job. I'd broken up with Wyatt, and I suspected Bart knew who I was. I'd be stupid to stay, but the thought of leaving Hank broke my heart.

And *that* was what finally broke me.

I started to cry.

"Carly, come out here and tell me what's goin' on," Hank called out.

I had to tell him sometime, so I might as well do it while I was already upset.

Carrying my glass of water, I went out to the living room and sat down on the sofa next to the recliner.

"Why aren't you at work?" he asked.

"Max fired me."

"*What?*" he asked with a mixture of disbelief and anger. "Why?"

"He's upset that I'm looking for Lula."

"Were you usin' work time to look for her?"

I blinked in surprise. "No."

"Then those aren't grounds to fire you. Why doesn't he want you to find her?"

I released a short laugh. "You really know how to cut through the bullshit."

He lifted his shoulders into a shrug and waited for my answer.

"I think he either knows something about why she's gone or had something to do with it. In fact, he was drunk off his ass this morning when Marco went by to talk to him, and we had to call Tiny to close the tavern."

"So you're really not workin' because the bar is closed."

"No," I said. "He fired me."

"While he was drunk. What are the chances he'll remember?"

"I'd say pretty good considering Wyatt stopped by to see why he was closed, and Max told him he'd fired me."

He pursed his lips. "What happened with you and Wyatt out there?"

"Same old shit, and shame on me for still fallin' for it." I set the water glass on the coffee table. "Hank, I need to ask you some more questions about Lula's parents."

His eyes widened in surprise. "What does that matter now?"

I sighed and sat back. "I don't know, but I have this gut feeling it does." I crossed my legs on the sofa. "I ran into Emily and Bart Drummond in Ewing this afternoon. Emily mentioned that Louise came to their house right before she shot her husband. She was there to see Bart."

He turned his attention to the television.

"But Emily said Louise also mentioned your name." I took a long look at his profile. "Walter Baker was working for you, wasn't he?" Thelma had sure thought so, anyway.

He released a snort. "Whoever told you that? That man was too stupid to tie his own shoelaces."

His reaction was so unrehearsed that I had to believe Thelma had gotten it wrong.

"Why did you look so surprised when I told you Louise was getting out of jail?"

"Because I hadn't thought of her in years," he said, shifting his gaze back to me. "Hearing you mention her name caught me off guard."

"I know you have a past, Hank. I learned that when we invited Bingham to take that dead body away."

"He wasn't the first man I killed, girlie, and I doubt he'll be the last."

I wasn't surprised by the first part of his statement, but I wasn't prepared for the rest of it. "Who else do you plan on killing?"

His gaze darkened. "Whoever shows up lookin' for you."

A cold chill washed through my body. "What makes you think someone's going to come looking for me?"

"I know you're runnin' from someone, and I'm prepared to deal with 'em when they darken my door."

A lump filled my throat. "You don't even know what or who I'm runnin' from."

"I don't need to know," he said in a gruff voice. "You're kin, and kin sticks together."

The irony of his statement brought a round of fresh tears.

He looked dismayed. "I didn't mean to make you cry again."

How had I been lucky enough to find this man? Then again, it was his grandson's death that had brought us together, and that hadn't been good luck for anyone. "Not all kin sticks together, Hank. I'm running from my father."

His cheeks turned red. "Your *daddy*? Why?"

"It's a long story, but I'll tell you this much: in August, I found out he's part of a crime syndicate in Dallas, and I took off and went into hiding. He needs me back to protect his share, and he'll do anything to get me. A few weeks ago, he offered a five-hundred-thousand-dollar reward for my 'safe' return, but I know I won't be alive for long after he gets me back."

"Did you see something you weren't supposed to?"

"It's complicated," I said with a sigh. "But yeah. That's part of it. I also found out that he's not my biological father. He found out when I was a kid and had my mother killed."

"You're thinkin' about runnin' again."

I locked eyes with him. "I lost my job. It will be awkward dealing with Wyatt, and I think Bart Drummond has figured out my secret."

He sucked in a breath. "The first two don't matter as they seem to at the moment," he said. "It's Old Man Drummond we need to worry about."

"I'll have to leave. I won't have a choice," I said, my voice thick with emotion.

"Not necessarily, girlie. Not necessarily. What makes you think Bart Drummond knows?"

I told Hank what Bart had said in the pharmacy and about his invitation to come to his house next week.

"He's not gonna pull anything before he meets with ya," Hank said, "but I suspect you're right. He knows something. Maybe we'd do best to see what he has to say, then go from there."

"You don't think I should run?"

His lips pursed. "Sometimes it's better to fight the devil you know, and I know Bart Drummond. Bart's ruled the roost around here for far too long. It's about time for someone to stand up to him. Besides, I ain't ready to give you up yet."

I smiled, but he was blurry through my tears. "Thank you, Hank."

I slid off the sofa and knelt next to his chair and hugged him. It occurred to me that maybe Wyatt wasn't the only one who wanted to knock Bart off his throne. There might be others in this town who would help me.

He was stiff at first then softened, wrapping his arms around me and patting my back. "There, there, girlie. You're my kin now. I'll take care of ya, one way or the other."

I pulled back to look into his face, wondering what that meant.

He must have understood because he gave me a tight smile and said, "If I think you need to run, I'll tell you. I'm selfish enough to want you to stay, but care about you enough to tell you to go if I think it's safer."

"Thank you, Hank. I really like living with you."

The phone began to ring, and I glanced into the kitchen.

"You better get that," he said.

But what if it was Wyatt? I decided the chances of that were slim. He'd taken off like a bee had bitten his bottom. He was on some secret mission or other, and I was probably far from his thoughts.

I got up and reached it by the fourth ring. "Hello?"

"You need to get your ass in to work," Ruth said in a snippy tone. "I'm opening in a half hour."

"I can't, Ruth. Max fired me."

"Too damn bad for Max. I'm the manager, and I overrule him. Get your ass in here." Then she hung up.

Replacing the phone on the hook, I said, "I guess I'm going to work."

CHAPTER TWENTY-FIVE

Max's was already open when I pulled into the parking lot in back. Tiny was in the kitchen, and I stopped in the doorway as I tied my apron. "What's going on, Tiny?"

He stood in front of the grill and shot a look over his shoulder. "Ruth went on a warpath when she found out we were closed. She didn't want to miss out on Saturday night profits."

"Where's Max?"

"Wyatt was upstairs with him when I showed up, and they left soon after."

"Both of them?" I asked in surprise.

"Yep. Got the impression Max wouldn't be back tonight."

"Where's Sugar?" It was Saturday night. We were bound to be busy.

He shot me a wry grin. "Ruth decided if she was takin' over, she was goin' full tilt. She called Sugar up and fired her ass."

Not that it wasn't warranted, but I would have expected Ruth to at least have the decency to fire her face-to-face. Which didn't bode well for her disposition this evening.

I shot a glance toward the dining room. "I take it Ruth's still pissed?"

His eyebrows shot up and he gave me a pointed look that suggested it was a stupid question.

"Is she mad at me for closing the tavern this morning?"

"No, I told her it was Marco's call, but she's still not happy."

I sucked in a breath. "Okay. Wish me luck."

"Just remember she's more bark than bite."

"Tell that to Sugar," I called out over my shoulder.

I walked out into the dining room and took a second to assess the situation. Three tables were filled with customers, and Ruth was behind the bar, filling a mug at the beer taps.

"I'm here," I said, hurrying up to the counter. "What do you need me to do?"

Her gaze jerked up to mine. "I've taken all the drink orders and the food order for table three."

"Got it." I hurried off toward table eight, but I only made it a couple of steps.

"Carly," she said.

I turned back to face her.

She started to say something, then stopped and started again. "I don't know what's goin' on between you and Max, but we'll get it straightened out." Her eyes turned glassy. "I need you. Max does too. We'll make it right."

"Thanks, Ruth."

It felt weird without Max there. I was used to him being off for a few hours at a time, but I'd never worked a full shift without him. We'd gotten a late start on the dinner shift, and I'd kept busy for several hours, then went right into the drinking crowd.

Jerry showed up at around eight and sat at the bar. I heard him ask Ruth why we were closed earlier, and she told him that Max had been under the weather but he'd encouraged us to carry on without him for the night. When a few customers asked me about Max's absence, I told them the same story. Everyone seemed to buy it, and I couldn't help thinking our lies were only enabling Max's drinking.

I'd think that through later.

Bingham walked in at around nine, shockingly alone. He stood at the door for a moment, his gaze slowly tracking from Ruth at the bar to me at the other end of the room.

Was he casing the joint because he was up to no good? Had I pissed him off enough for him to want retaliation?

My heart was in my stomach, and I could barely focus on taking my order as I watched Bingham approach the bar to speak to Ruth.

Her eyes widened and then flicked to me. She said something to him, and he sauntered across the room and sat in a booth. He took a relaxed position, but his gaze was intense when it landed on me.

Ruth beckoned me over, and I finished taking my order before I headed to the bar and handed her my ticket.

She looked it over and started filling a beer. "Bingham wants to talk to you."

Was he here about Lula?

She scanned the room, and I could tell she was tense from the set of her shoulders. "You haven't had your break yet. I told him that I can spare you for ten minutes max."

"A break?" I asked. "Have you taken a break? No. That's because we're too busy for *either one of us* to take a break."

Her lips pressed into a thin line. "Are you in trouble with Bingham?"

"I don't think so, but I *did* ask him about buying my junk car, and we couldn't reach an agreement on price. Maybe that's why he's here." Despite my argument with Max, I figured he was probably right about Ruth: it would probably be best if she didn't know I was looking into Lula's disappearance.

Confusion flickered in her eyes. "I thought Wyatt was takin' care of your old car."

"Yeah, well, I'm a strong, independent woman…and I decided it wouldn't hurt to get on Bingham's good side."

"Still, it's unusual to see him alone. He's a pack animal—the alpha, sure, but a pack animal nonetheless. This is…weird. I don't like it." She set the drinks on the counter. "Max isn't here, but Tiny's in the back."

I flashed her a grin. "You're worried about me."

"Of course I am. Just… be careful."

I considered making Bingham wait, just to prove he couldn't control me like he controlled so many others, but his presence was making Ruth and a few of the other patrons nervous. Better to deal with him ASAP and get him out the door.

I dropped off the drinks Ruth had pulled, then headed straight for Bingham's booth.

"Have a seat, Ms. Moore," he said in a slow drawl when I stopped next to the table. "We have some things to discuss."

I stuffed down my pride and slid into the seat opposite him.

"See there?" he said with a wide grin. "No mouthin' off. Just doin' as you're told. That wasn't so hard, was it?"

I clenched my fists under the table. "I'm here as you requested. You have five minutes."

His grin widened. "You like to think you're in control, but there's a long-ass ladder to climb to get to this level, Ms. Moore. The sooner you learn your place, the *healthier* you'll be."

A threat to be sure, but what was he threatening me about? Shane Jones?

Marco had said something about Bingham's limits, and I

knew I was in danger of pushing them. But I needed to talk with him. He was my number one suspect, and he was sitting right in front of me.

One thing I'd learned about Bingham was that he'd take anything he was given and many things he wasn't. If I kowtowed to him, I'd get nothing. "If you don't like me sniffin' around your boy, then perhaps he shouldn't be followin' me so closely."

His eyes narrowed. "What the hell are you talkin' about?"

"Shane Jones." Before I could think better of it, I blurted out, "I know you had him stalking Greta. Did you have him take her too?"

"What *the hell* are you talkin' about?" he repeated, sitting up straighter.

"Don't play stupid, Bingham. It's not a good look for you. I know Shane Jones is working at the nursing home in Ewing to keep an eye on Greta Hightower, and he followed her to the café last week to ask about Lula. She came back and disappeared again, so it stands to reason he took Greta in an attempt to recover something from Lula. Or maybe he thought Lula had given something to her."

He reached over and grabbed my wrist, squeezing tight, his eyes blazing with fury. "I'm gonna ask you one last time what the fuck you are talkin' about."

I glanced pointedly at my arm, then back up at him. His grip was tight enough to leave bruises. "You're damn lucky Max isn't here. Now get your grimy hand off me."

He gave me another squeeze for good measure and then released me.

So this was a pissing contest. Good thing I hadn't peed for hours.

"Are you trying to claim Shane Jones isn't one of your men?"

"He's not."

I reached into my jeans pocket and pulled out my cell phone, then opened it to the photos. "You don't know this guy?"

I held up my screen so he could see the grainy image of Shane's headshot.

"Why the hell would I?" he barked.

I narrowed my eyes. "Are you lying to me?"

His dark brown eyes locked on mine. "No."

Pushing out a breath, I exited out of the photos.

"Why would you think I took the waitress from Watson's?"

"Because she's missing, and currently you're my number one suspect."

To my surprise, he burst out laughing, which scared a couple sitting at a table a row away. They got up, snatched up their coats, and left.

I gestured toward them. "They just walked out without payin'. You're gonna cover their tab."

"The fuck I am," he said, but his tone wasn't as gruff as before. It was almost droll. "Let me get this straight. You think I took Greta Hightower to question her about Lula. Why the fuck would I give a shit about Lula?"

He was the very last person I should tell about her pregnancy, so I had to take a different tack. I still hadn't asked him about the packages, and it seemed like the time was right.

"Did you have Lula deliver a package for you?" I asked. "Maybe you're waiting on payment."

His eyes darkened again. "No one, and I mean *no one*, questions my business dealin's."

"Greta said Lula's been delivering packages when she goes away. Greta has no idea what's in them or who's behind it."

He grinned, but his eyes were intense and unamused. "So basically, you're sayin' she doesn't know shit."

"Obviously someone *thinks* Greta knows. That's why she's missing."

But saying it out loud, the theory started to ravel. Why would Lula's kidnappers have cared about getting information from Greta? Or had they taken her to keep her quiet about Shane's snooping? But I wasn't sure that made sense. It stood to reason that Greta had already told her friends about her odd encounter with him at the café. Sure, he could make her disappear, but it would only draw more suspicion, not minimize it.

What if there were *two* parties involved in this? What if the first party had Lula and the second party wanted the packages and took Greta thinking she might know about them?

I had to rethink everything.

Because the more I thought about it, the more I believed that the person who took Greta didn't have Lula.

So who did?

Bingham looked me in the eyes. "And you think this Shane Jones took her."

I shook myself out of my musings. "Yeah."

Of that I was sure.

He glanced over at the bar. "Do you think he took Lula too?"

Did I share my theory with Bingham? I suspected the information highway with Bingham was a lot like Wyatt's—one way. Better to keep as much to myself as possible. "I don't know yet. There are more clues to follow with Greta. I'm hoping it leads us to Lula too."

"Us? You and the deputy?" He grinned, but it didn't reach his eyes. "You been deputized, Ms. Moore?"

"No. I'm just a concerned citizen lookin' for two missing women, with a deputy on medical leave who has been kind enough to come along as backup." I purposefully diminished Marco's role. The last thing he wanted was for Bingham to set his sights on him. I cocked my head, then added, "Does Tim Hines work for you?"

"Do you think I go around publicly announcing all my associates?"

"Fair enough," I said. "Then tell me this—did Greta come to you last August or the first of September asking for your help with Tim Hines?"

"And if she did? Why would you want to know?"

"If she did, I suspect she gave you information in return for making her life easier. You were dealing with Carson Purdy's gang, and I've heard Greta's sister was working for them."

"And your point?"

"I need to know if you got Hines to back off," I said. "The details of the transaction are between the rest of you. I'm only interested in whether he's a credible suspect."

"In the waitress's disappearance?"

"She has a name. Do her the courtesy of using it."

He glanced at the bar again. "Hines moved on soon after *Greta* left him. I'm not at liberty to go into the details."

I pushed out a breath. "Is there any chance he decided to get her back? Maybe kidnapped her to help convince her?"

"Hines is with someone else. Anything is possible, but it's not very probable."

I nodded. "What do you know about Lula's mother killing her father?"

His gaze jerked back to mine and a flash of surprise filled his eyes. "Now, what makes you want to go into such ancient history?"

"I think it might have something to do with what's going on now."

He chuckled. "You're reachin'."

"Maybe," I conceded. "But I'm checking it out nonetheless."

"Rumor has it her mother shot her father."

"That's what's floating around, but I suspect you know more."

He winked. "Lula's father's murder wasn't exactly pillow talk when we were together, if you know what I mean."

"I highly doubt Lula would want to chat it up with you about her father's murder…considering your involvement." This was another reach. I didn't know that he was involved, but I figured this was a possible way to find out.

His eyes darkened, and I involuntarily shrunk back in my seat. "What are you talkin' about?"

Not an admission, but definitely not a denial. "Your father was dead. You were trying to build your kingdom, brick by brick. Hank and Bart were the big men in town. The guns to go after."

"And your point?"

"I suspect Louise Baker had a reason for telling Lula to stay away from you, and it had nothing to do with your reputation now."

He glared at me for several seconds. "The past is in the past. Where it belongs."

"Why would Walter Baker drown his daughter? Did he have a history of abuse?"

"How the hell would I know?" he snapped.

"When I mentioned the whole thing to Hank a few days ago, he said there was more to the story of a mother protecting her daughter. And Emily Drummond said Louise came by looking for Bart the day she shot her husband." I decided to leave any mention of Hank out for now. "What do you think she wanted?"

"Why don't you ask Louise Baker herself?" he sneered.

I paused. Why hadn't I thought of that? But that would mean going to Nashville, and that wasn't happening in the near future.

He clasped his hands on the tabletop. "Chalmers is right.

There's more to the Baker murder. Someone must have had it out for Louise, because they made damn sure she was put away for a long time."

"Like they wanted to get her out of the way?" I asked.

His brow furrowed in thought. "I always thought it was a vendetta. Louise Baker pissed off some people, and as corrupt as the whole justice system is… it's not outside the realm of possibility someone paid someone else to make sure the sentence was a stiff one."

I decided to go for broke. "What if it was something else? What if Louise killed Walter for Bart Drummond?"

Shock covered his face, and then a knowing look filled his eyes, as though I'd just given him a long-lost piece to an unfinished puzzle. "One of his famous favors."

"You never suspected?" I asked.

He grinned. "Turns out you're pretty helpful, Ms. Moore. Perhaps havin' you around isn't such a bad thing after all."

I hadn't realized that he considered me troublesome. "Then you can repay me by giving me four thousand dollars for my car."

He burst out laughing again. "That piece of shit isn't worth more than two grand."

"I just gave you a useful piece of information, so perhaps that deserves compensation, but back to Louise… why would Bart Drummond want Walter dead? Someone told me Walter used to work for Hank, but when I asked him about it, he told me Walter was too stupid to do anything for him."

So why had Louise brought up Hank's name when she'd gone to the Drummonds' house?

Shit. "Oh…*Louise* was working for Hank."

"I suspected but didn't know for certain," Bingham said. "Even so, Hank didn't have a reason to want Walter dead…that I know of, anyway, and I can't think of a single reason Bart would. It's an intriguin' story, but that's all it is. A story."

"What did Louise look like?"

He snorted. "You think I'm carryin' a photo of her around in my pocket?"

"Lula's a pretty girl. Was her mother pretty? Did she get a lot of male attention?"

"Is that your delicate way of asking if she was a slut? No. She slept with her share of men, but she did so one at a time. Everybody was shocked as hell when she married Walter Baker. He was dumb as a stump and worthless to boot. Louise was the brains of the two, so if anyone was doin' a job for Hank, it was her."

I wasn't sure what to do with this information, so I added it to the growing pile of clues and facts in my head, hoping to sort it out later.

"I didn't have anything to do with either of them disappearin'," he said, more earnest than I'd ever seen him, "and I definitely didn't know about the packages Lula was deliverin', but something's obviously goin' on under my nose." He paused. "If you come across information that you think I'll find useful, I'd be happy to pay for it." For a brief moment, I could see concern in his eyes, and I realized he still cared about her. Then he added, "Lest you think I'm planning to retaliate against the girl, I assure you that I won't touch a hair on her head. Someone was usin' her, and I know who."

"Her mother?"

"She's a master manipulator, and I can guarantee you that Lula wasn't doin' shit without Louise's say-so."

Which meant I really needed to talk to Louise. I just didn't know how to make that happen.

The look on Bingham's face suggested he was done, and the

customers were getting restless.

"This has been very helpful, Mr. Bingham. Thank you. Now if we could reach an agreement on my car, it would be a very fruitful evening."

"Thirty-five hundred," he said. "Not a penny more."

"Thirty-seven fifty," I countered. "And we keep the lines of communication open."

His brow shot up. "You want to exchange information again?"

I had two choices when it came to Bart Drummond—I could run or I could stay and fight. Despite his initial promise, Wyatt clearly wasn't inclined to include me in his plan, which meant I had to make a plan of my own. But fighting Bart Drummond would mean sinking to his level, and if I had to fight dirty, I'd need temporary allies like Bingham. Maybe I was being naïve, but I didn't have a lot of time to second-guess myself.

"I'm going to bring Bart Drummond down," I said, "and I might need more information from you to help me make that happen."

"Why are you goin' after Drummond?" he asked, all pretense gone.

Obviously I wasn't going to tell Bingham the real reason—the last thing I needed was yet another dangerous man knowing who I was—so I hoped my explanation would convince him. "Because he reminds me of a bigger asshole I know, and I'm considering takin' Bart Drummond down for practice before I take on the other."

True enough.

He grinned. "*That*, Ms. Moore, is an agenda we can both agree upon." He extended his hand. "Four thousand for your car, and we have a deal."

I shook his hand, knowing full well what I was getting into.

Hank was right. It was better to deal with the devil you know.

CHAPTER TWENTY-SIX

"I'll have an associate drop by with the check on Monday," Bingham said. "Just let Wyatt Drummond know that my men will be pickin' it up."

"Will do, but don't you want to know about the title?"

He grinned. "I don't need the title."

"Okay…"

He started to get up, then settled back on his seat. "You got paper and a pen?"

"You giving me a bill of sale?" I asked as I pulled my order pad and pen out of my pocket and pushed them across the table.

"No." He wrote down a phone number. "This is my direct number. It's a satellite phone. I get reception just about everywhere."

A satellite phone? Why hadn't I thought about that? Bart had brought a cell carrier to town, but Bingham probably wouldn't want to use it on principle alone, not to mention it didn't reach far outside of Drum city limits. "How much do those cost?"

He laughed as he slid the ticket over to me. "More than you can afford. Don't call this number just to shoot the shit. You better have something important to discuss. And don't share it with another damn person. It's for you only. Got it?"

I picked up the paper and folded it in half. "Got it."

Then he stood and walked out the door.

I got up and started making the rounds. When I made it to the counter, Ruth gave me a look of disbelief. "Well? What did he want?"

"I was right," I said. "He was here to make a deal about my car. Four thousand."

Her eyes narrowed. "Todd Bingham came here all *alone* to make a deal about your car?"

"Yeah."

"And it took y'all that much time to reach a deal?"

I shrugged. "What can I say? It was a tough negotiation."

"What were you showing him on your phone?" she asked suspiciously.

I hadn't seen Shane in the tavern the night before, but it occurred to me that *she* might have. I slid my phone out of my pocket and pulled up his photo. "Did you see this guy in here last night?"

She took the phone and squinted at it. "Your phone takes crap pictures."

I rolled my eyes. "Yeah, I know, but did you see him?"

She pushed out a breath and held the phone closer to her face. "Maybe?" She looked up at me. "Where the hell did you take this photo?"

"Greener Pastures nursing home in Ewing."

"Are you lookin' for a replacement for Wyatt?"

"At the nursing home?" I asked in disbelief. "No, but I think this guy kidnapped Greta."

Her mouth dropped open. "Greta from Watson's Café?"

"Yeah." Which wouldn't mean much to her unless she knew

everything else. I'd thought it best to keep my worry about Lula from her, but maybe that was a mistake. Ruth knew a lot about Drum and the people here. She might be able to help. Besides which, she was my friend, and it felt wrong to keep this from her. It concerned her too. I took a deep breath, then added, "And it's somehow connected to Lula."

Her eyes narrowed. "What are you talkin' about?"

"Lula didn't just run off this time. Someone took her. Even Marco thinks so. We've been trying to figure out what happened to her, and after we questioned Greta, she disappeared too. She came here last night to talk to me, not Max. She answered some questions about Lula, but then she saw something that scared her, and I had Max walk her out to her car. But she never went home, and her sister and her coworkers say she's not dating anyone, so they have no idea where she is."

Worry filled Ruth's eyes. "Did you talk to her cousin?"

"Ginger? Yeah. And I even went to Greener Pastures to talk to her nana, which is where I got the photo." I pointed to the picture on the screen and explained what I'd learned about Shane Jones, holding back that I'd seen him today at the garage.

"So he was stalking her?"

"I think *he* thinks she knows something about Lula."

She stared at me in disbelief. "Like what?"

I knew police usually held back information, and it didn't seem like a good time to tell her about Lula's packages. "I don't know, but he's looking for something."

Frowning, she looked at the photo again. "I think I may have seen him a few months ago, but his name wasn't Shane. It was Charlie. I don't know his last name. He came in with Dwight Henderson."

I gasped. That was the link I needed.

Dwight Henderson had been part of Carson Purdy's gang.

We got busy again after that and stayed that way until well after midnight. We closed at one, and I realized Max still hadn't returned.

"Should we be worried?" I asked.

"Normally, I'd say no," Ruth said. "But in this instance, I don't know. Tiny said he left with Wyatt. He's never done that before. Why don't you call Wyatt and ask him?"

I shook my head. "I can't. We broke up."

Her mouth dropped open. "For real?"

I nodded.

Worry creased the corners of her eyes. "Does this mean you're leavin' Drum?"

"I'm not just here for Wyatt. I like living with Hank. And I like working here with you and Tiny and Max. If I still have a job." A lump filled my throat. "I want to make things right with Max. I hate being at odds with him."

She put her hand on my arm. "Don't you worry. We'll make it right." She gave me a little squeeze, then said, "Now, what happened with you and Wyatt?"

I'd kept so much from her, I wanted to be as honest as I could about this without giving too much away. "Wyatt keeps his past locked up tighter than the gold at Fort Knox. He won't tell me hardly anything. Nothing about his past girlfriends. His family. Not even why he's at odds with his father and Max."

She started to say something, but I sighed and held up my hand. "Before you tell me that we've only been together a month, I'd like to point out that I've shared very deep, intimate things about myself, and he hasn't even come *close* to reciprocating."

She tilted her head and gave me an *are you finished* look. "I was *tryin'* to say that the very same thing was part of what broke us up. He'd gone out with Heather for years. They broke up, and about a month later we started seein' each other. We were together for only about three months, but he never told me why they'd broken up, or anything about anything. It was like he was dropped onto Planet Earth without a past. It's hard to get close to someone who won't share his life. And then I found him kissing Heather in the back room." A wry grin twisted her lips. "And *that* was the other part of what broke us up."

My mouth parted as her words sunk in. His reticence to share his past hadn't come out of some need to protect me, and this had all gone down before his time in jail, so it wasn't just that his incarceration had changed him. This was a pattern.

"That's part of my beef with Lula," she continued. "I don't dislike her, really. It's more that I don't trust her. I can't help but think Wyatt never opened up to me because I was the filler until he got back with Heather. Why waste his time and make himself vulnerable? Right or wrong, between her runnin' off and keepin' her business to herself, I can't help thinkin' it would be a waste of my time to get to know Lula better."

While I understood why she felt that way, I wondered how deeply Wyatt had hurt her for her to still be so affected.

She pushed out a sigh of exhaustion. "Go home and get some rest. Since we're runnin' with just three of us, we'll open at four tomorrow. Enjoy your partial day off."

We walked out to the parking lot together, and Ruth followed me home until I turned off at Hank's. While we'd never discussed that I might be in danger, it was like she was making sure I got home safely. It made me even more grateful for her friendship.

I was exhausted, but my thoughts kept tossing around, refusing to let me sleep until well into the night. I had set my alarm for seven thirty, but I hit the snooze button a few too many times and woke up after eight.

Hank was on the porch again, so I took a quick shower and

washed my hair and blow-dried it into loose, fluffy waves, then went out to make him some oatmeal and fruit.

I brought his food out on a tray and set it on the small table between the chairs.

"You don't get too cold out here?" I asked. "I can get you another blanket."

"Stop your fussin'. I'm fine."

We were silent for a few moments, watching the birds, before I said, "I'm goin' out with Marco again, so I need to change your compression bandage before I leave."

"I already did it," he grumped, then shoveled a spoonful of oatmeal into his mouth.

"Then I want to take a look at it before I go."

"I've got to learn how to do some of this myself," he said. "You're workin' doubles and cookin' and cleanin' and takin' care of me." He turned to look at me. "Since Ginger's gonna help out a few days a week, I don't think we need Wyatt comin' out here anymore. He upsets you too much."

"But you like Wyatt. He keeps you company while I'm workin'."

"And maybe he can come back at some point, but for now, I think it's best all the way around if he's not hangin' around."

"Hank...I'm sorry. I feel bad."

"Don't feel bad. It ain't nothin'."

It was plenty of something.

"Hank," I said carefully. "I have some follow-up questions after our chat last night."

"Okay..." He sounded leery.

"I know you said Walter Baker never worked for you, but what about Louise?"

He sat perfectly still while the birds on the feeder released a melodic call.

"Hank?"

"I don't like dredgin' up old memories."

"And I hate to make you dredge them, but this is important."

"She worked for me some. She helped process the pot after it was harvested and bag it up. I fired her because I suspected she was spyin' on me for Drummond." He took a sip of his coffee, then made a face. "Cold."

"I'll get you a fresh cup, but first tell me when she worked for you in relation to the murder."

He took another sip of the cold coffee, and his look of disgust was so dramatic I knew he was stalling.

"Hank."

"I fired her the day before it happened."

Oh crap. "So when she showed up at the Drummonds' looking for Bart and mentioned your name, it was because she was letting him know she was no longer in a position to spy for him."

"Likely," he admitted.

"So she *did* ask Bart for a favor," I said, not all that surprised. "And the payment was to spy on you. But what did she get in return?"

"Hell if I know," Hank said. "She could have just been reporting to him for the hell of it."

"You seriously have no idea?" I asked.

"It all happened over a decade ago, girlie. You need to let it go."

I could see Marco's SUV through the trees next to the road. Hank was going to luck out of the rest of this conversation. At least for now.

"You got something goin' with the Roland kid?" he asked with plenty of attitude.

"No. We're just friends lookin' for another friend." Or two.

"I'm not sure when I'll be back, but there should be enough leftovers for dinner tonight. I'll make a pot of chili tomorrow."

Marco pulled onto the property and drove toward the house. When he stopped, he rolled down his window. "You ready?"

Hank looked fit to be tied. "Don't you know it's not polite to pull up to a lady's house and honk, expecting her to run out for your date?"

Marco's eyes widened.

"Hank, I told you it wasn't a date," I said in exasperation. I sent Marco an apologetic glance. "I'll run in to get my bag."

I brought Hank's dirty dishes inside, setting the oatmeal bowl in the sink and filling it with water while I got him a fresh cup of coffee. Then I grabbed my bag and purse and headed out the door.

"Maybe don't have Wyatt stay away today," I said. "It's gonna be a long day all by yourself."

"If you're gonna keep gettin' rides, then I can start drivin' again," he said. "It'll be nice to get out. Maybe go to church."

I blinked in surprise. "You want to go to church?"

He'd never once mentioned it.

"What? You think I'm gonna catch on fire if I cross the threshold?" he grumped, his gaze firmly on Marco.

"Of course not, but I could have taken you. It's part of my job. And I'll be getting my own car soon enough," I said, handing him the fresh cup of coffee. "I sold my old one to Todd Bingham last night for four thousand dollars. We're going to Ewing today. Maybe I'll look for a new car while I'm there." Although I had no idea how Hank would go about driving without a right leg. I'd call the doctor's office tomorrow.

Hank gave me a frown. Did he think I was more likely to leave if I had my own car? I leaned over and kissed his cheek.

"Thanks for caring, Hank. I haven't had someone who cared for me like this for a very long time."

Not since my mother.

He gave me a warm smile. "Be safe today. I have a feelin' you're pokin' some big hornets' nests with sticks."

That was twice I'd been told this very thing, and boy was it true.

"You know it," I said with a grin, then bounded down the steps and got into Marco's Explorer.

When I got inside, Marco said, "Did I hear you say you sold your car to Bingham last night?" He shot me a dark look. "Did you go out to his property alone?"

"No. Ruth opened the tavern around six and called me into work. He came by to see me. And he was all alone."

He backed up the SUV and headed to the road. "That's not like him."

"Yep. I asked him about Shane Jones and showed him my photo, but he claims Shane doesn't work for him. However, I showed the photo to Ruth and she *does* remember him. He came in a few months back with Dwight Henderson."

"The guy who worked at Mobley Funeral Home?"

"That's the one, but Ruth knew the friend as Charlie. We know that Dwight was having drugs smuggled into the area in caskets delivered from Atlanta. We need to ask Pete Mobley, the funeral home director, if he recognizes Charlie." I turned to him. "Did your friend at the sheriff's department find anything?"

"No, but if his real name's not Shane Jones, then I'm not surprised." He turned onto the road. "If we don't find out much from Mobley, then we can stop by the nursing home and ask for more information about Charlie from his boss."

"Sounds good." I said, my mind whirring on to the next concern. "Have you talked to Max since yesterday morning?"

"No."

"After Wyatt took me home, he left to check on Max. Tiny said Max left with him, and he hadn't returned by the time we closed up."

"Did you call Wyatt to check on him?"

"No. With the way we ended things after he dropped me off, it doesn't seem like a good idea. I think we need to take a break from each other." After what I'd learned from Ruth, I felt even less optimistic about our prospects. But I'd come to the conclusion that my feelings were much too complicated to sort out while we were looking for Lula and Greta.

When Marco didn't say anything, I said, "No comment?"

"What's there to say? You two seem to fight more than you get along. Maybe it's for the best."

"Maybe." I needed to change the subject. "I'm still trying to figure out the dynamic between the Bakers, Bart, and Hank. Turns out Louise worked for Hank for a short time, processing his pot, but he fired her after he figured out she was spyin' for Bart. He fired her the day before she shot Walter."

"So she probably went over to the Drummonds' to tell Bart she'd been fired."

"I'm presuming, but what did he do for her? And why was Walter drowning his daughter? I still have so many questions. Bingham suggested I talk to Louise herself."

"Go to Nashville?" he asked in surprise. "That's probably a good idea. I'll get her attorney's information. See if maybe we can get her to call you and save a trip." Then he grinned. "I'm starvin'. Let's get some breakfast at Watson's, then head to the funeral home."

I wasn't looking forward to going back there, but I was hoping Mobley would have some much needed answers.

CHAPTER TWENTY-SEVEN

There was nothing appealing about the Mobley Funeral Home. It was a one-story brick building in the nondescript style typical of architecture from the 1960s and 70s. The asphalt parking lot surrounding the building was empty except for two cars on the side of the building—an older green sedan and a shiny black Lexus.

"A Lexus?" I asked when I saw it. "In Ewing?"

Marco shrugged as he pulled into a parking spot in front of the building. "You were with Hank when he buried Seth. Did you ever hear how much the funeral cost? It takes a small fortune to bury a body these days."

"I never heard," I said softly. "Wyatt paid for it all."

"Really?" he asked, turning to me in surprise. "Where'd he get the money?"

"I don't know." My mind was racing. I knew the garage didn't bring in much of a profit. Where had Wyatt gotten the money? It struck me that I didn't even know where he'd gotten the money for his garage. He hadn't said, of course, and I'd presumed it had come from his father in some way. But Marco and I were here for our investigation, and I didn't have time to think about Wyatt's secrets just now. "I take it the Lexus belongs to Pete Mobley."

"I don't know for certain, but it's a good presumption," Marco said. "The question is why he's here on a Sunday morning."

My eyes widened. "You didn't expect him to be here?"

"No. It's Sunday morning and a funeral home director needs to have a good reputation in town. Which means he should be in church, especially since one of his men was caught smuggling drugs into the area using the caskets he uses to bury the townsfolk."

I'd only been in the area for a month, but I'd already learned one of the stark contrasts between Ewing and Drum—other than spotty cell phone coverage—was that the people in Ewing weren't as blind to illegal activity as the citizens of Drum. Perhaps it was because Ewing housed the sheriff's department. Whatever the case, I was sure Marco was right. Pete Mobley needed to polish up his reputation, and being seen in a church pew was one surefire way to do it.

"If you didn't expect him here," I said, "then what are we doing here?"

"I wanted to talk to some of the employees about Charlie, and get their take on Dwight and Mobley. I figured we'd take what we learned and go to Mobley."

"Wait," I said, turning to him. "You're not just asking to find Greta and Lula. You think Mobley had something to do with those drugs."

His jaw tightened. "You're damn right I do. I never bought that he was a victim."

"But he was cleared of all wrongdoing."

His brow lifted. "And look who cleared him."

"Hensen County Sheriff's Department." I pushed out a sigh.

The corruption in this area ran deep. Fighting it felt like pushing a boulder uphill. "So what do you want to do? Wait?"

He stared at the building for a few moments. "No," he said, "but we need to think of a reason to be here asking questions." He shot me a glance. "What if we ask him something about Seth's funeral?"

It was a good idea, but what could we ask about that he wouldn't see through in a second?

"Oh," I said. "We never found the guest book. I told Hank we should call and ask about it, but he said one of the ladies in town likely had it."

"That's perfect," Marco said, his eyes glittering. "Let's go."

He got out of the car and grabbed his crutches from the backseat. When I met him at the front of the SUV, I said, "No overdoing it today, Marco. You're no good to me if you're half dead."

He grinned. "But I've still got it even when I'm half dead… which reminds me that your clothes are still at my house. I meant to bring them to you and forgot. Want me to call Wyatt to come pick them up?"

I shot him a glare.

"You know he's jealous as shit, don't you?" he asked. "He hates that you're hangin' out with me. Especially with my reputation."

"Maybe so, but that wouldn't stop me. He doesn't have any say over what I do." Especially now.

I started to walk toward the front door, but he blocked my path with the tip of his crutch.

I looked up at him in exasperation. "Marco. This doesn't seem like the time or place to be discussing Wyatt."

His gaze held mine, his expression unusually serious. "If you find yourself in trouble, you call him. Broken up or not, that man will drop everything and come runnin'. Got it?"

His statement humbled me. He was right. Things were

different today. We were getting closer to the truth, which also meant we were getting closer to whoever had kidnapped and maybe hurt two women. And while I might not trust Wyatt Drummond with my heart, I could trust him with my life. "Yeah."

He'd left his coat unzipped, and I noticed the dark brown leather strap across his chest. Given what he'd just said, I knew what it meant.

His gaze dipped to his chest before rising back to my face. "I'm carryin' today, but we can't count on me to save us. With these crutches and my lack of balance...if things get hairy, I need you to do as I say. Can I count on that?"

I nodded. "Yeah."

"Okay. Let's go in."

We walked across the parking lot. I could tell Marco was feeling better by his faster gait with the crutches, but it wouldn't be smart of me to forget how quickly he'd lost strength yesterday. The same thing could happen today if we weren't careful. I held the front door open for him, the tinkle of the bell on the door announcing our presence.

Mobley appeared in the long hall to the back within moments, popping through a door. While I'd previously guessed him to be in his late fifties based on the gray in his dark hair, he looked much older now. His eyes were sunken and bracketed by deep wrinkles, and although he was dressed in an immaculate dark suit and pale blue tie, his posture was slumped. The Dwight incident had aged him.

"Carly Moore," he said in a friendly tone as he approached, but I sensed hesitation. "I hope bad news hasn't brought you to my door."

"Oh, no," I said, forcing cheerfulness into my voice. "Nothing like that. I happened to be in Ewing and decided to stop by and ask about the guest book for Seth's funeral. Hank and I want to send thank you notes to everyone who attended, but we can't find the book."

"Hmm." He tilted his head to the side, the wrinkles around his eyes deepening as his face screwed into a look of concentration. Something must have dropped into place because he finally straightened and said, "I'm fairly certain we gave it to the sister of the minister. I think her name was Paisley?"

"Miss Patsy," I said with a smile. "I'll check with her. Thank you."

"No problem," he said, his eyes turning wary. "But you could have saved yourself a trip and called."

"And that's exactly what she wanted to do," Marco said, pinning his crutch under his armpit as he reached out and put his hand on my arm. "But you know us men. I wanted to take the more direct approach." He dropped his hand. "Go straight to the source."

"There's something to be said for frankness, Deputy Roland."

"You know who I am?" Marco asked. He'd kept his tone neutral, but I could feel the tension in his body.

"How could I not?" Mobley asked. "Your face was all over the newspapers. They called you a hero shot down in the line of duty." He glanced between us. "Are you together now?"

It seemed like an odd question. What difference could it possibly make? Then again, Marco seemed to be purposefully creating that impression. I suspected he wanted to discourage Mobley and whoever he was working with from messing with me. Even in a place like Hensen County, there was still some protection to be had from being a cop, or being with a cop.

Marco leaned closer and snagged my hand, lacing our fingers. "There's something about trauma that draws people together."

Mobley's gaze dropped to our linked hands, then darted back up to our faces, completely devoid of emotion. "We find comfort where we can, especially after a tragedy. I tell my clients that there's no one-size-fits-all approach to grief, so if they find someone soon after the death of a spouse, it means no disloyalty to their lost loved one." He took a step back. "If you'll excuse me, I have something I need to attend to."

Marco dropped my hand and took a step forward. "On a Sunday morning? I don't envy your workin' hours, Mr. Mobley."

"Well, the dead don't sleep," Mobley said with a short laugh.

"Some people would say they sleep eternally," Marco said.

Mobley blinked, though it looked more like a flinch, then took another step back. "Yeah. I guess so. Now, if you'll excuse me…"

He turned and started walking back down the hall.

I shot Marco a frustrated glance. We hadn't gotten a single piece of information. Why was he just letting Mobley walk away?

Marco had already spun around, however, and he flicked his eyes toward the front door.

He'd insisted I follow his lead, and I'd agreed, so I gritted my teeth and walked out, holding the door open for him. I waited until we were in the car to let loose.

"What the hell, Marco? Why didn't you ask him about Charlie?"

"Because it's plain as day that man is guilty of something, and we're gonna tail him." He started the car and steered us out of the parking lot. "Carly," he said when he saw I wasn't appeased. "We weren't gonna get a confession out of him."

"We could have tried!"

"No," he said, turning toward downtown Ewing. "This is better. We made him nervous, which means he thinks we know something about him. Mark my words, he's gonna run scared like a chicken from a fox." He shot me a glance. "And we're gonna follow him."

Once we were out of sight of the funeral home, he turned left onto a side street.

"What does he think we know?" I asked. "He only landed on our radar because Ruth remembered seeing Charlie with Dwight."

"That's the question of the year. Like I said, I always suspected he was more involved in the drug smuggling than the department determined. But we didn't press him for information, and it seems odd that he'd freak out at just the sight of us together. Which leads me to believe Charlie *does* work for Mobley, and they know we've been looking into Lula's and Greta's disappearances." He turned again, heading down a residential street that would lead him back toward the funeral home.

I released a sharp gasp. "You think Mobley has something to do with their disappearances?"

"Maybe." He snuck a glance at me before returning his attention to the road. "What if those packages Lula was delivering were for Mobley?"

"Why would she do that?" A sick, slimy feeling washed through my insides. "Oh. No."

"What?" Marco asked in a sharp tone.

I shifted in the seat to face him. "Remember the other boyfriend? Lula was sleeping with an older man." I paused and choked out, "A man of great importance."

His face twisted in disgust. "You think Mobley's a *man of great importance?*" he asked in disbelief.

"God, no. I don't, but someone like Lula might. He wears a suit. Owns a business. Is considered respectable. Drives a *Lexus.*"

"Shit." He ran a hand over his head. "That is so disturbing I might have to bleach out my brain. How old do you think that fucker is?"

"I don't know. Maybe early to late sixties?"

Marco shuddered. "Too old to be a new dad." His eyes widened. "Too in need of the community's respect to knock up someone other than his wife."

"You think he took Lula because he doesn't want to be a father?"

"That's been one of our working theories, so it's not outside the realm of possibility."

"But it's Pete Mobley," I protested. "Is he capable of hurting her?"

"Maybe not. That would be a reason for hirin' someone like Charlie. It sounds like maybe he *is* capable of such a thing."

My stomach churned.

The funeral home came into view at the end of the street, the Lexus fully visible. Marco pulled over to the curb and put the Explorer in park. "Mobley's reputation is already on the line with the drug smuggling. If word gets out that he's been cheatin' on his wife with a woman in her twenties, and he got her pregnant to boot? I'm not sure he'd recover."

I swallowed bile. "So he took her to keep his dirty little secret."

Which meant she was dead.

"Hey," Marco said, reaching over and snagging my hand. "Don't think the worst." But I heard the hopelessness in his voice.

"He runs a funeral home, Marco," I said flatly. "His business is taking care of dead bodies."

"Yeah," he admitted. "I know."

"Greta." My voice broke, and I couldn't stop a tear from falling down my cheek. "If Charlie took her, it's because I was talking to her." I released sob. "What if I got her killed, Marco?"

"Hey," he said, turning in his seat to face me. He was still holding my hand and squeezed it. "Let's not think like that."

"It's hard not to."

"We don't know that they're dead. He might be keepin' them alive somewhere. When he leaves, he might lead us right to them." Which meant we were back to the original theory that the same people had taken them both. I hadn't told Marco my new theory, and I decided now wasn't the time. Mobley certainly seemed to know something. Hopefully, he'd lead us to at least one of them.

I nodded, only because I couldn't bear to consider the possibility of them being dead. But we had to look at this practically. What purpose would Mobley have for keeping them alive?

"Carly," he said with an authority I wasn't used to hearing in his voice. "Worst-case scenario, if Greta is dead—you did *not* kill her."

A fresh round of tears filled my eyes. "Is this when you tell me that I didn't pull the trigger, or however they killed her?" Oh God. What had they done to her? I couldn't let my mind dwell on it.

"No, although it's true. You have to remember that Charlie has been watching Greta for weeks, probably since Purdy's death, based on when he started working at the nursing home. And he was in the café last week asking about Lula. He would have taken her whether you were askin' questions or not."

I nodded.

"*Carly.*"

I jerked my gaze to his.

"This is *not* your fault." The compassion on his face was nearly my undoing.

I nodded again but didn't answer.

He pushed out a breath, probably realizing that was the best response he was going to get from me.

Movement out of the corner of my eye caught my attention, and I realized Mobley was in the parking lot, practically sprinting to his car.

I sat up straighter. "He's on the move."

Marco sat up too, shifting the car into drive. "Showtime."

CHAPTER TWENTY-EIGHT

Mobley headed out of the parking lot as though he were being chased by a pack of wild dogs.

"He isn't exactly cool under pressure," Marco said. "That will definitely work in our favor."

Marco slowly drove down the side street parallel to the funeral home parking lot, staying back several car lengths, as Mobley sped out. The Lexus barely slowed down before Mobley turned right onto the four-lane highway, narrowly missing a car, and heading away from town.

I curled my upper lip in disgust. "I get the impression that a life of crime might be new to him."

"Maybe," Marco said. "We've definitely put the fear of God into him." He turned right at the stop sign, pulling up behind a pickup truck, several car lengths behind the Lexus.

We followed behind the truck for several miles until Mobley turned into the parking lot with a faded sign for Mountain View Lodge and Spa.

"Marco..." This was where Lula had met her man of importance.

"Yeah," he said, his voice tight. "I get the connection." He drove past and I turned in my seat to watch Mobley's car head around a two-story motel that looked like it had been built many decades ago. Mobley was driving down a lane that went between the motel and a smaller building that had the word *spa* in faded letters on the side. I was shocked Bart Drummond owned this dump. Then again, the tavern and the Alpine Inn weren't exactly nice. Sure, Max was now the owner of record for the former, but Bart had owned them both back in the day.

"He's driving around the back."

"I'll pull a U-turn up here," he said, swerving into the left lane. He drove about twenty feet, waiting for an approaching car to pass us, then jerked the car around in the opposite direction, heading back toward the spa.

I held on to the door and the dashboard as he made the three-point turn. When we reached the resort, he turned into the parking lot and drove around back.

"There's his car," I said, pointing toward the black Lexus parked in the middle of the lot. The only other cars around were a blue Hyundai and a rusted green minivan. Trees crept up to the back side of the parking lot, making me feel closed in.

Marco drove to the very back of the lot behind the spa and parked in a dark corner.

"What do you think he's doing in there?" I asked, my stomach in knots. "Do you think that's where he's keeping Lula and Greta?"

"I don't know."

"Should we contact the sheriff's department?"

"And tell them what?" he asked. "That Pete Mobley sped away from the funeral home and pulled into a motel parking lot?"

When he put it that way… "If they're in there, we can't just sit here, Marco."

"That's exactly what we're gonna do. Sit here and wait to see which room he comes out of and if anyone's with him." He shot me a frustrated look. "We can't go from door to door, Carly."

"But what if we freaked him out and he's going to hurt them?"

He grabbed my hand and squeezed. "I'm just as frustrated as you are, Carly. Trust me. But there's nothing we can do but wait."

I pulled my hand free and grabbed a tissue out of my purse.

"We could be here a while," he said. "He might be in there for hours or he might be in there for five minutes."

I had to do something, and my worried mind turned to the next concern on my list. Max. I was willing to suck up my pride for some peace of mind. I pulled out my cell phone. No service. "I'm worried about Max."

"If he's with Wyatt, he's fine."

"Do you have cell service?"

He pulled his phone out of his jacket pocket and checked the screen. "No."

Another danger to add to our list. We wouldn't be able to call for backup even if Marco decided it was a good time to move.

I shifted in my seat, antsy and frustrated.

"Carly," Marco said with a sigh. "Take a deep breath and try to relax."

I shot him a dark look.

"You're gonna drive me crazy," he grumbled.

"I'm sorry. It's just that my imagination is running wild about what's going on in there."

"For all we know, he's up there meetin' his new mistress for an afternoon delight. Try gettin' that out of your head." He made a face and shuddered.

It wasn't a pretty image, but I'd rather think of Mobley's sex life than worry about Greta and Lula. Bottom line: Marco was right. We had no idea which room Mobley had slipped into, and there was absolutely nothing we could do but wait.

"So you really sold your car to Bingham?" Marco asked.

"Yep. For four thousand dollars, which means I have money to buy a new one. Got any suggestions where to go?"

"Yeah," he said in a dry tone. "If you're wantin' a used one, Wyatt is the best source."

"Then how come he never offered to help me find one?" I asked defensively.

"Hell if I know. Maybe he didn't think it was a priority. You've been driving Hank's car."

"Well, Wyatt's not an option. Where else can I go?"

"I'll make a few calls," he said, then leaned forward, his body stiffening. "He's comin' out."

I swung my gaze to the motel and saw a man in a suit walking out of a room at the far end of the bottom level. He shut the door behind him and hurried toward his car. Alone.

"What are we going to do, Marco?" I asked. "Follow him or stay and see what's in the room?"

"Follow him."

"I can stay and check the room," I suggested. "While you follow him."

"No freakin' way," he said. "We stay together. The other two cars are parked at the opposite end of the lot, so they're likely not connected to this. We'll follow Mobley, then come back and check out the room."

"How will we get in?"

"My lock pickin' kit."

"I thought you were a deputy."

"Well, sometimes you need a little help."

Mobley's car whipped backward in reverse, and he drove just as erratically getting out of the parking lot as he had coming in.

Once he was between the buildings, Marco started his pursuit.

Mobley headed back to town this time. I wondered if he was returning to the funeral home, but he drove into a residential neighborhood and pulled into the driveway of a ranch house.

Marco parked down the street, and we watched as two children ran out the front door, shouting, "Grandpa!"

Mobley leaned over and gave them both hugs, then let them tug him into the house.

I glanced over as Marco pulled out his cell phone and started swiping. Apparently he had service again. "This is Mobley's address of record. He lives here."

"We scared him. It makes sense that he'd run home, but why did he go to the motel first?"

Marco put the car into drive. "We're about to find out."

He didn't waste any time driving to the motel, and I was a nervous wreck. Scared of what we'd find in the room. Scared we wouldn't find anything.

Marco drove around back and parked a few rooms down from the room Mobley had emerged from.

"Wait in here," he said, reaching for the door handle.

"You're crazy if you think I'm not coming with you." I opened the car door and got out.

He opened the back passenger door and got his crutches out of the back.

"Carly," he groaned as he reached me.

"We're in this together, Marco. That was our bargain. I didn't insist on getting out when you told me to stay in the car with you."

He gave me a grim look, but he didn't try to talk me out of coming. I walked next to him as he hobbled over to the motel room. The number 134 was nailed on slightly askew in the middle of the wooden door.

"Wait over there," he whispered, gesturing to the side of the door opposite the doorknob. Once I was in position, he knocked and then reached into his jacket and withdrew his gun.

My heart beat double time.

When no one answered, he shot me a glance, so I knocked on the door.

No answer.

"You ever picked a lock?" Marco asked.

"Do I look like the kind of person who picks locks?" I asked in disbelief.

He grinned. "Kind of."

I rolled my eyes, but our exchange had helped settle my nerves.

He slipped his gun back into his holster and retrieved two long metal tools from his jacket pocket. Balancing on one foot, he handed me his crutch, then glanced around to make sure no one was watching. He leaned over and inserted the tools into the keyhole, and I realized we were lucky Bart Drummond had been too cheap to upgrade to an electronic locking system. Seconds later, Marco turned the knob and pushed the door open a crack, staying to the side of the door. He quickly slipped the tools back into his pocket.

Pushing the door open with the tip of his crutch, he called out, "Hello?"

My heart was in my throat as he pushed the door open wider. He stayed in the doorway, taking in the sight of the room, and I leaned around him so I could get a look.

The room had two full-size beds and the typical décor of an old motel room, complete with the stained carpet and the framed nature prints. But no people. No sign of anything unusual.

Marco walked into the room and I followed.

"I don't get it," I said, looking around. Even the beds were made. "What did he do when he was in here? We haven't been gone long enough for someone to come in and clean the place up."

"There's a pair of gloves in my jacket pocket," he said. "Put them on and start opening drawers."

We checked every drawer, the closet, and even under the beds, but he'd left nothing behind.

"Look there," Marco said, pointing his crutch toward the bed. "There's an indentation."

I moved closer and noticed a dent in the bedspread. "It looks like he sat down here."

Marco stared at the spot on the bed, just beneath the pillow, then shifted his attention to the nightstand. "I think he was makin' a phone call."

"Why would he come here to make a phone call?"

"I don't know," he said as he leaned over to examine the phone. "But cell service sucks in this area, so maybe he uses it as a burner phone. He can make calls and receive messages without fear they'll be traced back to him."

"That's crazy," I said. "Who would do that?"

"Got a better explanation?" he asked.

"No."

We were silent for a moment.

"Let's go try to rent this room," Marco said.

"What?"

He grinned. "Trust me."

The office was on the other side of the parking lot, a long walk for Marco, so we drove over in the SUV and parked closer. As we headed in, he said, "Oh, by the way, we're deeply in love."

"What?"

He opened the door and said, "Look, honey! The office looks exactly like it did when we were here on our honeymoon."

I glanced around the small space. If he'd claimed the wedding had been thirty years ago, I suspect he would have been challenged about our age, not about the unchanging décor.

"Sweetie, you're so right," I gushed.

"I told you this would be perfect. Exactly like it was five years ago."

The woman at the front desk watched us with interest. "Can I help you?"

"I sure hope so," Marco said with a cheesy grin as he hopped toward her. "Jessica and I were here on our honeymoon. We're celebrating our fifth anniversary, so I told her I wanted to come back and relive the magic."

"Oh, isn't that sweet," she said, beaming. I could tell she was a fan of romance. "And with you on crutches too!"

Marco leaned against the counter. "The thing is"—he glanced down at her name tag and lowered his voice—"Sarah, Jessica and I are goin' through a rough patch and we're tryin' to recreate our honeymoon, so *please* tell me that room 134 is available. That's where we stayed before, and we loved the view of the woods through the window."

I wrapped my arm around his shoulders and leaned my temple against him. "It would be awesome if we could have that room. *Please* tell us it's available."

She frowned. "I'm so sorry, but that room is already taken."

"What?" Marco said in dismay. "You didn't even look. Are you sure?"

"Unfortunately, very."

"Will it be available tomorrow? Or any time this week?" He tilted his head and gave her a pleading look. "We *really* want to stay there."

"I'm so sorry," she said. "But it's a long-term rental, and I have no idea when it will be available. The manager rents it out month by month and it's paid up until after the first of the year."

"Is that even possible?" Marco asked. "I've never heard of such a thing."

She leaned forward and lowered her voice. "Tell me about it. We've never done anything like that before, and what's weirder is the beds never look like they've been slept in."

"Do the guests make them themselves?" I asked eagerly, like I was excited to get some juicy gossip.

"No!" she exclaimed. "The room never looks used at all. Not even the toilet paper, but the phone gets messages and someone shows up to listen to 'em. The weirdest thing I've ever seen here, and that's saying something."

"Must be some rich bozo," Marco said. "Who else could afford to rent a room they never use?"

She leaned her head closer and whispered. "It's the local funeral home director, only I shouldn't be tellin' you that. At first we thought he was bringin' his mistress here, the one he was screwin' this summer, but we ain't seen hide nor hair of her. Just him. And like I said, lately the beds are never used."

I shook my head as if disgusted. "I bet she has platinum blonde hair and is barely out of high school."

Sarah's mouth dropped open. "You're right on both counts. It's like you're psychic."

"Nah," I said, "I just know from experience. Most home-wreckers are blonde, and if he's a bigwig, he'll want her in his bed." I shot Marco a glare, hoping he'd pick up on my cue.

Marco's body stiffened and he said in a tight voice, "Jessica. I told you I wasn't havin' an affair with the blonde from accountin'. I swear to all that is holy that I have no idea how photos of her naked boobs got on my phone."

I turned to him with a glare. "Are you pullin' that same bull-shit again? This second honeymoon is officially *over*."

I spun around and stomped to the door but then waited for him, shooting him an aggravated look as I waited for him to limp out.

"I hope you two work things out," Sarah called after us, her voice trailing off at the end.

We got into the Explorer. Marco waited until he'd pulled out of the parking space and was headed toward the highway before he turned to me in amazement. "That went better than I could have hoped. Not only did we find out that Mobley's rentin' the room by the month, but thanks to your quick thinkin', we got confirmation he brought Lula here this summer."

"Sure, we found out that he's usin' the room to get messages, but we still don't know where Lula and Greta are."

"But we're closer to findin' them than before," he said.

"So what do we do now?" I asked.

"Next we stop by the nursing home and try to bluff our way into getting contact information for Charlie."

"Okay," I said, "but we have to make one short stop first."

"Where?" he asked.

"The Dollar General."

CHAPTER TWENTY-NINE

Greener Pasture's parking lot was busier today. Turned out that Sunday afternoon was an active visitors' day. Everyone attended church in their finest, went out to eat for lunch, then came out to the nursing home to do their familial duty.

The crowded recreation area meant the staff was busy, and I wasn't sure if that would play in our favor or not. Judging by my last visit, they weren't overly helpful at the best of times.

"Where's the photo?" he asked.

I led Marco down to the hall of headshots and he frowned as he looked over Charlie's photo. "We need his employment file."

"I suppose they won't just hand it over, will they?" I asked.

He pursed his lips as he scanned the other photos. "Maybe if I flashed my badge, but I can't do that since it's not an official investigation."

"So what are we going to do?"

"Try anyway."

"I might know someone who can help us. Let's go back out into the rec room and see if I can find her."

He gave me a questioning look. "And does this source have anything to do with what's in the bag?"

Marco had stayed in the Explorer for my Dollar General errand, and I hadn't told him what I'd purchased.

I glanced down at the plastic bag. "Let's just say I'm not above bribery."

"I like how you think."

We headed to the recreation room, and I quickly found the two women I'd spoken to the day before. Grumpy Lady was sitting at a table with a middle-aged couple and two teenage girls, looking even grumpier than the day before. Cotton Ball was sitting by herself at a small four-person table, working on a jigsaw puzzle of a covered bridge.

I headed straight for her.

She glanced up at me in surprise. Then her gaze drifted to Marco behind me and her eyes lit up with excitement.

"You came back."

"I brought a friend with me," I said, taking a seat at her table.

Marco stood next to her and extended his hand. "Hi, I'm Marco."

"Gladys," she said as she shook his hand. Turning to me, she said, "He has a firm grip. Is it true what they say about firm hands?" She winked. Subtle insinuation clearly wasn't her strong suit, because she followed up with, "The firmer the handshake, the stiffer the boner."

My cheeks started to flush. "I… uh…"

Marco laughed as he sat next to me, easing onto the chair and leaning his crutches against the table. "A lady never screws and tells, Gladys."

She chuckled. "And who said I was a lady?"

Marco laughed again and I shot him a grin. He had a nice

laugh, rich and warm, and it had a way of making you feel included in a joke but never the butt of it.

When had I become such an expert on Marco's laugh?

"So," he said, leaning forward, his eyes twinkling. "I hear you're one of the experts on this place."

Her chest expanded and she looked inclined to start strutting around like a peacock. "Some people say that."

"I need information on one of the new employees."

A scowl crossed her face. "Shane Jones."

"That's the one."

"I don't know a whole lot about him," she admitted. "He's only worked here a few weeks, but he's a menace. Like I told your girl, he's been stealin' things, and the staff won't do anything about it."

"Well, maybe I can help with that," Marco said. "But first I need the scoop on him."

"You're wanting to look at his employment file," she said with a sly grin.

Marco rolled his shoulders in a lazy shrug. "Perhaps. And if I was lookin' for it, where do you suppose I might find it?"

"You'd think it would be on a computer," she said in disgust, "but this damn town is stuck in the Dark Ages."

"So new hires fill out a paper application?" Marco asked.

"Yep."

"And where do they keep those?"

"Office down in the west wing," she said. "And good thing for you that no one uses it on Sunday afternoons."

"Lucky for me indeed."

"But the door's locked." Gladys glanced up, her eyes twinkling. "What's a key worth to you?"

Marco released a short laugh. "Gladys, you're quickly becomin' my new favorite person." Then he winked at me. "Sorry, Carly."

I grinned back. "Hey, priorities." I pulled one of the puzzles out of the bag in my purse and slid it across the table to her as if it were a hundred-dollar bill. It was a 1000-piece puzzle of a mountain.

She slid the box over to her. "Got any more of these?"

I took out another 1000-piece puzzle of a still life with a ceramic water pitcher and fruit.

She reached into a pocket of her pants and pulled out a key, setting it on the table. "This is a master and gets into everything."

"You just carry it around with you?" Marco asked in disbelief.

"This place is boring as shit," Gladys said. "Sometimes we like to get into things." She held his gaze. "Like the employee lounge. That has lockers."

"And where might those be?" he asked in a conspiratorial tone.

"Next to the office."

Marco put his hand over the key and picked it up. "Carly, wait here."

I leaned over next to his ear. "Wouldn't it be less noticeable if I search?" I asked quietly. "You're bound to attract attention on your crutches."

"But if I get caught, I'm fairly certain I can talk my way out of it," he said. "I might be on medical leave, but I've still got the badge."

Reluctantly, I agreed.

He got up and moved down the hall, leaving me to stew in my nerves.

"Let's open a new one," Gladys said, her eyes lit up with excitement, and I felt bad that I'd used the puzzles as a bribe. I should have just given them to her. I used an ink pen in my purse to break the seal on one of them while Gladys swept the old pieces of the bridge puzzle into the well-worn box. We'd spread all the pieces on the table and had started sorting out the edge pieces by the time Marco returned about ten minutes later.

He set the key on the table and gave Gladys a slow nod. "Thank you."

"You gonna get the bastard?" she asked.

"I sure as hell plan to," Marco said, his voice gruff.

"Then go get 'em, Deputy Roland," she said with a sly grin. When surprise washed over his face, she said, "I read the papers." She shot me a glance too. "Now go get the bastard."

I got up and started to leave, unnerved that she'd known who he was and hadn't let on.

Marco and I were both silent as we left the building, but when we reached the parking lot, I looked around. No one was watching us, so I asked, "You find what we need?"

"Yep. Address. Phone number. Emergency contact. Employment history. I made copies of it all. It's in my pocket."

"He was working here under an assumed name. You think he gave them real information?"

"One way to find out."

We got inside the SUV and Marco pulled several folded papers from his pocket. Glancing at the top one, he plugged an address into the Explorer's navigation system.

"Are we headed to Charlie's house?"

"We're gonna do a drive by and go from there."

"Why'd you put his address into the maps when coverage is so spotty?"

He shot me a grin. "It's spotty with a cell phone, but the car uses satellite."

Like Bingham's satellite phone. I considered mentioning that to Marco, but Bingham clearly made him uncomfortable. He'd be pissed if he knew I'd offered him information. Instead, I grabbed the photocopies and looked them over. Charlie had a Ewing address, but the street was listed as *County Road* and the navigation system said it was fifteen minutes away.

"Rural address?" I asked.

"Yep."

We were both silent as Marco drove out of Ewing and up a mountain road, passing only a few houses, most of them run-down and abandoned. Finally, the GPS said we'd arrived, but there weren't any houses within view—only an entrance to a private lane that was blocked by a gate with a sign that said, *No Trespassing*.

"I don't like this," Marco finally said, his hands gripping the wheel.

"Can we get the gate open?" I asked, but then I realized it was locked with a heavy metal chain and a padlock. "Do you have bolt cutters? Or can you pick the lock?"

He stared at the gate, a wide array of emotions flitting across his face. Anger, frustration, worry. Fear.

"We can't do that."

Outrage exploded in my head. "What do you mean we can't?"

"Even if I had the means to open that gate, we can't go down that lane. Not with the No Trespassing sign."

"But you're a sheriff's deputy!"

"It doesn't fuckin' matter, Carly!" he shouted.

"What if they're down that road, Marco?" I choked out, pissed that I was close to tears again.

"I know, goddammit, but we still can't go down there. I've got no probable cause."

"What the hell are you talking about, Marco?"

He turned to me in frustration. "It's all circumstantial, and on top of that, this isn't an official investigation." He slammed the heel of his hand into the steering wheel. "Dammit!"

We sat there, his car stopped on the two-lane county road, both of us breathing heavily as we tried to rein in our emotions.

"I'm sorry," I said, running a hand over my head. "I know your hands are tied."

"*Our* hands are tied, Carly, in case you're getting some crazy-ass idea about getting out of this car and running onto the property."

I hadn't considered that, but I was also smart enough to realize it would be foolish for me to attempt such a thing on my own. I was an intelligent woman, but I was no criminal mastermind. I had no delusions that I could outwit a hardened criminal. Sure, I was mouthy with Bingham, but like Hank said, the devil you know. I had no idea what to expect with Charlie. "So what do we do?"

"You're not gonna like it."

"I'll hold my peace until you've said yours."

He nodded. "We head back to Drum." He glanced at me, his brow raised as though waiting for my outburst. When he saw it wasn't coming, he continued, "I'll take you to Hank's, then I'm going to call Detective White, see if I can convince her there's something here. It hasn't been a full forty-eight hours since Greta went missing, but it's close enough."

"She's the detective who handled the Carson Purdy case, isn't she?"

"She'll be sympathetic to our case, especially since we have more information tying Lula and Greta to both men."

"Okay."

His mouth parted in shock. "No protests?"

"I'm no police officer, Marco. I can't storm the property and demand he produce Lula and Greta. I'd likely get them, you, or myself killed. I have no problem handing this over to professionals, as long as they actually do something with it.

"If they still won't open an investigation, I'm going to keep workin' on it, Carly," he said defensively. "I'll find aerial photos of the property, look into the owners' history, and I can check out the references on Charlie's application. They likely lied for him, and we can find out why. I won't just let this go."

"I know you won't," I said. "And I'm sorry if I implied that you were."

"We're both frustrated. But let's see if we can pull the big guns in."

CHAPTER THIRTY

Once we got back into Ewing, Marco tried calling Detective White on his cell, but her phone went to voice-mail. He called the sheriff's department next to see if she was available, and they told him she was off until Tuesday.

"Shit," he said when he hung up. He sucked in a breath and blew it out. "It's two o'clock. Let's head back to Drum, and I'll go to the library to start my research."

"It's closed on Sundays."

He gave me a wry grin. "I have a key."

I shook my head. "What's with all the older women just droppin' keys into your lap?"

"It's my charm," he said, but it lacked his usual laid-back tone.

"Can you tell someone else in the department?" I asked.

"Honestly, Carly, other than Marta, I'm not sure who I can trust with this. Purdy had his hooks in the sheriff's department. Mobley obviously didn't give up the operation. For all I know, he and his goon still have someone on the inside." He glanced at me. "Don't give up. I'll figure out somethin'."

We picked up lunch to go and headed back to Drum, neither

of us in the mood to sit in a restaurant. We were quiet during the drive, both of us lost in thought. I shared my theory that Charlie had taken Greta but not Lula, but Marco quickly nixed it.

"I might have considered it if it weren't for Mobley. His involvement indicates they took Lula because he found out she was pregnant."

"So why take Greta?" I asked.

He snorted. "You saw Mobley panic after we dropped by. I suspect Mobley and Charlie thought Greta was going to blow their cover. They took her to cover their tracks."

"Yeah," I said. "I guess it makes sense. I mean, taking Greta wasn't the smartest move if they wanted to keep this quiet, but Mobley's clearly not some criminal mastermind. Why do you think Lula was so worried when Bingham walked in Thursday night?"

"Maybe he caught wind she was carryin' packages for Mobley. Or maybe she was worried he'd figure out she's pregnant. If she's five or six months along, then people are bound to start noticin' soon."

"He still doesn't know, or if he does, he's not letting on." Call me naive, but I was going with not knowing.

I barely touched my lunch because my stomach churned every time I thought about what might be happening on Charlie's property. Were they out there? Had we made the wrong call?

"You need to be careful," Marco said as we were approaching Drum. "In fact, I'm not sure you should be drivin' alone. How about you come to the library with me until it's time to head to the tavern?"

"Yeah," I said, spooked out that Charlie or someone else might be watching me. "Maybe it makes me a coward, but I don't want to be alone."

"Not a coward, Carly. It makes you *smart*."

But when we drove past the tavern, I saw the open sign was in the window. I'd planned on going to the library with Marco, but it was already three thirty. I'd only have about twenty minutes or so to do some digging before I had to quit.

"Can you drop me off at the tavern instead?" I asked. "Ruth's already opened, and unless Max came back, she's covering the bar on her own."

"Yeah. No problem." He turned and pulled into the back parking lot. "I'll watch you go in, then come by later to take you home."

"Thanks, Marco," I said as I grabbed my bag out of the back. Before I left the car, I searched his face. "You be careful too. You're not at 100%, which makes you vulnerable too."

He patted his chest over his jacket. "True, but I've got a gun."

"Still."

A smile cracked his mouth. "I will."

When I got inside, I quickly changed into my Max's Tavern T-shirt. Tiny was working at the grill, but my heart sunk when I found Ruth behind the bar.

"Still no Max?" I asked, tying on my apron.

She frowned. "No."

"How long have you been open?"

"Not long, so get that guilty look off your face."

"Has anyone called Wyatt to see how Max is doin'?"

"Yeah, I called him this morning. He said Max is better, but he's keepin' him out at his place until tomorrow."

I nodded.

"This is *not* your fault, Carly," she said in a stern tone. "Max has had a drinkin' problem for years, and we've been sweepin' it under the rug, pretendin' it doesn't exist. If Lula hadn't set him off, it would have been something else."

I gave her a tight smile. "Yeah."

She put her hand on my arm and gave it a gentle squeeze. "Why don't you go call Wyatt and talk to him yourself? Maybe Max'll talk to you. The sooner you two make up, the better."

As much as I hated to call Wyatt, I really needed to hear Max's voice. I had to reassure myself he was okay. "Yeah. I think I will. I'm going to call him from the office."

"Good idea."

I got settled in Max's office chair, then took a deep breath and dialed Wyatt's number.

Wyatt answered and launched into a tirade. "For the umpteenth time, Ruth, Max is fine."

"It's Carly."

The line went silent, and I was starting to wonder if he'd hung up when he said, "Are you callin' to check on Max?"

Had he hoped I was calling to talk to him? "Yeah. I'm worried about him."

"He's feelin' like shit right about now, but he'll be much better tomorrow. Sober at least."

"That's good."

"He feels terrible about the things he said to you. Do you want to talk to him?"

"If he's willing."

I heard muffled voices in the background. Then Max's voice came over the line. "Carly, if you never speak to me again, I'll understand."

"No," I said, covering my eyes with my hand in relief. "We're good. I promise."

"You're not fired."

I released a short laugh. "Well, that's good, since I've been working. Just get better and come back. We miss you like crazy."

There was so much unsaid, but it wouldn't feel right to talk our issues over on the phone, especially not on Wyatt's phone. We said our goodbyes and I hung up, taking a moment to let my emotions settle. I was still sure that Max knew something about Lula, so why hadn't I pressed him? Was it because I was scared to find out he'd done something bad? Or was I worried he'd reject me again?

I was considering calling him back, but the phone rang again. I picked up and said, "Max's Tavern."

A recorded voice asked, "Will you accept a collect call from the Tennessee Prison for Women?"

The blood rushed from my head and it took me a moment to choke out, "Yes."

Marco had intended to request a call from Lula's mother, but as far as I knew, he hadn't gotten around to it yet. So why was she calling?

I heard some clicks and then a woman's raspy voice said, "I need to speak to Lula."

"Louise?"

There was a pause. "Ruthie?"

"No," I said, putting a hand on my chest and taking a breath to slow my racing heart. "This is Carly. I work with Lula."

"Never heard of you. Put 'er on the line," she said impatiently.

"I can't. She's not here."

"What do you mean she's not here? She works every Sunday."

Had she been scheduled to work today? She'd only been missing for a few days, but it felt like much longer. "Ms. Baker, Lula's missin'."

She took a beat before she said in a neutral voice, "She never came back?" Then her tone turned harsher. "You her replacement?"

I'd really hoped Louise would give me some insight on what had happened to her daughter, but I got the impression she'd be tight-lipped. "No, but when she took off last time, Max hired me to help cover her shifts. When she came back, Max kept us both on."

"There ain't enough hours for both y'all."

"We planned to make it work," I said evenly. "Lula and I worked together one night, but the next day she didn't show up for her shift. Most people think she took off again, but I don't believe that. I think someone took her." I purposely kept Marco's name out of it. While including him would lend credibility to my concerns, I had the impression that mentioning his name would make her shut up tighter than a clam. This wasn't a woman who'd want anything to do with the police.

She didn't say a word, so I took a chance and added, "I think it had something to do with the packages she was delivering when she left."

Complete silence hung on the other end of the line.

"Ms. Baker?" I asked, terrified I'd scared her off. "Are you still there?"

"How do you know about the packages?" she snapped.

"It doesn't matter how I know," I said. "The important part is that I do."

"Does the sheriff know?"

"No."

"Keep it that way." Her voice was hard and calculated. Not the voice of a mother worried about her only child.

"Do you know who took Lula?" I asked. "I'm trying to find her, and anything you can share with me would help."

"Why in the hell would *you* look for her? You said you only worked with her for one day."

"Maybe so, but I felt protective of her." I suspected she'd only give me information if I threw her off, so I added, "Especially after I learned she was pregnant."

"She told you?" she blasted through the line. "Who else has that stupid fool told?"

I gasped in shock. "Ms. Baker, I believe your daughter was kidnapped and is in danger. The sheriff's department doesn't seem inclined to take this seriously, and I'm worried she's living on borrowed time." If she was still alive at all. "I need you to tell me what you know so I can find her."

"I ain't tellin' you shit," she snarled. "You stay the hell out of my daughter's life."

"Louise," I practically shouted, "I'm worried she won't have a life. Now, who do you think took her? The father of her baby? Is it the same person who had her deliver the packages?"

She burst out laughing. "You really are stupid."

"So fill me in." She wasn't going to volunteer anything, but she might confirm information if I offered it. It wasn't a great plan, but it was better than nothing. "Lula was having an affair with Pete Mobley. Maybe he's the father of the baby. I'm guessing she broke it off when she figured out he wasn't going to leave his wife for her, but she did it before he noticed her expanding belly."

She remained silent, which I took as a good sign.

"I wasn't sure about the packages," I said. "At first I suspected Bingham, based on the way he stared at her the night she came back. She seemed terrified of him and he seemed anxious to talk to her. When I asked her about it later, she told me to leave Bingham alone. That he makes people disappear. And the next day *she* disappeared."

Her voice was tight as she asked, "You think Bingham took my girl?"

"No. I've since decided he had nothing to do with it. I think he was watchin' her because he misses her, and he's pissed she broke it off." Then the truth hit me. "I think he's in love with her and wants her back."

"He's a fool. They both are."

"But you broke them up. Why?"

"Because Mobley was sniffin' around, and I needed her to focus on him."

"Why?"

She snorted. "You think I'm just gonna confess everything I know?"

"I would hope you'd want to save your daughter. Just like you saved her the day you shot her father."

A peal of hysterical laughter rang out in my ear. "You think you've got it all figured out, but you're a fool just like the rest of them. You really believe that shit?"

"Your husband wasn't drowning her in the creek?"

"Her *father* was drownin' her, but it sure as shit wasn't Walter. He showed up and tried to stop the man."

The blood rushed from my head.

"That stupid girl didn't remember shit about that day after she came to, so when my sister brought her to see me in jail, Lula believed me when I told her that her daddy did it. Broke her heart. She couldn't believe her daddy would try to kill her. That man always treated her like the sun rose and set on her. And then Lula started rememberin' bits and pieces she'd forgotten. She recalled another man was there, one who was furious to find out he was her real daddy."

"But she didn't remember who the man was."

"No. That drowning took some of her common sense, you know what I mean? So she bought it hook, line, and sinker when I told her back in July that Todd Bingham was her daddy."

For a split second, I felt struck dumb by the notion of Bingham being Lula's father—had he knowingly slept with his own daughter?—but then I processed the rest of what Louise had said. "But he's not her father. You just didn't want her to be with him. Why?"

"I tried to hook up with that man years ago, but he wasn't interested," she spat. "I wasn't about to let him have my daughter. And I'm sure as hell not going to let him lay claim to my grandchild. Thank God Lula isn't too smart with the logistics of determinin' due dates."

I couldn't believe she was confessing all of this to me. "Who is Lula's father?"

"Didn't you hear me?" she cackled. "Walter was a simple man and believed he was her daddy. I think he might have realized the truth, but he loved her too much to care. He put up with me sleepin' around just to keep that girl. He was weak."

"He was a father."

"And it got him killed in the end."

"Her biological father didn't know?"

"No. I purposely kept it from him, plannin' to use it against him at some point, but I'm not a patient woman. I'd been needlin' 'im, and he figured it out. His solution was to get rid of the evidence of his indiscretion. He was more worried that people would know I'd slept with him than the fact he had another kid."

Which meant he had at least two.

"Louise," I said in what I hoped was an authoritative tone. "Who is Lula's father?"

She scoffed. "I've kept his secret for twenty years, and I sure as hell ain't tellin' you."

Not that she needed to. She'd made it clear enough.

"But you have other plans to tell," I said. "When you get out."

"Let's just say I've learned patience, and I'm ready to collect what's mine." Then she hung up.

I stared at the phone in amazement and horror. Louise Baker

was using her daughter as a pawn, at the expense of her happiness and her life.

Sure, I had more information, but I felt even more helpless to find Lula.

Then I realized I knew someone who wasn't constrained by the law, someone who'd be even more motivated to find Lula given the information I'd gained.

I dialed the number I'd memorized, and when he answered, I said, "Bingham. We need to talk. *Now.*"

CHAPTER THIRTY-ONE

He didn't waste any time getting to the tavern. He told me he could be there in twenty minutes and to meet him out back. I didn't bother asking Ruth if I could take a break. We weren't very busy, which meant I wouldn't be missed for a few minutes, so I slipped out the back door. A truck was parked opposite it, and it didn't surprise me to see Bingham behind the driver's wheel. Alone. Not allowing myself time to think of all the ways this might be a bad idea, I hurried over and got into the passenger seat.

"This better be important," he said with a growl, "or you might not have the opportunity to call me again."

"It's more important than you know." I'd spent the past twenty minutes trying to figure out where to start, and I'd decided I'd do best to start with what meant the most to him. "I know how Louise Baker got Lula to break up with you."

His hands gripped the steering wheel so tightly his knuckles turned white. "You got me to come runnin' over here to discuss my *damn love life?*"

His anger rattled me in the close quarters of the truck cab, but I pressed on, deciding to cut to the chase. "Lula's pregnant. I'm pretty sure the baby's yours. Her mother somehow convinced her it wasn't—and also that you're her biological father."

"*What the fuck?*" he shouted, turning to me in disbelief.

I turned to fully face him. "I know it's a lot to take in, but you strike me as a rip-off-the-Band-Aid kind of guy, and I think I might know where Lula and Greta are being kept."

He took a deep breath, and when he spoke again, his tone was calmer. "Go on."

"First, I need to know if you love her."

"Back to my damn love life?" he snapped. "It's none of your fuckin' business!"

"Like I said, I'd bet good money she's pregnant with your baby. I doubt you'd planned on having kids, but it's too late to change anyone's mind about this baby. She's six months along, so it *will* be coming. I need to know that you're goin' in to save and protect Lula. Not to retaliate for some perceived wrong."

"Perceived wrong?"

"Those packages we discussed. You told me you wouldn't hold it against her because her mother put her up to it. Did you mean it?"

His jaw clenched and unclenched. "I could lie and tell you what you want to hear."

"And that's why I had to see you in person, to look into your eyes as you tell me. Anything you say will stay right here in the cab of this truck, because I know how dangerous it is for you to admit you care about someone. She'd become your greatest weakness. The last thing I want to do is save her now only to put her and the baby at greater risk later."

His face remained expressionless, giving nothing away. "You say that as though you have experience in the criminal world."

"I do. I have a friend who's pregnant with a crime boss's baby. I know how dangerous this is for both of you. So I need to know, Bingham. Do you love her? Will you try to protect her and her baby? *Your* baby?"

His gaze held mine, and I was surprised at the flicker of emotion in his eyes when I mentioned his baby. "Yes." Then his face turned into a scary mask of rage. "Now tell me where she is."

I was thankful that rage wasn't directed at me. "I think they're on Shane Jones's property outside Ewing. Only his real name might be Charlie. It's rural and a perfect place to hold someone against their will. We got the address from a—"

The corner of his eye twitched. "I don't need to know the details of how you got the information, Ms. Moore. Only the address. Can you manage to give it to me without a story?"

I reached into my apron pocket and pulled out a piece of paper and handed it to him. "The GPS will lead you to it. The drive is blocked with a padlocked gate."

He looked over the address and slipped it into his jacket pocket. "Won't be a problem."

"Will you let me know when you have them?" I asked.

He gave a sharp nod. "Now get the fuck out."

I tried not to take offense as I climbed out and watched him tear out of the parking lot. If he was truly a man in love, and he seemed to be, I didn't blame him for being in a rush. I headed back in and returned to my tables. Ruth didn't seem to have noticed my absence, or if she had, she didn't comment.

Marco came in around six, looking spent. I rushed over to greet him at the door and led him to an open booth. "You've done too much again, Marco."

"I haven't done near enough," he said. "We're still no closer to gettin' someone to go out there."

Oh crap. I couldn't keep him in the dark about Bingham

anymore, not after everything that had happened this afternoon. "Marco, let's sit down for a moment."

He gave me a funny look, but he slid into the booth all the same, propping his leg on the seat.

I sat opposite him. "Louise Baker called for Lula this afternoon."

"Here?"

I nodded. "She admitted some interesting things."

"Go on."

I told him how the conversation went, and frustration covered his face. "Why the hell didn't you let me know earlier?"

"How was I supposed to reach you? Would you have answered the library phone?" If I could have even found the number. His mouth pursed, answer enough. "Your cell phone doesn't work, and you made it clear you don't think I should be walking around alone."

"You're right," he grudgingly admitted.

I groaned. "Sometimes I hate that this town is so stuck in the past. A simple working cell phone would make all the difference."

"It is what it is," he said. "Now we need to figure out what to do next."

I swallowed, suddenly unsure of myself. In the moment, it had seemed essential to act immediately, but Marco might not see it that way.

"What?" he asked warily.

"I called Bingham."

He stared at me as though he was still waiting for a response.

"It makes sense, Marco. He's got a vested interest in this, and he's obviously not beholden to the law."

"I want to put these guys away, Carly," he said darkly. "In prison. Not seek vigilante justice."

I leaned closer, whisper-hissing, "I know. I want the same thing, but our hands are tied and their lives are in danger. I called the one person who might move heaven and earth to free Lula. To free them both."

"We should have discussed it, Carly. We were doin' this together. You might have been able to sway my thinking in the end, but now we'll never know, and you can be damn sure that Bingham will kill anyone who's involved and destroy any evidence I could have brought to the sheriff's department."

He was right. I should have discussed it with him. But if I'd learned one thing over the last months, it was that the law had its limitations. As much as I hated the thought of Bingham possibly killing people without due process, I cared about those two women more. I would do anything I could to save them.

"Well, in a perfect world, we wouldn't be doing this investigation on our own," I said, squaring my shoulders. "The sheriff's department could bust in and get them, but no one will touch it. You can't go because of your leg, and I'd be useless, so that left me with one option. And yeah, I should have talked to you about it, but I was trying to save their lives, Marco," I said, pissed when tears stung my eyes. "And I refuse to apologize for doing whatever I can to save them. Even at the risk of destroying evidence we don't even know the sheriff's department would use."

He pushed out a breath and stared down at the table. Finally, he put his hand over mine and met my gaze. "You're right."

My brow shot up.

"Truth be told, I've been doin' this partially for selfish reasons. I've been hopin' to prove I'm detective material, but if Bingham's gettin' involved, we'll have to keep it all on the downlow. The sheriff's department will be none the wiser."

I wrapped my hand around his. "I'm sorry."

"Not your concern." He pulled his hand free. "I'm beat. I know you're gonna hate this, but I'm gonna ask Wyatt to take you home tonight."

"No," I said. "I'll get a ride from Ruth. Bingham's takin' care of the situation, so I'll be fine."

"Okay, but let me know the minute you hear from Bingham."

"Will do." I took his to-go order and turned it in, and I realized Ruth was watching me like a hawk. Since I'd been ripping off Band-Aids all night, I decided I might as well tug off one more.

"Out with it," I said. "I know you have something to say."

She pursed her lips. "What's goin' on with you and Marco?"

"I told you. We've been looking for Lula and Greta."

"What's with the hand holdin'?"

I shrugged. "Marco and I had a small disagreement, and that was his way of apologizing." I leaned in closer. "There's nothing between us, Ruth. Sure, I broke up with Wyatt, but that doesn't mean I'm ready to jump into a relationship with someone else."

She studied me for a moment. "Why not? Marco's unreliable, so he's definitely not long-term material, but I've heard he's good between the sheets."

"There's nothing wrong with Marco." My instinct was to defend him, yet she wasn't wrong. He was the first to admit he didn't get serious with women. "But that's beside the point. I've been hurt by so many men in the past. I thought Wyatt would be different, and he wasn't." I pushed out a breath in frustration. "I don't trust my judgment with men, so I think it's best I go manless for now."

She gave me a long, serious look. "Then we need to get you a vibrator."

I broke out into laughter. "Ruth, thank God I have you in my life. You keep me sane."

"Same for you," she said, then nodded her head at a table. "Looks like table six needs refills."

"On it, but before I forget to ask, can I get a ride home? Marco dropped me off after our trip to Ewing."

"Of course. No problem."

I checked on table six, then got Marco's order and sent him home. As the evening progressed, I got increasingly antsy. Why hadn't I heard from Bingham yet? He'd had plenty of time to storm the property. Had he found them?

I was on the verge of calling him, consequences be damned, when Ruth called out from behind the bar, "Carly, you've got a phone call."

My eyes widened, and I said, "I'll take it in the office."

I hurried into the back and picked up the flashing line. "This is Carly."

"They weren't there," Bingham said, his voice heavy. "We searched every piece of that land, and there was no sign of the girls or any kind of drug operation. The place was a run-down, abandoned house. No sign of anyone living there for years."

I resisted the urge to cry. We were back to square one.

"Any other idea where they could be?" he asked.

"No." I felt like I was going to be sick.

"If you find out anything—anything—let me know."

"I will."

He hung up and I immediately called Marco to tell him the news.

"So we have no idea where they are," he said.

"I guess not." Then I said, "You never told me what you found at the library."

"I checked on his references. The people who answered sounded like they'd genuinely never heard of him, which says a whole lot about Greener Pastures' screenin' process."

"And the fact there's a thief workin' there," I added.

"The property on record belongs to a Dennis Jones, who does have a son named Shane. Our guy could have perpetrated identity theft, or he could have just given his father's property address to throw off anyone who might come lookin' for him. Maybe Charlie's the assumed name."

"So their operation is run out of another location," I said. "We just need to figure out where."

"It could be the funeral home," Marco said. "Or it could be some place they rented, which will make it harder to find. It would be easier if we had the resources to tail them."

I pushed out a breath. "Okay. We start fresh in the morning."

"That's the spirit," he said with forced cheerfulness. "We'll find them. I swear it. But it's not safe for you to go home with Ruth tonight. I'm gonna pick you up."

I almost argued that we'd be fine, but the last thing I wanted to do was put Ruth at risk. "We're not very busy tonight, and there's a new snowstorm coming in. Ruth's planning on closing early. Can you come around eleven?"

"See you then."

I hung up and headed back into the dining room. Ruth looked curious about my call, but she didn't ask questions. She surely would have if she'd recognized Bingham's voice.

Jerry was at one of our few remaining tables, talking to a couple of older men, and they waved me down to get their check.

"We need to get home before the snow hits," one of the men said.

His comment made me remember the coat I'd gotten Jerry but hadn't given him yet. "Don't leave yet, Jerry," I said, setting the ticket on the table. "I got you something in Greeneville last week, and I keep forgetting to give it to you. It's in the back. Let me run and grab it."

I hurried to the back room and pulled out the Target bag I'd stuffed into one of the empty lockers. It was really jammed inside, so I gave it a hard tug. I pulled it loose but stumbled backward and into something firm.

A person.

A hand covered my mouth as I felt a sharp jab in my thigh. I glanced down to see a hand holding a syringe against my leg.

"Time to go nighty-night," a man whispered in my ear.

I felt woozy and started to slump to the floor, but a strong arm held me up against a hard chest.

And then everything went black.

CHAPTER THIRTY-TWO

When I came to, my head felt fuzzy and my body shivered from cold. I released an involuntary groan.

"Carly?"

It took me a moment to recognize Greta's voice.

"Greta?" I said, but my mouth felt like it had been stuffed with cotton and my voice came out as a croak.

"Yeah," she said softly.

"I feel like shit." Everything in my body ached, from my head to my toes. I was lying against something cold and uneven. The air reeked of mold and pee.

"If they dosed you with the same drug they used on me, it's one of the aftereffects. It's probably gonna get worse before it gets better."

Great.

My eyes were adjusting to the darkness, and I could see slivers of pale light shining through rectangular slats on the wall. The dirt floor was damp beneath me. "Where are we?"

"Some sort of shed. It's not insulated."

My hands were tied behind my back, and my fingertips tingled from cold. "Why are we here?"

"They're lookin' for Lula."

I struggled to keep my eyes open. "Lula's not here?"

"No. But they want her. Bad."

A wave of nausea rose up, and I pushed up on a shoulder and turned my head as I vomited violently.

"That's also part of it," she said sympathetically.

I vomited again. After the last spasm passed, I tried to sit up, but my stomach muscles ached too badly, so I rolled away from the mess, toward Greta. I began to shake and she edged closer to me, pressing her jeans-covered leg against my bare arm. My eyes were still adjusting to the dark, but I could tell she was wearing the thick sweater she'd had on the night she'd walked into the tavern. Her left eye and her lips were swollen. She'd been beaten.

"You're gonna freeze to death," she said, her voice full of concern.

Whoever had taken me from the tavern had dumped me in here without a coat. "Who took us?"

"That guy who came into the café askin' about Lula," she said.

"Shane Jones," I said. "Only some people know him as Charlie. I found out he works at Greener Pastures. I think he was the one who took your wallet. Marco got his employment application. We got his address, and Bingham and his men searched the property, but they didn't find anything. Do you know where we are?"

"I was unconscious when I got here too. I don't leave this shed, so I have no idea."

"They don't take you somewhere else to question you?"

"There is no *they*. Just that guy. He asks where Lula went, I tell him I don't know, and he knocks me around. Over and over."

"Do you hear any sounds?" I asked. "Cars? Planes? Water?"

"Birds," she said. "Just birds…and leaves."

"No people talking?"

"No."

"Have you tried the door?"

"He locks it from the outside. I think it's a padlock."

I finally managed to push myself up to sitting, my back resting against the wall, wood splinters digging into my skin. Another wave of nausea rose up, but I swallowed the bile and then took several breaths through my mouth.

Greta leaned against me. "It takes a few hours to recover."

I wasn't sure I had a few hours. It was freezing outside, and I thought I could see snowflakes through the slats of the shed. I was only wearing jeans and a short-sleeved T-shirt.

I'd gone to the back room at around nine thirty. Marco wouldn't show up until eleven, but it wouldn't take Ruth and Tiny long to notice I was missing. What would they do? Call Marco? Wyatt? Would they assume I'd just walked out? Even if they contacted Marco, how would he find me?

Bottom line: I couldn't wait for someone to come rescue us. We had to save ourselves.

"Are your hands tied behind your back?" I asked.

"Yeah."

"Get them to the front. We're breaking out of here."

"But the door's locked," she protested.

"We're not using the door." Another wave of nausea hit me, and I took several breaths through my mouth until it passed. "We're going to dig ourselves out. Is there anything in here we can use to dig?"

"I…"

"Think about it while you work your hands to the front." I braced my back against the wall and lifted my butt. Sliding my hands underneath me, I then concentrated on unthreading my arms from my legs.

Greta's voice shook with fear. "If he sees we've done this, he won't like it."

"We won't be here when he comes back." With my back to the wall, I pushed up to standing, then waited out a rush of dizziness. Greta seemed to be working on slipping her hands to the front.

I turned and pressed my eye to a crack between the slat. The ground was clear for about ten feet and then it hit the woods. I took a step toward another wall and my legs nearly buckled underneath me. I caught myself against the wood slats and waited for a new round of nausea and pain to subside.

"What the hell did he give me?"

"Some drug they created but it didn't work out for recreational use. Obviously. It's brutal, Carly. You need to sit and rest."

No fucking way was I going to sit and rest. Unless he was stupid, he didn't care if I survived or not, otherwise he would have given me a coat or a blanket. "No. We need to find something to dig with."

I looked out of the slats in the second wall and saw more woods. The third wall faced the side of a small wood cabin. A black truck was parked out front. Mud was caked on the sides, and I realized it had double wheels in the back.

"Charlie/Shane's the one who was at Lula's property," I said. "Only she must have seen him coming and run out into the woods." I moved to the wall with the door and saw a narrow road curving from the house and into the trees. "We need to go out on the side opposite the house. Toward the back," I said, nodding in that direction. "We'll dig a depression big enough for us to slip through, run into the trees, and run parallel to the road until the house is out of sight. There's bound to be another house somewhere close." I hoped.

It was a solid plan. We just needed to find makeshift tools and hope that the asshole didn't come out to check on us.

"We can't do that, Carly. If he figures out what we're doin'…"

"He's not gonna figure it out. Not until after we're long gone."

I found a metal coffee can full of screws on the ground, so I slowly dumped them out, careful to make as little noise as possible. Dropping to my knees in front of the back walk, I gripped the lip of the can and pushed it into the ground as hard as I could. A small amount of soil got scooped up, and I tossed it into the corner before going in for another. The ground was hard, but we'd get through it.

Greta found a small garden shovel, and I suggested we use it to cut our wrist bindings before we started digging.

It took multiple attempts for me to get the angle and pressure right, but I finally cut through her bindings. By the time I finished, my hand was shaking, and I dropped the shovel to the ground and took a few seconds to recover.

She shook out her hands and released a soft moan, then wrapped her arm around me and hugged me tight.

I sank into her for a moment, soaking up her body heat, before I reluctantly pulled free. "Me next."

She nodded and picked up the shovel, and I got a good look at her as she started working on the rope. The band of her ponytail had slipped a few inches from her head, making the hair around her head loose and messy. Her face was more swollen than I'd realized, and her sweater was covered with splotches of blood.

"What does he ask you when he comes in?" I asked, the words taking more effort than I'd expected.

"He asks where Lula is," she whispered. "Where she put the money. I don't know anything about any of it, of course, but he doesn't like that answer." She gave me a wry smile, but it stretched her swollen, busted lips, and she winced. "I'm not surprised you're here. The last time he paid me a visit, he asked about you and if you were workin' for Bingham. He thinks you know something about Lula." She paused for a moment, looking up into my eyes. "Carly, he'll try to beat it out of you."

The hairs on my arms stood on end, and a new wave of energy flushed through my veins, pushing away the exhaustion. We had to get out of here before he came back.

Greta was almost through the rope, so I pulled my wrists apart and broke through the final cords.

I rubbed the rope burns on my wrists and said, "Let's get started."

It was slow going. The ground was packed, but we were determined. We worked in coordinated silence as I kept pushing back against the overwhelming urge to lie down and take a short rest. If I closed my eyes, I had no idea when I'd wake up. I prayed the adrenaline rush continued to hold off the darkness in my head.

The deeper we dug, the more freezing winter air filled the shack. The snow continued to fall, adding to the dirt we were scooping. After we'd been at it for twenty minutes or so, we could clearly see the outside. The ground was covered in a light dusting. Panic hit me when I realized we were going to leave tracks pointing to our escape route. We needed to get out of here as quickly as possible so the continuing snowfall would hopefully cover our tracks.

"Stop," I said, closing my eyes for a second as a new round of nausea and dizziness hit me. "I think we're close. Let's check the depth."

The depression was about a foot deep in a half circle. Freedom was so close I could taste it, but it made me anxious too. If he decided to come in and check on us, it would be difficult to hide what we'd been doing. But the hole still wasn't big enough for us to escape. "I think we only need to go a little farther."

"Okay." She continued digging while I took another few seconds.

The movement had warmed me up some, but my head was killing me and my balance was off, and a new worry took hold. I was going to slow Greta down when we got out. I wasn't sure I could run, let alone walk without falling over.

After another five minutes of us working in silence, I checked the hole again. "I think it's good enough. Greta, you go first."

She stared at me in wide-eyed terror. "I can't."

"You can," I said. "*And you will.*"

"What if I get stuck?"

"Then I'll dig you free. *Now go.*"

My bossiness must have overridden her fear because she got on her stomach and started to put her head through first.

"Stop," I said. "Put your hands through first so you can pull yourself up."

"Yeah. Okay," she said as though giving herself a pep talk. She did as I'd suggested, threading her arms into the hole and then her head.

I realized our mistake straightaway—we should have given the hole more of an incline, but it would work in a pinch. Greta had gotten the top half of her body through, but we hadn't made it wide enough for her hips. She was stuck. She started to panic, struggling against the blockage, but I put my hand on her lower back and said, "Calm down. He'll hear us. You're okay, I'll dig you free."

To my relief, she settled down and I used the shovel to dig

around her hips, trying to not jab her despite my growing sense of urgency.

We were so close.

Just when she was on the verge of wiggling free, we heard the squeaking of poorly oiled door hinges. Greta pulled her legs the rest of the way free and turned around to stare at me through the hole with pure panic in her eyes.

"Carly!" she whispered.

I doubted I'd make it through the hole in time, and I was still unsteady enough that I'd never outrun him.

Grabbing her hand, I squeezed it hard. "Run for help. I'll keep him busy."

"How?" she asked in disbelief.

"I've got some weapons I can use," I said. "He won't be prepared for them. *Now go!*" I gave her hand a shove, and after giving me a look of hesitation and guilt, she ran soundlessly into the trees. Leaving clear tracks behind her. Hopefully he wouldn't see them before he came into the shed.

I planned to buy her as much time as I could.

A man was whistling a happy tune, and the sound got louder as he came closer. I suspected he was taunting us, something he confirmed when he called out, "Carly, I'm comin' to see you. We're gonna have some *fun.*"

And I would be ready for him. If I'd had time, I could have refilled the bucket with screws and swung it at his head, but I really needed to use the element of surprise.

I grabbed a handful of the screws, pulling out the longer ones and placing them between the fingers of my right hand, the ends pointed outward, while I held the shovel in my left hand.

"Carly?" he called out again, sounding entirely too happy to suit me. "Are you awake yet?"

I remained silent, trying to formulate a quick plan. I'd never taken self-defense classes, but I knew one of the most sensitive areas for a man, so I crouched next to the door and waited.

"Hey, Greta," he said next to the door. The padlock clunked against the wood. When she didn't answer, he grew pissed. "You stupid bitch. Answer me."

My pulse was pounding in my head, and adrenaline flooded my system. I gave this a twenty-five percent success rate, but I reminded myself of my main goal: buying time for Greta. Anything else was pure bonus.

There was a thud on the ground. The sound distracted me, and I realized too late he'd dropped the padlock on the ground. The door was already swinging open, and a beam of light shone against the back wall.

"What the fuck?" he snarled, turning around.

This hadn't gone as I'd expected. I'd thought he'd walk in and I'd punch him in the balls with my fist full of screws, but obviously that plan was blown to bits. He hadn't taken a single step inside the shed.

Time to improvise.

"Hey, you fucking asshole!" I shouted, still crouched on the other side of the door.

"Carly?" he asked, spinning around and shining his flashlight into the shed again. This time he took a step. "Where are you, you stupid bitch?"

He hadn't walked all the way into the shed, but at least he was standing still. I thrust my arm between his legs, but he shifted to the side and the screws sunk into his left thigh.

He screamed out in pain and started to reach for my arm—which was when I jabbed the garden shovel into his bicep, slamming the screws deeper into his leg as I did so.

He fell to the ground screaming in pain. I'd temporarily incapacitated him, but I'd neglected to take into account the fact that he might block the door. If I tried to go over him, he'd hurt me. But every second I hesitated gave him one more second to recover.

He sat up and pure rage covered his face. "I'm gonna beat the ever-lovin' shit out of you."

Keep him talking.

"Is that what you did to Greta?" I asked.

"Honey," he said, grabbing a screwhead and pulling it from his leg. He threw it against the wall, where it pinged then fell to the ground. "What I did to Greta's gonna look like patty-cakes. I promised her sister I wouldn't hurt her too bad, but I didn't make no promises about you."

The thought that Melody knew he had Greta filled my head first, but it was quickly replaced with an image of Greta's bruised and swollen face. If he called that holding back, I wasn't sure I'd survive long enough for Greta to get back with help.

"What about Lula?" I asked. "What did you do to *her?*"

"I didn't do shit to her. I'm trying to *find* her, so it worked great when you started lookin' for her too. But then you sniffed too close in my direction. That's when I knew it was time to shut you up."

"You realize I only got to you because you took Greta. If you'd left her alone, I'd have been none the wiser."

He released a long growl of frustration as he pulled out another screw and threw it hard against the wall.

"What about Marco?" I asked. "You gonna shut him up too? And what about the sheriff's department? You have enough people on the inside to keep them out of it?"

"The sheriff's department's not lookin' into this," he said, taking several rapid breaths to deal with his pain. "I checked this afternoon." He reached for another screw but hesitated as though psyching himself up to deal with the pain.

Part of me wanted to tell him not to remove the screws, that doing so might increase his blood loss, but this man intended to hurt or kill me. If he was injured, it would work to my advantage. "Marco won't let this go. He knows about you. He'll find me."

"There won't be nothin' left of you to find. Unless..." A grotesque grin spread across his face. "Unless you tell me where Lula is."

"You know I have no idea where she is."

He laughed. "Well, all right then. Now I can kill you with a clean conscience."

Obviously his conscience was messed up.

"You're workin' for Pete Mobley, aren't you? Lula was delivering packages for him, but she didn't contact him after this last run." I was grasping at straws, trying to goad the truth out of him.

"You really don't know shit," he said as he pulled out the last screw and threw it in my direction.

I batted it away as I shrank against the back wall. "If I don't know shit, then tell me how it happened."

"She called him and told him she wasn't makin' no more deliveries, and on top of that, she was havin' his baby. Then she left town. He's a respected man in the community. He couldn't let the truth get out, so he asked me to take care of it. I suspect he meant to pay her off, but Lula knows more than she should. She's a liability. Just. Like. You."

He got to his feet, sagging against the doorframe. "You like to dig holes so much, I think I'll have you dig your own." He pulled a gun out from behind his back and pointed it at my chest. "Come on."

He motioned for me to walk past him out the door, but I didn't trust him. He was going to make me pay for causing him pain.

"I said *come on!*" he shouted at the top of his lungs. "*Get the fuck outside.*"

"I'll go," I said, hoping I was buying Greta more time. "But first I want to hear where Mobley fits into this situation. Is he the mastermind behind it all?"

He laughed, filling the doorway. "*Mobley in charge?* Mobley couldn't be in charge of a clusterfuck. Hell no, he's not in charge. Purdy was, and now it's fallen to me by default."

"But it only works with the stuff coming in with the coffins," I said. "And now that everyone knows…"

"I'm working on a new site in Chattanooga," he said. "Lula was deliverin' samples. They're about to come on board, but Lula's a loose thread."

"So after you kill me, you'll hunt her down and kill her?"

"That's the plan. Now *let's go.*"

I could let him try to come get me or I could walk over to him. He didn't seem to want to shoot me in here, or else he'd have already done it, so I decided to make this as difficult as possible for him. "No."

An evil grin filled his eyes. "Fine by me." He aimed the gun right at me, and I knew I'd made the wrong decision as soon as I heard a gunshot and the smell of gunpowder filled the air.

CHAPTER THIRTY-THREE

I pressed my back against the wall, waiting for the inevitable pain, but Shane dropped to the ground like a rock, revealing Todd Bingham standing about ten feet outside the doorway. Several men were fanned out around him.

"Where's Lula?" he barked, his gun pointed right at my chest.

I'd gone from one monster to another.

Something inside me collapsed, like all the air had been let out of a balloon. I wanted to sink to the ground, sobbing in fear and pain, but I wasn't going to back down. Not with him.

Somewhere deep down, I found the last of my strength and straightened my back. "I don't know."

"You said she was with Jones!" he shouted. "You said he had her!"

"He didn't," I said, still standing against the wall. "He was lookin' for her just like us."

"*Then where the fuck is she?*"

Who else would want her? Her biological father?

Pure panic raced through my blood. If *he* had her, I had no doubt that he would kill her.

Unless...

Did Max know the truth? Had he told Wyatt? Were they all holed up together, the two brothers stepping up to protect their half-sister and trying to figure out what to do next?

Suddenly, I knew where Lula was—or at least who she was with—and the truth hurt so badly I doubled over in pain. I leaned to the side and vomited bile.

Bingham's voice wavered. "Did he hurt you?"

"Drugged me with some failed concoction. I feel like I've been run over by a truck, but I think I know where Lula is. Give me your sat phone and I'll arrange for you to see her."

"What the hell are you talkin' about?" he demanded.

I sank to my knees. "Which part? The drugs or her location?"

Then I realized I was six feet from a dead man, his blood slowly seeping toward me on the hard ground.

That man would have killed me if he'd had his way. It was all too much. Still, I forced myself to swallow the sob rising in my throat.

You can't fall apart now, Carly. Not in front of him.

"If you lend me your sat phone and give me some privacy, I can confirm my theory. I think I know where she is."

He seemed to give it some consideration, then said, "There's someone you might want to see first."

Oh God. Had he taken someone prisoner to use as motivation? To convince me that I'd better guess right this time?

"Let him out," Bingham said with the flick of a hand.

It was then I noticed an SUV behind him—a dark Explorer— and Marco got out of the car, flying across the ground on his crutches. My first thought was that he was going to slip and fall in the snow.

"*Carly!*" he shouted.

I found the strength to get to my feet, forcing myself to walk over the dead body on the ground. Marco reached me a few feet outside of the shed. He dropped a crutch and engulfed me with one arm, holding me so tightly I could scarcely catch my breath.

"You're freezin'," he said, releasing me to shrug off his jacket. He balanced on one crutch as he wrapped the jacket around my shoulders. Leaning down to look at my face, he said, "Are you hurt?"

I shook my head, dangerously close to crying. Part of me wanted to collapse into him and sob, but I couldn't fall apart. Not yet.

"Where's Greta?"

"We dug a hole to escape, but he was coming out of the house, and I was still too unbalanced from the drugs he gave me to run. So I sent her to get help." I lowered my voice. "Can we trust Bingham?"

"As much as anyone can, but he won't hurt Greta, if that's what you're worried about. Which way did she go? I'll have him send someone to go find her."

"Through the trees, parallel to the road. I need to use Bingham's sat phone, Marco. I think I know where Lula is."

He searched my face. "Did Jones tell you?"

"No."

I held his gaze, and he must have seen something in my eyes because he simply nodded and led me over to Bingham. "Greta escaped toward the road. We need to send someone to find her. And you need to give Carly your sat phone and let her make her call."

The two men had a staring contest for a few seconds, and it ended with Bingham reaching into his jacket pocket. "Ty and Pitch, go look for Greta. Try to be as nonthreatening as possible."

Two men jumped into a truck and drove back down the lane, but Bingham still held the phone in his hand. "I'll listen in."

"If I'm right, I'm giving you Lula, Bingham, and asking for nothing in return. All I ask for is some privacy."

His eyes darkened. "You have five minutes."

I took the phone and he walked away, leaving me with Marco.

"I need to sit down," I said, my legs shaky.

"Let's go over to my car."

I didn't think I'd make it that far, so I sank down onto the snow-covered ground, a wave of dizziness washing over me.

"Carly?" Marco cried out, tossing his crutch and sitting next to me.

"I just need a minute." But I didn't have a spare minute. Bingham had only given me five of them. I blinked a couple of times, trying to see the touchpad, but it kept going in and out of focus.

"I'm sorry," I finally said. "I can't see the numbers. I need you to press the buttons."

He took the phone, giving me a worried look.

"I'll be fine. Greta warned me that it takes hours to recover." I told him the number, pleased that I remembered given the state of my head.

When he finished, he handed me the phone.

I could hear it ringing. Then Wyatt's hardened voice cut in. "Wyatt Drummond."

"Wyatt, it's Carly. I know what you and Max are doing, but I need to speak to Lula."

He hesitated, then said, "Where are you callin' me from?"

"It doesn't matter, Wyatt," I said, my voice breaking. Then, lest he think I was calling under duress, I added, "I'm with Marco. Now put Lula on the phone."

More silence, and I knew he was torn between lying to me,

again, and protecting his newly discovered sister. My heart felt ripped in two.

"I know she's with you," I snapped. "And I understand why, now just put her on the damn phone."

"Okay," he finally said, "but then we need to talk."

"I can't discuss this now, Wyatt," I said, choking up. "Just put her on the line."

There was a rustle of distorted voices. Then Lula said into the phone, "Carly?"

I leaned my forehead against Marco's shoulder, fighting the urge to break down. He wrapped an arm around my back and rested his chin on my head.

Sucking in a breath, I sat up. I'd made it this far. I wasn't going to let myself fall apart yet. "Hey, Lula. You have no idea how happy I am to know you're okay."

"Max said I couldn't tell anyone where I was."

"He was trying to protect you," I said in an even voice. "But I spoke to your momma this afternoon, and I found out that she lied to you about your father."

"You talked to Momma? She told you?"

"She didn't totally confess, but she admitted to lying to you about Bingham being your father."

"I know," she said in a tiny voice. "Turns out she lied about a lot of things."

"She also lied when she told you that Mobley is the baby's father. You should have the baby tested, but I'm pretty certain Bingham is the father. Your mother confirmed it."

She started crying. "He is? But the baby…"

"He wants it, Lula, and he wants you. You should see the lengths he went to trying to find and protect you."

She continued to cry.

"He wants you, Lula. The question is do *you* want *him*?" I said, lowering my voice. My vision was turning hazy and it was diffi-cult to focus. But this was important, so I poured all of my remaining energy into finishing our conversation. "He's a crimi-nal. A hardened one at that. As your friend, I feel like I need to tell you it's a bad idea, yet I know the heart wants what the heart wants. What does your heart want?"

She was silent for a moment, then took a deep breath. "I want Todd."

"Okay," I said, and it sounded like I was speaking in a well. "I'm gonna give the phone to Bingham so you two can work out the logistics of getting together."

"Carly?" she called out as I pulled the phone away from my ear.

"Yeah?"

"Thank you."

"I'm just glad you're safe," I said, handing the phone to Marco. What little energy I'd mustered to get through the call left me, and I slumped against him.

"Bingham!" he shouted as he wrapped an arm around me. "Lula wants to talk to you."

Bingham strode over with a dark look, but his expression softened at the sight of me.

"Lula's on the phone," I said as my vision faded.

"Carly?" Marco asked, sounding panicked. "Talk to me."

But everything went black.

CHAPTER THIRTY-FOUR

I woke up screaming, but Marco was at my side, gathering me into his arms, stroking my hair and soothing my fears. "You're safe. I swear you're safe."

I fell asleep again, and the next time I woke, my entire body was shuddering. Marco was still holding me tight.

"We should take her to the hospital," he said in a wavering voice.

"No," another man said. "It's part of the detox. They can't do anything other than give her a saline IV, which we're already doin'."

"You're only sayin' that to save his ass," Marco sneered.

"No hospital."

I pried my eyes open to stare up at him. "No hospital, Marco." Then I tried to crack a smile. "I don't have insurance."

"Jesus, Carly. That's the least of my concerns."

"Easy for you to say," I teased. "You're not the one paying."

I fell asleep again, and when I woke up, I was drenched in sweat. Sunlight filtered into the room. I felt more lucid this time, and I recognized my surroundings: they'd transported me to

Marco's bedroom. He was asleep in an armchair next to the bed, his leg propped up on a kitchen chair. An IV pole stood next to the bed, the tube running to my hand.

"Marco," I said, but my mouth was dry, and it came out garbled.

He heard me anyway, and the sleep left his eyes in an instant as he sat upright. "You're awake."

"Either that, or I'm dead and I didn't make it to the Pearly Gates."

Relief filled his eyes, bringing his good humor with it. "I'll have you know that a fair number of women have claimed to meet God on that bed."

I closed my eyes and groaned. "Then I hope you put some antibiotics in that IV."

"Can I get you anything?" he asked, sitting forward on his chair.

"A glass of water?"

"Comin' right up." He walked out of the room, using one crutch, and returned a couple of minutes later with a glass of ice water that sloshed with every step.

He sat on the side of the bed and set the water on the nightstand. Then he lifted me to a sitting position, propped up some pillows behind me, and handed me the glass.

I took a drink, then glanced down and realized I was wearing one of his T-shirts.

"Yours was wet and covered in dirt. This is the second one you've worn since you got here," he said unapologetically.

"What time is it?"

He hesitated. "Around two." Then he added, "You've been out for nearly two days. It's Tuesday afternoon."

"Hank!"

"He thinks that you're stayin' with Ruth while Franklin's out of town."

I nodded. That was probably for the best. "What happened?"

"Lula and Bingham met in the Laundromat parking lot, and I hear she left with him. Before he went to meet her, he had some of his men bring us to my house. I wanted to take you to the hospital, but Bingham said his medic could counteract the drug's side effects better than any hospital. His guy stayed the entire first night and has been out multiple times to keep an eye on you. We've gotten you up a few times to pee, but other than that you've slept."

"I don't remember any of that."

"The medic said you probably wouldn't."

Then a new horror hit me. "Did I talk while I was out of it?"

"Only gibberish," he said. "Nothin' that made sense."

It scared me that I'd been so vulnerable—even more so because I remembered so little of it. "What did Charlie/Shane Jones give me?"

"Something Mobley and the others brought in from Atlanta. A bad batch. Jones gave some to Greta, and while she suffered, she said it was much milder than your reaction. Bingham thinks you were lucky to survive." Then he added, "It's the same drug that killed Hank's daughter."

"I thought it was supposed to make you high. All it did was make me feel like I was coming down with the flu."

"Like I said, bad batch."

"What happened with Jones?" I asked.

He released a bitter laugh. "Bingham enacts his own justice, and the sheriff's department is none the wiser."

My heart sunk. "I'm sorry, Marco. I know you were hoping to do this the right way."

He gave me a tight smile. "The important thing is that you're safe. Greta and Lula too."

Something about his tone caught my attention.

"He blackmailed you, didn't he?" When he gave me a blank look, I said, "He wouldn't let you take me to the hospital, but it was pretty generous of him to provide medical assistance, so I'm sure he got something for it. He asked you not to involve the sheriff, didn't he?"

"Don't feel bad," he said. "You saved my life. I saved yours. We're even."

So why didn't it feel like that?

Because he hadn't just saved my life. For my sake, Marco had given up his morals and his aspirations for the sheriff's department.

"Are you hungry?" he asked.

"No. My guts feel like they've been scrubbed with sandpaper."

"The medic says you probably won't be able to go back to work for a few days."

That sobered me some. "I'm not sure I'm going back to the tavern."

"Max said you have your job back."

"I know," I said. "But if Max had just been honest with us, then we never would have gotten this deep."

Wyatt too, but I didn't want to say it.

"He and Wyatt did what they thought was best given the circumstances. They think you've got a bad case of the flu," he said in a tight voice. "They don't know how many times you came close to dyin' over the last few days. We didn't tell them about what happened with Jones. Greta and Lula have sworn they won't tell a soul."

"How are they explaining Greta's face?"

"She's tellin' everyone her ex kidnapped and beat the shit out of her, but she refuses to press charges. Hines is Bingham's man, so he won't make a peep."

"And Mobley?"

"Disappeared." He swallowed, then said, "But Bingham paid Mobley a visit and got the location for where Charlie Jones was keepin' you and Greta."

"And then Bingham shut him up permanently," I said. It wasn't a question.

Marco didn't need to respond, and he didn't.

"How did you end up showing up with Bingham?"

"Ruth called me and said you'd disappeared after going to the back room. She was scared, saying you disappeared shortly after Bingham came to see you. Charlie was careless when he kidnapped you, because there was an obvious sign of a struggle and your coat was still there. So I went to Bingham's property to tell him you'd been taken. I demanded he give you back if he was the one who'd taken you, but he swore he didn't have you, which put Charlie Jones at the top of the suspect list. Seein' as how Bingham's not bound by the law, he drove straight to Mobley Funeral Home and demanded answers."

"You were with Bingham when he questioned Mobley?"

"No, but I was in my car in the parking lot. I'm still an accessory."

I closed my eyes and tears leaked from the corners. "Marco. I'm so sorry."

Marco pulled me into a hug. "I'm not. I'd do it all over again, and then some, to save you."

The whole nightmare replayed in my head. I started to sob. He let me cry myself out, gently wrapped me up in his arms, then tucked me back into his bed when I got sleepy from the exertion.

The next time I woke it was late evening. He gave me some chicken broth and then helped me into the bathroom. He gave me some privacy, but returned to sit on the toilet while I showered in case I needed help.

After that, I was awake more often, and the next day I could get out of bed on my own. I'd moved out to the sofa, and we were watching an action movie that Marco had picked from his satellite dish lineup. I was leaning into his arm, dozing off and on, when his body stiffened. He jumped up, grabbing his crutch, and hobbled to a window overlooking the front yard.

I could hear a car engine coming closer.

Marco picked up a shotgun lying on his kitchen table and headed for the front door.

"Marco?"

He ignored me, opening the front door and lifting his gun as a greeting to the approaching vehicle.

"*Marco.*"

I started to get up, but he shot me a glance as he lowered the weapon. "It's Lula and Greta."

I sank back into the cushions, pulling the blanket on my lap higher to ward off the chill from outside.

"Is it okay if we see Carly?" I heard Lula ask.

"She's still recoverin'," Marco said, "but I know she'd be happy to see you both."

A few seconds later, they both bustled inside and hurried over to me. Greta was carrying a vase of flowers and Lula had a handful of magazines.

Relief flooded my veins. "You have no idea how happy I am to see you both."

"We've been dyin' to see you," Lula said. "But Marco said you weren't up to visitors yet."

"I suggested that you wait until tomorrow," he grumbled, shutting the door and laying the gun on the table. "She still needs her rest."

"I'm glad you came," I said, even though I felt a little self-conscious. Lula's face was glowing with an inner joy that made me slightly jealous, and while Greta's face was still bruised, she'd covered it up with makeup and had on a cute shirt and jeans. I was wearing one of Marco's long-sleeved T-shirts and a pair of sagging jogger pants. I hadn't brushed my hair since my shower the night before, and I knew I had a serious case of bed head from lying against Marco and the sofa back.

"We brought you some things as a thank you," Greta said, holding out the vase of mixed red, yellow, and white flowers, "even though it's pretty lame in comparison to what you did for us."

"Thank you," I said with a soft smile. "I love flowers, but you didn't have to bring me anything but yourselves."

They set their gifts on the coffee table, and Greta took a seat to my right while Lula got settled in the armchair. Marco offered them drinks, but they declined. He hung back in the kitchen, giving us space but ready to step in if I needed help.

Lula stared at me for a few seconds, clearly wanting to say something but hesitant to do so.

"It's okay, Lula," I said. "Feel free to say what's on your mind."

She glanced down at her lap before looking up to meet my eyes. "No one in this town thought to look for me except you. Max was countin' on that." She grimaced, then shook her head. "The no one lookin' part. Not the part about you lookin'."

"I gathered that," I said, the scab ripped from the wound of his betrayal. "What happened after I dropped you off at home? How'd you end up with Max?"

"I went home and started a fire before bed. I was getting ready for work the next morning when I heard a truck comin' down the lane. No one comes to see me, so I knew it was probably one of Carson Purdy's guys wantin' their money. The thing is, I did something stupid, Carly. When I got to Chattanooga, I stood by the river, looking down at the water, and it was just so beautiful. I thought about taking my baby there someday, and suddenly I couldn't stand the thought of going through with the deal. I threw the drugs in the water. I knew I couldn't come back after what I done, but then I heard about Carson Purdy, and I figured maybe it would be okay to come home. I didn't think Pete would hurt me because of the baby. But when that man showed up on my property, I realized I'd thought wrong. I grabbed my shotgun and ran out the back to the creek, then hurried down it a ways so he wouldn't see my footprints."

"Weren't your feet wet and freezing?" I asked.

"I was wearin' my snow boots."

Lula was obviously a whole lot smarter than I'd given her credit for.

"I wasn't sure what to do or where to go, so I decided to go to Max. He's always been nice to me. Momma had hinted that maybe Bingham wasn't my daddy after all, that maybe it was Bart Drummond. She knew I was wantin' to quit workin' with Mobley, and she thought I'd keep doin' it if I thought there was a pot of gold at the end."

Which meant Bart was likely behind the operation after all.

"Did you call Max to come get you?"

"I had to get to a phone first. I stuck to the trees, so it took me most of the day to get to town. I wanted to stay hidden, so I let myself into one of the rooms at the Alpine Inn by pickin' the lock. That's when I called Max. I told him someone was after me. He said to stay put, that he'd come get me after closin', but then he called and told me to get out of there. To go hide in the church until he could come get me."

I nodded. "I saw Neil Carpenter coming out of one of the

rooms at the inn, and it freaked him out. He must have thought his father was lookin' for you." I made a face. "Your father."

I glanced up. Marco was leaning against the opening to the kitchen, watching me with concern in his eyes.

Her hands twisted in her lap. "I hadn't given him any details at that point. Anyway, he brought me back to the inn and put me in the second room from the end. He said he'd fortified the locks and no one was gettin' in. He left me a burger and fries and then went back to the tavern. He called me later, after he walked Greta to her car, and said this was gettin' serious and I needed to tell him what was goin' on. I was scared he was just puttin' me up temporarily, so I told him. Just blurted it out. 'I'm your baby sister,' I said. And Carly, I'm not proud of this, but since I didn't know what else to do to get his help, I lied to him. 'We have the same daddy,' I said, 'and I think he wants me dead.' He told me to stay put and he'd be over after he closed."

Had Max made that call from his office? He'd been gone a long time and then acted tight-lipped afterward.

"He hated that you were lookin' for me. He thought that tellin' you Ruth wouldn't like you lookin' would make you stop, but he said he underestimated your stubbornness."

Marco grinned, but he stayed in the background, giving us our space even though it was his house.

Earnestness filled her eyes. "Max wanted to tell you, but I made him swear to keep it a secret. It's my fault he kept it from you."

"How did Wyatt get involved?"

"He knocked on my motel door and gave me a blanket to wrap around my head and told me to get into the backseat of his truck and stay down. Max was sittin' in the front, smellin' like puke."

"Late Saturday afternoon?" I asked. After Wyatt had taken off running.

"Yeah."

I nearly asked if they were worried about being seen, but then I thought better of it. Downtown Drum was pretty dead on the weekends.

"Wyatt took us both to his house, and after Max showered and had some coffee, we just talked." She gave me an apologetic smile. "Wyatt had already figured out that Bart was my daddy, and he knows about five others. He has a notebook he keeps notes in."

I smothered the involuntary gasp rising in my throat. He barely knew Lula, but because they shared DNA he'd told her more than he'd told me. After everything we'd been through.

Marco made a move to come into the living room, but he must have thought better of it because he stopped and turned toward the table, easing himself into a chair.

"Wyatt said we needed to take the weekend to think things through and figure out how to handle the situation, 'cause they still thought it was Bart comin' for me. The guilt just ate at me, so I told them the truth on Sunday. That it was Carson Purdy's guy who was after me, and I'd been smuggling drugs to Chattanooga." She paused. "Wyatt didn't take it well, sayin' he'd thrown away the best thing that had happened to 'im in a long time to save me, but Max told him to calm down. That you'd understand. Look at what you'd done to try to find me. Then they argued about tellin' you the truth, but Wyatt said he'd do it in person on Monday. They'd figured out that Ruth had opened the bar by then, and Hank had said you were workin'." Tears filled her eyes. "Then you called around midnight that night, and Wyatt didn't get the chance."

I was dangerously close to tears, and I searched for Marco's warm eyes. He nodded slightly, and a soft grin lifted the corners of his mouth, his silent message loud and clear. *You've got this, Carly. You're stronger than this.*

"I'm sorry I wouldn't let him tell you," she said, tears tracking down her cheeks. "I'm sorry you were nearly killed tryin' to help me."

I gnawed at the inside of my cheek, hesitating. "Marco said Wyatt and Max don't know the truth about what happened, that you wouldn't tell a soul. But you didn't...?"

She shook her head. "As far as they know, you came down with the flu and you're stayin' with Marco until you recover so you don't get Hank sick. The only reason they let me out of their sight is they know Todd will protect me."

I nodded.

"You look tired," she said. "I only wanted to tell you thank you and let you know that Wyatt was helpin' me. Both of the Drummond brothers were."

I gave her a tight smile. "Lucky for you that you have them on your side."

"Yeah," she said with a wistful smile. "I am."

Greta had been silent, but I turned to her and said, "Greta, there's something I need to tell you."

Then I told her what Charlie had told me about her sister.

"Don't worry," she said with a soft smile. "I already moved out and into a small house outside of town."

"That quickly?" I asked in surprise.

Lula gave her a conspiratorial smile. "It helps havin' friends with connections."

I lifted my gaze to Marco's, and the look in his eyes confirmed we were both thinking the same thing—Bingham had helped Greta find her new place.

They got up to leave soon after, and I stood to see them out.

They both gave me hugs, and just as Lula was getting ready to walk out the door, I said, "Lula?"

She turned back to face me.

"Do you remember much of the day your mother shot your father?"

Storm clouds filled her blue eyes. "I don't like to think about that day."

Then she turned around and walked out the door.

I watched her and Greta get into a car driven by a man with serious muscles and an even more serious expression. Moments later, they were gone.

It stood to reason Bingham would give her a bodyguard.

"I forgot to ask if she was still workin' at the tavern," I said softly as I watched the car disappear around a curve.

"I think you know the answer to that. I'm surprised Bingham let her off his property long enough to come see you. I expected him to make you go to her."

I closed the door and turned to face him, still sitting at the table.

"Did Wyatt try to come see me?" I asked quietly.

He hesitated, and pity covered his face. "No."

"Did you talk to him at all?"

"Max came by on Monday, and I quickly shooed him out. I told him you had a bad case of the flu, and I wasn't sure when you'd be back. He's called to check on you every day, but I haven't heard from Wyatt."

Tears filled my eyes and I walked over to the sofa. He got up and hobbled over to sit next to me. "I don't know what's goin' on with you two, but I think he was probably your closest friend in town. After Max kept me in the dark, turns out, I've lost my closest friend too"—his voice wavered—"so how about we agree to be that person for each other? The one person you can turn to, no matter what."

He held out his hand, fingers flexed.

Biting my lip, I held back tears. "Just friends?"

"Just friends. Turns out sex complicates everything."

I released a laugh. "I didn't even have sex with him."

"Really?" he asked in disbelief. "Sorry, none of my business."

I turned to look up at him. "Isn't that the kind of thing best friends tell each other?"

He grinned. "Yeah."

"I have one rule, Marco. No secrets. That's why I broke up with Wyatt. I couldn't trust him. I need you to be honest with me, and I'll tell you everything in return." I held his gaze. "Everything."

He held out his hand again. "That's easy enough. I don't have any big, dark secrets. You're the one with something to lose, but I'll be honored to the day I die if you trust me with yours."

I grabbed his hand, linking our fingers and holding on to him as though he were my lifeline.

And then I told him everything.

CHAPTER THIRTY-FIVE

On Thursday, Marco took me back to Hank's. He took one look at me and knew I'd been sick, and the tables turned—he started waiting on me instead of the other way around. By Friday, I could make it through the day without taking a nap. Ruth stopped by to see me. She was surprised by how poorly I still seemed and suggested that I see a doctor, but I told her I was on the mend and would be as good as new by Monday.

Marco dropped by multiple times over the weekend, and I was sure it was partially out of boredom. Hank seemed to enjoy his company, but on Sunday afternoon he suggested it would be good for both of us if we walked the property—Marco so he wouldn't end up a one-legged man like him, and me so I'd be in good enough shape to return to work on Monday.

We were close to the road when a car pulled into the driveway and the driver's window slowly rolled down. The man at the wheel was a stranger. "Carly Moore?"

Marco took a step in front of me. "Who's askin'?"

"I have a message from Bart Drummond."

I moved around Marco. I'd been expecting this. In truth, I was surprised it had taken so long. "I'm Carly Moore."

He handed me an envelope, then rolled up his window and backed out onto the road and drove away.

Taking a breath, I opened the envelope and read the hand-written note.

Your presence is requested at the Drummond residence on Monday at eleven a.m.

Bart Drummond

"You don't have to go," Marco said.

"Yeah," I said, but we both knew I did.

The next day, I put on a dress and makeup, and left early enough to stop by the tavern first.

Max was in his apartment, but I'd warned him I was coming, so he met me downstairs. Concern filled his eyes when he saw me. I'd lost five pounds and my color still hadn't returned. Makeup helped, but I still looked like I'd been on death's doorstep.

"Are you sure you want to come back to work tonight?" he asked.

"I've missed a whole week of work. I need to make some money, but I'm not sure how long I'll last."

"Lula's workin' tonight, so don't you worry about that. We'll figure it out."

"Lula's workin'?" I asked in surprise. "I thought for sure she'd quit now that she's with Bingham."

"Well, I'm not sure how much longer she'll stay. I suspect she's doin' it to cover for you. I wouldn't be surprised if she quits soon after you return."

"That makes sense." I gestured to the dining area. "Can I sit? I'm still not—"

"Of course." He led me to a table like I was about to collapse, then ran and got me a glass of water.

When he sat down next to me, he turned serious. "What really happened to you, Carly? Greta had to take a few days off from Watson's too. Only when she returned, her face was sportin' bruises she said came from Tim Hines."

"It was a really bad bug."

"One that makes you disappear out of the back of the restaurant? Marco told us all you had the flu, but we're not stupid, not to mention I stopped by Marco's last Monday and saw you in his room with an IV pole and Todd Bingham's personal medic injecting something in your IV."

"Did you ask Marco?"

"He said you had the flu and refused to address the Bingham part."

"Well, there you go."

"But it seems quite the coincidence, considerin' Wyatt and I delivered Lula to him shortly after your call."

I didn't respond.

"Wyatt thinks there's something between you and Marco."

"I can't control what Wyatt thinks," I said. "And frankly, it's none of his business since we aren't together. But for the record, Marco and I are just friends. Very good friends, and nothing more."

"Wyatt cares about you, Carly."

"I know." I cared about him too, but it wasn't enough.

We were both quiet for a moment before he cleared his throat. "About Lula…"

"She came by to see me and told me everything."

"We know there are others," he said, looking down at the table, "but Lula… she's special."

"I know," I said.

"I felt bad not tellin' you, and I felt even worse when I realized Greta was missin'. You and Marco were gettin' in deep, but I didn't think I could tell anyone. It seemed possible Lula's life was in danger, and I didn't know if it was because of our father or if someone else was after her. Then Wyatt showed up and took charge, and we all went out to his house to figure out what to do."

"Did you come to a conclusion?"

"We told our father that we know the truth, and that Lula wants nothing from him. We told him to leave her alone."

I doubted they knew the full truth, but I wasn't going to be the one to tell them. At least not yet. "Do you think he will?"

"Only time will tell. But we're ready to jump in if need be."

"Lula's lucky to have two big brothers like you and Wyatt. Does anyone else know?"

"No. We're keepin' it quiet for now."

"Don't worry about me. I won't tell anyone."

He narrowed his eyes. "You sure you're ready to come back to work tonight?"

"I'm goin' stir-crazy, so yeah."

After we said our goodbyes, I drove to Wyatt's garage. I was worried about this meeting, but it needed to be done, and I wanted to see him before I met with his father.

I pulled into the parking lot and walked toward the building. The garage doors were open and both bays had cars. Wyatt was standing next to one of them, but he turned as I approached him. He started to walk toward me, a guarded look on his face.

"Carly, I hear you've been feelin' under the weather."

"You heard correctly," I said, already feeling winded and I hadn't even met with Bart yet. Maybe this had been a mistake, but it was too late to turn back now.

"What happened?" he asked, but there was an accusatory edge to his voice.

"What exactly are you asking, Wyatt?"

"Why did you stay with Marco?"

"Are you serious?" I asked in disbelief. "What happened to fighting for me? Where were you last weekend?"

He looked away. "We had a family emergency."

"Funny how you've known about all of my emergencies, yet I don't know anything about yours."

"That's not fair, Carly," he said in exasperation.

"You know," I said, utterly exhausted, "you're right. We've known each other for a month, so yeah, it's unreasonable for me to expect you to share your secrets with me, but the fact remains that you know far more about me than I know about you, and you've made it clear you don't plan on leveling the playing field anytime soon."

"Carly…"

"This argument is getting old, and I'm exhausted by it too. So I'm here to tell you that I have no expectations. Not anymore. You said you wanted to work with me to make things right with our fathers, but I accept that you changed your mind."

"Why do I think this isn't as good as it sounds?"

"Because bottom line is you don't trust me, and I can't be with someone who doesn't."

"Carly."

"I deserve a man who trusts me."

"You deserve a lot of things, Carly," he said with a tight voice.

"Yeah," I said, "I do." My voice broke. "I thought you were different."

"Is this about Lula? We had to wrap our heads around finding out she was our sister before we could tell anyone."

"I'm not supposed to be just *anyone*, but to top off the insult, you knew I was looking for her."

"You mean you and *Marco* were lookin' for her."

"We were *both* looking for her. Max put Greta's life in danger by keeping this secret. She was kidnapped and almost killed because of what Charlie Jones thought she knew about Lula. But *you* put *my* life in danger, Wyatt. You left me vulnerable all because you couldn't trust me."

"How did you get hooked up with Bingham on Sunday night?"

I released a bitter laugh. "No. You don't get to ask me that."

"What were you really doin' at Marco's house?"

"I had the flu."

"You still look like crap," he said. "I don't believe that for a minute. Ruth said you disappeared from work on Sunday night. But hours later you called me up, askin' to speak to Lula. First of all, how'd you know she was with us? And second, what kind of fool do you have to be to join forces with Todd Bingham?"

"For your information, I figured the Lula part out all on my own, thank you very much, and as for hooking up with Bingham —how dare you! I'd be dead several times over if not for that man. I was poisoned and almost shot, so fuck you, Wyatt Drummond." I pointed my finger at him, my voice breaking with tears. "Fuck. You."

"What the hell are you talkin' about? Nearly shot?" His eyes widened as though he was finally realizing how sick I'd been. "*Poisoned?*"

I shook my head and took a step backward. "*No.* You didn't trust me enough to tell me to call off my hunt for Lula. Which means I no longer trust you with the details of my life." I drew a deep breath. "Now if you'll excuse me, I have an appointment with a man who thinks highly of himself and likely won't appreciate it if I'm late." I turned and started walking to Hank's car.

"You on Bingham's payroll now?" he called after me.

I spun around, so hurt I could hardly take a breath.

"Thank you for saving me from any regret. But that reminds me—I sold Bingham my car, so let his associates take it when they show up. I know I still owe you money for the work you did, but you can just send me a bill."

He closed the distance between us. "What the hell happened to us?" he asked.

"I grew a backbone. That's what happened." I reached for the car door and got in. He raised his hand as if to call me back, but I ignored him as I drove away.

The smart thing would be to leave this town behind, but I knew my next stop would likely prevent that from happening.

CHAPTER THIRTY-SIX

I'd never been to the Drummond property before, but Marco had given me detailed directions. My stop to see Wyatt had made me a few minutes late.

The two-story house had rough stone siding and looked more like an estate than someone's home. As I parked in the circular drive, I tried to imagine Wyatt and Max growing up here. Neither of them seemed the type to live in such a place.

I approached the front stoop, but a woman greeted me at the front door before I could knock. She looked like she was in her late fifties, and she wrinkled her nose at the sight of me. Then again, I suspected she was the kind of person who always looked like she'd caught wind of a bad smell.

"Mr. Drummond would like you to use the side entrance," she said, pointing toward the end of the house.

Score one for Bart Drummond. He was sending me to the servants' entrance to drive home that he considered me trash. Fine. As I headed to the door, I found myself wondering if Louise Baker had approached this same door years ago.

I rapped on the wood and waited nearly a half minute before

a younger man in jeans and a T-shirt opened the door. He didn't look any friendlier than his coworker. "Mr. Drummond'll see you in his office."

He led me down a short hall, then stopped at an open door. I entered a large room with walls covered in animal heads. Bart sat behind an oversized desk with wall-to-wall bookcases behind him. To his left was a large window overlooking his land...and also a view of my car.

He'd watched me walk up. What a creeper.

"Hello, Carly. Thank you for agreeing to meet with me." He stood and walked around the edge of his desk. "I had hoped to meet with you last week, but I heard you were under the weather."

"I'm feeling much better," I said with a forced smile. "Thank you for asking."

He grinned at my cheekiness. "I heard you had the flu." The way he said it made it clear he knew it was a lie.

"Something like that."

He gestured to a grouping of sofa and chairs opposite the desk.

I sat down in the chair in case he got any ideas about what might happen on that sofa. He sat on the sofa opposite me and crossed his legs, resting his hand on his knee.

"I'm sure you're wondering why I invited you here."

I didn't answer. I wasn't volunteering anything.

"We all have secrets," he said.

I still remained silent.

"I have secrets," he said. "One of those secrets came out last weekend."

"Max said that Lula's not his only half-sibling. You were a busy man," I said. "Building empires in every sense of the word."

A forced grin spread across his face. "I love that you under-stand me."

"I understand you better than you know," I said.

"Maybe not, Caroline. Maybe I understand *you* perfectly."

I gave him a blank look. "Sorry if you were hoping for more of a reaction, but I'd already figured out that you know who I am. The real question is why I'm here."

He blinked in surprise.

"You could have turned me in, but you haven't, which means you want something from me. What is it?"

Score one for Marco. He'd coached me to come on strong and put Bart on the defensive.

"How do you know I don't plan to turn you in?"

"I'm sure you will when it's advantageous to you, yet for now you'll wait and try to get something from me. But I've heard of your famous favors. Perhaps you consider keeping my secret as my favor. The real question is what you'll ask of me and when."

"Whatever I deem appropriate," he said.

"No," I said. "You have something in mind, but you're keeping it to yourself for now."

He sat back and rested his forearm on the arm of the sofa, taking an easygoing pose. "You seem very certain of yourself, but you'd be foolish to underestimate me. I've destroyed more lives than you can count, and I'll rip yours to shreds if and when I feel like it, so wipe that smirk off your face."

I would never kowtow to him, but I'd let him figure that out later.

"If you were plannin' to leave town," he said. "I suggest you reconsider. If you try to leave, I'll be forced to release informa-tion that will put Hank Chalmers in prison for the rest of his life."

What did he have on Hank? Given Hank's past, it could be

anything. "And if you use it, I'll be forced to tell the world you tried to drown an eight-year-old girl in a pathetic attempt to destroy evidence of your affair."

"You've been talkin' to Louise."

"We had a lovely chat," I said. "Very informative."

"Louise can speculate all she wants," Bart said. "But she has yet to prove that Lula is my daughter."

"It's not difficult to determine such things," I said. "A simple DNA test will sort it out."

"And I've already had one done," he said. "Negative."

"Forgive me if I don't believe you."

He shrugged. "Believe it or not, I still have it and plan to show it to anyone who asks for proof."

And it would be just as easy to counter his claim—any home DNA kit would do—but that issue wasn't pressing at the moment.

He stood. "I brought you here to let you know that you have been noticed, and at some point, I will require your willing and able service. The less fuss you make, the better for all, especially poor Hank. I wonder how they deal with one-legged inmates?"

He smiled, but his eyes were dark.

I got to my feet and looked him square in the eye. "This has been such an informative meeting. Thank you."

"I'm happy we could reach this understanding," he said.

Oh, we'd reached an understanding, just not the one he'd meant. I'd do everything in my power to protect Hank.

Bart Drummond had finally met his match.

The dead can't speak

After months of living in the Smoky Mountains town of Drum, Tennessee, Carly knows firsthand the financial hardship the citizens face. Still, she can't muster the same excitement as everyone else when town patriarch Bart Drummond breaks ground on his new resort that promises more jobs and money.

But the project comes to a screeching halt when the construction crew unearths a grisly discovery—an unmarked grave. The discovery threatens Carly's ex-boyfriend, when the authorities learn the body belongs to his old girlfriend who had supposedly left town…and Wyatt is suspect number one.

Carly's sure Wyatt's innocent, even if the rest of the town, and more importantly, the sheriff's department, is ready to lock him up. Carly has moved on from Wyatt, but now he's asking for her help to clear his name. In exchange, he'll tell her what he knows about his father. Information that will help her bring Bart down.

But danger lurks around every corner, and as Carly puts her life on the line to help the man who betrayed her, she begins to question everything and everyone around her...especially Wyatt Drummond.